MERDRAGON

By Laura A. Lahtinen

Copyright © 2021 Laura A. Lahtinen
All rights reserved

The characters and events portrayed in this book are fictitious. Any similarity to real persons, living or dead, is coincidental and not intended by the author.

No part of this book may be reproduced, or stored in a retrieval system, or transmitted in any form or by any means, electronic, mechanical, photocopying, recording, or otherwise, without express written permission of the publisher.

ISBN-13: 9798519794428

Cover design by: Laura A. Lahtinen
Printed in Canada

Contents

Prologue 1

An accident, intentional, and not 4

A foggy forget-you-not 45

Is she or is she not? 48

Back to reality 64

Money, money, money 70

Breakfast at later 83

A day at the museum 93

A little light nightclub drama 103

O, bee-have 112

Ice fishing 115

Scene, set and go 121

Moonlight sailing 129

Sneaking 'round the Forbidding Palace 142

Wishful thinking 150

As phone calls go... 155

Back to fanta-sea 159

Swimming with the current 194

Gravity? 209

Enlist in more 233

What's going on? 250

Singing in the dark 258

Epilogue 263

Acknowledgement 264

About the Author 265

Prologue
(2000 BC, give or take)

Deep inside the ocean, three creatures lounged about in a room large enough for their individual wings, tentacles, and tails. The room had a dark view of the ocean around them—a view they mostly ignored. Water in, water out, made no difference.

"Who have you scheduled for today's questioning, sister?" one creature asked, lion tail swaying as she groomed her feathers. The water had no effect on her breathing, but she still felt the need to groom. As a sphynx who'd inspired more than one statue, she curated her own appearance.

The question stirred the other sister into an uneasy sway in her half-shell swing. "Do try to be gentle on this one. He's only a child." The bubbles rising from an air vent fluttered the tip of her tail—a large fan deceptively capable of prehensile behaviour. She had no feathers or fur, but dragon wings and fish tail to hound the sky and sea.

The first sister purred in amusement, "A child? Aren't they all?" She spoke in question, always, almost. Giving information was not her modus operandi.

A low and high-pitched rhythmic sound came from the third member of the party--laughter. The tentacled sibling only partially lolling inside the room. The majority of his bulk rested outside, darkly visible through the wall-sized window that allowed a dim, unimpeded view of the oceanic valley. He had never flown or trod on dryland, and few understood his speech.

Sister number two shifted in her swing and scolded the third one's laughter. "Brother, I know too well that you are not given to any grave sympathy toward the main staple of your diet, but do try to keep to the larger, and proven guilty specimens."

The thick glass thrummed with the reply of a solid triple thump. Laughter again—he was hungry and had little care for his youngest sibling's soft heart. Instead, it amused him.

"Squeamish, sister?" mocked the first speaker, teeth gleaming sharp. "Aren't you the precious hunter-scout that found and retrieved him?" As the interrogator, seldom did she hunt. That privilege had been given to the dragon-winged sibling. The sphynx had more skill dissecting a mind than catching a body.

Air bubbles swirled as the creature in the sling flexed her scaled tail. A song-wail lilted behind each word. "But he's a child. At eighteen rotations around the sun, they are curious and easily misled."

A barely comprehensible mash of sounds resolved into three syllables from the one they called brother. "Sssuck-u-leeenT." Finally, he spoke. Unpleasant in sound and content.

"I care not for a description of your diet's tenderness, brother. And, sister, I simply ask that you do not base your decision upon brother's appetite." Her translucent wings loosened and countered the sway her tail had started, stretching a little too far into the sphynx's territory.

A sharpened claw brushed against the outstretched wing of the second sister. A sudden yelp, and a mob of bubbles stampeded—away from a fireball. The placid water devolved into a maelstrom of talons and tentacles, fins and wings, flashes of fire, roars, hisses and whistles.

Then, a nearly unintelligible scream and thrum, "D-d-dee-ssssisssssT!"

Abruptly the engine of the melee was split. Two totally dissimilar faces planted against the ceiling by two rather sturdy tentacles.

A muffled spit came from one sister, a wriggle from the other. The tentacles pressed harder. "rrrrRRReeessPeh-K-T!"

"Those better be your hand tentacles you're using," muttered the scaled sister.

Before the other sister could actually purr in agreement, a bell sounded. The tentacles swiftly withdrew. The first of the sisters flashed her teeth before she leisurely swam down to her previous resting place. The second wiggled from top to bottom, realigned all her parts, sniffed and returned to her swing.

The bell sounded again, twice this round. A door located in the center of the ceiling space spiraled open. Down from the opening descended the child that had sparked the contention. The door spiraled shut. Unbound, he floated before them, scars on his arms evidence of the second sister's capture methods. A line of missing scales on his tail added to the story.

A purr stirred the waters, and the child's scales clenched tight. The sphynx flexed a paw, and asked, "Where did you think you were going, slave?"

The child moaned. Tentacles drifted closer, suckers pulsing, tasting blood.

Again, the first sister spoke, "What lies did you hear to lure you away from your home with us?" Rumours had been spreading like algae; she had orders to find the source.

The child shivered, then whispered through gritted teeth, "They're not lies."

Merdragon

A smile curled back from long canines, "Indeed? What have you heard?"

Later, early morning sun glittered across the ocean waves as a lone figure, high above, wings outstretched, sought out a rainstorm. A rainstorm to wash off the tears and the indecision. A bit of lightning might help to ignite the rebellion.

An accident, intentional, and not
(A hot, modern today-ish)

In the middle of a blue space of ocean, a middling island airport sat with some importance. More than one arrival and departure inside the hour kept it busy, and a mix of southeast Asian languages established its general global location even if one—anyone—were to be jet-lagged and travel numb.

Confidence and camouflage are key when walking in such a human stream of busy people, and Min Soo had both in plenty. Han Min Soo, or Min Soo Han, depending on which culture he happened to be in, had the hood of his hoodie draped over the hat on his head, and the hat's brim shaded his sunglasses which overlapped his face mask. A slouch masked his profession, and, as a solitary traveler, his mouth stayed shut. Slim as seaweed, he maneuvered through the crush without being overly overt.

His phone rang and the camouflage suffered with the first words out of his mouth, "Yes? He what!?"

The volume created a bubble around him. He'd broken the flow. And the baritone voice was twigging a sense of familiarity in the ears of one or two travelers as they passed. He could see it in the tilted heads and the side-eyes. Paranoid as only those who've been labeled "celebrity" can be, he immediately lowered his head and slouched toward a window.

Min Soo glanced around, then cupped his hand over his mouth to interrupt the flow of words at the other end of the connection. "Yes, I'm at the airport, but what does that have to do with Lee Joon Ho? What happened? Is he going to be okay?"

In the quieter area around the window, the other end's words rang clearer, "Don't worry about Joon Ho, he'll live. The doctors are working on reattaching his toe right now. But I heard you managed to finish your shoot early. This is going to work out great with the client. They probably wanted you in the first place, but we couldn't fit you in because of your schedule. There's a helicopter waiting. Check with information and they'll get you in touch with someone who can direct you. Your manager will meet you at the site. Got that Min Soo?"

"But I, president, I don't even know who the client is. You know Joon Ho handles stunt shoots," Min Soo warned.

Merdragon

"It's a referral from one of our bigger clients, and if we get this first shot rock-solid, they'll be paying a small fortune to sign a long-term contract. Go slay 'em for Joon Ho."

Min Soo glanced around again and saw one of the announcement screens displaying a weather report. He frowned to read it. His eyes widened.

"President! There's a typhoon coming, this is crazy, I can't..."

"Get going, Min Soo, it'll be fine. I'll be waiting to hear rave reviews." Overruling any protests, the company president hung up to harass someone else.

Min Soo stared at his phone in disbelief. "A typhoon, president, a typhoon. Ah, man." He shook his head and sighed. Straightening up from his slouch against the window, he spotted an information desk sign. He glared at his phone and, sarcastically this time, muttered, "Yeah, yeah, president, whatever you say."

A father's distraction blurred the usually sharp mind of the helicopter pilot. A small hair ribbon fluttering unobtrusively to the left of the control panel provided additional distraction. Already seated inside, he had a clear view of Min Soo's escorted approach, and the signature stride eating up tarmac, both which should have alerted him to a change, but distinctive strut or not, the pilot proved oblivious. He merely nodded as his passenger opened the co-pilot side door. Once Min Soo had hauled himself up into the co-pilot's seat, the pilot handed over a headset.

Running through his checklist, the pilot touched the hair ribbon briefly, then glanced over at Min Soo and asked, "You all set?"

Bemused he hadn't been asked his name let alone why he wasn't Lee Joon Ho, Min Soo responded with a visible tug on the five-point seat belt and gave a thumbs up, "Ready."

"Good," the pilot replied tersely, started the engine, and radioed the tower to let them know he was ready to leave. Min Soo quietly listened as the pilot received instructions and clearance. The pilot's responses came quick and succinct—a man not given to banter.

Blades doing their job, the helicopter rose, and they headed out over the blue waters off the island. Observing the progressively deepening shade, Min Soo shifted in discomfort. His gut was not happy with the whole of the present situation. He still didn't know where they were going. The company president hadn't felt it necessary to fill him in on the details. One of the islands between Okinawa and Taiwan? That covered a lot of territory. Vast. And who was the client? He glanced over at the pilot, but something grim and determined about his face dissuaded Min Soo from asking.

The day had been long. Time-zone crossing long. Night, day, night long. He shrugged fatalistically, crossed his arms and closed his eyes. If they happened to be flying a little off-kilter from a north easterly direction, closed eyes made him oblivious. Knowing wouldn't have made any difference anyway.

The pilot managed to peel his eyes away from the horizon at one point to check on his passenger. His eyebrows rose in surprise to see him sleeping.

"Nerves of iron! Glad I'm only flying you in. I'd rather deal with that typhoon than risk that island's protective shield. Or the one inside."

Elsewhere, in a plain windowless room, an older man and younger woman sat on foldable chairs beside a radio set and a computer.

"You've tested it?" asked the man.

"Dad, this is the test."

"Yes, Darya, but you did input the information I got from…well, you know…into the simulator, and it worked?"

"We wouldn't be doing this if it hadn't, but one thing I couldn't input is any of her, um, possible modifications to the system. The island shield programming is complex, but…" *The woman scratched at her leg nervously.*

"You mean, if she tried to hack herself out?" *the man asked and frowned at her mindless scratching. The young woman tracked his frown to her hand; she casually patted her leg as if to emphasize her next words.* "That's right. We all know she's got the credentials."

"Don't remind me," *he growled in sudden anger.* "That test-tube wretch. Even her banishment managed to mess with my plans. With her supposedly imprisoned on that island, it gave them the excuse to seal it from anyone else."

A countdown suddenly flashed on to the computer screen and both parties shifted their chairs closer. The grey-haired one grabbed the radio and the woman started typing.

Back in the helicopter, the pilot spotted the island and the air halo around it. He radioed out, "This is Blue Three. Island in view, over."

An old man's voice responded, "Blue Three, understood, we're still a go. Ten-minute countdown starts in three, two, one, mark. Don't forget to keep an eye on your altitude. "

Merdragon

"Understood, Blue Three out," he said, the timer counting down on the instrument panel.

The pilot shook his head at the still sleeping Min Soo and questioned himself, "Hmmm, should I wake him up for this?" He considered it, but then, "Ah, forget it, nothing he could do anyway. Less distracting this way. Here goes."

The helicopter approached the island that in no way resembled the busy tourist spot where Min Soo's manager was most certainly searching frantically for his charge. If anything, it more resembled one of the many islands where fictitious pirates always seem to get stranded with a few cases of rum, only less populated. Plenty of foliage, possibly a volcano, but no cannibals.

Forty-nine meters above sea level, -00:00:02 on the timer, the helicopter suddenly freak slid across thin air. The pilot's eyes widened in alarm and his hands clenched the controls, muscles strained to hold the helicopter sane as the impossible happened outside.

Min Soo's head banged against the door and he woke up as confused as possible. "Where's the stunt double?!"

The pilot didn't answer, gripping the controls, trying to contradict the skid. No go. He tried to go up, it threw them a-kilter to the left, he tried going right, they went tail up. Every move screwed them over, fin over flipper. Then sudden stop, the helicopter was stuck. On thin air. Min Soo's punched out lungs gasped in a full breath—and whooshed out again as the helicopter flipped upright, then started a slow falling spin downward.

The helicopter pilot, cursing through his teeth, fought hard. The yellow ribbon cheered him on. Min Soo clenched his jaw and gripped the safety harness with fists gone white. Blue sky, green trees, and dark blue ocean blurred into one.

"Blue Three, Blue Three, status report!" yelled the older man into the radio handset, over and over, but there was no response.

The woman stared at the computer screen, frozen. A cellphone ringtone interrupted her shock. Fumbling, she reached into her pocket to pull out the phone and answered, "Hello?"

She listened intently, then without saying a word, she swiped disconnect and slid the phone back in her pocket.

"Dad?"

"What?" he snapped.

"Our man's in the hospital."

"What?! Are you crazy? We don't even know what happened yet."

She swiveled the chair to face him. "No, our guy, Joon Ho Lee. The guy with the plastic surgery. The guy with the legs. The guy whose been plastered on as much media as we could manage. The guy who's supposed to be on the helicopter and fake a stunt accident. And supposed to get close enough to use the blade that's supposed to render her manageable. Mr. Marvelous is right now having surgery. A stupid accident at his modelling cover job. He never even made it to the airport."

The man's face had progressively gone from pale, "Wait," to rage, "then who was Blue Three transporting?" His voice snapped granite, "Find out."

The helicopter had somewhat landed on the island. At least part of it. The rest hung precariously off the edge of a cliff. A hefty tree had caught them mid crash, unfortunately impaling the pilot, but redeeming itself partially by keeping the helicopter itself from falling into the rocks and the grinding waves below.

Min Soo, not dead, but concussed, hung from his five-point harness, oblivious to the shear drop below the hanging-by-the-hinges door. Getting out…well, that would take someone with fully functioning mental faculties.

A groan emanated from the now not so unconscious Min Soo, regretfully reducing his chances of survival. Especially regretful for all his world-wide fans. Blindly his fingers felt for the buckle of his harness. Fingers curled around the edge and pulled…and went slack. Instead of a click, the buckle had jammed, mercifully. The grey waves far below crashed against the cliff, disappointed.

The helicopter groaned. A face appeared peering down into the cockpit from the pilot's side. A woman's face. A face copy and pasted with the same grim determination previously plastered on the pilot's, but the transfer had been corrupted; hers held zero terror.

Rosie the Riveter arms wrenched open the pilot's door. The woman had a rope wrapped around her waist. A thick rope that stretched out along the length of the helicopter hull, past the tail to encircle a stout tree. Monkey slick, she slipped inside the cockpit. Efficiently she inspected the pilot to confirm that he had, indeed, been done in by the aforementioned tree; she dismissed him with scarcely a facial twitch. A man without a heart wasn't inclined to have a pulse. She jimmied herself past him, pushed what parts she could out of the way and clambered closer to assess the other passenger, Min Soo.

A gamut of undefinable expressions flickered across her face the instant she got a good look at him. Recognition. Suspicion. Admiration. Anger, confusion, disgust, worry. They all danced in the mix along with a few less obvious. She shook her head to clear the mental mess and refocused on the rescue.

Merdragon

Laying her ear to his chest, she heard a steady heartbeat and lungs laboring against the life-saving straps. Positive signs according to her approving nod. One of her hands stretched around to feel the back of his head and came back bloody. A hiss slipped past her teeth and she eyed the culprit with censure—the tree. It had thumped him on its way to skewering the pilot. She leaned back, eyes narrowing, analyzing the positioning of all his, thankfully, fully intact parts and their chances of being trapped, but then nodded to see the straps were the only restraining factors.

Making her decision, the woman secured herself with her back and feet braced against the control panel and seat, then untied the rope from around her waist. She wrapped the rope around the unconscious Min Soo in imitation of the five-point harness currently holding him. Then, with the indifference of an ibex traversing up a desert canyon, she climbed back out of the cockpit, scrambled back to the tree at the other end of the rope, and there she secured the rope taut.

Hurrying back to the cockpit, the woman swung inside and pulled out an antique knife. Old, yes, but the blade gleamed like new and cut through first one, then the other straps with ease. As the last strap surrendered to the blade, the taut rope held. Min Soo hung loose, and the woman breathed a sigh of relief. The helicopter was now free to take a dive any time it so pleased.

With that hurdle cleared, the woman sought the radio and transponder. A bonus while it lasted. Turning it on with skilled hands, she glanced over at both pilot and Min Soo, then covered her mouth before calling out.

"Mayday, mayday!" Her voice came out in a foreigner's English with some gruff and husk. "We've crashed...," she flickered with the switch, feigning radio damage, "...island...pilot's dead...storm...safe...over." Fully releasing the switch, she added in a more natural voice, "Let's see who's sending out ravens."

A voice came back, sooner than expected, asking for status, coordinates, and any additional information she could give. Her eyes narrowed. Gruffly she responded with artificial enthusiasm, "Oh, freaking aces! ...good...have supplies...clue where I am." Instructed by the voice at the other end, she read off the call numbers of the helicopter, then added, "...on edge of cliff...have to leave helicopter." The voice at the other end mentioned waiting until the typhoon had passed, so she dropped the handset not bothering to reply. Instead, she eyed Min Soo. "Villain or dupe, either way you're mine, for now."

With the mayday sent and Min Soo secure, the woman set to dragging him free and clear. It took some wrangling, and repeated runs to the tree as the rope grew slack. Halfway through the procedure, she reached a point where she had enough rope to reach and pull on the other end of it while staying with her rescued ragdoll.

Sweat dripped down her face in the thick, humid, storm heavy air. Grunting, she pulled him along the helicopter hull, bare feet slapping hot metal. A final pull and he thumped onto solid ground. She laid him out in a relatively comfortable position, then ran nimbly back to the cockpit.

Swinging herself inside, she patted the dead pilot's shoulder sympathetically. The sympathy passed quickly. She fished through his pockets and salvaged what she could of his belongings, a watch, belt, pen, and other bits and pieces.

The ocean beneath the helicopter's slap-dash position had increased in its roiling and foaming at the mouth by the time the salvage operation finished for the day. She stashed the bounty in a safe place on the cliff top, then walked over to stand over Min Soo. Hands on her hips, finger tapping, she considered options. Transporting a man, a hand taller than her own above average height, was a problem.

The woman crouched down beside him, hair glued to her face from sweat, knees grimy below her equally grimy shorts, and the pilot's belt wrapped around her waist. Her face was a study in contemplation. Multiple solutions presented themselves one by one, moral and otherwise. With a roughened hand she reached out to touch his face, then leaned over to put her ear to his chest, listening for his life beat. She lightly slapped his face to try and wake him, but no fluttering eyelids or hand grabbing ensued. She wrapped her arms around her knees, sniffed at the changing smell of the air, then pursed her lips. Her head dropped to her knees and she whispered a prayer.

A short one. She concluded her mental processing with a nod. From a kneeling position, she first raised his limp form into a slumpy sit, pulled his arms over each of her shoulders, then with a grunt, she stood up in one smooth heft. Bending forward, she hiked him onto her back until his chin threatened to bruise her collar bone. Stooped over like an old woman, holding his arms around her like the empty arms of a sweater, and with his feet brushing against the ground, she carried him down a steep trail that led away from the cliff's edge.

The island had its own convenient lagoon. At its craggier end, the width of sandy beach narrowed, and the land rose steeply. Several steps from where the sand thinned out in a battle between itself and stubborn brush, a crack in the

Merdragon

rising rock played formal entrance to a surprisingly dry cave. Out of reach from the tides and high seas, and large enough to hide its far reaches from the light.

As the long arm of the oncoming typhoon set the tropical trees and palms swaying, the pair reached the cave. Worrisome waves lashed against the shores like heralds, and a frown of urgency was etched on the woman's face. Inside the cave, the woman stumbled to a makeshift bed located against the wall most protected from the elements and half-dropped Min Soo on it.

"Fish food, but you're heavy," she gasped. She slid to the ground and stared at one of Min Soo's legs hanging free of the bed. She pointed at it firmly and remonstrated, "You, no hanging about." She giggled, then shook her head sharply. "Fatigue hysteria, no time for that, get it together." A big breath and she hopped to her feet to make quick work of the escaping limbs. "Done. Now to make sure that storm doesn't invade this space. It's going to hit heavier with the shield gone." A shot of suspicion in Min Soo's direction, "Wonder who I should be thanking for that?"

While the diminishing light still provided some illumination, the woman prepared, bringing out a bucket of water from one dark recess, herbs and a bottle of something from another, and clean rags from still another. Earlier she had tied a few of the scavenged things to herself, and among these things, a battery-operated heavy-duty torch. Another item, an emergency first aid kit. These she set beside Min Soo's bedding, turning on the torch as she bent down to see what she could do for her freshly rescued patient. Gently she turned him on his side to examine the bump on his skull.

Her first inspection of the damage had shown superficial cuts, and now, inspecting it with greater care, she confirmed her initial findings. Still, the site needed cleaning to prevent infection. Fingers deftly parted the hair around the bump. First, she wiped what she could, before pouring a viscous liquid from the bottle onto the wound. With the cloth in hand, she wiped the excess clean, keeping the majority of the liquid from drifting too far.

The site cleansed of blood and dirt, she felt for the full size and shape of the goose egg. She stood up to pace, glanced back at him with a frown, paced some more, then glanced back again. A gust of wind ran over her bare feet like a scouting mouse. A wet and whistling one.

She snapped her fingers. "Right!" she exclaimed, and dropped the torch to dart toward the back of the cave, disappearing into darkness.

The cloud laced sun had withdrawn several degrees back from the cave's interior when sounds of something large being dragged along stone added to the scouting wind and heralding waves. A huff of human breath. A scrape. Hard place against rock. From inside the cave. A glimpse of blue glow and then the woman, drenched in sweat, gasping air, dragging a thick wooden slab, somewhat door-sized.

She slumped against a wall, still on her feet and one arm straight to prevent the slab from falling over. The wooden slab gleamed in patches, phosphorescent splotches glowing in swirls and carved curls, partially rubbed out in random sections, hinting at a sensible pattern. The slab was a single, solid piece of wood nearly a hands width thick and a meter by a meter and a half high at the top of its rounded edge. The woman reset herself, and arms and legs straining, she pulled, shoved, and begged the slab to the cave's entrance.

Goal reached, she didn't stop to rest. The wind threatened unfriendliness. One edge of the slab she aligned to one side of the entrance and ran her fingers along the edge of the dirt covered walls to reveal ancient hinges. Hinges that matched the sockets in the slab of a door. With a fine time of wrestling and wrangling, using this and that piece of rock, wood, and foot, she leveraged the massive door into its long-ago reserved place. The hinges groaned and screamed as she swung the door closed for the first time in many a tree's memory.

The sound made her wince. She spun 'round and dashed to one of the small dark recesses. Out from a dark cavity she pulled a bottle. Tossing the dingy thing up in the air, she grinned and practically skipped back to the source of her ear's irritation. She uncorked the bottle and liberally poured fish oil over the hinges. Her nose wrinkled at the smell, but when she swung the door back and forth a few more times, she smiled at the silence.

With the winds growing fierce, and the day's light nearly gone any which way it pleased, she decided to close the door for the night. So long out of use, it failed to seal completely, but she nodded in satisfaction regardless. The gap beneath the door would maintain a draft if she wanted to start a fire, and putting fresh leaved branches or rags along the seam would keep the majority of rain from successfully seeping in, if it proved necessary.

Why the door had been separated from the entrance remained a mystery.

Immediate environmental dangers covered, the woman returned to check on Min Soo. The light in the cave had become decidedly endangered so she turned on the torch light again. Min Soo groaned and his eyelids twitched. Encouraged, she shone the light directly in his face. He winced and his hand rose from the surface of the bed. It only made it halfway before collapsing on his chest. Experimentally she shifted the light away from his face then swung it back. This time his head turned away and his mouth moved in soundless words.

She switched the torch from one hand to another, then reached out with the free one to tap him on the shoulder. "Time to wake up, starfish." Her accent leaned toward American news broadcaster with a touch of melodic.

Words grumbled from his lips, and then he stilled. Eyes still closed, his fingers began fumbling over the unfamiliar surfaces beneath them, especially the makeshift bed with sheets not made of smooth cotton. His head shifted to one side and he winced, groaning as the bump on his head rubbed against the rough pillow. The hand that had failed to cover his eyes before, swung up now to clutch his forehead, and a moan hummed deep in his throat.

The woman tapped him on the shoulder again. "Hey there. You awake now? How do you feel?"

She shifted the torch away and set it aside to light their corner of the cave.

His eyes flickered once, twice, the third time dark black eyes blearily peered out for a moment only to close again in pain.

"Ah, akfjd jgjagd..." he mumbled, unintelligible. His hand slid to cover his eyes.

"O dear, that sounded like it might have been Korean." She scratched her head. "I am sorry, but you wouldn't happen to know English by some remote chance, would you?"

Min Soo grunted something which she took for a potential positive and so continued.

"You've been in an accident. Do you understand? Do you know who you are?"

He lay silent, and she waited for him to decipher and digest the words. Then, with eyes still closed, in an English vaguely suggestive of time in Australia, Min Soo responded, "Where am I?"

She clenched a fist in a silent yes! but calmly answered, "We're in a cave on an island. You suffered a hit to the head."

"What, how?... who?"

She leaned back on her heels and crossed her arms in front of herself. Under her breath she muttered, "What are you, a reporter?" In a more audible voice, she asked her own question, "You don't remember the helicopter?"

"Helicopter?" he asked, his voice wavering in confusion.

She rose from her squat and sat down beside him on the bed. She laid a hand on his forehead, testing for heat. "Sorry, I don't know a lot of first aid, but I think you may have lost a bit of memory with that thunk to your head. Do you know who you are?"

"Han…Min Soo Han," he enunciated carefully. Enough wits to manage the order change of his name.

In one swift motion she pulled his hand out of the way and leaned over to stare intently into his face. Complex emotions flitted across her face. His eyes blinked open in her shadow. Her eye colour shouldn't have been visible, but green stared into black.

Brokenly he asked again, "Who. Are. You?"

Matter-of-factly she ignored the question, as she'd done before, and leaned in even closer to inspect one eye and then the other. He tried to lean back but winced instead.

"What. Are. You. Doing?" he asked.

She sat back and replied, "Doctors always seem to do that, and I thought I'd see if I could find what they were looking for."

His eyebrows rose in clear disbelief.

She continued, "Oh, don't worry, I didn't see any dancing llamas in there or anything. To answer your previous question, my name's Ellia Nighe and I'm a storyteller in my spare time so you probably shouldn't believe a word I say, but we were sharing a flight in a helicopter to an island which I suspect is not the one we crashed on. Can't be sure since I was snoozing on the way, but considering I haven't seen anything looking like a five-star resort schmoozing up to the only beach, I'm pretty confident it isn't, unless you know something I don't."

She didn't give him a chance to express any possible insider knowledge of events which were entirely concocted inside her own head. Standing up, she began pacing, spinning the story. "Unfortunately, the pilot didn't make it. Somehow I survived, mostly scratch-free, although I've got a few bruises that are going to blossom brilliantly, and you, lucky dog, were the recipient of a glorious bump on the head."

While she spun her tale, Min Soo's eyes followed her, blinking repeatedly as she passed in front of the torch, back and forth, back and forth. Her words flowed over him in a steady stream, and eventually his blinking eyes slowed their pace.

Ellia, as she'd named herself, suddenly drew close and crouched down so that he had to turn his head to look at her. In her hands she held a traveler's coffee mug. "Would you like some water?"

Eyes glazed, he didn't respond. She gestured with the mug. He dry-swallowed, then nodded. He struggled to lift himself up. Ellia recognizing his efforts, scooted up onto the bed beside him, placed one arm behind his shoulder, and leaned him against herself so that he could drink without drowning himself. Two gulps down and he abruptly stopped.

He shifted in a disguised squirm. "Ah...toilet?"

"Ah...perhaps you forgot my comment about the lack of five-star resorts...and the typhoon?"

He coughed. "Typhoon?"

She patted him soothingly on the shoulder. "Don't worry about it, we're safe, but outdoor activity is a little, erm, risky, hmmm..."

The issue had been voiced however, and Min Soo's clenched fist revealed the rather urgent nature of the problem. "I could..."

"Let's see if you can walk first, hmm?" she interrupted with an optimistic peppy tone of voice. Optimistic for more than one reason.

Now it was his turn to put in effort to move his considerable length, slim as seaweed or not. Ellia grabbed for him as his forward motion went downhill instead of up. He crumpled by the bedside and clutched his head. Then he moaned and covered his mouth.

"Dizzy? Nauseated?" Ellia asked in concern as she helped him crawl back onto the bed.

She stood beside the bed in visible consternation, leaned over and rubbed his shoulder, consoling, "No big deal, you just stay there, and I'll think of something." She pursed her lips and scanned the cave as if it were unfamiliar. "The good news is that it's better you than me. Give me a moment and I'll find you a bucket or chamber pot or, or something."

It didn't take long to find the something. She handed him a large tin can. "Here, careful of the edges, I'll just step over to the door. Let me know if you, uh, pass out or whatever." She paused, considering. "You think you can manage it yourself?"

White-faced, he nodded and blinked his thanks. She turned away so he could take care of business.

To assess the storm's current status, Ellia opened the wooden slab of a door. The wind blew in with a hurrah, breaching the fearsome door's defenses. She stepped out into the dark elements and raised her arms wide into the wind to let the wild energy rush around her in a flurry. The rain fell, still thin, but sharp now, and once she'd had enough of its bite, she snatched one last gulp of rich air into her lungs and stepped back into the cave's shelter. The wind insisted on overstaying, but with a firm, legs braced against one wall determination, she closed the magnificent door once again.

The sudden change cleared the pensive expression off her face, and she returned to see that her patient had managed to complete his business and now lay slumped on his side, a hand still on his zipper and an honest smile of relief on his face. A smile echoed across her lips as she took in the scene, empathizing. Nurse steps took her to his side, and she checked both his pulse and breath. Checked the bucket with a quick glance to see he hadn't voided his stomach in his nausea. She rearranged his limbs until he lay fully on the bed again, head slightly raised. Throughout the ministrations he refused to do more than call his "ommaa" in protest, asking for something she couldn't translate but sounded a lot like "mom".

Done, she stood back to consider her work and to consider this unexpected guest. A surprisingly gleeful smile crossed her face. She tilted her head. No way of knowing whether he was a villain or dupe, but she could still admire him a little. He had a beautiful face. Not conventional with its long nose, but the surprisingly big eyes, unfortunately closed now, balanced the look. Compelled, she raised a hand to touch his rice paper white, warm marble skin, but a finger's distance away she stopped. Her toes curled against the cave floor. She shivered.

"What are the odds that a prime specimen like you, all long, lean and famous would end up here? It's a shame to see you so…still." Her eyes narrowed. "I hope and pray I don't have to kill you." A pained grin crossed her face and she added morbidly, "I hope I can if I have to."

The words went ignored and she concluded that he was well and truly out. Suspecting he'd be sleeping for a while, she narrowed her eyes at the tin can. She sniffed. Emptying that seemed a priority. She gave him one last glance, threw her braid over her shoulder, whispered a prayer for his survival, grabbed the tin can gingerly, and switched off the torch. In the fading phosphorescence, her soft footsteps disappeared from the sounds of the storm.

During Ellia's absence, Min Soo gasped awake into solid blackness. Desperately blinking, he nearly poked out his eyes trying to see his own hand. The darkness played with his mind. Banshee screams slid like spiked bobsleds down blackboard tracks. He choked out Ellia's name, but no answer. He grabbed at his pounding head. Terrors flashed through his mind. His heart shivered; his imagination mocked him. Ellia, a hallucination his dying mind had conjured to comfort him in his last moments after the crash. A crash. What crash?

Merdragon

He passed out and his pulse settled. But he woke again in cold sweat...and passed out again, and again, and again.

Mercifully, his moments of delusional wakefulness were brief and had an end in the morning hours. A morning still being trounced by the typhoon. He stirred, and this time his opened eyes saw more than utter darkness. The relief was profound. The torch had been turned on. Gingerly he turned his head and saw Ellia, not a hallucination, stretched out on the ground beside him. The cloth on his head slid off. He hadn't felt her place it there during the night.

Heart beating its normal steady beat, his head feeling a little better, and his senses already recalibrating to reality, he studied her. He tried to categorize her into a familiar box. He suspected at least some part Caucasian, the facial features suggested it, along with his memory of her green eyes. The difficulty lay in her frazzled brown hair and the tanned skin blotchy from smears of sweat and dirt. And her bare feet confused him. They didn't look soft.

Thinking hurt. He carefully laid his head back to stare at the ceiling of the cave. It was grey. And dusty. His Adam's apple bobbed as he tried to swallow. The sound of the rainy winds outside was making him thirsty. There'd been a cup of water yesterday. He craned his head around to try and spot it. There, on the floor. Within arm's reach.

Carefully he reached for it, but a wave of light-headedness set him swaying. Wisdom advised he take his time, leisurely. Trying to keep his head straight, awkwardly he stretched... Success! His long fingers wrapped around the cup, and pulling it carefully to himself, he breathed a quiet sigh of relief. Too soon. He fumbled the cup halfway to his mouth. Water spilled onto his shirt, and an unintelligible exclamation spluttered from his mouth.

The sound woke Ellia, and in the predatory manner of all those who've had a late night, she opened her eyes and glared at the source of her stirring. A blink, and the glare disappeared. Sleep surrendered to waking memory. She rose to her feet and hurried over to help.

Trying to brush off the water while simultaneously trying to get up, Min Soo didn't notice her approach until her hand slid across his back. His free elbow jabbed into something not-bed, and his normally nimble fingers lost all their skill. Her fingers working fine, she deftly grabbed the cup with a quick practical nab before its contents could cause any more damage to him or the bedding.

Flushing, he turned to say, "Thank y—", but knocked heads instead. He moaned as the sudden impact spun the room dark.

A cool hand brushed away the hair from his clammy forehead, and he felt her hands gently rearrange his limbs and the bedding around him. He lay there, vision dark and starry, but still conscious of his surroundings. Including the wailing banshees providing mood music.

Her voice came soothingly somewhere above him, "That was some head-butt. Relax a second. I'll get you some more water." Her voice faded as he heard her walk away. He thought she added, "Blooming algae, you may look fae ethereal, but there's some solidness to that handsome head of yours."

His ears practically swiveled to follow her around the cave. He heard a clatter of wood and metal objects, then, "Ah ha! What's an abandoned rustic getaway without a few utensils hiding around."

Listening to her move around the cave, he heard her quietly muttering under her breath. Blind, curious, he followed her sounds like a blind and weak puppy; trying to understand this unfamiliar world to which he'd awakened. Eventually the dark clouds that had threatened a full loss of awareness began to dissipate.

A blow hit the cave's stalwart door. The typhoon's thug winds wanted in. Blindly he raised a hand as if to hold it back. He clenched his fist. He'd lost track of Ellia.

Before his face completely forgot its typical cool as a cucumber expression, he found her again. Beside him, tsking, "Easy, easy. That door's solid."

He took in a calming breath. His nose filled with the perfume of wood fire smoke and seawater. The gentle hand that landed on his shoulder next connected the dots. It was her. Lungs froze mid breath as he felt her arms wrap around him. Then pull him up. Mystified, and frankly unable to do anything about it, he waited as she seemed to rustle around with something behind him. Done, she gently leaned him back against what felt like a giant pillow. Her weight shifted off the bed then depressed it again. He gave opening his eyes another try.

Concerned eyes watched him. Then he noticed the cup and spoon in Ellia's hands.

"Tilting your head back to drink might give you a bit of nausea so," she wiggled the spoon, "since we don't have any straws at the Deserted Islands Resort, perhaps a spoon will suffice?"

The spoon in her hand resembled more an antique ladle from some yester-lore's Spanish noble's table, but it shone in the firelight, freshly polished clean. Wait, firelight? His eyes darted past her and caught the site of a small fire Ellia had started while he'd been blind. His eyes darted back to the ladle in her hand. He licked his lips and leaned forward, lifting a hand to take the spoon, ladle, whatever. Waste of effort. She brought it to his mouth.

He swallowed convulsively, then again as she offered another spoonful for him to drink. On the fifth spoonful he raised a hand to stop her. "Thank you."

She set the cup and spoon aside, then asked, "Do you want to lie down again?"

He shook his head carefully and placed a hand on his midsection. "Is there anything to eat?"

A cheeky grin lit her face. "The chefs at the Deserted Island Resort left a few decades ago when they heard that a typhoon was coming, but we do have fruit." She frowned. "I'm not sure how your stomach will react... You haven't thrown up yet and it's probably best if you don't start now."

Her lips twisted and she tapped a finger against her chin. Tired, Min Soo closed his eyes while she pondered. He opened them again when he felt her get up. Out of a sack on the ground he saw her pull out what he assumed was the helicopter's first aid kit. Opening it, she gave her second, "Ah ha!" of the day, and hurried back toward him with a small object in her hand.

"Emergency energy bar," she declared, brandishing her discovery. "It's not bread or rice, but it'll help until I can go find out if there are any bananas or plantains on this island. But not durian." She frowned to herself. "There'd be a guaranteed vomit-fest with that. If not you, me." An idea lit her face, and as she handed him a small piece of the bar, she added, "Maybe I'll learn to fish."

Skeptical of the idea, Min Soo gave her a raised eyebrow, but the energy bar piece she'd given into his hand distracted him, and he focused his energies on taking a bite. He hoped his digestive system wouldn't have a typhoon of its own.

First, he took a little crumb of a bite. He rolled it around in his mouth. It tasted...dry. He swallowed and waited for it to reach his stomach. He waited. Nothing. So far, so good. The next piece was a little bigger. He repeated the rolling, tasting, swallowing and the waiting. Nothing.

For some forgotten-in-an-instant reason, he raised his eyes up and caught Ellia's eyes on him. He took a breath to relax, then licked his lips. They were dry, again. The motion broke her stare, and she proffered the water cup and spoon to him, again. His dark gaze stayed glued on her as he took a cleansing sip. He blinked as he swallowed. The spoon trembled in her hand almost imperceptibly.

Not sure what to make of it, he shifted his attention back to the small piece of energy in his hand. He popped the whole thing in his mouth, screw the consequences, and chewed it. A small piece, but with emergency energy bars being infamous for a reason, it took some heavy-duty masticating. His eyes closed, he swallowed the final crumb, and drifted off to sleep.

Ellia saw his body relax and she whispered his name, "Han Min Soo? Hello?"
She tsked to herself, tapped his limp hand a couple of times, then when a stronger tap on the shoulder failed to stir him, she concluded he was well and truly out.

The next few days were not good. Min Soo's morning of lucidity had been a spot of paradise, an eye in the storm. A fever arrived to send shivers coursing through his body, sweat and words spilled randomly. Stillness would take over, then his eyes would fly open, and he'd begin tossing about in distress. His already slim body grew increasingly gaunt.

Feeding him broth brought from dark places, holding his hands from breaking against the cave walls during his thrashing, and tending to his overall care, Ellia no longer left for more than a sprinted minute. Her own face grew paler, and shadows grew under her eyes. When days later he developed a grey stillness, Ellia began pacing. To and fro, from the rear of the cave and back to Min Soo's side. Back and forth, indecision in her every step.

Seven times she traversed the short distance each way; on the eighth she stopped midway, nodded to herself, and with decisive steps she headed to the rear entrance of the cave. The home of the wooden slab. A sigh stopped her.

Her eyes widened and she ran back to Min Soo's side. She placed her fingers on his carotid artery, feeling for a pulse.

"Han Min Soo? Can you hear me? Min Soo?"
His eyelids lifted. She bent closer, searching for sentience. He blinked. His mouth opened but nothing came out. Dryly he cleared his throat and croaked, "Wha-?"

Carefully Ellia spooned a few drops of water in his mouth. As he swallowed, she updated him.

"You've been out for about three, four days, and I think it's because of that goose egg lump on your head. Or maybe that energy bar in the first aid kit passed its expiry date in the last decade. I'm not sure, I'm no doctor, not even a nursing student. I'm very glad to have you back."

She brushed a strand of hair away from his eyes. "I don't think I'd be good at digging graves."

Merdragon

He gave her a strange look, but the effort made him wince—strange looks being difficult endeavors at the best of times. The scruff he'd developed over the last few days did help.

"How are you feeling? More water?" she asked. He nodded and struggled to get up. As she helped, the blanket slipped down, and he suddenly tightened his grip on her arm. "Ah..." he started.

Reading his expression with full fluency, and honestly not wanting to discuss it herself, Ellia shook her head and charged over the subject before it could start, "You look pretty lucid right now, I hate to leave you just when you've woken up, but since you're awake, and going on the fifth day of broth, something a little thicker might be in order. I can't have you getting any more skeletal than you already are. Typhoon's passed so you don't have to worry about me blowing away."

He looked up at her, and she slipped a spoonful of water into his mouth before he could say anything. Dark eyes stared at her as he swallowed.

In some awe, she froze for a moment, then shook herself. She stood to her feet, muttering as she escaped without saying a coherent good-bye. "Puppy dog eyes? Pah! That's a professionally trained seal pup."

Left behind, alone in the cave, Min Soo waited to make sure Ellia was well gone before assessing his current state of being. First, he slowly reached back to feel for the lump on the back of his head. A slight smile curled his lips as he happily realized it had nearly disappeared. Tender, yes, but no longer an unasked-for body modification. "Hope that's a good thing."

Leaning over to try and get a better view of the entrance, he listened for any footsteps before he used what little strength he had to swing his legs over the side of the bed. He followed that with an attempt to sit up. Nothing doing. His brain's puppet master strings no longer had the ability to move a single limb. He groaned and closed his eyes.

Five, ten, thirty minutes? He couldn't be sure when he opened his eyes again. The twisted marionette position probably the only reason he hadn't continued to sleep. He took a couple of breaths, prepared himself, and gritted into a sitting position.

Big breaths, he sat on the edge for a minute or two, modestly happy with this accomplishment. The happy slipped into a frown. His arms were bare. Weakly he swung out a leg. It was bare too. He pondered the situation with the blanket wrapped around him.

"I definitely remember still wearing clothes the last time I woke up."

Too tired to do anything other than continue sitting in consternation, he dragged the lumpy pillow closer so he could lean against the wall and wait for Ellia to return.

"I have some questions," he mumbled as his eyes closed. They flew open as he tried to stay alert, but too heavy, they drifted down, and he slumped against the pillow into a natural, restful sleep.

The smell of frying fish tickled the end of his nose, and he tried to brush away the cruel fantasy. The sublime smell persisted, and he opened one eye. No luck. No fancy interior decorating. However, a less dirt-streaked Ellia sat on her heels beside a cleverly crackling small fire, on top of which a whole fish lay, soaking up the flames. Leaning forward to catch another whiff, the blanket slid off thinned shoulders unnoticed. Past the cooking fish he spied a veritable mini smorgasbord of fruit on an antique tray which sat on a dilapidated wooden chair.

His movements had caught Ellia's eye, and she cautioned, "Trying to move around on your own could get you in serious trouble. Wait for me next time, will you?"

He pulled the blanket back up, and nodded, salivating.

Ellia moved the position of the fish and adjusted some of the firewood. Eyes on task, she added, "I found an old chair of sorts and set it outside, not too far away, with a bucket and some water, so when you're feeling a little stronger you can get some, ah, air."

The stuffing of the makeshift bed rustled, and Ellia added, "Focus on the good news."

"Good news?" A hint of wryness tinted the question.

Poker faced she pointed to the ground beside his bed.

Blanket clutched to his chest, he pulled away from the pillowy supports, and peered over the edge of the bed. His breath caught at the sight of his carry-on luggage.

He raised his eyes to see her watching him with a glint in her eyes. All he could say was, "My clothes."

She stood up from her crouch, and asked, "I hope you weren't too attached to what you were wearing before."

He shook his head.

"Good," she continued, "they've already been buried."

Merdragon

Casually she picked a small bundle off the ground and came close to kneel on one knee in front of him.

"What are you doing?" he asked, curling his toes away.

Without explaining, she split the bundle and revealed a fresh palm leaf woven sandal. She placed it and its partner on the ground in front of him. He eyed them curiously, and then, relaxing one set of toes after another, he slipped his feet inside.

Letting his feet adapt, he asked, "What happened to my shoes?"

"Unfortunately, they fell off when I lugged you here, but the other good news is that I found those too, but," and here she pointed to the far wall where he saw them hanging off the edge of a ragged cupboard, "they're soggy as a Marshwiggle's footwear, so while they're drying I hope my weaving skills hold up."

The sight of the cupboard made him take another look at the cave. With sunlight coming in through the entrance, he realized the cave had been a home to someone, somewhen. Considering the cabinetry and furnishings, a slightly mad-cap pirate and the remnants of his shipwrecked ship. With very eclectic taste.

Ellia interrupted his inspection. "You ready to try them out?" Wrapping an arm around his waist and draping one of his arms over her shoulder, she said, "I'll help you up. You can sit in that chair in the corner so I can change your bedding a little more thoroughly."

Warily he settled his arm more securely on her shoulder and then, as he stood up, leaned rather more heavily on her than he would have liked.

She continued her running monologue as they shuffled across the cave floor. "Once I have you settled, I'll bring you something a trifle more civilized than the blanket you're trying to wear like a mummy."

A wistful tropical draft of beautiful fresh air came in to inspect the cave. Min Soo lost his focus on the chair and turned toward the open door like a hound catching a scent. Ellia steadied him out of an aborted stumble, and wordlessly led him to the doorway. He put out his free hand to lean against the cave wall and stopped.

Awed, he gazed in wonder at the beach and lagoon. The island was recovering from a typhoon hangover. The ocean stretched nonchalantly far into the horizon. Min Soo's frame and chest stretched as his lungs filled with clean, oxygen-rich fresh air. Threatening to break his own neck, he craned around, trying to see more of the island.

"Feel like sitting outside instead?" Ellia asked from beside him.

Immediate awareness lost to the view, he nodded distractedly.

Jostling him out of his distraction, she gestured with her chin. "Over to the left, here is where I have things set up."

He refocused, and although he still had to lean on Ellia, the fresh air had invigorated him, and each footstep was well planted before taking the next.

The dirt trail rose at a mild incline, and the spot she brought him to was itself sheltered by a tall brush and tree, separated by a breathing space from their mad jungle family. The quaint chair Ellia had previously mentioned, a short bench with a hole in it, and a hole beneath that, caused Min Soo's eyebrows to twitch. Beside the bench sat a bucket with a small frilly cloth draped over the side. A larger, misshapen cloth hung on a branch of the lonesome tree.

Ellia spoke up first. "If you feel strong enough to take care of business on your own, I'll go make sure the fish hasn't gone up in flames and bring some clothing from your luggage. Think you can manage, or would you like some help?"

Already tiring, he reached out to lean on the back of the bench and shifted his weight from off her shoulders. Secure, he imperiously gestured with a flick of his hand.

Concerned, she cautioned, "If you need me, yell and I'll hear you."

He gestured again.

"Hmph, I'm going, I'm going. Remember to yell and I'll be back before you fall." With that admonishment, she turned away and left him to his doubtful devices.

Min Soo's head slumped, too tired to move from the spot, even to sit down. It felt good to be outside the cave. Every breath, exquisite.

How she knew when to come back, even Ellia couldn't have explained it, but, with impeccable timing, she jogged into the clearing and found Min Soo holding on to the tree, wrapped in the oddly shaped towel, hair wet, eyes closed, and shivering in the heat.

"Not good, not good," Ellia muttered to herself as she hurried over with clothes in hand.

He opened his eyes hearing her approach. He didn't move. It was going to be tough getting him back inside.

She took a big breath. "Okay, necessity dictated I take a few liberties in the last few days, but I've done my best to maintain your, ah, modesty thus far." The tan didn't quite cover the blush. "If you keep hold of that towel, I'll help you with the shirt and, er, getting on your pants."

Merdragon

Too tired to do more than grunt an affirmative, they did as she'd suggested. Finished, he sighed, "Thanks," then slumped against her shoulder. The sudden weight nearly knocked her over, but she braced herself, recovering. "Sorry," he mumbled.
"No worries, let's get you back. My mistake, not yours. Ready to go?"
"Hungry."
"Make it to the cave on your feet and there's a feast a-waiting."
Taking a firmer grip on the arm draped over her shoulder, and with her arm wrapped around his waist, they tottered back to the cave, one step at a time. The sun began sending farewell tendrils low across the horizon and they paused in sync to watch it fully set. Turning the corner into the cave, the small fire paled in drastic comparison. The smell of fish compensated somewhat. Min Soo's stomach grumbled to be fed.

The next few days, Min Soo managed to step outside on his own a few times, but mostly slept between meals. Ellia spent the time crisscrossing the typhoon slammed island, dealing with the mess left behind. Regardless of what she'd told Min Soo, she'd been here a while. Certain places functioned better without dead trees and rubbish strewn about. On occasion, the rubbish turned out to be useful, but only if found soonest.
Finding food too, not only for herself, but for Min Soo, took extra thought and arranging. She crouched down beside a small stream and let her fingers dip down into the water and waited. It didn't take long before a froglet swam past. She allowed it to pass.
"Lucky for you, I don't think Min Soo likes frogs enough for me to determine if you're poisonous or not." She tapped the sole of its hide foot. "Hurry along, little one, before I get hungry."
The frog darted away and Ellia laughed standing up. "I do hunt better when I'm a tad peckish." Still laughing, she strode down a faint path through the brush and tropical trees. The path led upward and soon glimpses of the ocean glinted between the greenery.
Storm debris and food hadn't been her only concerns. The helicopter had survived the typhoon's mayhem. Ellia'd decided it would only be decent to grant the pilot a burial.
Grave digging was far from glamourous. She stood over the grave she'd dug, legs planted wide and arms crossed, filthy from head to toe. Her lungs had long recovered from the heavy exertion stage.

"I pray your girl remembers you fondly. This was the risk you ran with your choice." The jungle quieted momentarily at the words.

The noise had fully returned to regular business hours when she shut it down again. "God help her forgive her father and find a better cause than he did."

She bowed her head briefly, then turned away. "And God, please let Han Min Soo be innocent of all this."

All the running about the island left Ellia spent by evenings' end, and combined with Min Soo's propensity for nodding off at irregular intervals, only the basics of societal conversation managed to cross their lips. The state of the day, the state of the food, the state of one's health, these served well enough for five-minute bouts. The few leading questions Ellia attempted to slide in, slid right out again, most often accompanied by a snore.

On the fourth evening, Ellia had managed to complete most of her projects with energy to spare, and Min Soo had begun exhibiting the beginning symptoms of cabin fever. Safe in the cave, the two sat slightly opposite each other, facing the low burning fire between them. Min Soo had developed a penchant for dragging his bedding off the creaky cot and closer to the fire. A gentle draft drew the smoke out the open entrance, allowing them to enjoy the faint warmth without choking to death.

The repetitive dialogue had been exhausted. Min Soo no longer resembled the classic patient, and Ellia was drifting from the caretaker role. The change threatened to generate an uncomfortable silence, one between strangers constrained to be acquaintances in a broken elevator. Ellia took up the challenge.

"I have a suggestion," she blurted.

Min Soo's years of modeling experience allowed him to give the impression of raising an eyebrow without, in truth, lifting it more than a hair.

"Instead of asking embarrassingly personal questions about our former lives, what if we agree to lie?" she asked.

Not a stupid man, career stereotypes to the contrary, but clearly under the mistaken belief that she was a fellow castaway and that she didn't know his public persona, he replied, "Lie?"

"It's either that or soon we're going to be discussing shampoo, politics, how much I really want a green tea ice cream banana split, and your second cousin twice removed who always seems to find a way to steal every girlfriend you ever had, or hoped to have, since preschool."

Merdragon

Concussions can have a prolonged effect; he could only blink at the string of words.

Helpfully, "Let me demonstrate. Ask me a question."

She figured it had to be no-brainer for him, being a celebrity who'd been interviewed and been known to ask a question or two during show hosting duties. He offered the line, "Tell me who you're wearing... I mean, tell me about yourself."

"Shall I?" she replied with a grin. Then, reorganizing her face into a pleasant poker face of an expression, she proceeded with, "Well, you won't believe me, and I don't blame you, but I'm not entirely human."

The pause for effect was Min Soo's cue to ask a follow-up question, "Really?"

"True story," she answered, full of sincerity, "I'm a hybrid, crossbreed, an amalgamation, if you will... a mermaid dragon cross; a merdragon."

Min Soo coughed and waved his hand in front of his face. It seemed a random mini gust had back-drafted smoke from the fire.

After making sure it didn't seem too serious, Ellia continued, "Never would have guessed, huh? I was pretty darn flabbergasting to the neighbours, too. Believe me, when a merchild starts belching fire—underwater no less—people notice."

Serenely she waited as more smoke appeared to send Min Soo into another coughing fit.

"You see, my father was a bit of a sea-rover and when he came to visit the merKing—not to be confused with the word lurking, which the merKing never does." Caught by the thought, she gazed upward to blindly contemplate the cave roof. "Murky, murking? What else would you call lurking in a murky place?"

Tears appeared to be the next stage of smoke inhalation for poor Min Soo. Streaking down his slightly ashy, but much healthier face, the tears had a devastating effect.

Ellia shook her head to dislodge the effect. "Anyway, let me continue. My father was visiting the merKing, yes. Single, with one new piece of baggage, me. No recently acquired pregnant wife, an indiscretion with a girlfriend, or scandalous one-nighter. Most people assumed she must have died and pitied the little motherless merchild."

The fire had lost some of its flame so Ellia stirred it around to liven it up a bit. Her eyes glistened. Min Soo frowned. She leaned closer over the fire. And belched. Fire. Min Soo fell back, slamming a hand on the ground.

Ellia peeked over at him, doll-eyed, then covered her mouth and winked with an "Oops."

Ignoring Min Soo's glare at her supposed slight-of-hand, she leaned back in her spot, folded her hands in her lap and continued, "That's pretty near how they reacted too. It took some wheedling, but eventually dad told the merKing that he'd taken a nap on some rocks that weren't, and well, accidentally fertilized them."

That was that. Min Soo couldn't take it anymore. Ellia watched him stumble and trip out of the cave, all modelling techniques in shambles.

"Yes, run. Keep lounging around inside this cave like a piece of meat and I will roast you, hmmm." She smirked. "Definitely not the reaction I'd expect of someone who knows the truth."

A noise at the entrance warned her. Hair wet and face streak free, he'd obviously required a full head dunk. A few well positioned drops obeyed gravity, and the rivulets compelled Ellia to close her eyes for a few well taken breaths, in through the nose and out. "Five, ten, fifteen…twenty years?"

Min Soo's baritone sent a shiver down her spine, "Could you pass me a towel?"

She grabbed the nearest cloth at hand; threw it to him and stood up. Wiping his face, he eyed her curiously as she hurried out of the cave. The ocean's evening breeze met her as she stepped out to make use of the wash bucket herself. "Has it really been so long since I last met anybody? How could I forget?" The water felt good on her face, sobering. "Girl, that boy is transitioning quickly away from patient status. Smarten up. A healthy Han Min Soo is a net load more lethal than the one at death's door."

It took a bit more water, but soon she felt suitably refreshed to return. Walking in she spotted Min Soo in his natural professional model form, laid out beside the fire. His eyes were closed, but hearing her entry, he first opened one eye and then the other. Gravity pools. Black holes.

"You're back. You okay?" he asked, his face a step beyond the default public face and into actual concern territory.

She raised her eyes up to heaven, praying for strength and reason. The drops of water down her back helped. She smiled, the gracious host, and replied, "I'm good, you?"

"Hmm," he sub-sonically replied with a nod. He laid back down, stretched his arms out and tucked them behind his head. The shirtless display was rather suspicious, chest muscles and abs strategically highlighted by the firelight, but his

Merdragon

face only displayed curiosity. He prompted her to continue. "What happened after your father confessed?"

Palpitations threatened, and she seriously considered walking out again with a glance toward the exit, but the storyteller in her couldn't resist. For a few eyes-closed moments, she meditated on glaciers and icebergs and then, with an internal grin, began again to create the biggest fib she'd thought up in years. The closer to the truth the better.

"Well," she started, "after dad confessed his indiscretion, and consequential new responsibility in the personage of me, the merKing first made sure there was only one of me, since dad had said rocks, as in the plural. Dad concurred, although he did say the thought had only just occurred to him, and he expressed a little horror at the possibilities. He did say that since he'd witnessed the hatching, he knew two had sadly petrified decades ago, two were apparently still waiting proper fertilization by an actual male of the species, if such a one still existed, and only one had been born besides me, a par-par-, what was it, again," she snapped her fingers, "right, parthenogenetic dragonette. No fertilization required.

"Momma dragon was furious with dad, and honestly mystified with what to do, so she sent dad off with me and a scorched tail. His."

Ellia snuck a peek in Min Soo's direction and dug her toes into the warm sand around the fire. Stress lines had been developing over his face, but now a faintly curving smile replaced the dangerous visitors.

"...and that's how we ended up visiting the merKing. And the merPalace neighbourhood is where I tried to grow up." Ellia sighed dramatically. "Other than having to use special fireproof burping blankets, babyhood wasn't too bad. Thankfully, my toddler years passed relatively normally. I couldn't belch on command, yet. Dad made sure to avoid anything that gave me any kind of gas."

Min Soo turned over on his side to face away from Ellia, and she could hear muffled sounds synced to the shaking of his shoulders.

When it looked like he might be able to breathe again, she continued. "In school I first started noticing I differed from the rest of the masses." She raised her two legs up as if contemplating a tail, curling and flexing her toes. "Nobody really knew what to expect when it came to the crossbreed me. My tail scales weren't shimmery pearlescent like everybody else's, instead they came in dull dark browns and greens." She sighed sadly, but then her eyes crinkled at the corners and gleamed with mischief. "But it was great for hide-n-seek."

"Hide and seek?" Min Soo asked, reluctant curiosity colouring his voice. He glanced over in her direction, but then threw his forearm over his face as if afraid to hear the answer.

"I don't know how you played growing up, but in mer-circles, everybody always has to make sure their tails are well hidden out of sight, shimmering faintly like they do, but me, I had a whole lot more options. Find a hole for my head and think like seaweed."

A hoarse grunt was the response. She waited. He moved the arm covering his face. His masterpiece inspiring eyes appeared miffed. "That doesn't make sense."

Ellia smirked. "And why's that?"

His diaphragm expanded and he rolled his eyes before answering, "What about your, ah..." and he gestured at his own torso.

She waved her hand dismissively. "O, us little sea monsters, we actually have scales up to our armpits before we grow out of them. As for my arms, I didn't mind getting messy, so I slathered them with sea goop."

He blinked a few times, "Then why didn't you slather your face too?"

Incredulous, she raised both eyebrows. "Haven't you ever met a dragon before?"

He pursed his lips, eyes narrowing. With a bit of snap he replied, "No, I have never met a dragon."

"Really? Then you don't know." She nodded sagely, head bobbing in sudden understanding.

Rubbing his eyebrows, he bit the bait. "What don't I know."

"Their eyes glow."

"Their eyes glow?"

"I'm surprised you didn't know," she sing-songed back, batting her eyelashes.

Lids half lowered, he studied her for a few breaths, then sat up into a cross-legged position. "So, you stuck your head in a hole because your eyes glowed?" His lips twitched inside the poker face frame.

Eyes guilelessly wide, she shrugged her shoulder. "What else was I supposed to do? Mermaids don't do sunglasses."

He turned away, fist firmly pressed to his mouth.

She readjusted her seat then stared pensively out into the dark. The crackle of the little fire had a sobering effect. The cave had an oddly regular and comfortable temperature. The fire concealed the discrepancy.

Merdragon

Min Soo hadn't yet noticed, despite his health improvements. She heard him stir. He'd composed himself enough to ask a question. He'd taken notice of her apparent distraction.

"Did you see or hear something?" he asked, hope pitching his voice upward.

"Hmmm?" She absent-mindedly turned to face his concern. Smiling melancholically, she shook her head. "The waves are so noisy above the surface…"

Closing his eyes, he shook his head in disbelief.

Taking a big breath, she rose to her feet. "I'm a bit tired. Do you mind if I go to sleep?"

"That's it?" He protested.

"What?" she said, turning back from plumping up her pseudo-pillow.

"Your story. How does it end?"

"It's no story, it's my life, true or not, and it's a long one. Longer than yours by more than a year or two. This bed is calling my name right this minute." She crawled in and tucked her legs under the patchwork blanket. "We have a few tides at least for me to unwrap my life's narrative." She closed her eyes and added, "Don't forget, you owe me a fable in return. And if you please, no celebrity fables." She heard him cough in response. Eyes still closed she wagged a reproving finger in his general direction. "You're definitely an ostracized scientist on a research mission for the rare frog-spider in hopes that it will provide the answer to protecting against cosmic radiation for interplanetary travel."

Silence.

A long silence.

She dared a peek.

Still cross-legged, a hand on each knee, he was glaring at her.

She smirked, shrugged, and turned to face the cave wall. The best lies slept with the truth. She could only hope his dreams would prompt a more elaborate story than his true fan-tasy life. His lies would reveal more truth than his honesty.

Considerably further into the night, closer to dawn than midnight, Ellia woke to a shiver traveling from her toes, up her spine and into her skull. She couldn't have been more still than she already was, but that didn't prevent her from adding to her efforts. Ears hyper-tuned to the noises of the night, she one by one dismissed each sound, searching for the one that had roused her.

There. She heard it, fully awake now.

One eye opened, scanned its field of vision, then the other eye opened. In her sleep she'd turned her back to the cave wall, and fortunately now faced the faint glow of the fire's embers. The embers illuminated the cave a shade away from humanly impossible to see.

What had slid against her eardrums, and now appeared in the crosshairs of her vision, hissed as it stole up Min Soo's leg, coveting his body heat. Nasty and fast, the habu viper did not play well with others, and Ellia's eyes grew deep-space cold as she analyzed the situation. If Min Soo twitched a hair, the viper would strike without question.

His model lashes fluttered and Ellia moved. Hand grabbing tail, she spun and snapped the snake like a whip against the cave wall. Flung the limp body zipping past the magnificent door. A faint splash of water messaged its landing spot.

She shuddered to the ground in reaction. Compulsively she began wiping her hands on one of the many small lumps of rock rising from the cave floor. A hand landed on her shoulder and she gasped voicelessly.

"It's okay, it's okay," Min Soo's blanket warm voice murmured in her ear as he held her from leaping to her feet.

He handed her a piece of cloth she couldn't immediately identify, and while she wiped her hands on it instead of the hard rock, he awkwardly knelt next to her, patting and rubbing her back, murmuring soothing English and Korean phrases all jumbled together.

The shuddering finally dissipated, and with a last outburst, she flung the cloth she'd been wiping her hands raw on out the entrance of the cave. The patting and rubbing stopped. A little embarrassed, she turned to face Min Soo and saw his troubled expression.

Chin lowered to meet her eyes, he asked, "Snake?"

"Habu," she specified with a remnant shudder. He didn't need to know it wasn't from fear.

He fell back on his rear. "A habu? As in fkajgafd?"

"Habu, yes. Not sure what the other thing you said was."

Shaken, he ran trembling hand through his hair. Bed head made even stranger by the flustered gesture. Ellia grinned in honoured amusement. Not many got the chance to see this vulnerable side of Mr. Actor/Model unless it was scripted. Internally she shrugged, there weren't many who would have successfully saved him from a venomous snake either. Or a freshly crashed helicopter hanging over an abyss. His reaction did help his innocent victim storyline.

To avoid giving him the wrong impression, she squashed the grin quickly and turned to assess their campfire; at this point the term camp-ember would have been more appropriate. A few judiciously placed pieces of firewood raised the illumination level in the cave by a few degrees, and both of them found comfort, for separate reasons, in the fire's visually hypnotic caress.

Before dawn could show her skirts, the two in the cave had one after the other shut their eyes and blearily curled up on Min Soo's bedding by the fire and, like two toddlers after a long day at gramma's house, fallen dead asleep. Subconsciously Min Soo placed himself between the entrance and Ellia, but then again, both lay with the fire between them and the entrance.

Dawn was well past dancing the cancan by the time the uncomfortable effects of adults sleeping like toddlers penetrated through to the sleeping pair. Min Soo, a hair ahead on the waking scale, stretched like a turtle might, coming out of its shell, and promptly clunked his head against Ellia's. It woke them both up lickety-split, both sitting upright to rub their respective noggins.

Abashed, Min Soo snatched a glance over at Ellia. The corner of one side of his mouth stole upward, dragging the other corner along with it. Daylight made the night's events less fearsome and more comical.

Ellia's eyes narrowed, and she scowled in his direction, but she couldn't hold it. Her own mouth curved in reply. "Good morning."

Min Soo nodded his head in her direction, rubbing the leg the viper had been traveling. "Hmmm, yes, thank you." He surged to his feet, shook the memory from the offended limb and stretched both arms above his head as far as they could go. Then, with a gentleman's charm and a model's panache, he offered his hand to Ellia. "This is the second time you've saved my skin. Thank you."

"You're welcome," she replied like a duchess and took his hand to rise to her feet. A grand gesture toward the entrance followed her rising, and she added, "Would you care to join me on the hunt for breakfast?"

He bowed and swept his hand around to let her exit first. Ellia stuck her tongue out at the magnificent door as they left for Min Soo's first proper tour of the island. Sure, it hadn't been closed, but certainly it could have done something to keep out the viper, couldn't it?

With all the tall tales Ellia told over the course of the next few days, Min Soo grew increasingly more curious over her subtle, barely noticeable, infrequent disappearances. This morning, face wet from rushing his morning shave, he spotted a minor disturbance heading further into the island brush. Grabbing his shirt, he hurried to follow.

Habu snake concerns and trickster roots slowed him down. That and trying not to sound like a tribe of rhinos. Affectionate vines tired him out until he finally stopped and sank into a squat. He ran one long finger down his nose. He pulled the shirt away from his chest, trying to create a draft. He'd lost any trace of her passing. Birds cawed and insects chittered or buzzed as they saw fit. The ever-present sound of the ocean filtered through the dense brush. Slowly he rose to his feet and tilted his head to listen to something brushing the very edge of his tympanum. He took a step, and another, testing his bearing with each one.

The sound grew louder, distinct from the sound of the ocean waves. Recognition came one step before entering the clearing. A minor waterfall. He tripped into a full stop. He scanned his surroundings with breath on hold...and let it out. No telltale piles of clothing lying around. He grinned and frowned simultaneously. Scolding, he asked himself out loud, "What were you thinking?" The sound of his voice instantly muted a component of the waterfall's song. Min Soo's attention rose a level and he immediately surveyed the clearing again. The rocks framing the waterfall had that sturdy, rough look about them that welcomed a climber. Accepting the open invite, Min Soo took to the rocks, testing each one for slime and security, and arrived at the top with scarcely a missing breath. As soon as his head cleared, he saw it, the missing component. Out of sight of the lower clearing, Ellia sat on a rock eyeing him. For once, she didn't have a story on her face.

Min Soo stood silent, catching his breath. Too much silence; he turned around to stall. The view behind him refined his reaction. His breath caught again as he witnessed the unhindered glimpse of the beach, lagoon, and ocean. At this rate he'd run out of oxygen.

"Wow."

Ellia's voice interrupted his viewing, "What are you doing here?"

Without turning around, he replied, "Following you." The waterfall gave off midnight fridge vibes. He threw a second question over his shoulder, "What are you doing here?" The grass suffered a scuffing as he turned back on his heels. He hesitated, but curiosity pulled him down the garden path. "What was that sound?" He took a step in her direction. "I heard you playing something."

She shook her head, dropping her eyes. "I wasn't playing anything."

He disagreed with a shake of his head. A frown. "You stopped when I spoke out loud down there," he said, pointing down to the waterfall pool below.

"I was singing," she clarified, face reddening.

Merdragon

Thick lashes swept butterflies of their flight paths as he blinked with some significance. Bees protested as he blinked again. A hummingbird caught in the draft scolded him on his third blink.

He plopped down on the grass in front of her and leaned forward to scrutinize her face. Satisfied that her red face was not a hallucination, he leaned back and asked, "How is that possible?"

Scarcely moving her lips, she mumbled, "Polyphonic singing."

"Poly-what?"

She raised her eyes to look him square in the face, and Min Soo could almost see the mental quill being dipped in ink to start another fable.

"It's what bad mermaids, aka sirens do to lure sailors to their deaths."

The black moons of his eyes eclipsed for a full five second count. Revealing their light again, disbelief purred up his throat, "And that's called polyphonic singing?"

Defiantly, "Yup."

"Fine," he sighed, engaging in the game, "then I'm the Dread Pirate Robert. Can I hear you sing again? But don't lure me to my death. I'm a good pirate."

Grimacing, she shifted her shoulders. "I'm sorry, I haven't quite mastered it yet, but...if you insist, you can suffer through my practicing." Voice softening to marshmallows, she added, "You're the first person in a long time who's listened."

"Really? You don't belong to a mermaid choir or something?" he asked with wry twist of his mouth, moving to sit beside her.

She bumped him shoulder to shoulder. "I'm a merdragon remember? The choir master couldn't get the fire growl out of my voice."

It didn't seem to matter how ridiculous and far-fetched a line she pulled, the next one always went a little further. Eyes closed, he tapped his nose three times and sighed. He took a big breath and opened his eyes again. With the dark moons of his eyes intent on hers, he commanded, "Sing."

She complied.

He couldn't hear a thing. Nothing. Not at first. He could see the carefully controlled effort, so he waited. A burr began to vibrate behind his ear. Indolent. Aggressively so. The fire growl stalked him. It curled its flames under each vertebra, up, around, and up, growling, growling, up, up his spine. He swallowed hard. The haunting sound of a siren's song stirred into a stream over his head. His jaw went slack. The hair on his arms stood up as the notes spiraled into his skull. His breath stuck halfway, and he waited for her to breathe so he could catch his own breath—but the notes would not stop. The song she sang had no words he could comprehend, and he could not stop his eyelids from lowering. Surrendering, he let the notes have their way. They danced in and out of the present dimension; he lost himself trying to decipher reality.

The final note returned to its own realm and closed the door behind itself. Time resumed its earthly passing. The earth resumed its turning beneath his feet. He could feel it. His eyes flew open. The ground was shaking!

Ellia grabbed his arm and pulled him to his feet. "It's the volcano."

He'd never been on, or even near, an active volcano this, well, active. All around them the trees swayed, and more birds than he ever suspected hiding amongst them, flocked overhead in alarm. He struggled to keep his balance as the ground rumbled beneath them. Ellia's hand slipped from his arm and they both stumbled to stay upright. Then it all settled down. Min Soo and Ellia stood braced for another wave.

Min Soo spoke first, "Is it over?"

Ellia nodded. "I think so."

"Are you okay?" he asked, shifting from foot to foot, testing his stability.

"Good as goldfish, you?"

"Fine. Did that seem weird to you?" he asked with a frown.

She shrugged. "I'm no volcano expert, I have no idea. Do volcanos have a normal?"

He took in the birds beginning to settle back in the trees. "I wonder. How active is this volcano?"

"Hopefully it was only letting off some steam," Ellia replied.

Min Soo eyed her sideways and frowned again. A hint of dark sparked in his eyes; he shook his head and wryly suggested, "Or a fire growl."

Startled, Ellia stilled beside him, then she eased out of her own braced position. Chiding, she slapped him on the back, and he ducked his head, relaxing from his judo position.

"We should probably go see if our things are okay," Ellia said as she pulled a stray leaf from her hair.

Min Soo agreed. A thought stopped him. A chill froze his smile. "The helicopter."

Not waiting for Ellia's response, he bolted, long legs sprinting into the brush.

Ellia watched him go, one hand half-raised, sighed, then turned in the opposite direction. She danced and hopped her way past a few boulders and tree roots, threw a glance over her shoulder and quick-shifted to the left to disappear into a new cave. Two steps in, the cave distinguished itself from the other with its claustrophobic dimensions and smooth lines.

She sang a quick flurry of notes and pictures flowed up onto the smooth walls. Another flurry of notes and a flow of fingers over some of the symbols.

"Ah, good, the safety vents activated on time." Another image popped up. "Not sure why I even worried. It's been doing this for jellyfish generations." Her face stilled and grew sober. One more picture flowed up on the wall, distracting her. "Hmmm..."

Elsewhere, crashing and bashing into trees willy-nilly, Min Soo ran through the jungle. Birds screeched, twice disturbed, insects flew off their meal tables, lizards scurried to save their tails. He pounded up the cliff trail sending rocks and sweat flying, reaching the top, lungs heaving enough to commandeer the oxygen from a dragonfly minding its own business.

Trees and brush blocked his sight of the mechanical dragonfly—the helicopter—, and impatiently he circumvented them to reach the cliff clearing. The glorious view of the sky and ocean nearly blinded him, but tears of frustration finished the job. The helicopter that had survived the crash and typhoon, had not survived the volcano's turning in its sleep.

Knees hit the ground. He followed with his fist, and a few other words of the less savory sort. The long fingers of his other hand pressed into his eyes as he felt the burn of the bitter pill.

He dared the volcano to shake him off and crept closer to the edge of the cliff; he had to see. To his right, a piece of the tail remained as the last lingering reminder of the helicopter; the raw marks left on the ground revealed its final struggle. Down on his stomach, Min Soo peered over the cliff's edge, searching for any markers of the helicopter's ultimate resting place. The waves below crashed furiously against the cliff wall and obscured any hope.

More words slipped past gritted teeth, his head slumped between his shoulder, and his forehead hit dirt. Some modicum of survival instinct directed him back from the edge. He struggled to all fours and then to two; he took a step back, then another. And fell to the ground as his strength left him. He stayed there until the sun began to wave a sad farewell.

The next day, the sea breeze did brisk business with the washed clothes Ellia'd attempted to hang on any suitable branches she could find. Early though it was, the sun had agreed to assist in the drying effort and shone brilliantly, fiercely. She draped a ragtag length of sheeting over a handy bush, and watched Min Soo exit the cave to set off into the jungle without even a hey-ho. His dejection at the loss of the helicopter, and its radio, evident in every step.

Hours later, he returned from his walkabout of the island with a long piece of deadwood he'd picked up along the way. A stain on his shirt showed he'd at least managed to forage for a minor breakfast. Brandishing the stick at arm's length, he asked if she thought it could be used as a spear for fishing. Before she could reply, he answered his own question, "Probably couldn't spear anything anyway," shrugged and dropped it on the woodpile.

The walkabout hadn't used up all his energy. He began pacing the long beach, randomly picking up rocks and sending them skipping across the water. It proved challenging against the ocean waves. Standing near a palm tree, a jackfruit under her arm, Ellia opened her mouth to scold him for scaring away the fish, but shut it again, deciding against it. Fish who swam the ocean could handle a few rocks, and the humans stuck on the island could handle a few days of fruit, and maybe a mini mammal, if catchable, and at last resort, if absolutely necessary, grubs. As it was, she couldn't be sure the volcano's rumblings hadn't already done some fish stock disturbing.

Near evening's sun-light's-out, Min Soo returned to the cave entrance and the fire Ellia had set outside it to enlighten their dinner. Mum, he settled down cross-legged on one of the woven seat mats Ellia had fashioned from fallen palm leaves. She handed him his cracked pirate's plate and contemplated whether she could come up with a clever enough story to explain how she knew rescue was a lot nearer, and surer, than his current expectations. His hopes had been set on the helicopter's transponder, and she hadn't told him of her own radio correspondences when she'd first rescued him. Now, with its loss, he sat like an automaton, eating without tasting, eyes blinded by the flames.

"Excuse me, Mr. Fellow island castaway, but what do you think will be the first thing you do when you return to civilization?"

"Huh?" Min Soo grunted, blindly focusing on Ellia through the flames.

She repeated the question.

The question side-swiped Min Soo's mental dead-end cycling. He scratched his sunburnt nose. Ellia winced, then jumped when he barked a laugh. "Have a press conference."

"What?"

He bent his head and rubbed his neck. "Two steps before we're off the boat we'll be blinded by all the camera flashes. I'll be the number one news item for an

Merdragon

hour or more, and my management company will be raking in the advertising project offers."

He froze.

Ellia curled her toes in the sand. Casually, "Then...it'll be good for the brand of Han Min Soo?"

Softly, "You...knew?"

She scooped up a handful of sand and poured it over her feet. "I'd have to be blind and deaf."

The waves shushed against the shoreline. A few more pieces of fruit disappeared from Min Soo's plate.

"What about you?" he asked.

"Me?"

"Mmm, Ms. Ellia Nighe. If you were really a merdragon you could have swum or flown out of here no problem, long ago. You said something before about being a, uh, storyteller... Do you write books, read to children in libraries or...?"

Eyes on her plate, but thoughts burrowing far beneath the sand's surface, she didn't even consider telling him the truth. She'd started with the fibs originally to suss out his true identity. Telling lies had worked for her this far, and there was no point changing tactics now.

"The first thing I'll do upon sighting any spot of civilization...? Eat a steak, drink a cup of the darkest, blackest black coffee with a hint of sugar, and find out who's been caring for my cat."

"You have a cat?" Min Soo asked, eyebrows raised.

"Hmm, a calico named Dandy."

"You didn't mention him before."

She threw him a grin, cautioning, "I warned you early on, didn't I? By sheer overwhelming practice at the art, storytelling bleeds into everything I say. Whether I have a cat or not, or if it's really a fish, it would take an asphalt roller to straighten out the truth."

He shook his head and bypassed her tales of the past with a question about the future. "What are you going to do about the interviews?"

She leaned back to gaze up at the star spread that had developed over the course of their meal. "I'll leave those to you."

Fire flickered up around the tiny twig Min Soo threw into the dwindling flames. "They're going to want to talk to you too, and won't it be good for your career?" Cynically, "Because of me you'll rake it in. They'll be offering interviews to spill all the goods. You could even get a book deal or maybe a movie script."

"I probably could, but for other reasons..." She met his scrutiny straight on, and for the first time since she'd shown him her face, she gave him a fully honest one, "Han Min Soo-ssi, when you return to your star-studded, hallyu world, don't mention me."

"What? Why?"

"I've taken care of you well, haven't I?" she asked, resuming her stargazing.

"True," he replied, nodding his thanks and running a hand over the former lump spot.

"As a favour then." Her smile was overly bright. "I'd rather not get lynched by your fans."

"What? Oh, uh, don't think I'm that popular." The sunburn on his cheeks hid the blush.

"Oh, is right. The media can and will spin things any which way to get more hits. I'm sure you've had some practice obscuring answers."

"Not sure I can match your level," he muttered, but conceded. "If we ever manage to be rescued by allies rather than a North Korean spy boat, I'll make sure to edit out your part in this adventure."

"Excellent. Now tell me, what do you call that constellation there?" she asked, leaning back and pointing upward at a group of stars directly above them. The fire had decreased in intensity by this point which helped Ellia keep her facial expressions to herself.

The next hour or so of digesting, they enjoyably discussed the sky, sharing cross cultural nomenclature and mythological tidbits, making up name and stories for constellations they didn't know. Min Soo managed to send Ellia into gales of laughter with his stories of the Great Rockstar and his wandering amongst the varied constellations, and the concerts he played accompanied by the wild Leo, the Flying Fish.

Wiping tears from her eyes Ellia raised a finger to her lips and said she knew another story about the Flying Fish and famous Andromeda.

"Poor Andromeda," she started, "she wasn't chained to a rock like they say, merely exiled to an island and metaphorically chained to the land. You see, she was no ordinary girl, our Andromeda, no sir. She was one of those rare, mysterious foundlings. Found on the beach, all baby cute and adorable, but all alone."

Min Soo listened intently to the story, a smile curling comfortably at one edge of his mouth. Her voice had entered storytelling mode. A sound he'd willing

Merdragon

choose to listen to for the rest of his life. A frown flitted across his face at the thought of spending a lifetime on the island; Ellia's voice wound its way past the thought and brought him back to the story.

"The Queen happened to be enjoying a morning stroll—and this must stay between you and me—but if it had been a plebe, they would have said she was moping, but queens aren't allowed to mope, so she did whatever queens do when they're doing the equivalent. The reason? She'd been unable to bear a child, and queen or no, she was a woman who desperately wanted one. No amount of power or money had made one ounce of difference. Then, lo and behold, a little baby on the beach. Who would have thunk it?

"Anyway, many schemes and deceptions later, Little Princess Andromeda is now dancing over Palace grounds and the Queen happens to glance over and comment to a visiting frenemy that her little girl, who by this time was in the teen span of years, was prettier than any of the Ocean King's basket of brats. Yes, you may well gasp. So did the frenemy, right into the ears of her maid, who shared it with the footman, who spilled it over ale at the local tavern on a really, really early Saturday morning where a travelling troubadour happened to think it a fabulous idea for a tune, who then wrote the tune practically over day while hitchhiking a ride with a merchant on a cart to the next town, who then, after some happy haggling, cried that his loss was so great that his daughter would have to wear ashes and never ever attain to the beauty of the Ocean King's daughters, let alone that of Princess Andromeda. That night, the buyer heard the troubadour's song as well, and even later into the night, he quietly slipped away in a merchant vessel to some unknown location.

"Result? The Ocean King's basket of brats couldn't stand to hear something so ludicrous and cried tears of cold diamonds that Daddy must not love them because he allows such horrible defamation to be spread near and wide across the lands and oceans. Didn't daddy know that this was a clear declaration of war?

"Well, seven princesses, shedding copious, finest saltwater tears of hurt and injustice may even move the great Ocean King. That or his ears were starting to bleed from the whining, but for whatever reason, fatherly love or harassed daddyyyyyy, Andromeda became persona non grata in the land of the living.

"Understand, Andromeda's papa had strong knees and a strong heart, but the people of the land came first, and so he stalled, and then compromised by sending her to get a little scoured of her beauty on a little old island in the middle of storm central. The Ocean King's daughters, incompletely appeased, insisted that daddy make sure that no one ever, ever, ever, really daddy, never gets close enough to even see the vague suggestion of her figure on the island. A few sharks, who happened to cross the Ocean King's path as he muttered about being cursed with so many princesses, took the brunt of the King's chick-pecked displeasure and were sent to swim in circles around and around and around the island. The King let them know that despite one of them being a great white, he'd hunt them down and feed them to his daughters if they ever broke faith. Considering his beautiful princess were known to occasionally enjoy truly fresh, literally still breathing shark sashimi, the threat carried enough terror to spike them into dizzying obedience.

Ellia paused in her narration. The sound of waves lapped at Min Soo's ears.

The pause lasted. Min Soo propped himself up on his elbow and sleepily asked, "What about the Flying Fish?" Ellia hadn't gone to sleep with her eyes open, had she?

She stirred from her thoughts. "Mmm? Oh, yes. You remember Little Miss Andromeda was a foundling? Well, years ago, Argo Navis was bobbing along the sky oceans, where and when the horizon's line between the here and there disappears, with the Flying Fish school doing what they do alongside it, when a storm squalled up. Incidentally, you can thank the Ocean King's daughter number six for that one. Sadly, the Flying Fish were separated from Argo, mistakenly following a moony sunfish instead of the real moon, and by some weird, even by mythical tale standards, one of the Flying Fish fry found her little baby-self washed up on a beach, transformed into chubby little legs and dimples a barren Queen would fall in love with.

"The whole incident with Andromeda getting exiled to an island spread through the oceans like an oil spill and something about the whole thing made the Flying Fish curious. So, they've been swimming in the vicinity of Andromeda ever since, unable to ever really see her due to the always hungry and cranky sharks. Understandable, considering swimming around in circles forever and ever would make anyone cranky. There's a remorseful sunfish that swims by on occasion, staying just out of the shark ring.

Min Soo waited for more, but after another pause, Ellia stood to her feet and started putting dishes and meal remnants in order, the remains of the fire included.

"That's it?" he asked.

Intractable, she glanced over her shoulder, "What? You want me to climb to the stars and straighten them out?"

Merdragon

He frowned at the sharpness of her retort and stood to his feet. A glint on her face caught his eye, "Uh, you, wait, uh..."

Brusquely she cut him off, "I'm tired," and left the now extinguished fire and conversation to enter the cave without another word.

In the dark his mouth stumbled around words to say, but they refused to coalesce into anything solid. After a few moments in the darkness, listening to the lapping of the waves, he followed her into the cave. A step inside, he stopped. The cave was dark except for the faint shimmer from the door, but he knew she was there. He'd never consciously noticed it before. He took three more steps and stopped at Ellia's cot side. The fingers of his right hand moved in slow indecision. A stray glint flashed where her face had to be, an optical illusion or random spark of starlight. His hand clenched. A dark breath. He released it with a sigh. Going by memory, he felt the short way to his bedding.

The glint reappeared and curved into a scimitar of light. It disappeared a few breaths later.

In their beds on opposite sides of the cave, they both fell asleep to the sound of the ocean's shushing.

The early morning breeze, up before the early morning light, came flowing into the cave and brushed Ellia's hair against her cheek, waking her from her light slumber. She rose quickly, stopped by one of the cabinets and withdrew a small vial. Holding it tight, she continued toward Min Soo side, lithe and deadly. She opened the vial and held it under his nose for a ten count, placed two fingers on his wrist to feel for his pulse—a satisfied nod followed.

She closed the vial, and after putting it away, she made her way to the cave's entrance. More specifically, to the magnificent door.

"You did a good job with the typhoon, but not so much with the snake. To regain your reputation, I'm going to have to return you to a more critical position. Please cooperate, eh?"

By miracle or vial induced deep-sleep, Min Soo stayed under despite the scraping and grunting warming up the air in the cave.

By full morning light, Ellia sat cooling down high up on the cliff, infamous for the helicopter's ill-landing. There she saw what she'd been expecting the previous evening. A military ship a ways offshore. Min Soo's rescue.

She waited until it had approached as close as it could, been anchored, and prepped a boat to depart toward the island. "Min Soo's going to be ecstatic," she whispered to herself, and as the boat hit the water, her feet hit the path at a run. If a drop of rain on a clear sunny morning hit the ground on the way, what could one say, but somewhere a fox must have had a reason to cry.

    Out of breath she entered the still dusky cave. With a catch in her throat, which must have been from the run, she whispered Min Soo's name. He stirred. She crept closer and whispered it again. His eyebrows twitched and he turned his head to the side. With a quick and quiet sidestep, Ellia whispered it once more with a word or two added, then slipped inside the dark tunnels Min Soo had never managed to notice. She watched only until he had swung his legs over the edge of the bed and sat up. The moment he stood, Ellia disappeared completely.

A foggy forget-you-not

A whisper pulled Min Soo from his cotton-grey dreams. "Min Soo, chingu, friend, time to return to the stars, there's a ship…"

There was something both soothing and enticing about the voice. He scratched his nose. What was that smell? He rubbed at his eyes. He swung his legs over the edge of his bed, they felt like lead. Why was he getting up again? Something important.

Suddenly he sat up, eyes wide open. Ship. Cave. Island. Crash. Ship. Ship! "Ship. There's a ship!"

He tripped to his feet and dash-stumbled to the door that, what? He blinked at the sun-warmed grey cave wall. Why did he think there'd been a door? He shook his head, it wasn't important, the ship, the ship was important. Raising a hand to shade his eyes from the sun, he spotted the ship in the shimmering distance. Squinting, he raised a hand to wave when he heard yelling farther down the beach. A landing boat was coming to shore.

Sand flew as he ran to meet them.

The first man out of the boat ran a few steps toward Min Soo and called out as soon as they were in hollering distance, "Morning! Mr. Min Soo Han?"

Min Soo made it the final few feet and clasped the outstretched hand of the man. "I am so glad to see you." The sand shifted under his feet and he swayed.

"Mr. Min Soo Han? Hey, you okay?"

Fuzzily he raised his head to answer. Wait. He pointed at his rescuers with his free hand. Three of them now stood in a semi-circle around him, military boots steady despite the swaying of the island. "You guys are really tall." He'd fallen.

One of them waived over a fourth member. "Hurry up, there's something wrong with him."

A man knelt down beside him and started checking him over. "Mr. Han? I'm a medic, can you tell me if you were injured anywhere?"

He laughed, "Me? Naw, I'm fine, it's the island. It won't keep still. It's a volcano, you know?"

The medic persisted, "What about in the helicopter crash? Do you remember if you hit your head? And what have you been eating?"

Min Soo ran his hand over his face. "Anybody have any sunglasses? Everything's so bright today."

The medic moved his hand out of the way and forced an eye open.

"Sir, his pupils are dilated. We need to get him back to the ship."

Min Soo snickered to himself, "Long as there's no llamas…"

One of the men knelt down in front of him beside the medic. "Mr. Min Soo Han, I'm Lieutenant Scott. I'm going to have my men help you to the boat so we can get you back to the ship to get you checked out. Before I do, can you tell us where the helicopter landed? You're sure the pilot died?"

A puzzled expression crossed Min Soo's face. He tried to meet the Lieutenant's gaze, but light flares drove daggers into his eye sockets. He rubbed at his eyes and answered, "The pilot, yes, he died in the crash. The helicopter, it, it's at the base of the cliff in the ocean. But, but there's someone else though…a woman, I think…" The shimmer was giving him a splitting headache. He gingerly held his head between his hands, confused. "I'm sure…"

Orders flew over his head while he tried not to give in to passing out.

He felt a hand on his shoulders. "You'll be fine as soon as we get you to the ship. Hang in there. Here," something was placed in his hands, "have some water."

"Thanks." He hadn't had anything to drink yet this morning. He sipped with his eyes closed, trying to think. The smell in his nose made the water taste strange.

If he passed out or just drifted off, he couldn't be sure, but what felt like only a minute later he heard the men return. He tried opening his eyes and sighed in relief. No more light-daggers and the island no longer rocked. He stood to his feet with the medic's help and accepted the proffered emergency bar.

All four of the men had returned, one of them with Min Soo's suitcase.

"We found this in the cave down the beach, but we didn't find any people."

Min Soo frowned, chewing. It tasted off.

The Lieutenant added, "Mr. Han, we've already spent two hours searching the island. We found traces of the helicopter crash, and the grave you dug for the pilot, but we couldn't find anyone else. We were told you were the only one on the island, and before we can search anymore, I have to get you checked out on the ship."

Facing off with the obstinate Lieutenant, Min Soo almost panicked. He clenched his fists, then relaxed his hand to run over his eyes again. If only the shimmer would stop messing with his thinking, and the smell, it wouldn't go

Merdragon

away. Maybe there really was something wrong with his head. He risked a glance at the ship offshore, opened his mouth, and snapped it shut again.

"Fine, I'll get checked out."

The Lieutenant relaxed and started ordering their departure. Min Soo allowed himself to be shepherded into the boat and listened quietly to instruction. The medic helped him with his lifejacket and settled him on a bench.

"You okay? Let me know if you start feeling sick or anything."

Min Soo nodded.

The medic glanced toward the ship. "The return trip is going to be choppier than the one in."

Min Soo didn't bother replying over the rumble of the engine. A fist was pounding on an imaginary door inside his chest. He was trying to attach an arm, a body and face to the fist.

A spray of water jolted him from his pondering.

"Hold tight!" the medic yelled over the noise.

How far had they come? Eyes glued to the water, Min Soo felt his gut clench. His eyes burned.

"Sun fish… flying fish…" He didn't think, he slipped his lifejacket and dove.

Is she or is she not?

"Idiot!" Ellia cried, as she witnessed his insanity. She'd been watching from a hidden vantage point, strategically out of the main ship's line of sight. She took off running toward the end of the cliff muttering, "He's not supposed to remember. He's supposed to get rescued, not whatever it is he thinks he's doing. He better not get that drop-dead gorgeous body dead. Idiot. There are sharks and other miscreants out there, you, you jelly-fish brain." Flinging off her clothes, she gave one teeth-clenched roar and leapt off the cliff.

She dove. And transformed.

The transformation happened fast. But not instantly. There was a lot to change.

Wind and wildling strands broke the hair-restraining braid. Flashes of light along her skin formed into gold flecked scales from face to rapidly developing tail, and a third of the way down her flight, wings of gossamer steel cracked open, snapping instantly back against her stream-lined body. A ridge formed along her spine all the way to her tail. Green fire licked the edges of her pupils, and as she stretched out her hands, reaching for the ocean waves, diamond hard, dagger sharp talons parted the seawater.

Webbing formed between each finger, and as she sliced through the water, red, jagged gills flared along her neck. The gossamer wings hugged themselves around her like a tight-fitting second skin. Her tail beat a rapidly increasing rhythm, propelling her forward, and her scales clamped tight as her speed increased, her hair streaming, seaweed green, slick against her back.

Ellia burrowed through the water, heat-seeking Min Soo; torpedo strong, speeding in the direction she'd seen him dive, determined to find him before the sharks did—or he simply ran out of air, despite, well, it didn't matter. In these choppy waters his rescuers would not find him in time. He'd timed his escape too well.

There! The sharks she'd been worried about. Shortfin Makos clearly off their dizzying guard routine, narrowing in on an interloper/escapee, aka acceptable prey. Prey currently treading deep underwater, struggling not to rise to the surface, holding his breath with the desperation of someone running near empty. In the roughening waters he hadn't noticed the sharks, yet.

Merdragon

Clenching her jaw, she inhaled saltwater, then screamed through her teeth toward the nearest shark. Startled, well near out of its hide, it tumbled as the sound wave hit. The other sharks took immediate notice of her threat.

The sound pierced through Min Soo's increasingly oxygen-deprived motions. Jerking around, he spotted the sharks. Eyes wide, he noticed her too. The shock proved too much; with a whoof, his lungs let out his air. Before he could compound the error and inhale, Ellia reached him, grabbed his arm and pulled him close to cover his face with her other hand. Her diamond hard nails dug into skin. His eyes filled with desperation as instinct screamed to take in air; reason bellowed against it. What spirit remained had him grabbing her arm but not fighting her restraint.

Eyeing the sharks, Ellia loosened her wings and raised them above her head, creating a shallow dome. Then the gills along her neck began to suck in water. Her lungs pumped like bellows, and her mouth opened to release a stream of air into the dome. Before Min Soo's grip had lost its strength, Ellia lifted him into the small air pool. His inhale of relief was potent.

Just then, something hit her below the waist. She snapped her attention down. One of the sharks had been bold. She smirked. That strike would have seriously injured a regular mermaid. Nothing regular about her though. Even though her scales had taken on the dark version of a mermaid's pearlescent spectrum, they had the invulnerability of her supposed dragon heritage. But—and here she frowned as she tracked the other two older and wiser sharks—working together they could distract her enough to, at minimum, drown Min Soo.

A glance up verified he had a firm grip on the frames of her wings. So far her party trick was working, but she could feel herself getting light-headed. Her gills flared with effort and she considered her options. Things were getting complicated. Too big a ruckus with the sharks would pinpoint their location to Min Soo's rescuers. The sound of the boat engine kept passing closer and closer.

One diamond clawed hand reached down to scratch the spot the shark had thoughtlessly struck. She could practically see the scheming behind their cunning eyes. Simpleton sharks had not been sent to guard her island.

A sudden tightening of Min Soo's hand on her wing directed her attention upward. Her eyes narrowed as she noted the air pool's rate of shrinkage. It appeared her party trick worked better in still waters. Now that she saw it, her tail twitched—the trickle of bubbles tickled her wing edges unbearably.

She pointed at him and mimed instructions to breathe in and release his death grip.

Skepticism and newly formed trust warred in his eyes as he gingerly did as she'd instructed. Without any warning she spun up and around, and grabbed him from behind. She tucked him against herself, wrapped her wings around them both, and began swimming like his life depended on it.

She felt like a pregnant whale! Every stroke twice, doubly hard, and the turbulence in her wake may well have belonged to a panic-stricken school of tuna. The sharks had stalled on their tails, caught off guard, but a quick glance behind showed them racing after her with Mako speed. And Mako grins.

Ahead, a great rock ledge signaled a change in the current. They'd turned a corner of the island. Instantly Ellia dove deeper. She tensed her wings, then began to push upward, hard. The transition from air to water was always easier than water to air. Her seaweed-green slicked head breached the waves, her wings curved up out of the water to grab air, and, with a mute word of apology, she dropped Min Soo.

The well-established laws of physics fought her efforts. Cliff-side air-lift countered with a loop-hole. A minor one, but it gave her wings enough. With winds nowhere to go but up, her wings took full advantage. She fought for every inch of lift. Time didn't allow for the luxury of a leisurely climb. Every beat of her wings gained her more traction into the air. Reaching an unmarked altitude, she twisted, spun around, and snapped her wings into a screaming downward glide.

Her flight trajectory led straight toward the struggling Min Soo. She scanned the water along their escape path and spotted the sharks nearing fast. One of the sharks had gained a lead on the others. She smiled a cruel smile, one predator to another; on this side of the island, without witnesses, she could do as she pleased.

Her eyes began to glow; a flame escaped the corner of her lips. Min Soo saw her coming and turned fully to face her. She nodded in encouragement, refocused her eyes behind him, then spat out a javelin of fire half a meter over his head. Instinct struck and he forgot to tread water; he flung his arms over his head. Having timed things rather well, Ellia grabbed his arms above the elbow, and with the speed she'd gained coming down, she pulled his soaking-self up out of the waves and began curving skyward.

The roasted shark distracted the other two sharks from their lost prey.

Ellia again used the wind currents smashing into the cliffs, but now she fought less for speed as much as she fought against Min Soo's additional mass. He coughed up water from his lungs, and she nearly pierced his skin to keep from

Merdragon

dropping him. It did little for their ascent. Her eyes narrowed. Their current weight distribution needed to change. The sound of the crashing waves below didn't make it easy for her to talk to him—never mind her every lungful being used to fuel their climb.

Halfway up the cliff she figured she'd gained enough altitude to risk a move. If he slipped, she'd have leeway to catch him and try again. The raucous avian audience both jeered and cheered on her struggle, circling with interest. A meal was possible.

Her wingbeats slowed. She tensed. Then, with one counter-swing of her tail, she strained backwards until Min Soo thumped up against her tail. She released air from her wings and pulled up on Min Soo simultaneously. Up he came, down she went, and the moment she was eye to eye, she grabbed him around the waist. As her wings pulled them up again, with an "umph", Min Soo clutched her around the shoulders in a desperate hug. A hug that allowed her to maneuver like a cargo plane rather than a hot air balloon.

Counterintuitively she dove forward rather than trying to fight her way up from their mid-air standstill. Min Soo clenched his arms tighter but didn't go for the classic strangulation technique. Without having to strain against a dangling Min Soo, Ellia tacked her way upward with a touch more ease.

Min Soo murmured something she couldn't hear, his face lost in her hair. The sudden absurdity of it set off a giggle—a hiccough in their smooth climb. Another murmured tenor, "umph" almost made her lose it again. A judiciously placed claw against the back of her other hand cooled the nervous laughter, a side effect from the adrenalin downturn. She refused to think about any other cause for the guillotined hysteria.

Nearing the top of her climb, she began flying alongside the volcano's exterior wall. She'd been climbing toward this, the tallest point on the island, the volcanic peak. The rare series of geological events that had created the island allowed her to keep well out of sight of the boat searching for Min Soo, and the ship further to sea. The cone of the volcano had been worn down into a slanted opening that rose high on the opposite side of the lagoon but dipped on this side. The birds avoided it with good reason. Or had until the shield had disappeared.

Ellia whipped her tail around and banked sideways into the cauldron. A cauldron full of water, clear and barely touched by the ocean winds. A shear edged cauldron with nary a dry surface in sight. She slowed and began to hover, the currents spilling off her wings, rippling the water's surface. The beat of her wings hush-thumped in the dead air. The huffing and puffing she tried to keep to a steam engine simmer.

She turned her face to speak directly into Min Soo's ear, "Min Soo, I have to let you down now."

The creature spoke? Startled, he raised his chin from drilling its way through her trapezius muscle. He'd injured that muscle once, the only reason he could name it. "You can talk?" And knew his name?

"Uh, yeah, but you're no feather," she replied with a bit more inhaling and exhaling than would be normal in a sitting room. "Don't worry, the water's not deep. Shallow and free of things trying to eat you. You're tall so…up to your waist maybe?"

"Who are you?"

Her grip loosened—in surprise? It nearly dropped him. "Um, okay, I have to let you down before my wings fall off. Will explain after."

He coughed, his chin hitting her shoulder.

"Do you dance?" she asked. "

What?"

She winked, and he coughed again as she gripped him tighter with one arm, releasing the other from around his waist. She raised her free arm into a classic ballroom dance pose.

The near drowning, and near mythic encounter, had finally cleared his morning brain frog. Nodding, he tensed his one arm around her shoulder and released the other to reach for her hand. As quick as a breeze she grabbed his wrist, tilted them forward and released the grip around his waist. As if they'd rehearsed, he smoothly slid down and hung by one arm, eyes on the water.

Above him—she resembled Ellia; couldn't be her, could it? She called out, "On the count of three. One, two, three!"

Her hand opened and down he went, the water cushioning his fall. He sputtered up out of the water, thankful for the surprising freshness. Flinging his hair out of his face, sopping wet he stood, flexing his toes on the hard rock floor of the cauldron, happy not to contend with sand. It made it easier to turn around with shaky legs to search for an exit point.

360 degrees later, his attention was back on, Ellia? Dark against the midday sun, she flew toward him. Did she intend to land right beside him? But no, her eyes were focused above and beyond him. He followed her gaze to a vertical shelf of rock rising from the cauldron floor. Only noticeable from a certain angle, it had

Merdragon

a concave top and reached a couple of meters upward and a meter or less from the wall. Slogging through water, he drew closer and spotted the grooves carved into it, hand and foot holds.

As she approached the obelisk, the beat of her wings created wavelets in the water. In the quiet of the cauldron, the sound of her wings switched off his survival mode stoicism. His knees gave way, the result of the last half hour's adrenalin drain. Water up to his neck, he could only watch as the creature set herself up on the pedestal, softly spiked spine facing him.

Taking a big breath, she stretched out her neck, shook out her hair and fluttered out her wings to their widest. She wiggled her bottom and flexed her wings a few times, the skin between each silvery bone stretching gossamer thin. Suitably stretched out, she retracted her wings, lowered her spikes and slapped her tail against the rock. She gripped the rock with her diamond clawed hands. Gleaming green eyes met his over a delicately scaled shoulder.

"Well, that was certainly an eventful series of events you instigated with that impromptu dive. What in whale tails possessed you to jump? You were in the middle of being rescued."

His mouth slapped shut, and so did his eyelids. Twice.

"Shock, huh?" She nodded in sympathy. "A fry different from stunt choreography and safety harnesses. At least you held it in this long." She turned away, then with the strength of her arms, managed to turn herself so that she sat facing him straight on.

He could feel the slackness growing in his jaw.

"Frankly, it's reassuring. Oh, and by the way, it is me, Ellia." She tapped her diamond tips against her lips, "I didn't want to over-narc you... Never mind, done is done."

His jaw dropped again, and he moved it around, fully intending to ask something, but he wasn't sure what. He snapped his mouth shut. So many questions. He pointed, and managed to say, "Tail."

"Mmm, this thing?" she asked, raising it in mimicry of the first time she'd told him...the truth?

A tail, a surprisingly supple one, and wings, two faintly green and translucent ones with fine veins that pulsed with life. And, and, he squinted. What had she said? Something about merchild scales stretching up to their armpits before they matured. Why did hers seem to continue down the full length of her arms and up to her jawline? And, not sure quite where to direct his attention, he dropped his eye back to the tip of her tail. Dark seaweed green and mobile. The movement drew his eyes slowly upward. Flashes of gold edged the scales. Around her hips the green shifted into earthier greens.

"Han Min Soo?"

His eyes snapped to her face.

"Merdragon, remember? What kind of bioengin-, I mean, uh, what kind of dragon would I be without healthy protection over my heart?"

He looked. She was right. The scales from her midsection shifted into earth tones, faded into tan as they ascended and finally into ivory, but darkened again as they framed her face and circled around her back. Fully protected from spears, swordfish, and immodesty? Intriguingly inorganic. His eyebrow twitched.

The living breathing, inorganic Ellia rearranged her posture, straightened up and stretched out her arms to the sun burning above her head. She tilted her head from side to side, loosened up her shoulders and shrugged off his contemplation. Like a bird she inclined toward him, clinging to her perch.

"It might be warmer than the ocean, but I think it's time you got out of the water."

He ran a hand over his face, the shock wearing off in layers. He staggered to his feet. "What...?" He glanced around. "How...?"

"Not the time for a long story. Have to get you back to being rescued." She gestured him closer and directed him toward the other side of her pedestal. "Please find the cauldron exit a few steps this way. A crack in the wall for your convenience."

He splashed his way past her eyrie, brushing his hands inches from her tail. His fingers itched. This close, the scales looked like marble laced with gold thread. The muscles moved beneath the scales, and he ran a finger over his nose instead.

The exit, he saw it now, really was a crack in the wall. About a metre above the water level, grooves had been carved in the wall for convenience, and a lot of rocks and sand and dirt in the crack to give it a level walking surface.

"Don't worry, the entrance is a little tight, but once you get inside it opens up." She sat above him, silhouetted against the sky's glare. "The ship's not going to hang around long. We need to get a move on."

Min Soo nodded and squelched his way up into the exit's entrance. The sun didn't reach far into the dark and he sniffed at the antique smell. Fully cognizant of potential dead ends and venomous denizens, he called back to Ellia.

"You did say 'we', right?"

Her voice came back, strained and tight, "Give me fifteen to twenty minutes or so."

Merdragon

Scratching his head, he leaned back out into the open and witnessed Ellia's wings spread wide against the blue sky. Wide and dissolving like moth-eaten wool. He mouthed a word in Korean. A whimper curdled his eardrums. It came from Ellia. He clapped a hand over his mouth. Her tail was dissolving along with her wings, tearing. Gold edged scales flaking off like embers, turning into ash as they drifted off.

He withdrew. Another whimper and he covered his ears. He leaned back against the wall, slid down, and lowered his head to put his head on his knees. Tense, he waited. No watch on his wrist, no cellphone to consult, the fifteen to twenty minutes went on interminably. A splash triggered a realization. Raising his head, his eyes widened, and he jumped up. His still wet shirt resisted his efforts, sticking to him like all wet things do, but he managed to pull it off in time. He wrung it out, and hearing wet footsteps, he held out the shirt blindly.

A tired, "Thank you," announced Ellia's arrival. A one-sided smile crossed his lips. He took a breath to ask, but she added, "I'm fine, it's normal...mostly. We need to move." He didn't wait to hear more. Rubbing his bare arms, he furthered his way into the darkness.

The way grew warm and soon he lost the wall to his left. Shuffling he took another couple of steps and lost the right side. A hand touched him from behind and he stumbled forward in a second of panic.

"Easy, it's just me," came Ellia's voice moving away. The sound of her footsteps shushed off to one side as he listened to her mutter to herself, "I know I left a torch in here somewhere."

A burst of flame lit the dark, and Min Soo rubbed his eyes to see Ellia holding an old-fashioned, non-electric torch. And wearing his shirt. Politely, he averted his gaze. Rubbing the back of his head he feigned interest in the surroundings. The torch light flickered over obsidian walls and grandfather seashells. The more he looked, the more his eyes caught glints of bling and, well, barnacles.

"This is your home," Min Soo exhaled in half question, half statement.

Ellia laughed in self-mockery, "A prisoner's treasure trove of storm-tossed salvage?"

"Prisoner?" he asked, spinning around again to inventory her trove. "It's still amazing." A thought stopped him. "Wait...prisoner? Do you mean, you? Voluntary?"

"Admittedly it is an odd sort of prison, I've puzzled over it more than a few years. Initially voluntary, but of late I've become a little leery about that adjective." She came up beside him. She'd donned a dry set of clothes while he'd been gawping. The torch light made her look thinner. In her hand hung a dry shirt.

Inclining his head in something more complicated than a simple thank you, he took the shirt from her and put it on. He tried not to think about who might have worn it last.

"A dry set of trousers I don't have."

"I'll wait until we're on the ship to get a violent cold."

Ellia snorted but didn't parry. Instead, she lit the way toward another narrowing of the cave. With her holding the only source of light, Min Soo didn't need an invite to follow.

The passageway began to narrow uncomfortably and forced both Ellia and Min Soo to sidle sideways. It stretched infinitely into the dark, and when it began to curve downward, Min Soo began breathing a little harder. Only the blaze of the torch and the shine of it on Ellia's glinting hair kept him sidling one shuffle at a time.

Ellia clapped suddenly and the torch went out. Min Soo froze.

"Ellia?"

"Tell me again," she whispered in his ear, "why did you jump?" A subvocal growl curled its way around his throat.

He jerked back, grunting as his head smacked against rock.

"Why did you jump out of the boat?" she asked again, and Min Soo's hairs shivered to full attention.

"S-sunfish."

Genuine surprise lilted her voice. "You saw a sunfish? That would have been odd. They don't usually swim so close to shore."

The lilt in her voice loosened his. "My head was woozy, like I'd been drugged, must have been something bad we ate the night before."

"Or something," she interjected.

"I knew there was something important I had to remember and then I saw a flash of something out in the water. It got me thinking. When we were maybe halfway to the ship, I saw the sunfish. I've never seen one before. That's what made me remember."

The voice he'd come to know well over the last weeks asked cautiously, "You remembered what?"

"I wasn't supposed to be on that helicopter...and you never were."

He heard her do a slow inhale. "What do you mean you weren't supposed to be on that helicopter?"

Merdragon

"You can confirm when we get back, it's still a little fuzzy, probably the concussion, but I switched with...with another model at the last minute. I seem to remember a freak accident causing the change in plans." He paused. "If I'd been clear in the head, I probably wouldn't have jumped, but I wasn't."

The darkness pressed hard against Min Soo, but with less death-threat.

"Hmm...dumb drugs...they were supposed make you leave without a fuss, instead...ah well."

"Uh, drugs? You drugged me?" Where had she found drugs?

She cleared the growl from her throat. "Ah, yes. We'll talk more on that later. Be thankful I didn't do worse. I've got good reason."

"Worse?" He edged away without any real plans to run. She blocked the only way out.

"Later. Something happened to the shielding around this island. Whether it relates to the helicopter accident or some gizmo on that military ship impatiently waiting out there, I might as well take my chances and catch a ride. This way they won't drop you in a padded cell the moment they spot you. I planned on waiting until they'd taken you well and on your way, but I don't mind the lift. If there's sunfish out there, they have protection. Who knows what else is circling the island other than gangster sharks. But, we stall in here any longer and they'll think you've permanently become part of the ocean ecosystem."

Strong fingers grasped his, and abruptly the green and golden glint of her eyes blinked in front of his nose. He stumbled to a halt. He'd brushed aside the memory of those eyes from that first waking.

"Hold my hand and I'll guide you through."

He hiccupped or laughed or both, he didn't know what to call it. "You can't relight the torch?"

A squeeze of his hand and a tug started the sidling again.

"There are some volatile and noxious gas pockets coming up, and I really don't like roasted human."

"You prefer us raw, like sashimi?" He joked, firmly resisting the claustrophobic hysteria trickling up his spine.

"Hmm, that does sound rather tasty... You do have your eyes open, right?" she asked out of the dark.

"Uh, I think so, why? Oh..." In the process of blinking to test if he really did have his eyes open, the difference between open and closed had become discernable. The difference between onyx and charcoal.

"Are we coming to the exit?" he asked.

Ellia's voice held an odd timber in it. "It's going to get a little snuggier—is that a word?—before we see the exit."

"Do I want to know?"

"Probably not."

"You're going to do the same thing you did when you left me in the water with the sharks?" It sounded sulkier and more accusatory than the sarcastic he'd intended. Suppressed panic was stripping niceties away like sandpaper on skin.

"The ceiling's about to drop down to less than one and a half metres, but the good news is it's only for a short distance, and then it will open up into a rounded roomy cave, but we'll have to scootch our way around the vent of noxious gas I know is at its centre while holding our breath, but there's a vent above that which goes all the way to the surface so at least you'll be able to see to avoid stepping in the vent below. After that, a few more steps onward through this tunnel and a slide down a water worn lava chute. Then there's the tumble at the end where I try to keep us both from landing in the crown-of-thorn bushes, followed by a snake pit and a tribe of cannibals..."

Hyperventilating sounded like a good plan. "You should have added a tiger to that story. I haven't seen any cannibal left-overs on this island."

"And you have on others?" she asked wryly.

"I admit, I have not."

"Ha! Well, you're in luck. I admit to a mild fallacy, partly."

"What? The part about getting out of this pitch-black vise at all?"

"O ye of little faith. The noxious gas can make you a bit woozy, but only if the vent is emitting. That's where we're going to climb up and out. No bitey things, thorns, snakes or human."

He stretched a hand upward and, "Ouch!" He clamped his mouth shut and cradled the injured finger.

"There are bitey lavacicles, tho'."

To distract himself, and disguise any pain-hissing, he asked, "What if the vent is emitting?"

"We see who can hold their breath longer?"

"How hard is the climb?" he asked, ducking as he felt his hair brush against a lava formed stalactite, or lavacicle as she'd called it.

He felt her hand squeeze his. "Time to start ducking Mr. Jack's Beanstalk."

Trying to duck while sidling sideways, sandwiched between not one, but two hard places, is a trick only snakes and professional spelunkers, and maybe octopuses, should attempt. All they seemed to worry about was fitting their skulls, or beaks, through a space.

"Ellia?" His normally velvet voice rose and cracked above status quo.

"Yes?"

"You're sure this is passable? I think I prefer drowning to being stuck."

"Alleviate your concerns, my young man, should the situation devolve, you may abandon all dignity and lie on your side, in which case I will drag you like I do my dragon appropriate dinners, aka tuna carcasses. How's that relieve your mind?"

"I'm being compared to tuna, great, and a dead one at that. My modeling career may never recover. That particular solution would require my dead body. This is ridiculous. You should've just dropped me in a tree or something." The ceiling lowered still more, and he contorted to keep up with the figure in front of him.

"Witnesses, witnesses," she reminded him, tugging him steadily through the dark.

"Better than this. How low did you say this gets?" he asked, breathing with great concentration, in through the nose and out through the nose.

"Only a few more breaths away. Stop," she sharply ordered. She slipped her fingers out of his and added, "Wait here."

He groaned. Now he was alone, sideways skewed, crimped between immovable forces. He rested his head against the wall, focused on every breath that flowed in and out of his lungs, and really, really hoped she'd been convinced of his genuine innocence. He'd rather not be a dead tuna. The scent of overwhelming claustrophobia lined every dusty lungful.

The next moment, he could see. A crack of light lit the shark teeth above and the impossibly narrow exit. Ellia's face abruptly blocked a portion of the light—and some of the despair—and called to him.

"Sorry about that, I caught a whiff of those noxious gasses I told you about. I've covered the hole as a temporary measure, but you'll have to hurry. The pressure and concentration are only going to increase and eventually leak through. We can't be here when that happens."

She ducked out of sight again, and he anxiously gauged the tunnels dimensions. He'd thought the darkness oppressing, but now he wished for ignorance. When Ellia'd been leading him on, he'd just trusted, but now? Now that he could see? Blind faith would have been easier to stomach.

"I... Ellia...? I don't..."

The silhouette of Ellia's head came into view again, and in the shadow of her face her eyes glittered like solidified emerald flames. She hissed between her teeth, "Come. Out."

It sent chills up his spine, freezing the rising terror. One shuffling step at a time he squirmed his way around each bump and curvature of the walls, the ever-lowering threat of the shards above pushing his spine, hips, and knees into ever more contorted angles. He thanked his parents, grandparents, chosen profession, and the days of unconsciousness for his present slim physique. The height was a problem, but dwarfism had its own kettle of fish to boil.

The crevice pressed hard against him, caught every loop, button, and wet seam in his clothing. His hands reached out for the approaching edge, and with relief, felt her hand take his to pull his twisted self out. He gasped at the hasty extrication, and for his reward, Ellia yanked his shirt collar up over his nose and mouth.

Min Soo pulled back from the scent of his own stress sweat, but Ellia stretched up on her toes to grab the back of his neck, stopping his retreat. Her mouth was closed tight in a line and he realized something was up. Brows furrowing, he questioned her silence. Jaws strained tight, she released his neck and pointed upward to the source of the light. A rough-hewn ladder, if it could be called that, rose to the open skylight, about three metres up. Unsure why that required having his face covered, he shrugged and chivalrously gestured for her to climb first. She responded with a glare and two-armed him up the rickety contraption.

Trying to keep the shirt over his face with one hand, and climbing with the other, proved hard going. The shaking of the ladder let him know she was right behind him. With one hand and one elbow he hauled himself up as quick as he could.

Reaching the top, he released his hold on the shirt, held his breath, grabbed what purchase he could and crawled up and over into the rocky clearing. The brush growing at a distance had stayed clear of the noxious fumes the skylight regularly emitted. But not too far. Min Soo could see there'd be heavy slogging through thick greenery to get to the beach, but he grinned. At least here he had an ally in the sun.

Open air safely achieved, Min Soo turned around to help Ellia up out of the hole. He grabbed her hand and pulled. And nearly fell backward seeing her face in the full light of the sun. Her face glowed an unhealthy yellow and her eyes burned red around the edges. Tearing her hand from his grip, she fell on all fours and raised a hand to warn him from getting closer. Then she began to cough.

Merdragon

Harsh, gag-inducing coughs, and with each one, mustard green smoke poured from her mouth. She hacked and hacked until he worried her lungs would turn inside out. Between gasps of air, she repeatedly gestured him away until, with a final burp and spit-vomit of unpleasantness, she crumpled down on the shale and gravel.

Min Soo hurriedly removed his shirt and swept the air around her to rid it of the lingering fumes, for both their sakes. He knelt down to check she was still breathing, then raised her into a sitting position. Still conscious, she weakly ran a hand over her mouth, wiping away residue.

She grinned weakly at him, "Shirtless again." The grin slipped, her eyes drooped. "Beware sunburn."

He sniffed the shirt, grimaced, then pulled it back on. "Happy?"

She didn't respond. Compared to some morgue residents, her pallor could have competed for deader. Rocks grinding into his knees he took her arms and draped them over his shoulder. Reviving lightly, she helped him out until he'd risen to his feet with her in piggyback position. He frowned. She felt like a skeleton made of gold filigree. Heavy but absurdly fragile. Still semi-conscious, she tightened her arms around his and he felt her smile. The irony wasn't lost on him either.

"My turn to carry you."

"Hmm, we're now two to one. Better hurry, the ship isn't going to stick around forever, regardless if they're here for you or me."

He didn't respond. Already her weight was draining the little left-over energy he still had. It had been a terribly long day.

Lazily Ellia pointed in the direction of a faint trail that he noticed as soon as she'd pointed it out. It led away from the mountain and into the jungle. "That leads to the beach."

He managed to quip, "At least there aren't any sharks."

A hmph of laugher was all he got back in reply.

Carrying her on his back, Min Soo started on the trek to the beach, every so often pausing to resettle her position. Concern coloured his face in uncharacteristic shades. He couldn't help feeling how thin she'd become. Thin, but gold bar heavy. He didn't know how the whole transformation thing worked, but it hadn't sounded easy, and then to take in the amount of fumes he'd seen pouring out of her… Her face rested against the back of his neck and it burned against his skin. He knew she could breathe fire, but he didn't think she should feel like fire. It didn't help that his legs were beginning to feel like they were on fire.

The path sloped down, mostly, at a gentle decline, rough and rarely used by Ellia or passing animals. Being taller than Ellia, or for that matter any of the island's other regular inhabitants, had its disadvantages. Unable to free his hands, by the time he could see the ocean through the trees, every root and tree branch had conspired to add a few more ugly welts to his face. His knees had begun to develop a definite shake.

Within glimpse of the beach, a tree invited him to take a rest and inhale a few gallons of oxygen. Such a polite request couldn't be refused, so he politely slumped against the trunk. Bark scraped against his shoulder and face, Ellia scorching his back. He craned his neck around and nearly dropped to his knees seeing her face. Gray-blue and gaunt, her death mask spiked in him his last adrenalin rush. He pushed off from the tree, hiked her up again, and took off at a fast walk.

The rush lasted past the tree line and halfway across the beach, but the loose sand defeated him. It ate up the last of his reserves and he collapsed to his knees. Ellia slid from his grip and flopped on to the sand. Strands of hair streaked her drenched, death-painted face. Her breath imperceptible.

On the beach, another landing boat had arrived earlier while Min Soo's rescuers had been scouring the water, but now it too was leaving. Min Soo scrambled to his feet and began yelling and waving his arms. One of the seamen alerted the others, and within moments three of them jumped out and began running. Min Soo slumped to the ground, sopping sweat.

The largest seaman reached Ellia's still form, dropped to his knees, and put a finger in front of her nostrils. There was still life. He bent down, scooped her in his arms and surged to his feet. In Min Soo's eyes she could have been a feather pillow for all the effort it seemed to take the massed-up seaman. A grunt and a stagger when he took a step however, validated Min Soo's struggle to get her here.

The two other men took stock of Min Soo and one of them asked, "Can you walk?"

Min Soo clasped the offered arm, and the two men hauled him up and half carried him between them to the boat.

The bodybuilder reached the boat first, splashed through the waves, and with the help of those waiting, he handed her in to be laid on the bottom of the boat.

Merdragon

Min Soo climbed in next, helped by a judicious push. The boat received its own push, and the engines had their tolerances tested.

One of the crew called in to the ship on his radio, "We've got Mr. Min Soo Han and an additional person. A woman. She's in bad shape."

Over the sound of the motor, the rush of the wind and the boat impacting the waves, the reply was unintelligible. The man called to him, "Sir, do you know what's wrong with her?"

A fifth percent of the truth ready on his tongue, he waved back toward the island. "Volcano's active. I found her, name's Ellia, knocked out beside a smoking vent."

The man relayed the information over the radio. Min Soo didn't follow the conversation. His attention was on Ellia. Yesterday she'd pulled him out of a funk. Sturdy for a woman, ready at the drop of a coconut with a bewilderment of quipped tall tales. Today she'd turned into a hardcore sylphic fable he'd never even imagined. But here and now? He reached over to pull a strand of hair from her mouth. How many times was it she'd saved his skin?

The crew man keeping tabs on her vitals clapped him on the back. "You did good, man."

Slumping forward, elbows digging into his knees, Min Soo murmured, "It's only fair."

"We've got a good doc on board; she'll get through this."

Min Soo rubbed his eyes. "It's only right that she should."

The crew men shared a look over Min Soo's back. A few hours ago he'd been a crazy loon jumping into shark-infested waters over a half-baked hallucination. Now? A crazy civilian with die-for loyalty they could appreciate. Even nod approvingly. But one of them sat between him and the edge of the boat. Safety measures.

Back to reality

When they arrived at the ship, medics were waiting for both Min Soo and Ellia. With drill training they first lifted Ellia up onto a stretcher and placed an oxygen mask over her face. They tried it on Min Soo, but he'd already regained some strength thanks in part to another emergency ration bar. He walked to the sickbay on his own two feet.

The doctor in charge questioned him as the medics and nurses fussed efficiently, lifting Ellia onto a bed, recording her vitals and inserting an IV into one arm. Seated, with legs swinging, on his own gurney, Min Soo kept craning his neck trying to keep an eye on her. He scratched the scruff he hadn't cleared in the morning and watched a nurse draw Ellia's blood. With the doctor interrogating him, a nurse checking his vitals and prepping him for his own IV-line, there wasn't much he could do without raising suspicion.

Eyes darting, his mouth continued to answer questions. His mind spun for traction. And slipped. The room fuzzed in his eyes. His mouth felt heavy. What was he thinking? Oh, sedative…

Down a few decks, a crewman hurried with intent along a busy passageway. A medic, coming down one of the ladders, nodded to him. The crewman nodded in reply and waited for the medic to get out of the way. As soon as the way was clear, the crewman brushed past the medic with mutual slight-of-hand and up the ladder he went.

Two decks up, the crewman paused in his steps, scanned the area, and saw his target. There was jollity in his greeting as he approached another medic entering the lab adjacent to the sickbay. Ever helpful, the crewman pushed open the hatch, flashed a smile that crinkled the corners of his eyes, and flipped the tray in the medic's hand.

He ignored the outraged cry and focused on catching the flying tubes of red substance before they could hit the floor. By some miracle he succeeded.

"I am so sorry," he apologized to the medic. Full of contrition, he opened the palms of this hands to reveal each tube safely whole.

Relieved, the medic collected the tubes and secured them. Then she forcefully pushed him out.

Merdragon

"I'm sorry," he said again as the door closed behind him.
Hours later, three tubes of blood that weren't missing, disappeared into a biohazard incinerator.

Min Soo woke like a machine from sleep mode; he'd slept past the post-drug-groggy and into natural sleep. The lights had been dimmed since last he'd had his eyes open, and now he did a visual 360. He'd been completely curtained in. Was that normal for a military vessel? A growling moan came from behind the curtain to his left. He rolled out of the gurney, grabbed the IV-stand tethered to his arm, and fumbled to find the opening to his fabric prison. Another moan. In frustration he bent down and yanked the curtain up and over his head.

In front of him, on her side, lay Ellia with an oxygen mask over her face. The moans stopped. Green eyes warily stared at his curtain draped face. Familiarity brought out a sigh. As he unbent to his full 180, the curtain rustled off his shoulders and draped itself on the tether. The nurses had secured the line well. He reached out with his free hand and touched the edge of her mask.

Ellia raised an eyebrow. An art she'd been practicing for years. He pulled his hand back. That gave her room to remove the mask. "I'm guessing we're on the ship?"

Min Soo nodded.

Gesturing at the curtains that surround them, she asked, "Would you open those up?"

This time Min Soo took his time to find the divide. He pulled the curtains back with a "shing" of metal on metal. The sickbay was empty.

"No one else's here?" she asked.

"We're the only ones. Want me to go see if there's a nurse or guard stationed outside?"

She shook her head, stopping him. "Help me out, will you?" she asked, raising herself on to an elbow. She used Min Soo's outstretched arm to pull herself up into a fully seated position and dangled her legs over the edge. Min Soo rescued her hair as she pulled the breathing mask off completely. About to pull the IV-line out, he placed a hand on hers, pausing the intent.

"I don't know what you had to do back there on the island, but I think you could probably use whatever's in that bag to recover."

She gave his hand a thoughtful moment. "You, you're probably right. Yes, I may have, uh, overestimated my substance."

"Overestimated...what?"

"Conservation of mass and energy. It's science. I presume you did learn that in school."

Min Soo withdrew his hand. "I didn't get top marks, but I didn't graduate at the bottom of my class either."

"So, certain things," she put a finger over her mouth, tugged on an ear, and tried to clue him into the chance of listening devices in the room, "require a proper accounting of resources. When resources have been utilized and discarded too abruptly to be recycled, less than required amounts are subsequently available."

The hum of the ship's equipment and machinery ran at odds with the years Ellia had spent in a near all-natural environment. Min Soo rubbed his thumb over his own IV-line.

Ellia gestured at the quarter-full bag. "I don't know about you, I, however, am thinking a toilet would help deal with some of the liquid that my systems been using to off-load unwelcome wastage."

"You do remember my first language is not English?" He shifted from one foot to another. "But I do understand the part about needing to use a toilet." The wheels on the IV-stand squealed as he spun it around to spot a possible door. He gestured toward it. "You think that might be what you're looking for?"

"Hmm, you could be right. Help me down, will you?" Her toes curled on floor contact. "Wowza, that floor is on the cool side. Never mind," she squeezed Min Soo's forearm, "that's just the fever talking."

She couldn't be sure which of the two choices his brain had been going for— find slippers or lift her back onto the cot. It didn't matter. The small door was her priority. She took a couple of mincing steps until her feet adapted. The coolness felt good. But it was short-lived. In the few steps it took to reach the mystery door, Min Soo had found slippers. Opening the door, she mindlessly slipped on the rudimentary footwear.

As she went in, he whispered, "They took blood..."

"A flushable toilet!" she squeaked. She clapped a hand over her mouth in shock. She was not the squeaking, squealing, eeek-ing type.

Min Soo swallowed a cough. "Hurry up, will you?"

"A-okay," she replied with a nod, trying to reassure him. She spun back to the 'head' with glee, hauled herself and the IV contraption inside and took care of priority business first. She really had had the need.

Merdragon

Washing her hands, she took a good look at herself in the mirror. She turned off the tap and heard the squeak of Min Soo's IV-stand being pushed back and forth in short stops and starts. To be fair she'd have to be quick. Staring into the eyes glimmering back at her in the mirror, she focused on the coolness of the floor, the cold ceramic sink, and the air vent blowing rudely through the gaps in her gown. The glints and flames subsided by flick and flare, down to a non-feverish pitch. She sighed. A surface human's shade of iris. Perfect.

She opened the door to catch Min Soo leaning against the wall in his legs-crossed way, the IV-stand inbound from its yo-yo-ing. He didn't need her thumb gesture to scoot past her into the facilities.

While he took care of his business, she sat herself down in a suitable chair and closed her eyes. The flames inside her core furnace still burned with the residue of the noxious gases she'd inhaled to protect Min Soo. She grimaced; the oxygen they'd given her had helped a tad excessively. Her lungs contracted as she breathed out and then held. Held her lungs until the darkness increased behind her closed eyes, until her lungs asked for water, and until the final flicker descended into a glowing ember. Then, and only then, did she carefully section off the furnace and allow her lungs to refuel. All systems near enough to standard, on the exhale, cool as the proverbial cucumber, she opened her eyes.

A stranger stood observing her. Strangers. She'd have to get used to those again. This one, a Medical Officer? Seeing her eyes open, he humphed, "You're out of bed. How do you feel?"

"Quite well, actually." She rose to her feet and reached out to shake hands. The sound of Min Soo exiting the head interrupted the polite gesture.

"And how are you feeling, Mr. Min Soo Han?" the doctor asked.

Wiping his wet hands on the borrowed gown, Min Soo replied, "Grateful, doctor. Thank you so much for helping Ellia." He rolled his IV-stand to Ellia's side. Hands still damp he chose to bow slightly, but not to an obscene degree. She added her own.

"Ah, yes, well, you seem to be recovering nicely." He glanced down at the clipboard in his hand. "Your blood results are fine." He frowned. "I may have to recheck them. Please take a seat on those," he gestured at the cots they'd vacated, "and I'll have the nurse take your vitals."

The door opened and a seaman holding a steadily reddening towel over his forearm walked in with a pained grin.

"Not you again? Nurse!" the doctor hollered.

Ellia and Min Soo sat down in a couple of seats to wait out a distracted doctor's attention span. Min Soo listed toward Ellia and muttered, "They took your blood." Ellia's eyes widened. "Did they take yours?"

Min Soo's eyebrows twitched through a few positions. He glanced down at his arm. "Uh, maybe?"

"Hákarl." It came out louder than she'd intended.

"Fermented shark?" It was the doctor asking.

"Is that what that word means?" Min Soo asked.

Ellia curled her lips. "I could use something to clear the taste in my mouth."

Min Soo stood to his feet. "Is there somewhere we could get some food? We didn't really eat well on the island."

The doctor gestured with a suturing needle to a second nurse. "Call someone to help them out. Including a spot to sleep."

"Yes, Doctor."

"Any nausea or dizziness, you have someone alert us right away," ordered the doctor, "and I'll want to see you back here before noon."

As Ellia and Min Soo trailed after the nurse, he leaned over and asked, "Fermented shark?"

"You're not as...clean as before."

Min Soo kept mum until they were left to wait for their escort outside the sickbay door.

"I almost drowned in the ocean and you're worried about my cleanliness?"

Ellia drew a finger down his forearm and rose on her toes to whisper three words in his ear. "In your blood."

Footsteps stopped further conversation, but Ellia could see the whirl storm of questions blurring in Min Soo's eyes.

Her eyes narrowed at their escort. He seemed the friendly type. She'd like to know who had covered her blood signature, but it wasn't like merkin sported identification tattoos—or loyalty stamps. Either they'd cleared Min Soo's blood too or the doctor had lied through fish lips. She asked a dozen or more questions of their escort, but not a single one that mattered; she couldn't ask the ones that did.

The two of them were never left unsupervised for any proper length of time. Meals and paperwork, happy phone calls for Min Soo, strategic ones for Ellia, and official questions, questions, questions. She'd had a surface presence before the island incident. She put it to use obtaining a conditional verification of identity.

Merdragon

Min Soo didn't need it. More than one magazine cover would have served as ironclad credentials.

Min Soo's actions had elevated him to civilian hero. A sufficiently vague remembrance of events due to near drowning and gas inhalation secured the truth. The tale spread until it began to eerily resemble one of Ellia's mythic ramblings. By intent it held little of her presence.

Officially, their rescue held few unpleasantries, but more than once Min Soo would rub the back of his neck. He got good at dodging Ellia's elbow. It distracted him from the pressure of observing eyes.

Money, money, money

Min Soo's arrival at Incheon Port generated celebrity gossip gold and reporters greeted him en masse. A strategic leak minus the official press meeting; zero sanctioning by authorities. A van waited for them past the crowd, and Min Soo glanced over at Ellia in her borrowed military fatigues, cap and boots included. Head down, she stuck close to Min Soo as he took all the attention, nodding and waving to the crowd. The van door opened, and she slipped in behind him and his manager. Somehow not a single reporter made any note of it.

Inside the van, Min Soo whooshed a big sigh, and with a stretch of his long arm, he pulled off Ellia's cap. "We'll find out soon enough if those reporters need to go to remedial training for missing you."

She shook her hair out and leaned back beside him. "What now, for you? The customs officials that met us on board kept me so long I thought for a bit I was going to get detained and miss your fan service arrival."

He flipped a mirror open on the separator to check his face. "Had me worried too." He test-flashed his teeth. Relieved with what he saw, he closed the mirror. "But all good now. I'm going straight to my apartment. My parents and little sister are waiting for me there instead of meeting up with all the cameras flashing."

"It's your arena," she commented with a shrug. "It's good you got to video chat with them last night. They must be ecstatic to have you back."

"Don't forget, somehow mother got a copy of that radio mayday you sent and interpreted it to mean I had a full-service hotel at my beck and call."

Min Soo's manager, Kim Do Hyun rustled for something on the seat beside him and then tossed Min Soo a small package. The van sped up as they merged onto the highway.

"So, I take it the sunburned face and the model-hollows in your cheeks were unexpected?"

Min Soo fiddled one-handed with the pack in his hand and shook his head. "I haven't seen mother that maternal in years."

"Does that mean she will or won't be checking your fridge for expired bottles of water?"

Merdragon

"Hey! I have a filter." He absently opened the pack but stopped when Ellia put a hand over his.

"Haven't had a craving since you woke up from your coma, have you?" she asked.

"I..." he started, then really looked at the cigarette in his hand.

"You've kicked the habit with a little help, it's going to get messy if you start again. Your choice."

He opened his mouth to ask for an explanation, but Ellia gave him the eye to remind him of his manager. A manager who'd been following their English conversation quite competently. He closed the pack and threw it back on the front seat. A sigh of resignation slipped past his lips; he tapped his mouth with a long finger.

Do Hyun glanced back with an uncertain grin. "I did have the cleaning ahjumma freshen everything up after..." Min Soo shook his head fractionally, so he finished with "...and I did stock the fridge with water 'cuz I didn't know about the filter."

Ellia started laughing as Min Soo tapped his fingers on the arm rest and twisted his mouth into a sheepish grin. He rubbed the back of his neck. "It's not as bad as it used to be, really." A smug smile crossed his lips. "Actually, I'm pretty sure the ahjumma must have put something in the fridge too. She usually does when I'm home. She makes some sick dishes. Hope mother doesn't throw them all away and replace them with hers."

"So, how big is your apartment?"

Face returning to neutral, Min Soo leaned deeper into his seat and crossed his legs. "It's comfortable. And mine. Don't worry, it is not a one room basement studio."

Ellia rested an elbow against the door to look out the window at the passing cityscape. "How about you give me the address and I'll meet you there?"

His legs uncrossed. "What? Why? I mean, aren't you, ah, do you have some place...?"

She jiggled one combat booted foot in the air. "If I walk into your building with you, dressed like this, I'm quite certain a reporter or two will catch that water current and start asking questions. That will lead to a lynch-mob. And don't forget your family reunion. Mothers of boys like you have their radars set on maximum suspicion."

"But what are you going to do?"

She gave him a coquette's chin to shoulder reply, "I may have been stuck on that island for far too long, but that does not mean I've always been stuck on that island for all my longer-than-you'd-think life." Nodding toward the view outside the van, she added, "Once we get to a neighbourhood still a good distance from yours, I'm going to need to borrow enough coinage for a public payphone, rare as I suspect they've become. Fear not, I should be ringing your bell before midnight."

He crossed his arms, then his legs and his mouth.

Rolling her eyes, Ellia promised, "I'll be at your door before midnight..." She threw a green glinting eye at the manager, then leaned over to whisper in Min Soo's ear, "... or at your window."

Min Soo coughed, uncrossing in a jumble. He reached over to tap the manager on the shoulder. "You remember seeing any payphones in Jang Su's neighbourhood? I think there's was one next to the park."

"There's was one by the 7-11."

Ellia jumped in, "That would be perfect."

With a frown, Min Soo added, "She'll need the money for it too." Turning back to Ellia he asked, "You sure you don't want a cellphone?"

"Of course," the manager bobbed his head. He clearly wanted to protest, but what could he say?

"Cellphones, smartphones, security... An anonymous payphone works better for this."

The payphone by the 7-11 was gone, but after a little searching, the manager yelped and swerved into a sudden right turn. Two right turns more and he pulled over to the curb beside a lonesome phonebooth. Ellia unbuckled her seatbelt while the manager pulled out his wallet for the necessary change. He eyed Min Soo as he placed the money in Ellia's hands; Min Soo nodded with a dismissive wave of his hand. Ellia's lips twitched at the exchange, clambering over Min Soo's lap to hop out of the van. She patted the pocket where she'd secured Min Soo's address and waved him off. The van door slid closed slowly even as the van accelerated away. The manager's tongue was not slow. Or quiet.

On the sidewalk, she tucked stray strands back under her hat and waited until the van had turned out of sight. She adjusted her shades. The tail hadn't moved. Reporter or other, didn't matter, she preferred literal tails to metaphoric.

The streets in this part of Seoul's grand metropolis easily accommodated her with multiple alleyways, random stairways, and half dead ends. An exchange of shirts hanging out on a clothesline helped. That and a few jumps that only winged, and social media 'like' junkies would care to attempt.

Down on ground-level again, she stood along a busy street, contemplating her choice of directions.

"'Water, water everywhere, nor any drop to drink.' Coleridge, you had no idea." Every other person, it seemed, had a phone in hand, but she'd lost hers.

She shrugged and turned right. It had been a good twenty plus years since she'd been lobbed into a foreign culture. A passerby brushed against her shoulder and her finger twitched. She took a breath. Her nose wrinkled but her legs kept moving like dual metronomes. One-by-one her senses processed the overwhelming nature of mass civilization. The incessant footsteps and mechanics, the mingling of cooking scents and petrol, the signs—the signs had multiplied since last she'd walked streets. It had been oh such a while.

She went through a variation of updos and shirt adjustments by the time a vending machine flagged her attention to a lonely payphone. It didn't look long for this world. She picked up the handset, and a tone indicated functionality. Her inner merchild wiggled with success. She squashed it with a little practicality, sliding the money into the payphone's earnest mechanism, and punched in a long string of numbers.

A professional female voice answered with the name of an international banking institution. Not a common one.

Ellia's spoke with a formal tone into the handset, "Mr. Bruener, please."

Without a hitch the voice responded, "Certainly madam. May I give him your name?"

"Ms. Nighe." It was a portion of her name.

This time there was a hitch. Then, "Thank you Ms. Nighe, let me transfer you through to Mr. Bruener directly."

Whether or not it was the same "Mr. Bruener" who'd spoken with her twenty years ago, she didn't care. Only the name mattered.

In one breath and out with another, the transfer went through. "Ms. Nighe! A pleasure to hear from you again. How may I be of service?" No need for an account number.

Her voice shifted again, this time to pleasant boredom. It encouraged disinterest while her portfolio encouraged extreme caretaking.

"Good day to you, Mr. Bruener. I'm hoping you can assist me with a small favor. I happen to be in Seoul, South Korea and I need you to direct me to a bank that will accept my biometrics as identification. Funds will need to be arranged as well."

A delay in the line for distance and human processing power.

"Ah, of course Ms. Nighe, please hold the line."

Leaning against the payphone shelter, she waited. Tapping the backs of her nails against metal, plastic, glass, she waited. Listening to the operatic hold music—an odd choice—she entertained herself, watching the comings and goings of the park across the way. Humans and animals. Predators of both lines appeared absent.

Finally, the music broke off, mid-aria, to the sound of Mr. Bruener asking, "Ms. Nighe?"

She straightened up. "Yes, still here."

"All the arrangements. Have been. Made." He'd been hustling. "The bank information is as follows."

She wrote the instructions on a mental notepad. Mermaids weren't known for carrying around pens and paper. And neither were dragons.

"Will there be anything else I can help you with, Ms. Nighe?" Mr. Bruener asked.

"That will be everything, Mr. Bruener. As always you provide exemplary service."

"My pleasure. It has been some time." The question hung in the air, inviting confidence, but prudence hung in there as well. Clients who utilized the name "Mr. Bruener" required a certain level of caution.

With a wry grin Ellia still managed to keep the bored pleasantness in her voice. "Has it? Good day, Mr. Bruener."

"And to you, Ms. Nighe."

Ellia ended the call with a click.

Knowing an address and getting to it are two very different things, exceptionally true in a foreign city. Seoul was not a tiny, thousand-person community. Nor a place she'd previously frequented. She grimaced. If she hadn't promised to be at Min Soo's place by midnight she would have walked—her favourite method of location imprinting. Public transportation had eliminated old-fashioned hitch-hiking.

So, catching a taxi it was.

Stepping out on to the street with a New Yorker's confidence, she waved down the first taxi she saw. She'd stored a few Korean phrases on her tongue, from varied sources, and used one to direct the driver to the address Bruener had given

Merdragon

her. The driver gave her the look people do when things don't add up. She widened her eyes and repeated the directions. He sighed, then reached over to start the meter. With a shrug and a shoulder check he set his chances into motion.

Internally Ellia breathed a sigh of her own, in relief. Taxi drivers were uncanny in their ability to deduce difficult fares.

The ride took a good half hour, but she knew he hadn't been randomly circling. An instinct well-developed in wide open waters and skies.

He pulled up in front of the bank.

"Keep the meter running," she said in English, opening the door, "I'll be back shortly."

Gambler's despair fell over his face. He jumped out of the taxi to chase after her, yelling, "Yah! You pay! You pay now!"

She had the head start and a stride that proved difficult to catch. Her hand was on the glass bank doors by the time he caught up. Pausing in the opening, she turned to him and spoke in English, "It would be difficult to pay you without first going into the bank to get the money." She pointed inside the bank, then gave the local hand symbol for money. "One door. You may join me inside or wait here until I return."

He glanced back at his taxi in the designated taxi spot. A woman, a bank client, arrived at their standoff, and taking a quick glance between the two, she tucked her purse under her arm and brushed past with as much space as possible. The taxi driver gave Ellia a dirty sniff and an aborted spit. He stomped back to the taxi. She waited until he had settled into a good lean against his livelihood. The glare he gave held some heft. Ellia shrugged with an amused apology, and, allowing a suited man to exit, she entered the bank herself.

Inside, she strode over to the information desk, and in her truly stilted, paralyzed even, Korean, she asked to speak with the manager. The clerk had the customer service smile cemented to her face, but her eyes dodged that small amount that any wild predator could ID as an herbivore's search for an escape route. Ellia cultivated a smile on her own face—cool and graceful to dissuade any suspicions of nefariousness. The clerk gestured toward a seating area and asked in simple English to, "Please wait for a moment."

It wasn't long, but longer than she knew the taxi driver would appreciate, when the manager belatedly arrived. Dressed in the standard black office worker's suit, and on the stout side, he scrunched his face as he did a millisecond's once over. Neutrally he introduced himself and asked how he could be of service.

He'd asked in Korean. That was his right. Impossible for her, and trusting Bruener's discretion, she replied simply, in English, "My name is Ms. Ellia Nighe."

The manager's whole body language changed in microseconds. His posture firmed up, his face shifted into respect, and he obsequiously gestured Ellia toward his office. Ellia didn't need to see the dropped jaws; she heard the involuntary hisses and gasps, and snaps of mouths closing. Tea was ordered. And her taxi driver's plight addressed.

"Of course," the manager replied in studied English, "I will have it taken care of immediately."

The taxi driver, who had been waiting while debating just how much fare he was willing to gamble on the foreigner, straightened up at the sight of a clerk rushing out with an envelope in hand. Reaching him, she asked if he had been the foreigner's driver.

He grunt-nodded.

"How much is the fare?" she asked.

He leaned over to check the meter and gave her a number. At her shocked gasp he threw up his hand in defense. "She was a long way out from here and then she told me to leave the meter running."

Reprovingly the clerk sniffed, then pulled out the requested amount from the envelope she had in hand. "I will need a receipt."

The money disappeared inside his jacket and he wrote the receipt with flare, then dared her to stop him with an, "I'm going now."

She nodded a quick bob and dismissed him. He grumble-skipped to the driver's side and slid inside with a grump's inside-the-cheeks grin. He had a story to tell with his buddies at the bar tonight.

The clerk spun back around toward the bank and her heels snapped at the pavement as she hurried to return.

Back inside, Ellia had been comfortably seated in the manager's office. A scanner had been settled on his desk and waited for her hand. The manager watched her place her hand on the machine and checked the information that appeared on his screen. He squinted, coughed, and grabbed a swallow from the paper coffee cup that looked like it had been there since the morning. He winced mildly as he set to typing and clicking madly.

Merdragon

He glanced up about a minute into his mad efforts and asked for an address. Ellia gave him Han Min Soo's address. He typed in the information, then gave her a second look and asked her to confirm. She did but declined to comment on it further. The wrinkle between his eyebrows deepened; it didn't stop him from typing.

Clerks hounded in and out of the office, documents were stamped, and tea lukewarm-ed, until half an hour later he sighed and stood up from his chair. He came around the desk and offered Ellia a hand to stand. "Ms. Ellia Nighe, thank you for your patience. Everything is in order now." A clerk walked in and handed him a folder. He handed them straight to Ellia. "Here is everything. Additional items, one or two days. To Ms. Ellia Nighe will be sent."

She nodded graciously and as he escorted her toward the exit, the words refused to be held in any longer. "The address you gave is new purchase or short-term?"

Stopping in the middle of the bank lobby, she turned fully toward him and encouraged him with an eye quirk to continue.

"It is...I hesitate to question your real estate agent, but don't they know about your other holdings? ... ah!" His face suddenly lit up with a realization. "Ms. Ellia Nighe owns the building, of course." He didn't know even the half of it.

She didn't explicitly correct him, but, "I dislike hotels." He could infer what he would from that. "Could you suggest the nearest suitable shopping district in the area?" she asked, redirecting the conversation.

"Shopping?"

"Yes."

He blinked twice as his mental gears ground down to a halt and ground up again in a new direction. A switch flipped and he nodded briskly. "Certainly, certainly. I will arrange a car service."

She raised a palm. "A taxi will do just fine." A small shake of her head pre-empted any arguments.

He personally escorted her past the other clients and to the curb. There he hailed a taxi for her himself. He held the door open for her, then leaned in to quick-meal-schpeal something to the taxi driver. Discrete as he tried to be, she didn't miss the paper that exchanged hands. Ah, the avarice that spins and stalls the planet.

The taxi driver didn't fail the manager's trust. Ellia stepped out of the taxi and sighed. She got back in. The manager had deemed it fit to have her delivered to the shopping district of the elite.

To herself she muttered, "Sure, I'll dress up in diamonds and no one will ask questions. That's why they stick Angelfish in tanks."

The taxi driver asked a question, then held out his phone to her. She looked down and saw Korean symbols and English beneath it. Ah, a translator app. She'd been keeping up with improvements as per media but hadn't expected them to be quite so real world active. The words written essentially asked if she wanted to go somewhere else. She typed a request to go to a place a little more ordinary, then handed it back to him. He thought for a moment and spoke something into his phone. He would take her to a mall.

This time when he stopped, she paid the fare before even getting out. She waved him off and dove into the mishmash of shoppers already engaged. Crash course in cultural immersion initiated.

It took hours of data collection, language muddling and shop hopping. Transit and outfit switching permanently left tailgaters with nothing but broken segments.

Late in the day, a nondescript nobody walked into an internet café. Even later, another nobody with the same name walked out.

Shortly after a dark eleven, shy of a broken promise, a woman arrived at the grand glass doors of Min Soo's building. In the twenty or so floors range, the building was plenty high enough to receive a baseball capped nod of approval. She punched in a code at the door and walked in giving the watching security guard his nod. Hair loose and healthy without a hint of saltwater damage, a pale peach blouse, crisp jeans, and white sneakers you'd never actually use for running, all added up to I-belong-here. The elevator doors opened before the guard could question her lack of familiarity.

At the nineteenth floor the elevator doors opened. Ellia peered out noting the all-clear and stepped out. As if the hallway was an everyday commute, she walked to Min Soo's door and began punching in the code. Keyless entries had their benefits, but one noisy number shy of open sesame, the door swung open to a Min Soo in sweatpants and a t-shirt still settling. He grabbed her by the arm, pulled her in, and rather firmly closed the door behind her. A stumble dropped her into an impromptu embrace.

Merdragon

Her arm wedged between them, and the other squished against her side; she felt a drop of water land on the tiniest area of exposed collarbone. The branded purse that had sealed the deal for the security guard hung heavy in her hand. Her nose inhaled his scent. He'd upgraded from the military supplied toiletries.

Abruptly he pushed her out to arms distance, hands on her shoulders, and looked down from his considerable height, and equally considerable length of nose, to say, "You're here."

"Expressive, aren't you?" She gave him a once over, stratosphere to basement.

He ignored the comment. "I wasn't sure if you were actually going to come. It's easy to get lost…"

She dropped the purse on the floor to the faint screams of fashionista penny-pinchers around the world, and wrapped her hands around each of his forearms, lifting his hands off her shoulders. "Yes, well, not saying I didn't, but here I am. Any parents or siblings present?"

Faint heat signatures rose on each cheek and he stepped back. He adjusted his shirt and, watching her warily, shook his head. Ellia took a quick look around the entry way and spotted the stereotypical slippers South Korean homes always had on foot. She didn't spot any visiting shoes. Wiggling her toes inside told her they were freshly purchased. The lack of shoes, his solitary presence. She left the purse behind and gently invaded Min Soo's territory.

The banker had sniffed things somewhat correctly. Despite her suspicions of Min Soo's impending invitation, she did not plan on staying. She was here to ensure Min Soo's safe space had not been compromised. Old friends had been notified. Ownership imminent.

This place had a modern, open concept flare. A bachelor lived here, one with an artist's eye, or money to pay for one. It had the frame of a minimalist, neutral colours and simple lines. His electronic toys had been well camouflaged, but a remote, and faintly worn knob, gave his habits away. In one corner sat an urn. It felt old, and family gifted. A large painting dominated a section of wall; too obvious to hide anything but a flat screen.

Ellia's fingers butterflied over an action figure from one of Min Soo's film roles. The one leaning against a performance award. Her eyes drifted toward the balcony doors. An area rug softened the shushing of her slippers, and she slid open the balcony doors to lean out for a breath. Night air heat greeted her with a smattering of pollution, over-watered plants and late-night fried chicken. The balcony had a respectable view and outdoor furniture to enjoy it. Feet still inside, she nodded approval and pulled herself back in.

Min Soo had parked himself against the back of a couch, arms folded and legs crossed, a bemused expression on his face. She ignored him to wander further in, and discovered an unexpectedly luxurious bathroom, practically a spa.

"How many parties have you had in here?" she asked, mostly to herself.

She didn't expect a reply and she didn't get one. Only a sardonic smile and an incline of Min Soo's drying head. A broom closet followed the spa reveal, a room she suspected only the cleaning ahjumma ventured.

The next door had been framed with an unusually grained wood, irregularly shaped and lightly stained to blend in with the colour of the wall. She paused for Min Soo's consent.

He uncrossed from the couch. "Please," he said with a permissive gesture.

With a lingering run of her fingers over the door frame, she entered.

No minimalism here. A wall had been removed from the three-bedroom apartment to make it two; the jungle had conquered the frame. A painted room divider held at bay a model's collection of gifts and impulses. A genius organizer had been put to heavy labour keeping the clothing assortment from devouring the empty spaces. Min Soo shrugged at her expression and ran a finger along his nose, but then he pointed her back outside and deeper down the hallway.

He led her to a driftwood framed mosaic of coloured glass and mirror shards. It stretched from floor to ceiling, an enormous statement piece highlighted by small spotlights on the opposite wall. Ellia leaned back to consider the odd non-monstrosity. A huff of amusement interrupted her thoughts and she turned to see Min Soo dangling a key from one long finger. Taking it, she turned back to the piece. There. A keyhole surreptitiously disguised in a "flaw".

The key clicked in the lock and the frame swung out to reveal a dark room. An error Min Soo quickly corrected with a flick of a switch.

A freshly prepared guest bedroom with the faint smell of paint and assembled furniture. Even a set of pyjamas on the double-sized bed.

Quizzically, Ellia pointed at the open and currently empty wall-length closet, specifically at the visible door within.

Low volume and register. "This used to be my walk-in closet."

"Ah, that explains the state of your bedroom."

"I had my manager get it done while we were getting back. It's technically a three-bedroom apartment, but I don't really have long-term guests." He rubbed the back of his neck sheepishly. "I had to pledge mother that tomorrow I'd go spend time at home."

"Hmm..." her response came distractedly.

Merdragon

His eye on the closet's door, he acquiesced, "If you don't like it, I can put you up in a hotel."

With Min Soo's focus distracted, Ellia slipped a handful of black bits into the bin by the desk. She'd need a chair to reach the one she'd spotted in this room. Then again, she might leave it for now.

"No, it's good. A step up from a volcano. Thank you." The abundance of electronics she'd squashed and crunched annoyed her. She'd be staying a day or two after all. "Now, how does one get a glass of water in this place?"

He straightened to his full height. "Of course, sorry. Have you eaten?"

She followed him out the door and closed it behind herself. "I managed to hustle up a bite or two, but I'm craving water with a touch of salt and that attracts the wrong kind of attention."

"Salt? I don't remember you drinking that on the island." He put one palm up, "Wait, you drank it straight from the ocean."

"Straight? Mmm, maybe a little filtered."

He shook his head and poured a glass of water from the fridge dispenser. A saltshaker followed.

A delicate tap, a swirl, and down the hatch the water went. "Delightful, thank you."

The rest of the evening, Min Soo puttered around, reconnecting with his apartment. He revealed the hidden television and his game systems, spoke of the urn in the corner, the family next door, the fan girl on the 15th and how he'd missed the area rug. Like a dolphin, cruel, she lingered on the couch in rest mode, flipping the pages of a recent fashion magazine in her borrowed pyjamas, rabbit trailing on the tablet he'd given her...waiting him out. The infomercials finally got to him. And the balcony doors were getting annoyed with repeat usage.

"I'm heading to sleep now," he stated. The clock on the wall directed the eye toward one and some.

She hmmm-ed acknowledgement, barely raising a finger of a wave. In her peripheral vision he retreated to his bedroom. A quiet click sealed the decision.

Fifteen golden moments of silence later, Ellia opened her eyes. Smoothly she rose from the couch she'd been imprinting, padded past his bedroom door just loudly enough to tickle the edges of his eardrums, and turned off all the lights. Assassin-soft she returned to the living room. Incrementally she slid the balcony door open and closed it just as gently behind her.

The nocturnal city greeted her. And gave up the spy on the ground. No facing building to worry about with decent rooftop sightlines. She stretched out on the lounger and fell asleep to the city's grumblings. The camera in her room could wait.

Breakfast at later

The next morning, Min Soo woke way too early to compensate for the late hour he'd eventually managed to snooze. Rubbing his eyes, he rolled out of bed, one thing on his mind. He navigated past the new partition, the cool floor broken by the area rugs that separated each organized display. His toes curled on their own. He stopped in front of the door. The door to his late closet. The digital clock by his bed progressed past more than one number while Min Soo stood, one foot cool, the other foot cozy.

The cool foot grew impatient and took a step forward. His hand knew better, and instead of turning the knob, Min Soo laid an ear against the door. Nothing. He listened some more, growing comfortable in the odd behavior, but the coolness of the floor finally reached far enough up the nerve chain to send a signal to his brain. A signal that stated he should absolutely, definitely, wake up, entirely.

He jerked back from the door, shook his head, and ran a hand through his bedhead. He rubbed his eyes again and blindly navigated his way back to the side of his bed. His waiting, not-put-upon slippers remonstrated with him over the slight. Or so it seemed as he struggled to slip them on, their shush-shush-shushing louder than he remembered as he shuffled out of his room.

First stop, the mosaic door. A knock and another gave him nothing, again. He tried the door and unexpectedly it opened. He winced in advance of a scream, but nothing. A squint of an eye revealed an empty room and an unslept bed. A frown replaced the squint.

"Where do you hide a dragon?" he asked himself, walking toward the living room, remembering to glance upward, just in case. It wasn't that he expected her to be in full scales and wings, but at the same time he somewhat hoped she would. Seoul reality was beginning to chip away at his island memories.

In the dawn-lit living room, Min Soo's eyes darted to the couch she'd been occupying the previous night, perniciously. It had plumped back into shape, fully restored by hours unburdened. He checked the bathroom, but with the door ajar she clearly wasn't there. Next, the entryway, but his inbreath sighed out with ease. Her shoes still awaited their owner.

Mystified, he scanned the living room and the open space connected kitchen. He rubbed the back of his head and swung around frowning at the empty suite. A thought arrested his restlessness. "She wouldn't have gone out flying, would she?" He turned toward the balcony and considered it. Then he looked closer. Squinting, he registered the shapely outline of something that didn't match his recollection of the balcony furnishings. A supine Ellia, obscured by houseplants and suspect lighting.

In a few strides he reached the balcony door but paused before opening it. She'd curled her hands into her body, and the memory of her gaunt skeleton flashed through his mind. He strode back toward his bedroom, gathered the covers off his bed, and returned to the balcony door. Trying to be as quiet as possible, he slid the door open, stalked to her side and gently, gently laid the blanket over her.

She stirred, but as he waited, mannequin-still, she simply snuggled deeper into the blanket and continued her dreamland adventures. Holding his breath, Min Soo ever so carefully crept off the balcony and slid the door closed again. He leaned against the frame of the door and breathed. Tilting his head, he wryly eyed her snoozing. Then he shook his head and shush-shushed to his room. Moments later the soft sound of the shower revealed his new location. Only then did a small smile play across Ellia's lips.

An hour or so later, Ellia decided dawn had passed and it was safe to have a proper morning. She opened her eyes.

Min Soo had returned. He leaned against the balcony railing in knee length red and black surfer shorts and an unbuttoned white shirt, sipping the hot cup of tea in his hand.

"Seaweed entanglement," she breathed.

He glanced over and coughed seeing her eyes wide open.

Two handed she raised the blanket's edge in a gesture of gratitude and said, "Thanks."

One long finger rapped a perplexed rhythm against the railing. "Why am I not craving cigarettes?"

Ellia sat up, draping the blanket over her lap. "Same reason you didn't drown."

"What do you mean? You did that air bubble thing," he said, shaping the air with his free hand.

She covered her mouth, yawning, fabricating, "I can't swim that fast. You still had some of the aftereffect benefits of the medicine I gave you. The stuff I gave you for the lump on your skull."

"Wait. What did you give me?"

Merdragon

"Simplest explanation? Considering I'm no doctor?" She shrugged, wriggled her toes into her slippers and stood up with a long, slow stretch. "I'm told it maximizes your body's own system to deal with the problem. Great for poisons and bugs, blood flow problems like swelling," she said with a pointed finger at the back of Min Soo's head, "and it increases the body's ability to clean things ups, like tar in the lungs. You're clear of the chemical addiction. The time on the island without, dealt with the habit."

"And the drowning?"

"Don't ask me how it works, but you were at near optimum cellular functioning. It gave you enough of an edge to survive and be rescued."

Wiping his mouth with the back of his hand, he provisionally accepted the explanation. He tilted his head toward the kitchen, "The tea's hot and there's a breakfast that isn't freshly picked from a tree."

A few necessities later, they sat at the kitchen table, munching on the breakfast Min Soo had pulled from the fridge and heated. He let her have a few sips of tea before asking, "Was the room unsuitable?"

"Unsuitable, no." She stared down at her plate and absently tapped against it with the stainless-steel chopsticks.

"Not enough sea breeze?" he asked with a wry sarcastic twist of his mouth.

She grinned. "We've been holed up in indoor sleeping spaces ever since we left the island." A shrug followed the grin. "In some ways you're not far wrong. I'm used to sleeping curled up in a corner of the ocean or the cauldron of a dormant volcano." Her grin faded, and pensively she added, "Your balcony's been my first chance since we left the island to sleep comfortably again."

"Ah, I hadn't realized," he said, leaning back in his chair. He crossed his arms and asked, "What if it rains?" He raised his hand, palm out. "Wait, don't answer that, sleeping in the ocean... What about snow?"

Deadpanned, "At this latitude? It's July. I'm no snow dragon."

"There are snow dragons?" he asked, intrigued.

"Maybe," she replied enigmatically, face at max Botox.

He tilted his head and narrowed his eyes, calculating his chances of learning more about the possible mythical existence of snow dragons. No, he recognized the storyteller surfacing. The truth surfed on the other side of her lips.

"Anything else I should know or warn PR about, like when the full moon transforms you into a dragon on my balcony and the media starts asking what kind of nefarious mystical arts I'm in to?"

"Merdragon, not weredragon," she said, correcting him. "And no. No involuntary transformations on my part...but there is one thing you should know. Talking about involuntary. The bedroom is bugged."

His entire body stilled in anger. "What?!"

"You do reassure me with those reactions of yours." With the smile of the gentlest angel, she leaned her elbows on the table and reached out to put a hand on his forearm. "Be thankful. It's the reason I stayed. I have a use for it."

"A use for it?"

"A case of the hunted becoming the hunter," she replied, a growl coiled around each syllable.

Min Soo shivered out of his stillness.

And choked on his tea when the doorbell rang.

Ellia released his hand as he grabbed for a napkin and hastily shoved the chair back. He glanced at the stainless-steel clock on the wall. Almost he furrowed his brow but stopped before it could cause any damage. There'd been enough of that this morning.

"It's alright," Ellia said, pushing back her chair, "nothing to worry about."

"The bugs or the door?" His answer dark against her reassurance.

Calmly she replied, "Neither."

"The bugs are your business, I understand, but that is my door."

With a grand wave she pointed at the intercom. "Then by all means, answer it."

Suspiciously he walked to the intercom, gave her side eye, looked back at the intercom. One long finger stabbed the intercom button. "Who is it?"

"Delivery for Nighe Ellia-ssi," came the reply.

"Ah, how did you?"

At his elbow, Ellia asked, "May I open the door now?"

His whole body swayed in a confused affirmative. A smirk crossed Ellia's face as she went to open the door. There, in all innocence, a regular delivery man with a dolly carrying four large boxes and several high-end boutique shopping bags looped over one arm.

"Nighe Ellia-ssi?" He asked, pronouncing the name unexpectedly well, and handed her an electronic signature pad.

"Nighe Ellia, yes," she replied, giving him a thorough once over. "Thank you." She'd already begun a high-intensity study of Korean, courtesy of the previous day's mer-tech access at the internet café, but it didn't guarantee perfection in one day, or even ever.

"Do you need help getting them inside?" A perfectly respectable question.

She gave him a wink. "Not this time."

The delivery man settled the shopping bags by the door, then shimmied his dolly out from under the boxes. Accepting back the electronic signature pad, he handed her a packing slip, doffed his hat, and left with an English, "Until next time."

"I'll be in touch."

Out of sight until the elevator bell indicated the delivery man had left, Min Soo popped his head out into the hallway. Ellia handed him a bag.

"Who was that really, and what is all this?"

"And you call yourself a model?" she mocked, ignoring the first half of the question.

Automatically he added, "slash actor." He put his hand out for another bag. "I'm serious, what is all of this?"

Wrangling the bags down the hallway to her room, she laughed, "I'm honestly, normally not an in-the-closet clothing obsessed woman, but these are the aftershocks of a clothing famine." A grey pallor shadowed her face in passing. "A long one." Like a minnow the shadow flitted away. "One does not merely require a tunic and shoes, but all the supporting accoutrements as well."

"Accoutre-whats?"

"Accessories, bells, whistles, and the niceties of civilization." She pulled out an electric toothbrush. "Including the items a person requires when they no longer have cleaner fish on staff."

An involuntary shudder ran through Min Soo. "I admit, I have tried some strange gimmicks, but that, hmmm, no."

"The one I have some qualms about is the tiny octopus. It seems so cruel to have them polish your teeth and then swallow them."

For a moment she thought he'd believe it, but "I'm not swallowing that line, Ellia."

"And it had such a good hook too."

"Here's the last box," he said, sliding it inside her room, then leaned a shoulder against the doorframe.

"If you're not going to bite the bait—no idleness allowed. Out, out, out."

He raised a hand in surrender and left with a lingering look. The door closed with a shh-click behind him. He paused to consider the unfriendly visitor in her room.

"She said she'd handle it." He shrugged and returned to the kitchen to clean up the remnants of their breakfast.

Kitchen clean, but no sign of Ellia, he plopped himself down on the couch, picked up the tablet resting on the coffee table, and began checking and browsing his email, and various social media accounts. News of his return, and requests for his attention, should have kept his mind firmly entrenched in the business of Han Min Soo, but too often his eyes would pause on a piece of click bait. On the tenth time reading the latest and greatest bit of nothing, he shook his head. And continued scrolling with a muttered something or other.

A thump from the bedroom and his head rose in anticipation. Nothing followed. He returned to his perusing of the tablet, his usual manner of unusual stillness, even in motion, shattered repeatedly as he resettled his seat, crossing and uncrossing his legs. He had a serious case of the fidgets.

The mosaic door opened, and he paused, casually glanced up, and swallowed to see her slip into the bathroom, bathrobe in hand.

Abruptly he stood up and began pacing, tablet still in hand. It might as well have been displaying vacuum cleaners for all the attention he paid it. His ears were using up all his powers of concentration. The sound of the shower stopped his pacing. He turned sharply toward the balcony and closed the door sternly behind himself.

On the balcony he breathed deeply, ran his fingers through his hair more than once and stared over the city. He stared a long time until the sound of the balcony door sliding open broke him from his meditation.

He glanced over to see a concerned Ellia watching him. A casually dressed Ellia. His eyes narrowed—with his days of modelling couture, and his professional skills insulted earlier, his eyes assessed her from slipper toes to collar tips.

"How do dragons convert their gold into local currency?" he blurted unintentionally.

She blinked in surprise. "What?"

"Sorry, that's not what I meant to say." He quirked his head and folded his arms. "But now that I've asked, I'm curious. You borrowed money to use a payphone yesterday and now... Those boxes and bags didn't come from a street-side stall."

Merdragon

Down at street level someone blew their car horn. A trio of athletic senior ladies gave the driver their disapproval. A snap of a fan and a few choice words. The delivery man double-timed it to his waiting van.

"Understandable. It wouldn't be good for your reputation to be associated with a thief. In your own home no less. To answer the question, I offer a storied answer. You've been warned."

An early morning runner on his return, passed the ladies, to their fan waving appreciation. An idler by the bus stop kept her eyes on the phone in her hand. The long-sleeved shirt and pants seemed an odd choice for the steadily increasing temperature of the day.

On the balcony Ellia continued, "Dragons, as you suspected, don't need currency, therefore they don't exchange. I received one measly coin from my mother before she sent me away with my father. When I reached my majority, dad gave me the other one."

Wise to her ways, he raised an eyebrow in full awareness of her serious leg pulling tendencies. The plants that had survived his absence listened in closely, eager to grow.

Down below, the idler snorted at something on her phone's display screen. A bus stopped to let off a passenger. The idler did not get on.

Min Soo shifted his weight, inadvertently ending a spider. An expensive one. The idler coughed.

Ellia leaned her hip against the balustrade and continued her fiction, flavouring it with bites of truth. "It is dragonkind tradition—one coin at birth, one coin upon reaching majority. Dragons hoard inanimate treasure, not progeny. Dad held that second coin in trust, since neither one of them intended to be reacquainted." She shrugged. "It proved sufficient. It seems my dragon heritage includes a knack for business. I have quite the portfolio above and below sea level."

"You're rich." It was not a question. "The coins are more of a metaphor for skills and something else, aren't they? Innate and...?"

"Mmmm."

The plants rustled giddily, innocently. A gentle breeze to clear the morning smog wandered in to greet them. Another bus arrived below. The idler stepped on this bus and raised the phone to her ear. The bus drove off.

"But you've decided to live in this apartment, sleeping on this balcony, and to share a bathroom with me." He realized what he'd just said. "I mean, not at the same time."

"It's a nice bathroom," she smirked, "but yes, as long as it proves suitable."

"I don't know what…"

She reached up to lay her hand on his shoulder. "Call it a whim if you will," on an aside she added, "but not a whip-or-will." She continued, "If it gets too burdensome, I'll take myself off your hands."

Opening his hands out in front, he absently echoed her words, "…off my hands…"

Ignoring the refrain, she changed the subject and asked, "When's your first interview?"

The question jerked him from his meandering thoughts. "First one's at 10:45, then there's one over lunch, and one later in the afternoon. Then it'll be time for the family triple interview."

"Call it as it is, it's going to be a family interrogation. How about the working gigs?"

"Proposals and contracts are coming in too. Already started when we were being shipped home. I have photo shoots later this week." He carefully ran a hand over his face. "Have to get some island-erasing done too. What are you planning on doing?"

Fire flicked deep in her eyes. "Well, while this dragon maid's been away, the catfish have been playing. Mud-eaters, blech."

Amused respect flitted across Min Soo's face. "I feel an odd sense of pity for the catfish."

He'd once been scuba diving at an underwater sculpture garden. In that instant her face replicated the experience. "Pity the dragon maid."

Without another word she pushed away from the balustrade. She left him behind on the balcony.

Min Soo stumbled quickly after her, bewildered by the sudden mood swing.

Behind them, unseen, the sun tangled on a distant pane of glass.

Inside, she had already reached the entryway. He stood by as she picked up her new brand-named purse and slipped on a pair of high-end sandals.

"Wait," he said, reaching to touch her on the back of the arm. "Did I say something wrong?"

One hand on the door handle, Ellia faced him and shook her head in the negative. "Nothing." She paused. "You reminded me I have business that needs quick attention." She opened the door and in a more matter of fact tone she added, "As soon as I've equipped myself with a phone, I'll text you. Thank goodness, you above-surfs don't rely on house-phones anymore. I'll see you later."

Merdragon

Min Soo grabbed the door before it fully closed and waited in the hallway until the elevator came to swallow her down. Door closed, he leaned against it in deep thought. He was home, safe, in his own territory, and questions were starting to come to mind. Lots of questions.

The sound of his phone ringing brought him out of his reverie, and he strode quickly over to grab it off the kitchen counter. On the screen it showed his manager's face; with a wry smile he answered it.

"Good morning, Do Hyun," began his answer, and off to a busy day he went, ignorant of the little "bird" that attached itself to his trail the moment he left the building. Questions occupied his spare moments; too many to notice his stalker.

"We lost most of the bugs we planted, and that idiot managed to step on the spider." The words came out in a sour tone. Min Soo would have recognized him as one of the reporters that had crowded around when he'd been hustled into his van. The faint whistle in his ese's would have revealed something entirely different to Ellia.

"Did you catch anything they said?" asked Darya, the one who'd been in on the helicopter disaster and most recently idling around the bus stop below Min Soo's apartment.

"At that distance?" He whistled in exasperation. "No. The air quality didn't help the lip-reading either."

Darya wrapped the scarf she had around her neck tighter.

"Sis, that's not normal. People are going to notice. You're supposed to blend in. What's wrong with you, wearing jeans and a sweater in this heat?"

"Riko, I'm taking care of it. Just focus on getting close to them. Find out who this Han Min Soo is. The whole story, not just his public stats. How much does he know, and can we use him to get access to the island basement?"

"Well, it is easier to follow him. She's got a nasty habit of slipping out of sight any time she so chooses. If we tail her any closer, we might as well hold her hand."

"Any clues regarding their relationship? Can we leverage him against her?"

"You mean if they're sleeping together? I don't think so. You wouldn't remember, but back home wasn't like here; casual hook-ups aren't really a thing. Anyway, I'm fairly sure she slept on the balcony last night from what we caught on our equipment."

"Sounds like bodyguard-duty to me. She's protecting him. If she's not sleeping with him, then why's she hovering?" Darya asked, absently scratching her leg.

"We'll keep tracking. Might even poke the bear and see if she reacts. You need to find a hot spring." The words and tone were sarcastic, but Riko's eyes held worry as he watched her leave.

A day at the museum

Days later, standing in the city heat, outside the radio station where he'd finished his most recent interview, Min Soo rubbed his grumbling stomach. A busy schedule meant irregular meals, and his fingers twitched for a cigarette while he waited for his ride. He pulled out his phone as a substitute. He tilted up his sunglasses to see the screen better—1:32. Mother had left a voice message.

A van pulled up beside him as he went through the painstaking process of checking the message she'd left instead of texting. He reached for the door handle. And yanked his hand back at the blast of a horn. Wrong van. He scratched his head and walked toward the van that had pulled up behind the one he'd almost entered. His manager scowled at him through the windshield.

Inside, the manager Do Hyun shelled out a lecture worth it's volume in gold as Min Soo tried to retrieve the message he'd accidentally deleted. No luck. He'd return the call after Do Hyun finished the diatribe.

In an entirely different neighbourhood, Ellia paced along an aquarium lined hallway with her eyes on a tablet. The receptionist barely glanced up as Ellia walked past again. The only creature still keeping her company up and down the hall was a little octopus, a young Giant Pacific Octopus; Ellia had named her Roberta.

A door opened, breaking the aquarium illusion. A nondescript woman of a nondescript age stepped out and whistled a complex set of notes.

Ellia immediately stopped, lowered her tablet, and whistled her own complex set of an answer.

The woman frowned with a touch of uncertainty. She held out the folder in her hand and uttered what seemed like an entire aria of cautions, whistles, clicks and mournful song.

Ellia took it from her hand and responded with soothing whistles and clicks.

The woman nodded, releasing her frown, reassured by Ellia's words. With a sway she bid Ellia fair currents and returned to her office. The walls resolved back to their aquarium appearance.

Ellia took advantage of the privacy desk set in the reception area and opened the folder. Inside were all the documents she'd need to satisfy government bureaucracy. Even an international driver's license—100% fiction; why fight traffic when one could fly? The tablet vibrated, an urgent message. A quick glance. She inhaled and the water rippled behind her. The octopus spat ink and disappeared.

The contents of folder were swept into her messenger bag, and with fingers sifting and typing on the tablet, she strode out of the office with barely a nod to the receptionist and the little crowd of fish that had gathered behind her.

Outside, Ellia paused under the building's awning. She stabbed at the tablet, directing her anger toward her stalkers. "Back off. This dragon treasures her persons with extreme prejudice." Her fingers danced over the tablet. They stopped. "Ah, well done, my good friend. You've anticipated and already have schemes in progress. I'll see you soon."

"Yes, mother, I'm outside the museum right now. I stopped to get a change of clothes but I'm here now." He paused, listened. "I'll pass on your greetings to Curator Oh." The call ended.

"Do you want me to wait for you?" asked Min Soo's manager with a touch of worry. The agency had also received a request for Min Soo's presence at the exhibit. It had been abnormally last minute.

Min Soo checked his face in the back-seat mirror. "Go get a coffee, or something nearby, and wait for my call." He smoothed his eyebrows. "I can't see this taking longer than an hour." He slid open the door and stepped out, adjusted his cuffs, and smoothed out any rebellious folds of his summer light suit.

In 'on' mode, he strode past the signs advertising the Artist Seung Gabriel—he paused to confirm he hadn't met him before—and into the museum. He slowed to a wander and accepted a glass of champagne. He'd gained a certain confidence from his recent adventure. The secrets had added to his air of mystery. It inspired more than a couple bold self-introductions.

A middle-aged woman dressed in a refined, subtly expensive outfit, approached Min Soo with a wealthy woman's smile.

"Han Min Soo-ssi, I'm please you were able to make it to Artist Seung Gabriel's exhibition."

Considering his mother had some relation to the woman, Min Soo paid her a more traditional respect with an abbreviated bow. "Thank you, Curator Oh for the invitation. Mother sends her greetings."

"Such a small thing, she needn't have. I'm the one who's grateful. Artist Gabriel personally requested your presence."

Merdragon

Off to the side a guest moved aside, and an art piece entered Min Soo's line of sight. He stopped breathing. A hand-sized dragon scale.

Curator Oh noted the distraction. "Come, come, take a closer look. It's a beautiful, deeply layered piece. See the ocean and fire imagery?"

It held more than ocean and fire. Menace?

"It is very, ah, passionate."

"Mmm, yes, he is quite marvelous. We were fortunate to be able to arrange this display on such short notice. But please, Artist Gabriel wanted to meet you. Allow me to make the introductions." Her jade bracelet swayed on her wrist as she gestured toward a gathering a short distance away.

Min Soo acquiesced and allowed her to lead him to the suspiciously creative artist. The larger-than-life dragon scale resembled Ellia's own, but instead of scales covering the person, a person covered the scale. A clever inversion.

Almost within loud speaking distance of the artist, an elderly gentleman intersected Min Soo's path. "Han Min Soo-ssi?"

Curator Oh turned around too late.

The man was vaguely familiar to Min Soo. "I apologize I don't seem to remember..."

"I've been to visit your father a few times over the years. Is he here?" He checked behind Min Soo as if Min Soo could have hidden his father somewhere behind his slim build. A moment of military bearing in the man's slouch caught Min Soo's eye.

"No, I came on my own. Did you wish to have me give him your greetings?"

The man gave Min Soo a politician's smile and shook his head, "I think I'll give him a call myself. I'll leave first." He hadn't given his name and Min Soo hadn't had a chance to ask or remember.

The man walked away, and Curator Oh Hyun Sook stepped back in with the facial expression of a mind scrolling through a guest list.

Those surrounding the artist parted to allow Curator Oh and Min Soo into the circle. She paused her mental search.

"Artist Gabriel? Is all going well?" she asked, sweeping into arm's length.

Grey streaks in his hair and a salt and pepper beard didn't prevent Artist Gabriel's charming smile from causing a few heart flutters in the crowd.

"Curator Hyun Sook, this is wonderful." He shared his beaming smile with the whole crowd. "Everyone, please meet Curator Oh, the wonderful lady who so graciously agreed to host my work and has done a marvelous job with all the arrangements." He took one of her hands in his and looked her in the eye, the old fox, "Have I expressed my gratitude sufficiently?"

"Dear me," she responded, flustered.

Mercifully, he spotted Min Soo and asked, "And who is this? An artist, a sponsor, a buyer?" He addressed Min Soo directly, "Have you found something of interest?"

Regaining her composure and her hand, Curator Oh stammered out introductions. "Th-this is Mr. Han Min Soo. The g-guest you added to the invitation list." She swung her gaze back and forth between them. "P-perhaps I was mistaken?"

"Han Min Soo?" Artist Gabriel's full brows drew together. He scratched his beard and did a walkabout around Min Soo. Desensitized to objectification, Min Soo held in the fidgets. "Madam, it was no mistake." He corrected himself, "Well, it could be a mistake, but the mistake does not lie in his attendance." He clapped a hand on Min Soo's shoulder. "Come, I'd like to show you around. I'm quite interested in your recent island journey, for artistic inspiration of course." To the crowd, "Please, you have come to see the art, not the artist, enjoy and excuse us."

The crowd dispersed good-naturedly, and Curator Oh Hyun Sook likewise excused herself. From her expression Min Soo could only deduce that Curator Oh had determined that the man he'd met early had most definitely not been included on the invitation list.

"Have you circulated the room yet to review my work?" Gabriel spoke, redirecting his attention.

"I saw the scale."

"Ah, yes, one of my more, can I say, imaginary pieces. What did you think?"

It felt like a test.

"It's pretty?" The old fox snorted,

"Pretty? Hah. Try again."

"What would you like me to say?" He didn't like tests.

"Mr. Han Min Soo...I hear you nearly went for an unplanned ride today?"

Min Soo stopped with a frown. Who was this man?

Gabriel clapped a hand on Min Soo's shoulder to nudge him to continue walking. "Just a few steps farther and here it is, the 'staff only' door."

They slipped inside, and Gabriel nearly lost his dignity tripping over an empty cardboard tube left on the floor. Min Soo caught his arm and brought him back to rights.

Merdragon

"Thanks, hard to be circumspect when you're raising a ruckus." He patted the sides of his hair and grinned at Min Soo. "Boy, you may have a fantastic poker face, but you can't fool me. I've lived too long."

"I don't understand. Who are you?"

"You know that scale is not as imaginary as I let on. Raised the hair on the back of your neck, didn't it? You're acquainted with Señorita Ellia, are you not?"

Min Soo's eyes narrowed. "Why do you ask?"

More than an artist's eyes scrutinized him for one, two, three breaths. "O these games of who know who and how much and what. Listen, Ellia doesn't like to make personal introductions. It's the way her father taught her. It's the way he taught me."

"You know her father?"

"Knew. And is that what intrigues you?" Gabriel asked, smoothing his well-trimmed beard.

A mental cannonball rolled down the inside of Min Soo's skull to connect with an unpleasant, green-tinged thought. Crossing his arms, he shifted his weight and eyed the older man. "..."

Gabriel glanced at his watch. "Sorry, my boy, but we're going to have to cut this conversation. Need to return to circulation or they'll suspect you of abducting me." He reached inside his sports coat and pulled a small envelope, the size to hold a few loose diamonds or a microchip. "This is for Ellia. A long list of bad news, pieces to a puzzle. We'll meet again soon." Putting his hand on the door he added, "Make sure you do a few rounds before you leave, appreciate some of the other artwork. You might like one or two. And mind the uninvited guests. Ellia'd have words with me if I let you get abducted under my watch. Took some charming to get you here."

The door closed behind the artist. Min Soo turned the envelope around between his fingers, lost in thought.

"That was three times he mentioned abductions..." He shook his head and slipped the envelope into his pant pocket. Time to make his own exit.

Timing it well by sheer happenstance, no one spotted his exit. A security camera may have caught it, but no harm. He wandered as instructed and greeted those who approached him, mostly the younger daughters of the matrons in the crowd. He tried to spot the man he'd seen earlier, but no luck.

While admiring the paintings and sculptures, champagne glass in hand, Min Soo tried to fathom the other man he'd met, the Artist Gabriel. Reading art did not come naturally; the process engrossed him. He didn't notice the approaching, fully jewelled, slightly over accessorized matron who'd had a few too many glasses of the bubbly. Neither did he notice the man whose name he still didn't know slip behind him and drop a rather slippery appetizer. The matron raised a hand to wave to another patron and simultaneously stepped forward, or rather slipped forward. Arms flailing and grasp, grasp, grasping, she caught the nearest object: Min Soo's sleeve.

A girl darted out from behind the matron and shoved Min Soo out of the way. Shoved him directly into another woman who'd been quietly contemplating the depth, or lack thereof, of the work she faced. Champagne flew from Min Soo's glass as he slammed into her. Momentum drove them toward the painting on the wall. His arms snapped out to brace against the wall and tried to prevent the poor woman from crashing into it herself, only it didn't happen. She'd anticipated and braced her hands against the wall on either side of the painting.

He bounced back and blurted a quick, "Sorry," turned around and spotted a red-faced mother and daughter being hustled away by one of the servers. The champagne glass slipped in his hands, but he caught it again, inches from shattering next to the mess on the floor. A quiet voice beside advised,

"Don't worry about it, Curator Oh's staff will take care of it. We have to go."

Min Soo's eyes widened and he spun back to face...Ellia? A fellow Korean wearing a fashionable face mask peered at him over the edges of a large pair of tinted glasses. Only, the eyes were Ellia's flashing green. Not a Korean. She tapped his arm with the program in her hand and started walking away as if nothing had happened.

"You?" he said, syncing up to her stroll. "Yes," she replied, "no need to introduce me to anyone." The words held an underlying shortness.

Min Soo studiously avoided contact with a nearing fellow guest and pointed to an apparently fascinating abstract painting of, "Is that a daisy?"

"Definitely a sea anemone," she corrected, "at a seahorse birth-day party."

"Are you sure?" he asked. Quieter words snuck out the corner of his mouth, "What are you doing here?"

"I'm enjoying my investment." Behind her mask she added, "and protecting it."

"What?" They paused at another display. He wasn't sure which line of the conversation he should follow. "This has got to be a...wave?"

"Yes. Extraordinary work, isn't it?" No meaning between the lines, she seemed to be genuinely admiring the wave sculpture. It rose half again as high as Min Soo, and so realistic, he edged away in preparation of it crashing down to soak the entire guest list. The rules were getting a little fast and loose, and he wasn't sure the wave might be the first to give.

A drop glistened in Ellia's hair, or rather wig, definitely a wig. Dark brown, gently wavy, almost wispy. He reached out to touch the drop only to realize it was a simple hair pin.

Ellia pulled back, cautioning, "Please, it's the only thing keeping this thing on my head." She leaned in close, and smoothed an imaginary wrinkle from his sleeve, "Appearances, appearances. You have your reputation to maintain." She walked with him, around the wave, eyes traveling. "Did you happen to see who dropped the slipping hazard?" A faint lick of fire coloured her words.

"I was focused on not smashing your head into the waves of diamonds and boulders you found so fascinating."

"That voice, you have no idea... Never mind, just keep it low. I'm not entirely sure how many unfriendlies we have gathered here, although I think Curator Oh managed to keep most of them out. He must be high-level."

"I'm sorry, what are you talking about?"

"Is your manager waiting for you or are you taking a taxi?"

"He's waiting at a café nearby."

"Good. Not sure how long I can convince them I'm a happenstance meeting. And dear Artist Gabriel doesn't need to know this particular guise." She gave him a giggle as if she'd said something flirty and nudged him surreptitiously toward the door.

He straightened from the lean he'd fallen into in his attempt to catch the quieter parts of their conversation. As he and Ellia meandered, casually drifting toward the exit, he did his own scan of their surroundings, but the display walls allowed for too many blind spots.

Clear, on the outside, Min Soo released the air he hadn't realized he'd been hoarding. "Who is Artist Gabriel? He used the word "unfriendlies" too, and an attempted abduction. How is my mother involved?"

"Let's clear the entry way," she said, leading the way with light steps. "To answer your question. He's an old friend and I send business, including some art (not my own), his way. He repays the favor by handling some of my non-monetary affairs, including securing the safety of people like you. His warning was no joke. I don't think you're in danger of being violently manhandled and stolen away, yet, but if you walk straight into their arms while staring at your phone, I'd expect them to take full advantage." She pulled the mask down under her chin. "Your mother, well, you'd have to ask Curator Oh about that." She played the disguise with an aegyo shoulder shrug. "I'm guessing their social circles overlap? Old school friends maybe?"

He shook his head and rubbed his eye.

"Something wrong?" she asked with a bounce on the balls of her feet.

He waited for a mini pack of middle-schoolers to pass. Lowering head and voice, he explained, "Your disguise is giving me double vision. Even your walk—". His phone rang in his pocket.

They stepped onto the grass and Min Soo quickly checked the display. Jackpot. It was his turn to be mysterious.

"Yes?" he answered, gleefully plastering on his model mask.

Ellia didn't bother trying to listen to the other end of the conversation as Min Soo went through the standard: Hey, whatcha doing, bro, waddaya want? etc. Her attention rested lightly on the youngish figure making her way down the other side of the busy street. Not a middle-schooler, she'd set off Ellia's subconscious perimeter alarm. The partner of whoever had planted the slip'n'slide hazard. A warning needed to be issued, soon.

Min Soo unexpectedly flashed his 10,000-watt grin. Ellia's radar went total fritz-krieg.

"Tonight? Yeah, I'm free. I have someone I want you to meet. No, nothing like that."

He listened again, a crinkle invading the corner of each eye. He startled Ellia again with a sudden laugh. She nudged him behind a hedge for additional privacy. Eyes were drifting in their direction.

The conversation continued until he closed it with, "See you then."

She brushed her bangs out of the way and asked, "I'm the someone?"

Min Soo slipped the phone back in his pocket, opened his mouth, closed it. His hand aimed for his hair, but he crossed his arms before it could make a mess. "You've been speaking Korean this whole time."

"Finally, you notice." She flicked a strand of hair back over her shoulder. "Hard to give the impression that I'm local if I don't speak the language." She tapped her glasses and the mask. "Just have to keep from having any extended face to face interactions."

He nodded thoughtfully. "Your Korean isn't a temporary thing, is it?"

Ellia put herself between Min Soo and the street as they continued walking. "What, you think it's like Cinderella or something? Midnight comes along and suddenly all I do is click and snicker like a dolphin?"

Merdragon

"Snicker…never mind. A few friends of mine are meeting at a dance club tonight and they invited me to join them." They walked a few steps in silence and Ellia managed a second glimpse of their follower. The family resemblance sang like electricity in the background. Min Soo's earthy voice grounded her back to their side of the street. "They're good friends."

"I'm intrigued. Are they models or actors too?" She flicked back a strand of hair. It settled right back where it started. Straight hair luck. A drop of sweat trickled down the back of her neck.

"They…do belong to the same agency."

"Hmmm…I won't press." The wig was starting to feel like a fur hat and the mask like a squirrel deathly afraid of identity theft.

"I should probably message my manager."

"Yes."

"Do you, uh, want a lift?"

"Came in a taxi, I'll leave in one too. Hopefully an airconditioned one." She fanned her face and spotted Do Hyun. "You go your way. I'll meet you back at the apartment. Have to remember I'm just some girl you may or may not have just met at the gallery, and who isn't me."

He threw his head back in a fake laugh. "Right. So, how do you want to do this?"

She covered her mouth and feigned a giggle. "How about we do a confused flutter of fingers, and then you hail me a cab?"

Words to actions and within minutes Ellia sighed in relief to have hit the A/C jackpot. She turned around in her seat to spot Min Soo raise a hand in farewell and take the two steps to where his manager had pulled up the van. The stalker had most probably stepped into a bush.

Ellia directed the taxicab to another neighbourhood, got off, walked a ways, took the subway, wandered around inside a shopping centre, purchased a day dress, quick changed inside a stairwell (wig removal included), hailed a cab to drive her to a boutique district, picked up a dress and shoes for the night, slipped into a small hair salon, took a ride on public transit, transferred three time and arrived at Min Soo's apartment an hour or so after dark.

She walked in and caught Min Soo, phone in hand, pacing.

"How long does it take to get from there to here by taxi? I was about to call you." He reached in his pocket and pulled out the mini envelope. "And before I forget, Artist Seung said to pass this on to you. He said it was probably bad news, pieces to a puzzle."

Hurriedly she slipped off her shoes and curled her toes into the chunky yarn slippers. A reminder of a different ocean. The constant mystification they caused Min Soo gave her an inordinate amount of secret glee.

"Thanks," she said, taking the envelope from his hand. "The last bus had some technical issues."

"What happened to the taxicab?" Min Soo asked. "Wait, you changed. And went shopping again?"

She speed-shuffled toward her room and he followed her in as she headed to the closet. "I may be a relatively plain Jane as, um, is, but since we're heading to a dance club to meet your friends, I figure a little upgrading might be in order."

His words came off dry as alcohol powder. "Yes, scales might be a bit much."

"Not to mention the, um, cape?"

He chuckled and shook a finger at her, "No breathing fire either."

She gave him a wink. "Exactly, now out, out, out. I've got a transformation to orchestrate thank you very much."

He got the hint. "Right."

She gave him a once over as she watched him walk backwards out the door. "Since you've got yourself in order, do me a favour and stick around within yelling distance? You know, in case I need a zipper or tooth pulled."

The door closed on his shifting face.

Ellia reprimanded herself. "Let's keep things friendly and above board, shall we."

The reflective mosaic piece glittered light and colours, but nothing useful, and Min Soo raised his eyes soulfully to the ceiling in a plea for patience, or something equally important. His long legs took him back to his own room to collect a pair of shoes from his considerable collection. They were harder to find these days since Ellia had taken over his closet.

A little light nightclub drama

A quarter, or half, or three-quarters of an hour, maybe a full one later, Ellia did a last check in the mirror. A little moue of disapproval crossed her lips. Makeup and the right outfit could drastically change a woman's appearance, but nothing came close to what a little merdragon transformation could accomplish.

She sighed and shrugged. "Ah well, no fire breathing for you tonight, dear." Puffing out her cheeks, she added, "At least no one will confuse you with a Día de Muertos participant."

Glittering heels hanging from her fingers, she stepped out and padded down the hall. Min Soo straightened up from leaning against the kitchen counter. His long legs leisurely uncrossed as he gave her his assessment. A nod indicated approval; a tilt of the head indicated a more in-depth analysis.

Choosing to ignore the reaction, Ellia attempted to short-circuit the loop and asked, "Time to go?"

Bemused, he nodded. He'd gone mute again it seemed. She slipped her heels on her feet, and, standing a little higher, she waited for him to slip on his own striking pair of footwear. In a pensive mood he stopped at the full-length mirror by the door and carefully tweaked an eyebrow, adjusted his collar, and finally did a full-body check to ensure that everything sat as it should.

"Narcissist," Ellia quipped. "

A well paid one," he quipped back, opened the door and gestured her through.

"Turning a flaw into a strength, well done."

They entered the elevator and Min Soo pointed at their reflection in the steel door. "Thank you, it takes hours of staring in a mirror."

"Oh stop," she replied, stabbing the parking level button.

"Alright, I admit the mirror doesn't get me the voice gigs." As the elevator went down floor by floor, he started counting out the numbers, each number a note lower than the last.

Min Soo grandly scraped bass, "Parking Level 2" and the elevator doors dinged open.

Ellia's knees wobbled taking a step forward and she smiled a bit shakily. "Still getting used to heels after a decade or so."

He offered his arm, but she declined with a shake of her head. They walked in silence toward his parked car. The sound of their heels clicked against the pavement, echoing in the parkade, his clicks more solid and slow, counter-balanced by her light and quicker ones.

The car doors unlocked, ending the duet. Next came the thunks of one door and then the other. Silence. A listening ear might reasonably expect to hear an engine start next, but the expectation of that sound hung in the air unrequited.

Inside the car, Min Soo rested his hands on the steering wheel. He angled the corner of his eye in Ellia's direction. He shifted in his seat and redirected his eyes forward again. He leaned his head against the head rest, fiddled with the side mirror controls. Checked the rear-view mirror.

Finally, he leaned one elbow on the door's arm rest and looked over at her. She gave him her full attention. "It'll do," he stated. Then he nodded in satisfaction, resettled his lips into his barley-there smile. Released from holding it in, he redirected his focus to operating the car.

They drove out of the underground parkade and Ellia smiled smugly to herself, unexpectedly pleased, and mouthed, "Of course," out the window.

Comfortable in silence, they rode to the club, streetlights and neon signs flashing their invitations as they drew closer.

A thought crossed Min Soo's face. "How old do your people live?"

"Merkind? Well, first of all, for the record, they're as human as you are, just a little modified." She ran a hand down her leg for emphasis. "As for their longevity? Well, with our current medical skills, most reach a hundred and twenty, on average. Some a little more, some less."

The traffic light turned red in front of them.

As casually as he could he asked, "And, uh, when were you born?"

She outright laughed. "Oh, where to start?"

The traffic lights switched to green. He released the brakes, more focused on her response than the road. Fortunately for them both, traffic behaved.

Ellia answered her own question. "Test tubes were involved in my creation. I think I'm human, doctors say I am, but my birthdate and lifespan are both unknowns. I could be forty or a hundred for all I know."

Min Soo's hands tightened on the steering wheel and he took a sizable breath in through his nose, and out again. Mercifully, they'd arrived at their destination. A lineup on the street led to a high-end club, and after giving the valet the keys to the car, Min Soo gave Ellia his arm, turned on his professional charm mode, and

Merdragon

walked past the doorman and bouncer with a nod. Those in the lineup nudged each other and whispers went up and down the line asking how, and why, and who, and who was that girl? The same questions rolled around like loose cannonballs in Min Soo's brain. He fought to keep his stride steady. The cannonball from the gallery had gained a few friends.

Inside the club, Min Soo led Ellia past the dancing crowd on the floor, the drinking crowd at the bar, up the stairs past another bouncer, and to a less musically and laser light overpowering private lounging corner. A few bottles and glasses already sat on the table, but it was the guys that sat in various degrees of relaxation on the padded seats that Min Soo wanted Ellia to meet. Now was not the time to unravel her newest revelation.

Keeping in mind their animal aliases, Mouse rose to his feet first and proffered a hand and English greeting. Min Soo watched her suspiciously. There was something slightly off about her reactions, hundred-year-old merdragon or not. He coughed in surprise when she replied to Mouse in accented Korean, different from the gallery. This carried an obscure tonal quality, emphasizing the foreign label, but different from English speakers. Ears twitched, intrigued.

A hint of smile grazed Min Soo's lips as he introduced Ellia to the rest of the group. Settling himself and Ellia down, he resisted responding to the subtle looks and nudges requesting an explanation for her attendance. Truthfully, even he wasn't sure why he'd felt the need to, what, show her off? He couldn't brag about her 'flying license'. Introduce her as a simple friend? Why hadn't he thought this out ahead of time?

A waitress came to their table with more drinks and to check on the newcomers. Min Soo accepted a beer.

Beside him, Ellia asked, "Mineral water for me."

The atmosphere teetered on a cliff's edge.

Min Soo gave her side-eye and a silent "?!?"

She promptly patted him on the knee. "Sorry, forgot to mention, I have zero tolerance."

Inexplicably she leaned in close only to brush something off his shoulder. He heard a sharp inhale from someone. Then, with pro accuracy, Ellia dropped a word only he could hear in his ear. "Careful."

She pulled back and his eyes immediately tracked the intense attention now on him. He forgot to ask, careful of what?

Panda, the youngest and natural born imp, decided to challenge Min Soo's "friend" description. Smoother than his name might indicate, he offered her a hand. "Care to dance?"

Expecting to hear a denial, Min Soo nearly uncrossed his legs when she rose to her feet. She gave him a wink and behind her back, where only he could see, she gave him a hand signal. What was she trying to say? No, wait, it was the band's symbol! She'd conned him.

Leaning against the balustrade separating them from the dance floor below, Lion teased, "Sure it's okay for Panda to take her? She might not come back."

"Ellia's free to do as she pleases. But let me tell you about…" and so he proceeded to distract them with an edited-for-friends version of his island adventure. For his interviews he'd rehearsed his story to keep Ellia out of it, and now he rehashed his script with a few added, not-suitable-for-public details. He couldn't figure out how Ellia had transferred herself out of the narrative and onto a non-existent woman. Most knew that a woman had been involved, but just didn't manage to connect her with Ellia. Oddly, in the public mind, she'd become an older, almost elderly woman whom he'd somehow rescued rather than the other way around.

"Okay, but why'd you bring Ms. Ellia Nighe tonight? Who is she really?" Monkey asked. Beside him Mouse seconded the question.

And that's when Min Soo had a stroke of genius.

"She's doing research. She's a storyteller." He'd stolen Ellia's own, maybe-true-maybe-false story.

"Like an author? Is she making your marooning into a book?" another one asked. "Wow."

"Nah, she's actually focusing on the woman, you know the one who was rescued with me. It's part of her full life bio." Hah, he'd wrapped it up all nice and neat.

A low voice asked, "Then why's she hanging around with you and not the old woman?" Dino, lip curled and eyebrow at the precise elevation required to label him an advanced level, professional mischief-maker. This dino ate meat. And whatever was in his shot glass.

Min Soo opened his mouth, hoping something intelligent came out, but Lion's sudden distracted gaze diverted the ill-attempt. Lion's eyes were on the dance floor. Min Soo glanced over. The cannonballs in his head all rolled to one side. Dino stood to get a better look. His glass remained full as he forgot to tilt and swallow. Ellia and the Panda had the dance floor.

Merdragon

Now Panda had moves, no question, and he didn't mind showing them off, whenever, wherever. Like right now. And he'd figured out pretty quick that Ellia didn't dance like most. A space had cleared around them. Min Soo rose to his feet. Mouse leaned over beside Lion to get a better view. They'd never seen a merdragon dance. Neither had anyone else in the room. There were no aerobatics or ostentatious gyrations, but her spine and spatial awareness differed from those of surface-dwellers. Min Soo could practically see her wings and tail as she and Panda bounced moves off each other, complexity increasing with each volley.

Something startled Ellia out of her flow. Min Soo saw the double-take catch her mid-step. Mouse noticed it too and scanned the room for a possible source. He grabbed Min Soo's arm.

"Panda's fiancée. She's going to freak."

Dino swore as alcohol spilled on his shirt. Or maybe it was the oncoming storm. Min Soo muttered something about seawenches under his breath and rallied the troops for a divert and avoid dismemberment mission. Monkey headed the charge down the stairs, and Dino played the charming clown. Lion disarmed males and females with his beach-time grin, and Mouse sidled up beside Panda. He flicked the proverbial switch and the equally proverbial spotlight split into five. Melt-down averted.

With a brief brush of the hand, Min Soo cued Ellia to the approaching fireworks. She nodded understanding and followed his taller than average self in the opposite direction of a potential re-ignition. Off the dance floor, he skirted past a few tables, and headed toward another set of stairs. He felt her tap his elbow. He glanced back. She wasn't looking at him.

Her head tilted first to one side. Then the other. Listening. Min Soo heard someone, a man, laugh above the club noise and immediately Ellia's whole body tensed. A second laugh triggered movement. Min Soo's mind flashed back to the snake Ellia had killed in the cave. His hair rose on the back of his neck. A split-second decision sent him after her killer footsteps.

Another burst of laughter twanged against Ellia's eardrums. Most wouldn't recognize the sea song weaved inside it, but eliminating it was harder still. Like forcing a drunk Scotsman to speak Texan. Some things couldn't be scrubbed from a childhood's vocal cords. She recognized these particular cords and their genetic connection.

The body encasing the cords held court in a dark corner, surrounded by an eclectic circle of persons. He'd dressed mostly in black, a high-end watch flashed on his wrist, and a fine gold chain glinted from the neck of his unbuttoned shirt collar. A smoky blue shirt that spoke of money. His face didn't give him away. It said South Korean. But something else said born out of country. His actions labelled him up and coming money-maker so make friends with him now.

He'd grown since last she'd seen him.

"Riko Danube," Ellia spoke his name low in her throat.

The man raised his chin in irritation. The same chin that had lowered at a sister's chilled habit. "I'm bus-sis-y… Oh, no." The ese miscarried and his chair scraped the floor as he drew back to his feet. "What, what are you…?"

"Oh, yes. You got carried away in your attempt to blend into the scenery," she replied, eyes narrowing. "Spy game's weak." For good measure she added a few clicks to the conversation. Clicks that didn't really translate. Clicks the equivalent of a literal sword.

He body-waved into a bow, merkin style. It didn't translate well without water. The stuttering was universal. "A-apologies, h-honoured one, please forgive the discourtesy."

"Sit," she ordered. The sucker fish that surrounded him drew closer. "Leave!"

Surprisingly loyal, one or two attempted to refuse the command, but Riko pushed the one closest to him and hissed, "Go. Now."

They left, sending Ellia resentful, and curious glares. In her periphery she saw them pass Min Soo with barely a hint of interest. He'd settled against a pillar and crossed legs and arms. Possibly his fingers.

"What about him?" Riko asked.

She pulled out a chair and settled down across from Riko. "I'm surprised you remembered the correct form of address. How old were you when your father decided to commit treason and implicate me?"

"You betrayed him first."

"Ha! I'm guessing you were what ten, twelve years old? I remember you." She added a few more clicks. Descriptive this time.

"That was you?" His voice shook.

"Foolish child." She dry-spat in disgust. "Getting caught in fishing nets."

"Twenty years on dryland. I'm no child." His voice was sullen. The music and lights camouflaged some of the fear. False bravado made him point out Min Soo. "Him maybe. Not much of a bodyguard."

Mongoose fast she snapped in close, a breath distance apart. A stream of clicks cracked against his ears and his face paled to fish-belly white. Drawing back finally, she added, "Do you honestly think I need one?"

Merdragon

Cold sweat dewed on his forehead. The chair scraped against the floor as he stood to do a quick, but low bow. "No, honoured one, my apologies."

Leaning back, she snapped her wrist. "Sit."

He sat. Uncomfortably. On the chair's edge.

"I earned that title. Be happy I don't speak it. Whether I'm a laboratory monstrosity or not, I am my own person. Not your father's pet. Never that." Her throat hummed, "I'm no soulless slave. You pay me lip service with your courtesy bow? Better to show me that courtesy by not kidnapping my people."

She spared a glance in Min Soo's direction. He'd plastered on his neutral face. It might take an icepick to crack it afterward.

Returning her attention to Riko, she clicked a few admonition notes. He wouldn't return her gaze and shook his head miserably, stiffly.

"I supposed your father's still hung up on my genetic keys, isn't he? Tell me Riko, what is he up to these days? Why is he stalking me and mine so fiercely?"

"I couldn't say," Riko replied.

Ellia tapped a finger on the table, "Curious… Give me your phone."

Hands slick with sweat, Riko dug in his pant pocket and half placed, half dropped the phone onto the table, sliding it to Ellia. Palm upward, Ellia waited. Two-handed, Riko picked up the phone, unlocked it and carefully placed it in Ellia's hand. She inclined her head in mock thanks.

Music pounding and strobe lights flashing in the background, Ellia perused the contents of the phone, her fingers quick and thorough. It didn't contain much; he wasn't an idiot. Finished, she handed the phone back to him. She eyed him for a few sweat inducing moments, then smoothly stood to her feet.

He scrambled to his feet and promised, "I won't say a word, honoured one."

Placing a hand on the table, she leaned toward Riko and allowed a hint of fire growl to dance along the edges of her words. "You are mistaken Riko-ssi." He winced as the words brushed the inner lining of his skull. "This is a blatant warning. I'm tracking the oil slick your father spilled and I will be setting it on fire. Careful you're not sitting in it neck deep."

She straightened up and stepped away from the table. "Remember, look, don't touch; you break, I bite. Don't change your number, you know how I like a good hunt. You came too close today."

A turn, a nod to Min Soo, and into the crowd she returned. She didn't glance back to see how long Riko managed to remain on his feet.

Clear of Riko's vision, Ellia slowed to make room for Min Soo to come alongside. She glanced up to see that the neutral mask wouldn't be needing an ice pick after all.

"Who was that?" he asked, perfectly reasonable.

"One of our friendly neighbourhood spies. They got too close today. I figured somebody would be here ahead of us to tail you. Turned out to be him. The bug proved useful."

"I thought you were staying under the radar. Why'd you confront him?" he asked, sidestepping a tipsy couple.

"It's the flush technique. Valued by predators everywhere. And like I said, they needed a rap on the knuckles." She pointed up to their previous vantage seating. "Think it's safe to return to your friends?"

Cluing into the closed info share, Min Soo used his extra elevation to scan the club's present frame of mind. "I think we're good. Let's head up."

A few tables from the staircase he leaned down to loudly whisper in her ear, "You know exactly who they are, don't you?"

She grinned up mischievously. "It's a pleasure to meet them in person."

He shook his head and sighed, "Says the mythical creature." He groaned and rubbed his nose. "If they ever find out…"

Ellia bounced on her toes and clapped her hands in near glee, "Oh, I have to be there to see it."

He looked at her in disbelief and ran his fingers through his hair. Frequent exposure to his exasperations, she barely blinked. The table nearby was less fortunate. Dribble may or may not have ruined an expensive dress or two, or five. Oblivious to the minor disaster, he offered his hand to Ellia and stopped their forward momentum.

"Was Riko the reason you told me to be careful earlier?"

"Oh, right. No. Completely different. I didn't think to warn you on our way here. Might want to keep the alcohol to a minimum. Your tolerance levels have been recalibrated, and there may be other effects. Did you happen to notice Riko's drink? Non-alcoholic. Blame it on biology. Hope you weren't a big drinker."

"Ah…I see. No, couldn't afford to be with what I do. Interesting." Min Soo nodded and took the first step to the second level.

Ellia followed. He'd taken the news better than she'd thought. She shook her head and took scope of watchful eyes. On him, of course. Her neutral appearance was proving practically an invisibility cloak for those who might have been tempted to throw, if nothing else, vicious dagger glances of jealousy. She sighed, taking the last step to the top. There had to be some benefit to not going full scale.

The rest of the night, after making nice with Panda's fiancée, Ellia enjoyed being thoroughly entertained by Min Soo's friends. Considerately she refrained from giving Min Soo anymore heart attacks of the panic sort. Heart attacks of the other sort were another matter. His friends bordered on the merciless. By the time she'd become everyone's older sister, she could see the Han Min Soo 24-hour-long-model-shoot patience had word down to a $500 pair of jeans. But shredded patience or not, at the close of the evening they all parted still friends.

Some more sober than others. Ellia and Riko topped the list.

Riko sat behind the wheel and called his father.

"What is it? We're about to break through." Waves and machinery filled the background.

"Already? Wow."

The next words bellowed inside the car, "Girl! Get your tail out of there. And get that *whistle* ribbon off your neck." The voice returned to phone-to-phone levels, "If her dad hadn't died in that helicopter, I wouldn't need her here, d—n genetics. Now why did you call?"

"It's about your headache. We had a...meeting."

"She's determined not to make nice?"

"Father, I don't think there's as big of a trench between the merKing and the honoured one as they'd like us to believe."

A squall of seabirds set off a distant racket. Riko could barely hear his father. He sounded distracted. "What makes you think that? Hey! That's worth nearly as much as your skin."

"She's not hunting the merKing."

"Hmmph, figures they'd pod together, hypocrites. Make sure she stays distracted on other things. Track all her connections. Can't have her discovering our new schoolmate. Or squealing to the merKing. The longer she's tripping over tailing us, the better."

O, bee-have

Min Soo drove into the church parking lot and couldn't help but smile. Saturday he'd awoken, late, in his own apartment, then popped out while Ellia still snoozed on the balcony. A few hours later, walking back in, he'd been surprised to see the fire alarms disconnected. He shook his head and shut off the engine; he laughed outright. She'd been expanding her fire skills, practicing by making crème brûlée.

He couldn't keep the grin off his face as he stepped out of the car and headed to the church. His heels crunched on the gravel. She'd had to whisper for the rest of the day; a consequence he'd advised she avoid in future by letting him take her out to explore the city's culinary offerings.

He pulled back on his smile to exchange nods and greetings to other congregants as he found his seat in a pew that only held one other, a middle-aged gentleman. A family running late slid into the same pew and the middle-aged gentleman shifted closer giving him an apologetic smile.

After the song service, the pastor took his place behind the pulpit and started his sermon. Min Soo kept losing the train of the message. It had been some time since he'd sat through a service. He blinked and subtly shook his head to clear it. His arm twitched and he shifted his shoulders. Without turning his head, he glanced down at his hands, then surreptitiously to his right. His eyes continued their way, and up, and returned to the pastor. Who happened to be staring directly at him in his moment of drift. His face warmed. Coming had been Ellia's idea, but she hadn't arrived; now he sat alone.

When the choir rose to sing the closing song, Min Soo's lungs released their iron hold. He rose with the rest of the congregation as the pianist began to play. Time came for the final prayer. The amen echoed through the church, and as he opened his eyes, the little boy, who'd been restrained from beginning to end, yelped and dove after his precious bumble bee.

A fat and fed bumble bee. Plump and happy to settle on Min Soo's neighbour's boutonniere. But little boys that smuggle forbidden pets into churches are generally not the type to behave like fat and fed bumble bees. The bomb-full of energy leapt up to recapture his pet. The man with the boutonniere stumbled

Merdragon

back at the impact. An usher grabbed Min Soo from behind and pulled him aside. Well-placed palms and a stern look at the young miscreant resolved the matter.

The usher passed a stern look at the parents as well, gently cupped the bumble bee in his hand and guided it back into the glass jar the boy had used for the smuggling operation. The parents apologized thoroughly, and with a firm grasp on the boy's collar, they forced him to offer his own bow of apology, the jar firmly clasped in his hands. Mr. Boutonniere and Min Soo accepted the apologies, and with all well in the world, the usher followed the family out.

Min Soo eyed his neighbor curiously.

Mr. Boutonniere laughed quietly, "Little boys. I think I spilled my mother's change purse once in the middle of prayer."

"Ah, yes. Thankfully it didn't happen during the service, although I did think I heard a buzzing," Min Soo replied, shifting his feet slightly.

"Oh, my, yes," Mr. Boutonniere nodded, "Yes, well, I'll be off first then."

They nodded mutually, and Mr. Boutonniere took his leave. An acquaintance stopped him halfway down the aisle to buzz about the incident. Min Soo watched for a moment, then shrugged. So, that was that. He nodded once to himself, straightened his shoulders, buttoned the single button on his suit jacket and took his own leave. A few greeted him with a smile and a nod, but no one stopped him in his tracks, not even the couple who couldn't seem to decide on something.

The woman was chewing on her lips as he passed, and he was sure he spotted her foot tap her partner. Her partner responded by taking hold of her hand and reassuring her. "Alright dear, I'll go take care of it. Make sure you get home safe."

"Don't take too long," was her response.

Min Soo didn't hear the rest of the conversation, but he did spot the man hanging around Mr. Boutonniere, and the woman drifted off after the family that had created the fuss. Not his business.

He stepped out into the sunny Sunday and found his way back to his car. Inside he tapped the steering wheel and thought. He sighed, took a breath, held it, sighed again. He leaned his elbow against the door frame and rubbed the back of his neck. The wheel received a few more taps.

Out loud, to himself, he commented, "That was weird." He nodded again.

His phone rang. It was Ellia.

"Hello?"

"Hey, Min Soo, how was the service?"

"Service was fine, shame you couldn't make it." He scanned the steadily emptying parking lot. "Afterward, yeah, there was a bumble bee, but it didn't go far, and, well, it was weird."

"A bumble bee? In the church?"

Nodding, he replied, "Yea…"

"Hmm, listen. The phone's fine, but the car might not be so wait until you get to the apartment to check your pockets."

"My p—? Ah, yes, ok, will do."

"And Min Soo?"

"Yes?"

"This too. I'm at the airport, on my way to Iceland. Keep it under your tongue. It's the reason I couldn't meet you at the church this morning."

Min Soo stiffened up. The steering wheel suffered. "What?! When? W-what, why? Now?"

He could hear the smirk in her voice, "And the how will be by conventional airplane. Sorry, I couldn't give you more of a warning. I did want to point you in the direction of an introduction. I'll be back in a month or less. Do keep yourself clean of bugs, bumbling bees or otherwise. Fair days 'til I see you." And she hung up.

His seat took the force of his slump back. He stared at his phone, sighed and shook his head, "Tch." The sound repeated in various forms all the way back to his apartment.

The door clicked behind him and immediately his hand dove into his pocket. Nothing. He checked the other one. Nothing. He frowned and started patting himself down. Almost he strip-searched, but it had been church. "Nothing." His well-coifed head suffered a run through. Off came his shoes. Something. A small slip of paper. He bent to pick it up, muttering, "Ellia picks her friends well." It had a sarcastic undertone.

He held the slip of paper at a slight distance as he opened it holding his breath. Inside it read, "Nice to meet you. See you soon. Beware trailing insects." Did he mean the bumblebee?

The usher reminded him of the delivery man. The "tch" was too big to get out.

Ice fishing

Keflavik International Airport was its usually international busy self when Ellia arrived. Not on the same level as New York or Beijing, but all the more pleasant for avoiding the top busiest list. She breezed through customs with her merEmbassy provided pseudo-official documents and passed the luggage carousel with her carry-on. Amidst the sign holders waiting, the name "Auður" stood out, written in thick blue ink, held by a young woman.

It wasn't her name, but it was the right colour and face, and her ride. With short work, they skimmed the pleasantries and stepped out into an Icelandic autumn afternoon. They stayed within common conversation until they'd entered the nondescript older vehicle and set on their way.

Ellia initiated the hot topic, "So, tell me, what's all the panic that I had to come see in person?"

Auður, the driver, kept her eyes set on the road. "It was very disturbing. I hesitate to make a guess. It is best for you to personally investigate."

The distance between international and national airports wasn't long, but time enough to hear a private report. And to open the paper bag she'd found on her seat; a snack pack of harðfiskur, aka fish jerky. The skyr drykkur helped wash it down, adding to the calorie count. "Blueberries?"

Auður nodded.

Mouth full of fish, Ellia asked another question, "The alert, it was something below the surface around Surtsey?"

"No one, except pre-approved scientists, are permitted to go there, you understand. Publicly this is because of the delicate nature of the emerging ecosystem." She glanced over at Ellia, frowning. "When rumours started that strangers had been given permission to visit, I learned that it was not a simple one-time permit." Her voice grew grimmer. "I have learned since that there have been visits to the area from before Surtsey's first rise to the surface in 1963. Last Saturday, the party that went, came back one short. There were reports of blood in the water." She paused in her telling, hands gripping the steering wheel. "There were additional rumours of something being stolen. I don't know what."

"Stolen?" Ellia had to pause to finish and swallow the piece of fish in her mouth. "If all this strangeness was witnessed, why hasn't Iceland's own taken care of all this? Why did you call me?"

"I heard the singing." Auður's hands clenched around the steering wheel. "It sounded just like the recordings we were given, thirty years ago. It was faint and brief, but definitely a match."

"Ah," Ellia sighed in realization. Absently she returned the empty container of skyr drykkur back into the paper bag. Didn't taste the same as the homemade stuff she'd had in her teens.

The nearest populated island to Surtsey, Heimaey, was in easy visual range and the reason witnesses were involved. Getting there necessitated travelling the short distance by conventional airplane; hiding in plane sight, so to speak. Time too, was not in her favour. The blood would be long gone by now. Other traces of evidence, however, might last a little longer.

Ellia shifted in her seat as the airport came into view. Mersong was the most incriminating evidence, but not one of the kinds that usually left traces, let alone witnesses. Auður should not be alive. Mersong so close to a populated area was the equivalent of an air raid siren.

"Instructions were to make contact immediately and avoid like nuclear fallout." Auður set the car in park; they'd arrived at the airport. "It isn't, is it?"

They climbed out of the car and watched as an airplane rose into the pale grey sky.

Ellia's voice rumbled with a hint of the growl Min Soo had first heard on the more tropical island. "Death follows as if it were." Min Soo had heard her sing on the island, but she hadn't been trying to kill him. The sailor stories held a grain of truth. Certain melodies precipitated intentional disaster.

They walked the rest of the way in silence; the plane ride to Heimaey, equally as quiet.

The two women arrived on Heimaey Island and headed to Auður's cousin's home to settle Ellia's gear. The family of three greeted her warmly, despite the late hour. A late bite to eat waited, as did a place to sleep. According to advance instruction, the late bite had some heftiness to it.

They all sat around the wooden table and kept Ellia company as she steadily downed her meal. Auður's niece had glued herself to her aunt's side; the adults kept their hands busy with a late-night cup of coffee. Unnþór, Auður's cousin, made a few efforts at small talk, asking about the journey. He owned a small sailing boat he occasionally chartered out. She'd be using it tomorrow.

Ellia asked, "You understood the message and what I need?"

Unnþór scowled, "I have the instruction, yes, but they did not make me happy. I do not want to be accused of murder."

Ellia choked mid-swallow. Eyebrows high, she asked Auður, "What exactly did you tell him?"

"Simply as you instructed. He thinks you are crazy and possibly suicidal. He thinks I am crazy and," he interrupted with an Icelandic word she translated, "dangerously irresponsible for helping you."

Ellia eyed him while he continued to focus on his cup with a grim intensity. A man determined to avoid aiding and abetting the suicidal intent, ignorant or otherwise, of his cousin's associate. Money and intimidation would not have an effect.

"Dropping me off, and leaving me on a secluded section of shoreline that is inaccessible by foot, is not an attempt on my part to end my life. I appreciate the concern, however, this is quite necessary for my investi- um, research."

Unnþór took a sip of his coffee, savoured it as it went down, then asked, "Research?"

"Yes."

Ellia took another bite of her meal and waited him out.

His wife, Kaja, poured Ellia another glass of skyr. Ellia noted the calluses.

"How long will you be?" Unnþór asked.

She wiped her mouth with a napkin and discretely burped behind it.

"Give me twenty-four hours. I'm well-prepared to overnight it. If I need you sooner, I'll give you a call."

In the quiet, Unnþór's swallow and the thump of his elbow on the table spoke eloquently.

"Auður," he addressed his blood instead of Ellia, "How can I do this thing?"

Auður replied in a steady tone, "Cousin, all precautions have been taken." She pointed to a half metre long shell discretely placed and secured on a corner shelf. "Remember the gift uncle received, what, like some fifty years ago?" She paused to let the spiraling, multi-faceted shell voice its speechless endorsement. "This is family business."

He grumbled something under his breath, took a last gulp of his coffee and stood up gesturing toward his daughter. "Time to go to bed. You will share your room with your aunt tonight."

Ellia guessed her at about ten and couldn't help smiling at the girl's glee. Auður rose at her niece's tugging on her sleeve and bid goodnight to the table. Kaja collected the dishes and, about to begin washing them, was interrupted by Unnþór. "I will take care of these. Show our guest the baðherbergi. She may not know how things work here."

Kaja glanced over at Ellia, then wiped her chapped hands on a dishtowel. Ellia hadn't heard her speak yet. Wordlessly Kaja led the way to a small room that held, of all things, a weaving loom. Skeins of yarn and spools of thread lined the shelves, beside books and a few trophies and medals. Some with Kaja's name. A long bench had been opened up into a cot-sized bed, a woven bedspread folded neatly at one end.

"Is this one of yours?" Ellia asked, indicating the bedspread.

Kaja nodded, and with hand gestures, indicated the clothes that had been arranged for Ellia as directed, hanging on hooks behind the door. She then urged her to exit from the room again and led her to the bathroom, or baðherbergi as Unnþór had called it. Kaja handed her a towel and some toiletries, and wordlessly showed Ellia the simple dos and don'ts of Icelandic plumbing.

"Takk fyrir," Ellia said, thanking her directly in Icelandic.

Kaja's eyes lighted up and she replied with, "þú ert velkominn." Then promptly closed the door to let Ellia prepare for bed. A good idea. She'd need every stored bit of energy she could scrounge and conserve for tomorrow's activities. As condoned, of course, by the shell.

Scowl-faced as he was about the circumstances, Unnþór had still done his darndest to find her a high-tide safe spot. The cliff did nothing to keep the sun out of her eyes as she waited for the boat to motor out of view. Wave after wave lapped against the edge of the rocks. A flock of gannets flew overhead.

"Not the season for puffins, is it," Ellia murmured to the clouds. The waves drew her attention back down, calling her to join them. "Mmm, I've missed you too."

The cleft to the left, indented into the cliffs, mimicked the shoreline, allowing for a shallow inlet of water. One glance around witnessed a clear coast, and in practiced hair-split seconds, she shimmied out of her human clothes into her shivering human skin, triggered the change and slipped into the shallow inlet. Partially enveloped by the water, she hand-walked herself in deeper. The moment her tail floated free of the rocks and sand, she submerged completely and set off.

Merdragon

Swimming deeper and farther, she took in the flavour, the sounds, the songs, and even the temperature. The ocean breathed differently around Iceland than it did in the South Pacific. For a few short moments the environment, and its denizen sea life, charmed her into coasting, savouring the differences. Then the sound of a nearing engine spurred her to her purpose. This was not the time to turn into a trophy.

Surtsey arrived almost too soon. Ellia curled her tongue around a piece of snack fish that had become stuck between her teeth. The reefs spread wide around the island, and she swam a cursory circle, scouting the coral neighbourhood. Juvenile growth surrounded the island from the toddler years, post volcanic. Small schools and solo venturers ignored her for the most part. On her second spin around the island, she slowed down to a leisurely tourist speed, stopping at every point of interest. The bright sun above made its way down to the shallows and each wave sent a secondary wave of light rippling across the nursery floor.

The muscles of her tail flexed, and she turned to twist down and under a small ledge. Iridescence! Her wings smashed against the ledge and coral. Ocean floor stirred into clouds of obscurity. Realizing her error, she wrapped her wings back in tight and stilled to wait out the settling sediment. The water slowly cleared, and she saw it again. A yellow iridescent tail fin. A tail fin detached from its tail; the only part left of a merkin's body.

Ellia held her breath and sank closer. Her fists clenched, talons biting, and her wings pulsed against her restraint. A moan bounced off the surrounding ledges; a whale's mourning song slipped past her lips. Bubbles blurred her vision. It was the tail-end of a juvenile, sixteen at most. Barely dull, it had happened in the last seventy-two hours, and been left, uncollected by her merkin.

The mourning song rose in pitch, grew in depth and then sank into silence. The echoes sang a new telltale. Ellia lifted her head to review. There. Disturbed coral. Fish darted out of her path as she swam closer to investigate. Cautiously she curved and circled, following a trail she hadn't seen before. It led to a bulge in the curvature of the island, a bulge with signs of tool damage.

She swam closer, and under a sheltering ledge she spotted an opening. Her eyes widened. A sealed pocket had housed something here. Something the volcano had pushed to the seafloor's surface. The tool marks included scars of something inside and out. Claw marks she couldn't categorize. Something that should have remained encased in the Earth's mantle.

"So, this was the cause of the mersong outburst? For shame. Merkin, what slave master device did you go searching for? Danube, whose child did you sacrifice? How many more will follow the Cult's deceptions?"

Scene, set and go

"Your first time visiting a film set?" Min Soo's manager asked Ellia, guiding her past wires, props, and crew running around with one urgent task or another.

It had been sixteen days, total incommunicado. She'd called Min Soo from the taxicab one hour ago.

"Min Soo asked me to meet him here, said it'd be okay." Do Hyun settled her down on a bench out of the way of the busy hubbub.

"Yeah, yeah, it's fine. It an advertising shot for, well," he pointed out the logos. "It's not a closed set or anything. I'll let Min Soo-ssi know you're here, but it may be a while, depending on how the shoot's going."

"I'll be fine, thank you." A nod set him free.

Iceland had been worrisome. The shoot's ordered chaos dissolved under the worry. The severed tail fluttered in the currents of her thoughts, the iridescent scales losing their lustre, the yellow ribbon she'd found in the helicopter syncing in her memory. She ground her teeth. Collecting evidence had been heart-aching. Unnþór had been kind seeing her face the next morning. She'd scouted the island a few more times and then gone further a-sea. Her first chance to rest was this moment.

The smell of crushed leather woke her to the murder she was attempting on her own purse. She relaxed her grip and relaxed into the bench, pulling the surroundings back into focus, disordered order and all. From one corner, Min Soo's manager came hurrying in a zigzag pattern with a towel and an ice coffee in hand. By anticipating his course, Ellia found Min Soo in the mayhem. A finger rested against her lips as she observed him. He held a script in hand, and when he nodded in response to something, she realized he was rehearsing with his female co-star.

Ellia let her eyes naturally drift away, now that she knew where he was, and began observing the rest of the crew. The dried fish she'd been snacking on since Iceland swam uneasily in her stomach. Much livelier than the living fish she'd consumed while on the hunt.

A moment of momentary ineptitude caught her attention. The slim girl from the gallery, maybe eighteen or nineteen? The potted tree sapling waivered in the girl's arms, but not as if it were too heavy. Ellia puzzled at it. The girl resembled a robot in her movements, lacking fine-motor skills. Then suddenly smooth muscle control returned. A quick glance around and the girl sight-lined on Min Soo. Back to young and nondescript in everything, including her work effort with not a moment of slack to catch another hardworking crew member's attention. Constant eyes, but no attempt to approach; more professional avoidance than a fan or anti-fan's moth to flame behaviour. Ellia frowned, tensing—her words to Riko must be holding, but why was the spy wearing a long-sleeved shirt in this heat?

A fraction of a second before Min Soo's hand landed on her shoulder, she relaxed her body. With all the sloth in the world she turned her head to face him. His nonchalant pose behind her revealed his secret, but slim hope, that she would have jumped at the sudden unexpected touch. He should have wizened to the fact that his cologne would sabotage his attempt. A scent she'd missed, unfortunately.

Having lost his slim chance at catching her unawares, he released her shoulder and stepped back a little so he could bend over to lean his elbows on the back of the bench. As he leaned in closer to keep his words clear of the noise around them, she disconnected the eye contact to face forward again.

"I have a favour to ask," were his first words.

No good to see you, no hello, no bubbles.

She gave him a look from the corner her eye.

Model mask in place. "Go on a date with me after the shoot."

Her look escalated into an eyebrow raise. Her heart rate might have matched it.

"Well?" he prompted.

Her eyes scanned the bustling crew and noticed eyes and ears surreptitiously turned in their direction. A lot of tea pots and kettles.

"There seem to a goodly number of people curious about our conversation," she stalled.

He glanced up, then returned his mouth to her ear. "I may have mentioned having plans with a woman tonight."

"With me? Who are you trying to avoid?"

"With you, yes, otherwise I'll have to add liar to my portfolio," he replied with a touch of a grin, the other question unanswered, "I believe that's more your arena."

"You could always go and spend some more time with your mother..." she opined.

Merdragon

"She's had enough of my company as is and she wouldn't enjoy where I'd like to go." This time his words held a touch of censure.

Curiosity made her finally turn to face him. Major personal face space invasion. A trifle short on oxygen, she asked, "and where would you like to go...with me?"

A little breathy, a little slow on the reply. "Night flying." She tilted her head toward the back of the bench and leaned a little closer for a cursory inspection of his back. "I don't see any wings."

"It's a surprise."

Her blouse shushed against itself as she crossed her arms and mused on his request. A nod precipitated her, "Alright."

The sudden smile on his face caused a breeze in the studio as all the women studiously not watching sighed.

Even Ellia's breath caught a little and thoughtlessly she reached up with one finger to tap his chin, "You know that's a lethal weapon, right?"

His smile faltered, eyes locked on hers.

Eye to eye they stayed as the set grew quieter.

Finally, he muttered, or was it stuttered, "If we were filming, this would probably turn into a kiss scene."

"Probably?"

"You're right. No probably. It would be a contractual obligation."

"In this room, surely someone has a smartphone set on record," she theorized.

"Oh, we've given them plenty of material already and I'm not going to be able to collect royalties from the wons they'll be making."

"In that case, you should probably back away," she advised.

A flustered panic rose in his eyes. "I would, but I, um, can't?"

The scent of crushed leather returned to her senses again. "O blowfish!" Ellia hissed. She blinked her eyes rapidly and averted her gaze.

Min Soo blinked a few times, shook his head and rose off his elbows shakily. He came around the bench, and cool or not, plopped down next to her. The set returned to functional as the moment un-crackled back to normal.

Careful not to muss the on-site hair stylist's work, he patted his hair instead of scratching his head and asked, "That, was what?"

"Hey, I'm feeling some peckish," she replied with a light hand clap.

Min Soo threw her a glance and crossed his leg in her direction. "What?"

Mentally dismissing the first class snacks she'd been munching on the entire trip back to South Korea, and the lunch she'd stopped to inhale on the way to meet Min Soo, she waved toward the fake food on the set. "It's a side effect."

Familiar with her prevarications and the side-stepping routine she'd been playing since he first met her, he didn't take her carrot-stick detour. He crossed his arms. "Explain."

She lowered her voice a notch. "It's a predator trait."

He sighed and waited.

Fine. "You know, paralyzing prey with eye contact...cobra-style."

He rubbed his neck and tilted his head trying to connect the dots. He stopped. His eyes widened. "Ah, that's why, what's his name, Riko didn't want to make eye contact?"

"Yes, intelligent prey."

He frowned. "I can't see that working very well underwater."

"Trust me it does, but it does work rather better on land animals, thank you very much, including the two-legged, upright kind."

He nodded, considering the possibilities. "That is. Useful."

She shook her head in disbelief. "Useful he says, when he could be the next meal."

It slipped out before he could edit himself, "I could handle a little nibbling."

Her eyebrows rose and his cheeks reddened at the slip. She narrowed her eyes and firmly stated, "Night flying should re-establish a healthy fear of crashing and burning."

He recovered with a cheeky, "We'll see." He smiled that lopsided self-effacing smile she'd forgotten she'd been missing on her Icelandic mission and stood up with his trademark fluid manner. He'd recaptured his previous confidence, and more, surrounded by the familiar, and carrying survival in his back pocket.

She watched him stride away and muttered to herself, "That man should wear a designer warning label."

Darya slipped out back to make a call on her phone. "Riko, she's back. I need more people."

"Who's back? Doesn't matter. This is not a good time."

"Look, the only reason I was sent to watch Han Min Soo was because, by himself, he's harmless. Now the," a quick glance around and a cupped hand over the phone, "the mer, you know, honour-whatever, is back. I almost lost it on set today and I think she marked me again."

A few unpleasant words soiled the airways. "Darya, I'm sorry, we're all suckers in action trying to contain Father's catch and keeping its tracks invisible from her eyes. Just keep her on your radar, but don't engage."

Merdragon

A hard expression crossed her face mixed with a little fear. "Riko, it's getting worse, seriously." She scratched angrily at her leg.

"What's getting worse?"

"There was the beginnings of a scale on my leg this morning."

A harsh sound made her wince. "Darya how long, no, never mind, listen to me. Forget the mission. Go home, now."

"What? No, I can't. I'm sure they're pulling something tonight."

"It's a medical condition that can affect merkin your age. I did some research. Father can't have not noticed. Uncontrolled reversion. He's going to descale me, but I'm coming. Go home. Take a taxi, don't drive yourself. You listening?"

Darya's chin might have been made of stone. "Yeah, I'm listening. I'll see you later, Riko."

She hung up and spoke to the exit sign on the back door. "I will exit stage right on my timetable. I have to find out what they're up to. Revision, reversion, whatever will have to wait."

By the time the shoot had finished, Ellia, chocolate croissant in hand and sugar and cream laden cold coffee concoction half empty on the bench beside her, had concluded that Riko's compadre was benign, for now. Keeping the spy in her peripherals, she'd redirected most of her attention to the tablet she'd brought along to surf. On the split screen, one side held names. Bless Artist Seung Gabriel and his skills. Practically a Cult membership registry—the names Artist Gabriel had given Min Soo. A third of which now showed their merkin details. She'd been busy on the flight, going by memory. The other names showed multiple links, connect-the-dots, and an occasional blank.

The other half of the tablet held financials—not even a smirk revealed the increase she managed while Min Soo played to the camera. The player, redressed in street wear, cleared his throat to announce his presence, and his readiness to leave. She put away her gadget and stood to join him.

Two steps toward the door and the spy engaged. Ellia swallowed the last of her croissant and licked the chocolate from her lip. She thumbed loose the lid of the coffee mess. It sloshed up against the rim when Min Soo uncharacteristically took her hand and wrapped it around his arm to bring her closer to his side. The pseudo-crew member slid to a stop in front of them, and Min Soo gave her his polite attention.

"Han Min Soo-ssi?"

"Yes?" He drawled out, polite face on.

"The director wanted me to make sure you didn't forget we're going out for some drinks. You must come and you can bring your, uh, friend."

Min Soo inclined his head with the freakish model grace of a swan. "Normally I'd be willing, but as I did mention before, tonight is a special night for me and my, uh, friend." The copy-cat phrase had a silky bite. Forestalling her protest, he continued, "I appreciate the offer, please convey my sincere regrets."

Beside him, Ellia narrowed her eyes. Hanging out with the enemy might have its benefits. She started to say, "It's still early...," but Min Soo gave her a sharp look. She shrugged and disengaged from the conversation. The opposition could wait, she supposed.

Min Soo winked at his spy-stalker. "It's a bit of a surprise."

As staff, Darya couldn't exactly pinch his ear and force him to join them. "Maybe next time?"

"Possibly." Final answer. He segued Ellia's hand from his arm and resettled it around his waist. The loosened lid cleared right off as Min Soo settled his arm around Ellia's shoulder. With a slight nudge he started them walking toward the exit. Fortunately the exit was wide.

Outside the sun had set, the parking lot sporadically lit. The open air cleared some of a certain drug from Ellia's mental state. "Wild guess, you suspected potential, what would you call it, advances of an improper nature, and decided you could use me to foil the attempt?"

He didn't remove his arm, "I was propositioned, semi-seriously, I think. By the director."

She nodded sagely, "Ah, a simple no thank you wouldn't have sufficed?"

"Can't get on her bad side. I figured my best defense was someone who had practice facing down sharks."

They hadn't been this snugly attached since he'd lugged her half-dead self to the beach. An older lady walking on the other side of the parking lot expressed a disapproving face as a streetlamp highlighted their connection.

"Propositioning director notwithstanding, I do believe this is a little more contact than this country considers publicly appropriate between the sexes."

Min Soo ignored the hint, leaving his arm where it lay. A whiff of garbage from a nearby dumpster breezed past. He sniffed and rubbed his nose. "Car's just over there," he gestured, then added, "The country will survive."

Under her breath she added, "But will you?" She moved her hand to pinch him, but his free hand arrested the attempt.

"Tch, that's expensive skin."

Merdragon

"And it will be safer at a distance," she sassed back. Bite nipped at the edge.

He slid his arm off her shoulder. They'd arrived at the car. He broke his posture to meet her eye to eye. "How was Iceland?"

Her face softened, eyes lowered. "Not good, Min Soo, not good." She turned to lean back against the car, one hand resting on the trunk. He leaned back beside her. Finger pads tapped a muffled pattern against the car. "I found…remains…and violence. Evidence of something that isn't, first of all, possible by," she glanced around, "our kind. Second, our kind was involved." Grief scored her voice, "Someone's lust for supremacy will bury him in power, and in the process devour all those around him."

"What are you going to do?"

"At this moment?" She tilted her head wryly, stuffing her worries back in their closet. "Right now, I intend on fulfilling the request you made of me earlier. I'm curious to see what you, my compatriot, have been up to."

"You sure? Alright then, I'll leave the underworld in your hands. Let's go."

He unlocked the doors and handed her into the passenger's seat. Seated, she pulled out her tablet to tap open a program. The driver's door slammed closed, and Min Soo settled himself beside her, immediately starting the car to get the air flowing.

"Problems?" he asked.

The schematic of the car displayed on the screen with a red spot flashing.

"We'll be fine, just an unwanted passenger."

Involuntarily he glanced into the rear-view mirror. He craned his upper body around to check the back seat.

Eyes still on the schematic, Ellia reached out to pat his forearm reassuringly. "A bug, a tracker, a nefarious device that is currently attached to the body of the car."

"What? Why?"

The question received 'the look' from Ellia. Well-deserved, and he blinked a couple times to process. "Ok, but this is my car. You just came back from Iceland today. Wait, how long has the bug been there? This is what you meant when you called me from the airport."

"Look, I warned Riko about interfering with your health and wellness, but I couldn't stop them from at least keeping an eye on you." She took a firm breath, then looked at him and gave him a smile, "But we are not going to let that stop us or worry us. We can always lose them when, and if, we must. For now, I've disabled the mic aspects."

Min Soo's fingers wrapped themselves around the steering wheel and gripped hard. She kept her eyes on him, silent, the sound of the running engine like white noise. A twitch of the foot against the gas pedal, revving the engine and he relaxed. "Alright. But how likely are they to do something? By now they know where my family lives, my friends, and at least one of your colleagues."

"There are rules, Iceland notwithstanding. Anything that could draw attention to the merkin is verboten. No side wants that attention. Harming your family or friends would cross that line." She tapped a finger against the screen of the tablet and shut it down. "Shall we go?"

A sigh. "Let's." A shift of mood along with the shift in gear, Min Soo pulled out of the lot and into traffic.

They drove in silence as he maneuvered through traffic and headed out of town. Ellia pulled out a high-energy bar from her bag and snacked away. Min Soo refrained from commenting. Not even when it turned into the third.

Passing another vehicle in the thinning traffic Min Soo suddenly spoke, "This is actually thanks to you. Artist Gabriel contacted me and verified the man who slipped the note into my shoe."

"You're talking about clever Cho Jung Sung?"

Min Soo threw her a quick glance and nodded, "Clever Cho Jung Sung, yes, that delivery man you kept smirking at and the usher at the church. I've met him a few times since then and he's designed something rather ingenious. I didn't ask, but is he like you?"

Emphatically, "No one is like me. But I understand the question. No, he's not merkin, regular human."

"With that tracker, will it be a problem that we're driving to meet him? I've already met him a few times."

"I suspect the place we'll be meeting him today won't be the place to meet him tomorrow."

Moonlight sailing

It was still today by a good margin, but a fully committed dark when Min Soo pulled off the main road, drove down a quieter tree-lined road, and past a dark field until a warehouse with a single streetlight came into view. A glow radiated faintly from a second story window. At the back edge of the building, away from the light, a cargo van sat waiting.

Still a ways off, Ellia tapped him on the shoulder. "Stop here and let me off." She wiggled the tablet in her hand. "We don't need to lead them to Jung Sung's door. I'll ink the signal." He didn't catch the reference. She added, "Like a squid."

"You're not going to meet up with him?" he asked, pulling over.

"This isn't the time. He knows we've been tracked, and he's got a long night of it after he meets with you." She closed the door and he watched her disappear, except for her glinting eyes.

He shifted into gear, "Those eyes, where have I seen that shade…"

Min Soo pulled up to the warehouse door, shut the engine, and went to knock on the warehouse door. Jung Sung was ready. They quickly exchanged greetings, Min Soo mentioned the trace which Jung Sung reassured him was old news and under control. With that out of the way, they got to work with setting up a roof rack for the car and then hauled out the little project Min Soo had commissioned.

Lifting it up together, Jung Sung commented, "Let me know how it works. Once you've test run it, I'll make adjustments. I tinkered with it a bit since last time we met, and I've already got a few more ideas on how to upgrade it, but no time now, can't keep her waiting and well, I've still got some packing to do, with the trace and all." He tossed Min Soo a pair of gloves and small, fist-sized case. "The gloves will give you better grip and that case holds goggles. They'll give you protection and altimeter readings. They'll help with the night vision too, so you don't fly into a cliff or a cloud of bats." He tightened a clamp on the roof rack. "She doesn't share the secrets to her gear, so if she gives you any suggestions, let me know right away."

Min Soo bit his tongue to keep back the surprise. "Sure, yeah." He tested the security of the project, "That should hold."

Jung Sung did his own test, then glanced down at a flash on his watch. "Good, good, now time to go." He raised a hand to wave at the practically invisible Ellia.

"Man, I'd love to be you tonight, testing this stuff. You remember where I told you to go? I think she'll find the airspace and terrain suitable."

"Uh-huh," Min Soo replied, tapping his forehead, "Directions are all in here."

"Good. Some days you know there's someone following, but as long as they don't get to your destination before you do, it's all golden." He handed Min Soo a small pouch. "Give this to Ellia, just in case it proves useful." Sandpaper hands gripped Min Soo's firmly. "Safe flying, bro, and I'll be seeing you again."

"I'm leaving, I'm leaving." And with that Min Soo got back in the car, started the engine and headed back toward Ellia's general direction. In his rear-view mirror he saw Jung Sung headed toward the cargo van.

He flicked his eyes back to front and slammed on the brakes. A pair of gleaming eyes met him above a wicked smile. They flashed and his heart managed a few beats before Ellia slid inside, closed the door and clicked the seat belt buckle into place. His heart reclaimed its resignation letter. He tossed her the small pouch.

"Jung Sung said you might want this." His hand trembled a hair as he put the car into gear. "He doesn't know you can fly on your own power, does he?"

"I did insinuate once, to test the waters, but there's never been a need to force him to see." She shrugged. "He's very clever and well, it seemed a shame to let his skills go to waste after he made a rather big, but unfortunately incomplete leap in thought on his high school science fair project. He should have gone international, but," she shrugged again, "life happens. I sent a scholarship his way and forgot about it. Five years ago I find out Artist Gabriel recruited him."

"Coincidence?" The gravel sound disappeared. They were back onto a paved road.

"Have you ever heard of reaping what you sow?"

"Okay, never mind about Jung Sung." He would have rubbed his hands together if they hadn't been on the steering wheel, "Tonight I finally get to test out our experiment."

Beside him, Ellia cautioned, "You do recall my limitations?"

Pointing to the roof, "That's what this is for."

"Well, they're your bones that will suffer." She'd resigned herself to his confidence. "Tell me, where are we going? Can't have people telling UFO stories."

"A suitable cliff." The answer wasn't much of one, the road had become curvaceous and now took more of his attention. He wasn't much of a countryside driver, especially in the dark. The thought of the tracker on their tail didn't encourage him to dawdle.

Merdragon

Several kilometres down and up various roadways, and a little closer to tomorrow, Min Soo pulled over into a scenic rest stop and shut off the engine.

"We're here."

Ellia peered out into the dark and asked, "And where is here?"

"Come out and you'll see," he said, nervous adrenalin beginning to flow. Last time he'd gone flying, drowning and sharks had been the fear factor. This time, thought and intent were involved.

Exiting the car, Ellia scanned the surroundings. Min Soo opened the trunk to pull out a lantern. He set it on the ground and turned it to a low setting. He reached up to unlock the driver's side clamps, and as Ellia came round to the driver's side, he came to hers to unlock the passenger side roof clamps. Back to the driver's side, he began taking the long bundle off the car. Relatively light, but bulky, difficult without Jung Sung's help. Once she'd observed how the bundle was arranged, she reached up to help ease the unloading process, laying it out on the ground for Min Soo to unpack.

In the faint light of the lantern, Min Soo unwrapped the bundle. A few unfolds and clicks pieced it into a whole. Ellia bent down beside him and felt the fabric.

"A glider, not a jet pack?"

"Oddly enough, a jet pack was one of Jung Sung's suggestions," he huffed a laugh, "but this requires no fuel and less explanations if someone spots me."

She rose to her feet and walked around the now fully extended frame. "I can't be entirely sure in the dark, but it doesn't look like the hang gliders I've seen before. This is sleeker."

"A little bit of Jung Sung's genius. I figured you'd see it. He's been studying acrobatic hang-gliding, and birds, like the swallow and hobby. It was something you said to him before which is why I was surprised he didn't know your actual skills."

"He's used a good portion of the materials I've sent his way." She bent down to do a heft test. "This thing's lighter than what your techs have in production. Good chance the materials in some laboratory somewhere, but not in public use yet." Her eyes caught the light of the lantern as she looked up at him. "Have you ever been hang-gliding?"

He grimaced, "Once. Tandem."

"Are you jellyfish addled?!"

"Hey, give me some credit. I've done repeated ground runs with Jung Sung. I've considered the risks and the reward is bigger." He crouched down beside her. "Sure, I'm not exactly on the list of actors who do their own stunts, but I've been working on it. Come on, Ellia. You probably don't get to go flying as much as you like out here." He raised a hand to her breath intake. "Not only that, but since when do you have a flying buddy? When I go surfing, I don't go alone. Since I've already gone flying with you once, your flying buddy might as well be me."

He pointed his nose at the moon, "It's a clear sky with a nearly full moon, and with your eyesight and the goggles Jung gave me, we should be good, as long as we don't do anything insane."

"This is insane."

"You'll see. With this gear, just think of me as a kite. If things go wrong, hospitals are nearer here than on that island."

"You might be better on the island," he thought she said. She bumped a fist gently against his chest, "You're still jellyfish and blowfish addled."

Parked by the side of the road, several kilometers from Min Soo's location, Darya scratched irritably at her leg and scrutinized the tablet in her hand. Frowning, she tried to see into the dark landscape around her.

"You're in the middle of nowhere. What are you doing? There's nothing here."

The missed call light blinked steadily on her phone. Riko had called more than once. The heater blew at max, but still she shivered.

"I need to find out what they're doing out here. We lost her for two weeks. Why'd she even come back? It's not like the guy's anything special. He's no scientist or connected to the military. Maybe good for fun, but..." she stiffened with a sudden frown, hand on the door latch. *"Is he blackmailing her?"*

The hang-glider was quite the thing, spring-loaded to open with a few flicks, and mostly ordinary in appearance. The only vaguely unusual piece lay in the rope attached to it. Ellia and Min Soo stood side-by-side, recovering their breath from hauling its awkward bulk together up the hill. While Min Soo took a few extra breaths, Ellia inspected the whole thing carefully. She trusted Jung Sung, but a second or third review didn't hurt. Reluctantly she had to give her approval.

"I haven't put it on solo yet. You'll have to help me," he said as he wrestled the glider into place and twisted to get the harness portion up over his shoulder.

"Believe me, even if you could, I'd be checking every strap twice." She came around behind him and hefted the glider into place. She held it until he had it secured, then came around to face him. A few tugs and one strong shake that threw him by a step or two. "I would hate to face your fans if you lost your life due to my oversight."

Merdragon

He grunted at the safety rattle.

She handed him the goggles. "Here. You know, once I take off, I won't be able to help you on the ground. And once we're in the air, watch me. We'll see what you can do with these wings." A quick bend and the lantern was flicked off. "We'll have to leave this here."

Min Soo could still see her, see the beginnings of more than a glitter in her eyes. He could hear the grin in her voice as she said, "I'm remotely fond of these clothes and avoiding indecent exposure charges tomorrow morning so," he could hear the wink, "time to close your eyes for a few fractions."

Her hair brushed against his face as she whirled around and ran toward the edge of the cliff he'd promised her. She stopped shy of the edge, his lifeline in her hands, a line of stars to mark its position. The stars fell to the ground and she spun back toward him. Passing him he heard her stop a few steps behind him and whisper, "Ready, fledgling?" The sound of clothes dropped a soft beat, cueing shut eye. He'd seen models in various stages of undress, but despite that, his face still heated up. The sound of bare feet on grass pounded past him and abruptly ceased. A whoosh of wings followed with an exultant, subdued roar.

His eyes flew open and instantly focused on the twin bomber fireflies diving toward him, fast. With glee, Ellia dive feinted him, then spun around in the air to come at him from behind. Quoting the best adventurers, she called out, "Run!"

He ran. Awkwardly. Like a stork. Dead of night with the moon alone as witness, untried wings fighting his determined balance. A meter from the edge he felt her slide over him, and saw the rope she'd snatched on her dive, firmly held in her clawed grasp. His foot caught the edge and he kicked straight off the cliff.

And down.

But seconds later the glider embraced the wind, and Min Soo released his own subdued exultant, "Wow!"

The moon beamed like a proud father, sharing its approval with the trees and river nearby. A few rooftops were included in the pride-wash. A caress of moonlight graced the merdragon's gossamer steel wings. Min Soo's eyes zoomed to the moonlit outline. It led him away from the mountain side, and so began his flight training.

The training mostly consisted of show and imitate. Little slips and slides, elevation increases and dives. One demo after another, Min Soo followed Ellia's instructions, and before long, the moon had wiled away an hour or so across the sky. Its interest was heading toward yawn territory.

Despite the coasting glide breaks, Min Soo could feel his energy slagging. Ellia noticed the slight strain in his face. "Time to return to earth flyboy." She carved the sky to turn them back toward the cliff top. Like a kite he followed obediently. The cool breeze ate up the sweat he'd built up chasing her from star to star. The glider faltered with his fatigue.

Together they approached the cliff top. His arms trembled on the controls. The trees loomed at the end of the clearing. He didn't have the strength to change the angle of his glide. The wings suddenly pulled backward. A gust of wind stalled him. No, not wind, Ellia. Rising above him, she'd back drafted him with reversed air pressure. Flying down in front of him, she gave a final wing flourish and circled back above. He landed, stumbled, and came to his hands and knees. Arms shaking, he flopped out on the grass.

Ellia watched from above, hovering over Min Soo in gentle circles. His breath steadied, and he finally regained enough strength to begin fumbling with the glider's harness. Relieved to see that he'd maintained enough reserve strength to help himself, she called down, "Min Soo, take your time, I'll be back in a bit."

An updraft snaked up the cliff side and lent her some lift to rise higher. To fly a scouting round. The moon had drifted off noon stage. She coasted sideways toward the road, spotted Min Soo's car, and farther down the road, a glimpse of another parked car. Nothing else. She grinned to herself, a slightly toothy grin. With a snap of her wings, she tight-banked back up toward the cliff top.

Fully stretched out, her wings touched stars at opposite ends of the horizon. Min Soo was on his feet, their packs on the ground beside him. He hadn't removed the night-vision goggles.

She pointed in the direction of her purse. "The thing Jung gave you for me. Throw it up, will you?"

The purse wasn't far and the container holding Jung's gift was easy to find by feeling alone—an absolute miracle. She banked back around and slowed to a hover, her back muscles straining to hold a steady air-hoarding pulse. Min Soo shook out his tired arms and tossed it up at a calculated angle. A release of wing tension and with a snap she had the pretty pigeon in her hands. A longitudinal spin, her head tilted back to spot on Min Soo. "I'll be back in a minnow's flight."

The digital clock in Darya's car blinked from 12:59 to 01:00. The only sound her chattering teeth. And heavy panting. A blanket lay wrapped around her, and the light of her phone reflected off her glassy eyes. She blinked.

Merdragon

Words ran one after another across her screen, her fingers shaky as she typed a stream of hypotheses. She shifted awkwardly, knees glued to each other, a dark stain seeping through the blanket.

"...speculations include possible reasons for her to return. Experimental work she may have done on the surfacer. He could be carrying anything in his blood. The surfacer may be more important than simply a way to keep track of her. Blackmailing has proved to be unlikely, but we could. Additional watchers should be set on him, and a team on standby to collect him if needed. Planted camera should be collected from this location." She grit her teeth and a whistle slipped through her teeth, broken immediately by their chatter. "Rik-k-k-o, it's so c-c-cold. So c-c-cold, c-c-cold.

I c-c-can't stay here much l-l-longer. Ffhhiivve mmmore minutes."

Skulkery wasn't easy when you were a three-metre-long mythical creature from outstretched talon tip to angelfish tail, not to mention the dragon wings and fire that went along with the package. It did help that falling off a cliff didn't cause quite the fear and trembling it did in most people. Their stalker had parked her car in an undesignated safe spot, a tad closer to the edge of danger than the department of transportation would have approved. Perfection for the half-landed merdragon attempting to place the device Jung Sung had given her to track the tracker.

Thinking stalking thoughts, Ellia hugged the roadside cliff, talons digging into rock cracks and dirt. She wiggled over the stubborn weeds, rocks digging into her scales, to reach a hand's breath closer to one of the wheel wells. Controlling her lung's shallow heaving, she stretched with the button-sized device on the tips of her talons and snuggled it under the passenger-side's rear door frame. Careful not to do the hula victory dance, she began the wiggle backwards, wincing as a gravel worked its way under her scale. They were not meant to go backwards. She shuddered and fell off the cliff...

...into a well-practiced push off and flip dive. Down she curled around trees, a wing tip brushing against a boulder. She snarled and craned up. Crash-landing was not an option. Her tail slapped against a tree branch; leaves flew off their handle in a train of stolen moonlight confetti. A sudden drop, a river's clear airspace, and bank ing into its runway she picked up speed to rise like a backfiring rocket ship.

01:43. 01:44. 01:45.

The phone played a whistling ditty, and played, and play– "He-he-l... R-riko?"

"Darya, what's wrong? Where are you? Just tell me where you are, I'm coming."

A shaking hand reached for the start button, but the car wouldn't start. "I, I, I'mmm" her mouth wouldn't form the words properly. Beneath the blanket, her legs moved as one, and grimacing she pressed the brake and tried again to restart the engine. This time it worked.

"R-r-k-o," whistle, "l-o-c-ate, mmmeee." The light from the phone shone through the webbing in Darya's hand. Two-handed she stuck the phone on the dash. Holding her right hand steady with the left, she pressed a button that immediately turned green.

Over the speaker Riko's voice came sharply, "I got it. Don't move, I'm coming. Your body is entering paralysis. Wait there."

"M-meet you," she managed through gritted teeth. Feet still on the brake pedal, she shifted into drive, and with sweat starting to collect on her skin, she ever so cautiously lifted her feet from the brakes and turned the wheels to head back down the hill. She didn't even try using the gas pedal.

"You stubborn girl! Father can't pat you on the head if you're dead. One of these days, one of these ocean-forsaken days, you'll see, and you won't be so determined to die. For all that's sacred, Darya, stay awake and please, please, just, just crash gently if you have to."

The road curved ahead and two-footed she slowed to a crawl. Arms strained to turn the wheel and straighten it again. If she could just make it down the mountain, she could turn off onto a side road and the merdragon would never know.

At the cliff, Ellia spotted a very relieved Min Soo waiting for her. It gave her a second wind to lift into a show-off.

First she extended her wings to their extremes and banked into a spiral, locked and loaded. An acrobatic snap back into level, a shake out into a roll and then up, up, up, stall, tail slide, hands to the sky, wings snapped closed. She flared her tail, allowed the air to force it up, bending her into a c-curve...and slapped into a loop, wings flicking out again, to caress the air waiting to catch her. The silent night's orchestra accompanied her calisthenics. An owl may have hooted, miffed at a missed mouse, but otherwise the night-flight predators took notes.

Twists and spins, dives and hard-won heights, she burned off Iceland's bitter taste, burned off frustrations, burned up the banked chemicals that had started giving her full bladder signals. Deliberately she rose higher, higher, higher. Her

Merdragon

back muscles strained with each pulse, each beat, each push upward. The air thinned at these heights. Radar became a real threat. South Korea was still at war.

She reached the night's limit. She stopped fighting. She shook hands with gravity and took a corkscrew's path down in a mellow descent.

She hated this next part.

A nearby cluster of rocks with a central boulder had caught her eye earlier. She coasted, drifted, feather swayed toward it. The backdraft of her wings blew against Min Soo's face and re-disheveled his hair, and maybe a few emotions. He came closer, hands raised to half-mast in the classic disaster readiness position all parents know. Parents and fairy tale princes.

With a thump and a mutter, Ellia planted herself on the boulder. Her tail slapped once, hard. She released her hold on the sky, her wings made balance adjustments, extended, contracted, collapsed around her. The wind sighed a farewell.

The deeper echo of the sigh drew her attention to Min Soo.

"Wow."

She sat high, Min Soo's head at the level of her knees—if she could be said to have knees in this form. He reached out a hand to run it over her scales. Her tail fin slapped against the rock. Startled, he pulled away. Ellia put her hand out to him in mute apology, and nearly lost her balance. Min Soo held out his hand to steady her.

"This really isn't your forte, is it?" He stated wryly, the mesmeration dissipating.

A growl slipped out from between her teeth and he outright chuckled. She went for another growl, but gave it up as a lost cause, and crossed her arms to patiently wait for him to sober up.

Taking a big breath to clear his tired head, he adjusted the night-vision goggles. "What can I do to help?"

"I'm hoping you can help me get off this lumpy, anatomically unsuitable granite heap."

Smart man, he thought it through. "Where we headed?"

Dubiously she calculated the clearing. "I don't suppose there's any way of getting me back to the apartment like this?"

"Nah, I didn't exactly prepare a disguise for a merdragon to be smuggled past all the building security."

"What if I flew straight to the balcony?" Exasperated, but sympathetic, he replied, "Too much light." A thought came to him. "The roof might work, but not this time."

She patted his head. "That's ok, I knew what I was doing. I'm stalling."

Her wings fluttered in and out in mental discomfort, her tail fin slapped against the lumpy boulder.

Resigned to the inevitable. "At least there's a grassy area here. Think you can carry me over to that spot over there?" She pointed toward a specific grassy spot growing off to one side of the gravelly rock cluster.

He gave her a look she couldn't decipher behind his goggles. "Have you ever used night vision goggles?" he asked. He didn't wait for the answer. "Trailing behind you in the air is one thing, but this close? Do you realize you give off random, I don't know what to call them, sparks? Fire in a BBQ, just before it goes out."

"Oh, just catch me, will you?" And as gracefully as a fish out of water, or swan on land, Ellia slid herself into Min Soo's quickly outstretched arms. She wrapped her arms around his shoulders and curled herself into him. He staggered at the weight, but gamely gripped her closer, steadying himself with a quick inhale through the nose.

Ellia whispered in his ear, "You okay?"

"Yup," came the terse reply. A careful step and then another methodical step toward the area she'd indicated. The steps could have been interpreted as staggers.

Reaching the grassy area, he oh so carefully lowered himself to one knee, then awkwardly set her down. He held the grunting down to a polite minimum.

Seated on her hip in the grass beside him, Ellia reached out and patted his sweating face. "One last thing, bring me my clothes and purse? There's a nice emergency blanket in there. While I transform back into a two-legged beast you can catch some sleep in the car. This time I'm going to take considerably longer to revert. Makes it less painful."

He stood up silently and fetched the items in question. Looming over her like a beanstalk, he handed over the purse and clothes, then walked, silent, back to his wings. He bent down as if to pick them up when instead he sat down inside the pocket between the frames.

"Han Min Soo, what are you doing?" Ellia asked.

Lying down, adjusting for the rods and joints, he settled into a pseudo comfortable position. He glanced at her over his shoulder. "I'm not leaving." He

Merdragon

laid his head on his bent arm, facing away from her to speak into the trees, "I'll sleep better this way anyway, fully stretched out—185 centimetres gets cramped in that car—and not worrying about you."

And apparently that was that. Ellia stared at the back of his head but didn't have the heart to protest. She could, however, give him some shelter.

First, she tossed the purse closer to the artificial wings. Next, she turned onto her stomach, set her hands on the ground and straightened her arms to raise her upper body. Moving forward, she was thankful for the darkness and Min Soo's back. Her movements were maybe just a tad more graceful than a seal trying to whomp itself up a beach. There was a bit more side-to-side wiggle in her movements, but not much. Thankfully, the distance was short.

Rustling inside her purse, she pulled out the blanket she'd mentioned to Min Soo and spread it out on the ground beside him. A whomp and a roll had her stretched out in quick order to settle into sleep. A tooth gleamed; a shot of mischief winked at the moon. Ever so delicately she loosened one wing and draped it over Min Soo. The speed his eyes flew open set a little night bug tumbling antenna over abdomen. Ellia held herself still and waited for his tired body to eventually conscript his brain into snooze land.

The moment his heartbeat had, for certain, settled into deep sleep mode she belly-crawled sideways a little closer. The glider frame created a bit of an obstacle, but she snuggled up against his back, as close as she dared, and, closing her eyes, she triggered the change. This was much the preferred method. It conserved more resources and nerve endings. With one final motion, she pulled the emergency blanket up and over the wing covering Min Soo. It wouldn't be there in the morning.

In the trees, a lost moonbeam caught on glass. A young owl momentarily mistook it for a large eyed meal but dismissed it quickly upon a closer inspection. Large eye, but no body.

Far down a side road, Darya found a spot to park. She hadn't the mental faculties to notice where. By the time Riko arrived, the light had begun to herald the sun's arrival. Already warm, early morning farmers had begun to gather at a nearby field.

Riko drove up to Darya's car, and, not seeing her through the driver's window, he momentarily panicked. He flung open the door and instantly spotted the tail draped over the center console. She'd crawled into the back seat when she could no longer fit in the front seat. He popped his head up to see if anybody could have been near enough to see inside. There was no way he was going to get her out and into his car without some serious questions.

He glanced back at his own car and pulled out his phone. A quick text message took care of its retrieval. Sliding into Darya's car, he pulled out a handkerchief and gingerly wiped the steering wheel. Residue from Darya's condition had left a slick residue. "The things I tolerate for you, little sis, you have no idea." He glanced at her in the rear-view mirror. "How in all the ocean water am I going to get you the treatment you need? Why'd you have to be one out of a hundred?" He slammed the steering wheel with his fist and swore. And swore a little more.

A press of the button and the engine came to life.

Solely for the sake of his passenger did he keep the take-off down one notch from a gravel spitter.

The next morning, mountain mist draped itself over the boulders, over the grass, and over a shiny emergency blanket. Min Soo's first sensation in waking was hard ground. Ground that wouldn't give, followed by the tickle in his throat that turned almost instantly into a cough. The warmth at his back stirred at the sound, and his eye automatically flicked over his shoulder to see...a brief glimpse of a very bare shoulder and the tickle turned into a strangled cough.

Again, the warmth stirred and no matter how hard he tried to keep his face turned in the polite direction, his peripheral vision steadily increased in scope as his natural instincts fought with his upbringing. Too late, or just in time, the blanket sped off him and a blur of motion resolved into a silver sheathed Ellia, bare feet trying to levitate off the wet grass.

Their eyes met. Then shot off in opposite directions.

"Not so skeletal this time around." Min Soo commented, ears tipped a faint shade of pink.

Hands on her hips, she addressed him sternly, "Min Soo…" A raised eyebrow came with a slow eye-wandering once-over, "Not so skeletal yourself."

He glanced down to see his long-sleeved shirt decorated with a collection of grass stains, twigs and splotches of black dust. A faint shiver confirmed that it was no longer entirely dry. A snigger from Ellia confirmed it was also no longer entirely decent. He hopped to his feet and groaned at the instant pain of strained muscles. Another snigger, and he lunged, pain or not. She dashed out of his reach, to the left, around, under his arm, and straight to the right. Her laughter followed her like cloud of bubbles until she was laughing so hard she could barely keep out of reach. Determination gleaming in his eyes, he made a valiant dive for her hand. And caught her.

He snapped her back to himself and held her tight inside his arms. Her laughing eyes rose to meet his. His senses stilled. Eyes focused. He wasn't shivering now.

"Ow!" He jumped back and hopped on the foot she hadn't stomped on. Not that it really hurt, he still had his shoes, and she still stood barefoot.

And now struggled to put on her shirt over the blanket dress. "Han Min Soo, you are sopping wet, and we need to get you back in the car with the heater turned up before your voice catches a frog."

"What about my toes?!"

"They may be pretty, but if they get ugly you can always hide them inside prettier shoes." With that she turned her back to him and began collecting the other bits and pieces of clothing, stuffing them into her purse. Face conveniently turned away, her voice suspiciously neutral, she added the common-place complaint, "And I'm hungry."

Min Soo felt like he'd attained a new level in a game he didn't know he'd been playing. An unfamiliar level. The pain of his injured toe already gone, the full body ache returning, he turned to collect his own wings, groaned with the bend, groaned with the lift. Ellia came over to help, shoes on her feet, and the silver blanket now a skirt. She picked up one end and led the descent back to the car. He trailed after her trying to remember the location of the nearest service station.

The room was dark. The shape of a man loomed beside a dark bed.

"What did you find out?"

A faint whistle answered him.

The man placed a hand on the bed and bent nearer to the whistler, Darya. "Try again," Danube Sr. ordered.

Glassy eyes met his, slim copper bands visible around her pupils. She tried. "Sheck. G.B.Sss. hissssto-yyy." Webbed hands flexed against the sheets.

"Anything else you can give me, come on Darya. How could you let this happen?"

Darya's whistled plaintively, her glassy eyes drowning.

Sneaking 'round the Forbidding Palace

"Bonsoir, madame," greeted the server at the rear entrance to Riko's modern-edged, posh-polished home.

"Good evening to you too, Hugh." An inside joke. "Any problems getting in?" she asked, brushing off the dust and twigs she'd collected climbing the wall defending the rear garden.

"You jest," he replied, a French maître' d's honour at stake. He riposted, "Shall I inform M. Riko Danube of your arrival?"

She quirked an ear and listened to the sounds echoing all the way to their corner of the house. "He seems busy, don't you think, with all his guests. If I find it necessary to speak with him, I'll be sure to find him myself. Now, show me how this place is laid out."

The passive tracker had connected to the house wi-fi and sent a here-I-am for Ellia to find. Conveniently, an event had been planned to which Ellia had self-invited herself with the help of Artist Gabriel's right-handyman of many names and talents. Now he pulled out a napkin from his breast pocket and spread it out on the tray held in the other. Ellia took the tray from him and scrutinized the surprisingly good sketch. There were some gaps, including the third floor, but at least she knew it existed.

"Thank you, Hugh." She handed the tray back. He received it and promptly poured a glass of water over it, dissolving the plan. "Learn that from your professor?"

"You've met." She'd surprised him.

Ellia gave him a thumbs up, and he simply bent at the waist a hair's degree, then turned to disappear down a hallway. According to the plans, it led to the kitchen where she could only imagine he was heading for another tray of either alcohol or appetizers. That, and to suppress the urge to run to the university and interrogate his professor.

While giving him a few head steps, she took the time to pull out a jewel encrusted barrette from her black jumpsuit and attached it to glitter the length of her chignon. The black, matte belt around her waist she flipped to reveal a shimmering turquoise pattern. Patting it in place, she then reached for one shoulder and pulled the sleeve off to give the whole outfit an asymmetric touch.

Merdragon

Time enough for Hugh to disappear, she followed him down the same hallway, but took the first door to the right. Immediately the sounds of the party she'd crashed grew louder. Her black flats glittered loudly to match the house volume but kissed the floor tiles silently.

Standard practice, Hugh had gossiped to his fellow servers as to which guests to avoid. Ellia's description had been slipped into the list so none of them bothered her as she slipped in and out of rooms, and guests, flowing in rhythm with the party's swing. Avoiding attention, and security, she dropped off a pleasantry or three, a nod, a stranger's comment and "Who's selling state secrets this week?" In a few instances she lingered alongside, eavesdropping on the conversations that held tasty tidbits.

Later into the evening, the fire flickering in the center of the main level great room, gently warming Ellia's left hip, she intentionally pretended to be fascinated with the words of a university economics profesora. However, what had really caught her attention was the brief utterance of the word "island" spoken on the walkway that crossed over the great room. Her position provided a convenient blind spot in the empty room. Empty of intel and recognition.

"Have you considered how you will handle your portfolios if the situation arises?" interrupted the profesora. Why was she even here? Her name was not on Artist Gabriel's list.

"Ah," Ellia replied, re-engaging in the conversation to fuel the next alcohol tipped monologue, "I'd say there's some security in foreign property acquisitions, even with a loss, but what would you suggest?"

The profesora's eyes flashed and she set off on a spiel.

Ellia focused again on the conversation above them, but other than the word "Maui", she heard nothing more. She rotated the fluted glass in her hand. No sound or sight of her tracker. None of Riko. Nothing of any person, place or thing. Her prey versus predator signals played ping pong. An itch was developing between her shoulder blades.

She raised the flute glass in her hand to her mouth as she casually scanned the room for her next direction. That's when she heard the voice coming up behind her.

"Profesora Hwang! Good of you to attend." A friendly pleasantry, warmly spoken, but a frisson of fear and rage electrified her spine. In the last twenty years she'd forgotten the cold that voice could elicit. She wasn't used to feeling cold. Without a thought, she "accidentally" threw the contents of her glass in the fire.

The flare she'd hoped for wasn't enough. She turned and nodded curtly to Riko Danube's father. Traitor, exile, and power-hungry giant hogweed. Pernicious, deceptive, blinding to those who fell under his influence. Expressions fell across his face like dominos. She didn't wait for them to settle.

A quick step right, an intentional flub into an inebriated circle of five. A spin, a fumble, her sleeve caught. Tore in Danube Sr.'s fist. Her jumpsuit tailored symmetrical again. She gave a little theatrical shrill of dismay to stir up a bit of tipsy testosterone and dodged off past a table and directly into Hugh's path. His tray full of glasses went up and over her head. She didn't wait for the shattering. A direct flight forward, a swivel and a left-angle into a hallway.

A server's dumbwaiter caught her eye. Hearing footsteps and the scrape of glass stuck to the sole, she flung the dumbwaiter door open, then whisked it shut again. And held her breath around a different corner. The scraping of glass passed the dumbwaiter, paused and retraced the thought. She heard the whisk of it opening and spun around the corner to slam the dumbwaiter door on Danube Sr's head.

Only he hadn't bent down to peer inside like she'd hoped. He stood facing her with a gun and suppresser.

He didn't hesitate. Neither did she. He fired and she dove diagonally toward him, grabbed the heavy glass vase from the hall table and threw it full force at his face. He flew back at the impact. She didn't wait to see if he'd recover. She continued her forward motion, fully passed him, and scrambled for the stairs. Two-stepping it, she flew up, wingless.

To the second floor, but it was too open, up to the third, the one Hugh hadn't managed to scope out. She reached the landing, took the second door on the right, and closed it behind her. The only light came from the exterior garden lamps. Shouts from below and more than one set of running footsteps; backup had been summoned.

But someone else had a gun to her head.

If she had to guess, "Riko?"

A shaking gun. She heard him swallow, audibly. "H-h-honoured one..."

A quick glance of the dim room revealed a great deal. "What's wrong with Darya? It is Darya, right? Your baby sister..." Artist Gabriel's list had been thorough.

No fool, Riko didn't bite the hook. The girl in the bed behind him moaned.

Ellia asked again, "What's wrong with her, Riko?"

A knock on the door, "Sir?"

Merdragon

Riko answered, eyes unblinking on Ellia, "What is it?"

"You okay sir?"

Ellia's eyes narrowed, then she sent a quick glance toward Darya. Riko opened his mouth to speak, but Ellia flipped her wrist, pulse side up. His eyes widened, and he swallowed his words to replace them with, "Fine. Bugger off."

Footsteps clattered around on the landing outside. Ellia and Riko waited.

Danube Sr.'s voice, "Did you find her?" The negative responses were either too quiet, or simple shakes of the head.

"Great Kraken breath take her, that elitist, entitled flying worm!" he cursed. "You two, stay here and keep watch, the rest of you, keep looking."

The kerfuffle subsided.

Ellia pointed in Darya's direction. Riko nodded but didn't lower the gun. Ignoring it, soft with her steps, she approached the foot of the bed. Ellia lifted the wet sheet to take a peek and realized she'd more appropriately arrived at the tail of the bed. She let the sheet down and rested a finger on Darya's ill-formed legs, or whatever they were, because as of now, they weren't wholly a tail either.

In scarcely a whisper she asked, "When did it start?"

"A year ago. She held it off, until two nights ago."

"That's why she left…"

His gun hand steadied. "What did you do to her?"

Ellia glanced up. Riko had her dead to rights. His eyes glittered in the dark, angry. And he'd been crying.

"If I had done something, it would not have been this. I value our anonymity. This is, you know it is, shall we say, a design flaw? I don't recall it running in your line. One in a hundred, although it does tend toward the hereditary. Hmm. The reasons and normal solutions don't matter now. It's kicked in, thank you, adulthood. Do you have a syringe?"

The gun lowered to a safer position. He jerked his chin toward the bedside drawer on the far side of the bed. Inside she found what she needed. And something else, tonight's rainbow pot. Her breath hitched up. But, in that same breath she made a decision and reached for the medical supplies instead, as she'd originally intended.

First, she swabbed a spot on her own wrist, ripped open the syringe packaging and placed the needle against her skin. A breath and in she slid the needle, deep. Biting her tongue, she grimaced as she sought the chemical pocket responsible for her ability to transform. The one at her wrist was the one most accessible, of the many that ranged through her system. She sighed as the needle found its mission target. As she pulled the plunger, amber fluid began filling the barrel, and Riko fully relaxed his gun hand.

At five cc's she stopped and pulled the syringe out. Gun back in its holster, Riko was free to hand her a cotton ball and a strip of medical tape. She gave him the syringe, pressed the cotton ball down hard on her wrist and closed her eyes, reaching a count of twenty-eight. A knock on the door interrupted her goal of sixty.

Riko spun around and secreted the syringe up his sleeve. To Ellia he mouthed, "Hide." She nodded and ducked into a ball down beside the drawer.

A second knock and Riko opened the door with a snarl, "What?! Wasn't the message clear last time?"

The security on the other side of the doorway took a step back, but with the message from Danube Sr. fresh on his ears, he recovered and stepped forward to peek past Riko's angry face.

"Sorry sir, we were supposed to check the rooms again in fifteen minutes. Make sure you were still ok."

"I'm not okay and neither is my sister." He opened the door wide and waved them in. "Come right in and make things worse, why don't you?" Darya moaned on cue as the light from the landing touched her face.

The second guard did a cursory survey of the room, then tugged the other guard's shoulder. He bobbed his head, "That's alright, sir, it looks like everything is secure in here. Come on bro, you know Riko-ssi's armed and wouldn't risk the Miss."

The first guard grunted, but allowed himself to be pulled back out. Riko closed the door with a frown. He turned, blind from the landing lights. And jerked back as the syringe slid involuntarily out of its hiding place.

"...best done quickly..." Ellia whispered darkly in front of him, the syringe glinting in her hands.

He blinked and rubbed at his eyes; his footsteps hesitant as he cautiously followed Ellia back to his sister.

"Help me turn her to on her side," Ellia instructed.

He did as directed, holding her still against her faint resistance. Ellia slipped the sheet down to inject the fluid into Darya's gluteus maximus.

"It's done."

Clean up moments later, Ellia and Riko stood by the window.

"It'll last about six months."

"Then what?"

Merdragon

"If your father doesn't kill me, I'll get her the stabilizer from the merkin medics."

"My father..."

"It wasn't your sin that put you, and especially not her, here."

He clenched his fist, "That's coercion."

"No, Riko, it's a simple case of supply lines." She leaned over to take a quick check on Darya. "It's in your sister's best interest that I succeed in stopping your father."

The shuffle of his feat revealed his discomfort. "What do you want from me?" A faint whistle from the bed interrupted them.

Riko snapped back to his sister's bedside and knelt down to meet her at eye level. "How are you feeling?"

Ellia cracked the window open, allowing in a breeze to cleanse the stuffiness of the room. Riko gave her barely a glance.

"Riko-ee-sae-eee," Darya whimpered.

"Shh, Darya, you're going to be okay," he soothed her, one hand reaching up to smooth her hair.

Ellia had a word of caution for Riko. Fire licked the words she whispered in his ear, "Keep playing in the shadow of your daddy's fins, Riko-ssi, but throw out a line when you see him setting off the maelstrom."

She didn't wait for the hairs on his arm to settle. Up, on to the window ledge and out, she added softly, "Take care of your sister and," she nodded toward the bedside drawer, "when she recovers you can always send me a thank you gift."

Deftly she ducked all the way out, closed the window behind her and began shimmying along the ledge. A loud knock and a door slamming open set her feet shimmying a little faster.

Danube Sr.'s voice roared loud through the closed window. "Where is that flying worm's spawn?"

Riko's quieter voice responded defiantly, "What the kraken spit are you talking about?"

Ellia pulled herself up onto the roof just as Danube Sr.'s head popped out like a vengeful whack-a-mole. The roof held a multiple number of folds and edges, convenient for hiding merdragons.

The next voice she heard was Riko's. "Darya came to and started pointing at the window, so I opened it. Wait, don't tell me that ruckus outside is about the merdragon? She's here?"

"Your sister's nearly comatose and still more helpful than you. Useless!" The bellow had subsided with distance. The slamming shut of the window followed.

Ellia lowered herself into a strategically sheltering crevice. Moonlight glinted on teeth where only the moon could see it. She'd flushed out a few secrets tonight. And planted a timebomb in Danube Sr.'s camp. What was Riko now, thirty or so? He was playing a dangerous game with his father.

The edge of an air vent dug into her thigh and she readjusted her position. The sound of footsteps in the yard drifted up with the scent of kitchen leftovers and overly strong perfume. Orders were issued and footsteps dispersed onto the street.

A little later, the sound of car engines starting cued her to the beginning of the end of the party. She shook her hair loose of the chignon and rose to a crouch. Avoiding displaying herself like a gargoyle, she kept low, moving close enough to the edge to spy on the departing partygoers. Handshakes, farewells and pauses to check their phones before driving off. Taxis, hired drivers, and on-staff drivers chauffeured the tipsy attendees.

It took several more hours for Danube Sr. to leave. She could guess he'd been organizing the hunt for her head, but when the scent had gone-with-the-wind, he finally resigned himself to leave. She pulled back from the edge with a yawn and lowered herself down even flatter against the roof.

Riko's voice floated up, petulant and fearful, drunkenly resentful, "I'll see you off, father."

"That's the least you can do for allowing that thing inside this house I let you live in." The scorn soured the apple tree in the yard.

"We can't even track her reliably. The merdragon is something I could stop?" Riko protested.

"If you had even an inkling of all we could lose to that self-important, lab-made clone of a traitor. I should have known she'd be a repeat when we made her. Your sister understands. Genetic tags restricting our roles in society? Bah! Serve under someone just because their helix has a crown? Even the surface dwellers know better. I want unobstructed waters to the top, and I'll use whatever I can get to get there. The island, history, whatever, son." He nearly spit out the word. "It's the only way we'll free all merkin." The car door opened. "Free to take a more direct role in surface matters; it's more than time we took control." The tone was smug.

The sound of one engine started, then a second and third. Danube the elder did not travel light. Not anymore. What percentage of his minions were in those

Merdragon

cars? Ellia sighed and pulled back even further. She found herself a comfortable niche. Now was not the time to give herself away. It had been years since she'd heard the free merkin rhetoric. Insidious because it struck a chord that reached all the way to the merKing. Deceptive because the chord was played by someone who only wanted that freedom for himself, at any cost. The life of a cloned tool fell well within his planned sacrificial offerings.

    She lay back to stare up at the night sky, stars and satellites dim and scarcely worth observation. An angry tear moistened the edges of her lashes. It dried as she lay awake and pondered. Min Soo would have the apartment to himself tonight.

Wishful thinking

Two days later, the sun rubbing its eyes awake, Min Soo slept, oblivious to Ellia's presence in his room. She sat in the corner armchair, knees drawn up to her chest, silent. She hadn't entered his bedroom since her first guided tour. A lost stray of sunlight bounced off too many reflected surfaces and caught in Ellia's eye. It broke her stasis.

She slipped off the chair and stood for a few more minutes at the foot of Min Soo's bed. Early dawn, fawn cautious, she circled the bed until she crouched down beside him. She hadn't watched him sleep since the island.

Mist quiet, she mouthed, "Be well, be safe," and whistled into the ultrasonic the sound of waves.

Min Soo stirred in his sheets, and the door opened and closed without a sound. He mumbled in his sleep and missed the light ding that should have played on the exiting Ellia.

A few morning dreams played until Min Soo woke out of bed and swung his legs over the edge. He slipped on his slippers. Reaching his hands up to stretch, he took a breath then frowned. He sniffed, tilted his head, then quirked his lip to half. "Tch," he mocked himself, stood up to complete the stretch, and groaned at the muscles that still had not fully recovered from the flight. He grabbed his dressing gown and headed out to take a shower.

Fifteen-minute routine completed, he came out of the bathroom, rubbing his head with a towel and went to the kitchen counter to pour himself some water. Glass in hand, he padded over to the balcony doors, but no Ellia snoozing away. She'd been preoccupied since the flight.

"Maybe she finally slept inside?" He went to knock on her door. No answer, so he cautiously cracked open the door a sliver. Then all the way. Not on the balcony and not in the bedroom.

Puzzled, but not too concerned, he walked over to the fridge to get himself breakfast. A tiny dolphin magnet held a note to the door.

"Gone for a day or few months. Should return."

The empty glass slipped from his hand and thumped on the rag rug. Ellia had placed it there the night before. He'd laughed and claimed she was marking

Merdragon

territory. Now? He stared at the unbroken glass, his brain a little slow in processing. The glass had failed to break. He knelt to pick it up, and, unseeing, he ran his hand over the rug. He slammed his fist into it. And slumped down to sit against the fridge.

"She knew yesterday…"

The phone rang.

He jumped up to get it like the floor was lava. "Hello?"

"Hello, Han Min Soo-ssi?" it wasn't Ellia, "I got the word that Señorita Ellia won't be around for a while, and in light of recent events, some additional information may be of use to you.

Min Soo glanced over at the glass and tapped his finger against his nose. "Okay, when and where?"

They settled for the end of the week. He slumped back into a squat and rotated a full circle, hoping to catch a bug so he could squash it. With prejudice. He and Ellia needed to have a word. More than one.

The meet turned into many more, two months' worth of intense training interspersed between his regular gigs. His slim build didn't bulk up more than his normal jobs required but became perhaps more usable. Early on in the sessions, meeting Artist Gabriel at a coffee-bookshop, Min Soo delivered a package he'd received from Riko.

"Can you get this to Ellia?" he asked, "but check it first; it came from Riko Danube. You know him?"

Gabriel took the foot long, slender box gingerly. "Riko Danube? Yes, I know him. He's a peculiar one." He slid the box into the tan shoulder sack he'd placed at his feet. "Did you take a look at what's inside?"

Min Soo shook his head, "No, I didn't have the suicidal urge."

"Wise. I'm inclined to agree with you." He took a sip of his coffee and nudged the sack with his brown polished oxford. "I'll have Ampara, I think, open it up."

"Ampara? Is that the foreign university grad student?"

"He's got the equipment we need at his disposal and a professor who's hoping to get some credit for being his teacher. Jung Sung's too mobile and doesn't have the facilities to deal with explosives and questionable gases."

"I never quite figured out where Ampara originated…"

"You could always ask him…" Gabriel chuckled at Min Soo's look of doubt, "but if that butler face of his puts you off, I will say Ellia's mentioned she found him in France."

"How long has he been here?"

Gabriel shifted in his armchair, "Let's say he had a sudden transfer just this fall."

"Hmm, that was handy." His knowing smirk faded, thoughts returning to the box. "If it's safe, it'll somehow get to Ellia?"

"The method might be convoluted, but we'll get it to her, don't worry."

Min Soo took another sip of his iced coffee. "Any chance I could deliver it myself?"

Gabriel leaned back and, at random, pulled a book off the nearest shelf. He flipped through it, first the western way, and then catching his error, he flipped through it in the opposite direction. "Still haven't quite got the hang of that. You spend years elsewhere and habits become engrained.

"I met a man, named Drayvin, in my early twenties while traveling through South America. I believe it was Lima, Peru. He couldn't have been more than twenty-five himself, but he saved my hide from some thugs who guessed rightly that I was an easy mark."

In telling a story, a little feedback goes a long way. Since Gabriel didn't feel like answering his last question, Min Soo asked instead, "Who was he?" Maybe Gabriel would get to the other question eventually.

Gabriel found the empty slot for the book he'd taken and replaced it. The mug grated on the table surface as he pulled it nearer, and then left it too close to the edge for Min Soo's comfort.

"Drayvin was a professional. An older brother. An enigma. A spy. A man with a fighting style I haven't been able to see since or name." He paused and fiddled with a napkin. "I knew him for years. He'd come and go, never asking anything illegal, but always something unusual in one way or another. Then one day a woman introduced herself to me with code words I didn't even know Drayvin had given me until she spoke them." He held up a hand to forestall Min Soo's suspicion. "I don't mean a hypnotic suggestion. Simple question-answer phrases Drayvin would say, casually. Things friends say. I met quite a few. Some did lean on the side of illegal, depending on the country, but only things that kept him hidden. And somehow, all that legal stuff I did for him ended up making me a fortune."

To Min Soo's relief, the Artist rescued the mug for a sip and then put it down again to reach for his sandwich. He took a healthy bite. Min Soo leaned back in his own chair and randomly tapped a finger against his thigh.

Merdragon

Gabriel swallowed another mouthful of coffee and cupped it in his callused hands. "Hah. He had the same bad habit as Señorita Ellia. Stop by for lunch, disappear the next hour. Buys the building you rent in, and does business in the area for a year, next thing you know he's gone, and you own the building. Free and clear, no strings, no contracts. Barely a note so you don't worry." He leaned forward and lowered his voice. "After about the fifth time, somewhere in my late thirties, thirty-seven I think, I planted a tracker on him."

"What? Really? Did he find out?"

"I will say this, when it disappeared a hundred kilometres off the shore in the ocean, the next two years of worry started this process," he pointed to his gray hair. "I never told him why I was so glad to see him at our next meeting. It was a short one and let me tell you, hah, that's when I met Ellia. He never did mention even having a daughter, and suddenly he's got a teenager on his heels."

The door jingled as a group of ladies on a book club date entered the café. Intense chatter, something to do with a book someone claimed had been written by a famous author under a nom de plume. Artist Gabriel reached into his breast pocket and fiddled with something inside. Actor Min Soo ducked his head and touched his hand to his ear. Gabriel nodded but didn't comment. There was a reason he hadn't felt the need to be circumspect with his words; one of Jung Sung's devices sat in his pocket. He continued.

"That's the last I saw of him, and only saw her a few more times before we started communicating primarily by every other means other than in person. I tried to ask her once about Drayvin, but never got a clear answer. Something about ocean currents and sirens." He clasped his hands together and gave Min Soo a speculative look. "None of us know the whole story, at least no one is telling. None of us know how to reach him or her directly, but things get where they need to go. You're a new type of puzzle piece. A bit of fresh blood in the waters." The old fox smiled.

Min Soo shrugged and crossed his legs. "I'm an accidental convenience."

The Artist huffed a laugh. "Accidental convenience, I like that. Might be true. On the other hand, she didn't ditch you the first chance she got. Dreams have been known to happen to some brief acquaintances." He shrugged. "Take it on the chin like the rest of us. You'll get used to it. Or maybe you won't have to. You are getting an unusually fast-tracked education."

Min Soo ran his hand through his hair and picked up his iced coffee. It crinkled a little in his grip. "What if she just disappears, like Drayvin did, and never shows up again?"

Clearing his throat, Gabriel picked up the tan satchel and stood to his feet. Min Soo stared up at him, black eyes burning.

Gabriel clapped him on the shoulder and gave it a double pat. "Time will determine if you need to be braver than I was."

Off in another drier part of the planet, Mexico maybe, a lone warehouse stood surrounded by dust and instant dry mouth. A hint of road caught shadows as the Earth rotated. Not a single window marred the four faces of the warehouse, but a glint on each side revealed a security camera mounted on each one.

Inside the warehouse the sense of barrenness continued—dirt floor, a dusty Land Rover, and a seacan shipping crate. The two guards at either end of the crate could have been effigies.

A radio-phone lit up against the wall. Neither guard stood up to answer it. Didn't even raise their heads. Didn't even blink.

A chuffing laugh came from inside the crate. "Couldn't you send something a little tastier?"

As phone calls go...

Each stride from the street corner to the agency doors made money for the trench coat makers lucky enough to have caught Han Min Soo's eye. The umbrella shared in the earnings, although less so indoors where Min Soo held it at a distance and left a trail of water while talking on the phone with his manager. Nothing gave away his awareness of his non-fan follower.

Intercepting him mid-hall, his agent's secretary took the umbrella from him with pursed lips and handed him a note. She darted a look around, then asked him. "I hope you're not thinking of leaving us Han Min Soo-ssi?"

Frowning, puzzled, Min Soo ended the call and opened the note. Inside it read, "Riko Danube, Lawyer. Call this number."

Min Soo shook his head in response to the secretary's query. "He called me, here?"

The secretary nodded rapidly. "He said it was urgent you get back to him. What's going on?"

"Nothing I know about," he replied with a shake of his head, "I need to use a phone." At the secretary's obvious glance at the cellphone in his hand, he made the excuse, "Battery's dying."

The secretary gestured toward a meeting room and led the way to open the door, "You can use this room."

"Thank you," he said, entered the room and closed the door behind him to the consternation of the nosy secretary.

Nosy secretaries have their place but being too nosy could get them gone so she left off eavesdropping at the door and simply went and told the boss who was in and what she suspected might be up.

Instead of sitting down at the table in the centre of the meeting room, Min Soo hooked a leg over the arm of the large plush sofa and pulled the hardline closer to the edge to return Riko's call.

The phone rang only once at the receiving end before someone picked up, "Gun, Danube and Associates, how may I direct your call?"

"Lawyer Danube Riko?" Min Soo replied, slightly caught off guard. Riko had not given him lawyer vibes. Not at all.

"May I let him know who's calling, please?" Asked the pleasantly cool voiced receptionist.

He didn't see any reason to hide his identity, considering he was returning the call.

The response included a hiccup, a pause and a warmer tone of voice, "I will let him know right away...Han Min Soo-ssi."

He could never decide whether to roll his eyes or grin at the reactions he got when his fans suddenly recognized him. A music bar's span passed before the phone went off hold.

"Han-ssi?" came Riko's voice. The form was rude.

Min Soo's warm dark black eyes nearly turned cobalt from the frost they developed. He'd only met Riko once before, but it hadn't been a good impression. Riko's greeting didn't improve it.

His voice hit the basement with the hauteur of an emperor, "Danube-ssi?" A pause. Then a chuckle. A nasty chuckle. "I'm betting she rolls with you for that voice alone."

If the phone in Min Soo's hand had been a mood ring it would have shattered. His next words carried Gobi winter winds, "Honoured ones only roll with the best. Now tell me why I'm calling you." He winced. Ellia wouldn't appreciate the insinuation or his lack of refutation. Why hadn't he?

"Some wits about you too, huh. Not just a pretty trophy she keeps on her pillow." He must have imagined Ellia's growl because he quickly added, "Well, never mind that. Ellia has to call me pronto."

"She doesn't," reminded Min Soo, Antarctica in the middle of July.

"Well then, treat is as a really, really strong suggestion," snarked Riko.

"Tell me."

"You? I don't talk to bedding," Riko replied with a sneer. "Wait... she hasn't bailed on you, has she?" he asked, drawing out the question.

"No." The answer came out firm; his thoughts rioted.

"No, huh? Let me tell you something, pretty boy." Min Soo had no clue why Riko seemed to thrill at needling him. "If she's gone, you better duck and cower. Play dumb. She's been making a maelstrom of a mess and a squall of barracudas is heading her way. Can't say when or where, but if they can't find her, you're their next target. We've had some complications, and they found out I sent her a package. Now they want it back. You're her last known contact point and they've got ammunition. Good sludging luck!" And with that Riko hung up.

Merdragon

Min Soo reset the phone back on its base and blinked at the room that remained neat and undamaged despite the violence in his thoughts. Riko's mouth had spikes like a porcupine in full defense mode. How had he allied himself with Ellia?

The message though, that concerned him. Ellia's phone wasn't picking up: no voice mail, no automated message. He wasn't sure how that was even possible, but that's how it rang; and texts came back undeliverable. His hair got the brunt of every ragged run through, and that's how his agent caught him, one hand scraping his scalp and a scowl sitting on his face.

"Min-Soo-ssi! Face man, face! You damaging that face for some part I don't know about?" His words rang like a carney who'd classed up.

Instantly Min Soo smoothed out his features, straightened his spine and inclined his head a touch. He offered a modest, wrinkle-free, pleasant stress-less expression, "Not at all, just heard something I'd hoped to buy has already been sold to some Bollywood director."

The agent replied soothingly, "I'm sure something else will come along." He waved his phone in demonstration, "Like the call I got from Producer Kim Sung Hun. The supporting lead in the new drama is yours."

"When does filming start?" Min Soo feigned interest. Careful of the lines of the trench coat he still had on, he pulled out a chair and took a seat.

"A month from now, they said. You'll be receiving a schedule in the next couple of days." He drifted over to the window to look out over the street. Still facing the window, he asked with a more serious note, "Secretary Soo Hwa said there was a lawyer calling you. Anything I need to know? Paternity lawsuit, bailing out a relation facing murder charges, changing companies?"

Min Soo leaned back into the chair, relaxed like a cross between a leopard and a sloth, "A private matter that has nothing to do with legal issues. That satisfy the president's curiosity?"

The words had a little more mental meat than Min Soo usually gave his agent. "It'll do." He checked his watch just as his assistant knocked on the door. He nodded and pre-empted her, mid inhale, "Yes, Soo Hwa, I have an appointment waiting, I know."

"Don't shoot the messenger," she shot back.

He waved her on ahead and urged Min Soo, "Call me if anything legal comes up, will you? I hate unpleasant surprises."

The door stayed open behind him and Min Soo stood up to head out, worrying about surprises too. What had Riko meant? He'd talk to Artist Gabriel about rotating his sleeping arrangements. What in all the skies and oceans was Ellia up to?

Back to fanta-sea

Far into one of those oceans, Ellia wondered the same thing. The dolphin pod didn't really care. They were trying their best to keep up. She circled one to tickle its belly and sent him into chittering laughter. Another tried to return the favour, but she slipped slipways, down, and up toward the surface, breaching with a wing assist. Two, then five, then more followed, whistling and chittering like toddlers at a waterpark. Slicing down under again, she sang a thank you for their delivery and whistle-chittered a good-bye.

The dolphin pod song followed her for a ways, blurring the thoughts of the past few months. She'd cracked a few windows with Artist Gabriel's list. Her gills pulsed for oxygen. Information had begun slipping past Danube's protocols. Secrecy was being sacrificed for speed and security increased elsewhere. Bubbles streamed past her as she groaned at the remembrance of Iceland. Remembrance of Darya. She couldn't wait any longer. The delivered item chilled against her sternum, secured by her wings.

The first evidence of MerCity's existence could have been dismissed as old surface wreckage. The cleanliness of the water, even less obvious. She swam past, staying below the ridges. The first line of defense and nothing responded to her crossing. As if she didn't exist. A dream visitor. She caught the sound of a domesticates school. No need to disturb the herders. Another ridge, cultivated with coral, marked the next trip wire. She slipped through. Again, no response. As expected.

Next level in, here lights and structures began to appear at more regular, less dismissible intervals. She aimed for the guard station. The day had darkened during her approach and the alerts would not register her arrival. This would take finesse and flamboyance.

She took a look around. Throwing a rock against a window wouldn't work. But, she nodded to herself, a dust cloud of rocks pounding against the front door should do the trick. This way they wouldn't have a target at which to lock and load. Taking the chill into her hand, she released her wings, stirred up the floor with her tail, and, with her wings, created a rock storm. It didn't take long to catch someone's attention.

Pocket lights scattered around the area lit up one by one, diffused light, perfect underwater illumination. She caught a glimpse of a messenger drone bolting through the dust cloud. A redundancy for the signal already sent. The escape hatch she'd spotted earlier creaked behind her. Task completed. She secured the chill against her sternum and wrapped her wings up tight.

A sharp crack of sound barked against her spine. The merguards. She relaxed her hands out to horizontal, and in the awkward pose turned to face her greeters. Regular sentry, they held sound cannons against her. The dust slowly settled.

The crack repeated. A word, "Identify!"

Ellia gave the underwater equivalent of a reluctant shrug. What would happen, would happen.

She sang her name. And title.

It wasn't anyone's fault. The merkin were a manufactured slave race.

They genuflected. The original version. Not what Riko had attempted.

Involuntarily. Grandly. Thoroughly. There were bubbles with a definite "blue" tinge.

Lightning struck her spine. Every muscle spasmed. She couldn't breathe. She couldn't think. Eternity in a single gasp. Eternity of white light and blank thought.

And it was gone.

Pain. She buried herself inside her wings and shook. And shook. And sang to herself, "Fish and freaking chips that hurt, hurt, hurt. But it's over. Yes, Ms. MerEllianna it is over and over and shake it off you can, can, can..." She broke off the hysterics and pulled herself in even tighter. "Sure wish Min Soo could haul me over his shoulders out of this one." A patchwork giggle. "Oh, I pray they don't have a tanker hammer. God, get me through this."

Who'd brought a flipping submarine prod?!

Gradually, a little tattered, Ellia loosened her cocoon and eased her head out like a sea turtle. The two sentries were floating several metres away, bodies limp and stunned. By the electric shock splash back. Her whole body ached. A tilt of the head, a stretch. A turn to see who had used a. Submarine. Prod. On. Her.

The emblem on his high-tech golden vest confirmed initial suspicions. A royal merguard. But here? A cautious one, he floated at a safe distance and a few degrees above her. An alarm was ringing in the distance and she could already see the regular sentry gathering.

He repeated the order the sentry had first given, "Identify yourself."

She shook her head and winced, "Dear me, I think not. I'd rather not get electrocuted again."

Merdragon

His nose wrinkled in confusion. "You are an intruder, you set off the alarms and then did something to the sentry. If you don't tell me who you are now, I will have to use this," he pointed the prod at her, "on you again. At a higher setting."

She let a string of bubbles rise from the corner of her mouth. "First of all, I didn't trip off the alarms. I jack-hammered them. Second, I did try to be as light in my self-identification as possible, but you know, genetics." She shrugged with a spin, working out the spasms. "Finally, seeing that, despite those robust chest muscles you're flaunting, you appear quite young to be a royal guard of the first order, I suggest you find your superior officer before firing that monstrosity again. It's meant for redirecting subs and occasionally putting them out of our misery." Her hair spun out into a dark halo and her arms landed firmly on her hips. "It may even be used for discouraging a sperm whale's careless melee with a colossal squid, but it is not meant for me." The last pronoun included a well-defined sound wave.

A more senior sentry guard arrived on the scene, blazing ahead of his squad with gills flaring from the exertion despite the underwater scooter. He spotted the royal guard first. "What are you doing here? Where are my sentry men?" His eyes panned toward Ellia and she caught the moment of instant recognition.

His eyebrows disappeared, his tail fin flexed out straighter than he'd managed in years, and his shoulder audibly snapped as he pointed at her. "You!"

Ellia raised a finger to her lips, "Yes, yes, it's me, I'm glad someone finally noticed. Someone who can spill my identity without my input." She flicked her wrist at the royal guard, "If he gets the itch, he might be tempted to trigger."

The senior sentry guard spun around, looked the young royal guard up and down. "Pftt, soon they'll have toddlers wearing that uniform. Pshaw."

Flustered, the merguard tried to regain some of his respect. "Well, who is she then? We're on heightened alert, and while I'm out on a perimeter run the alarm gets triggered near our third defense line." He flicked up a rock with his tail and skillfully fired it at distant boulder, startling something into burrowing itself deeper into its home. "I arrive to see a cloud of debris, and these two," he pointed at the guards being cared for by their fellow sentries, "in the middle of treason before this stranger who refuses to ID herself."

The senior guard's body waved in a surface dwellers equivalent of a head shake. "I know they teach you better than that. You didn't spot the wings, did you?"

Ellia allowed her wing tips to flutter out like a flared dress. They felt a little stiff from the shock.

"Wait," he gave her a tail to hair-strands scroll, then turned back to the senior sentry with a worried face. "Not...?" A little plaintively he protested, "Shouldn't she be bigger?"

Ellia rolled her eyes, and the sentry spluttered and choked on bubbles before asking, "Royal guard, what was your name?"

"Evansea Krakenkiller. Sir." Technically he was the sentry guard's superior, but experience has a way of adding invisible rank stripes.

"Well, Krakenkiller—that's a mouthful—I'll tell you what, we'll give you the benefit of the doubt that you meant her wingspan." He beckoned over a few of his men. "Now, we're going to escort the honoured one toward the MerPalace and into the more appropriate escort of the royal guard."

Ellia thought it best to interrupt with a hand waggle. "Reminder that I'm technically still in official exile."

The senior guard pfft-ed, "Honoured one, my name is Raf Ellis." He tapped one finger sharply to his head. "I've got a good memory, don't you worry. We'll keep this all nice and respectful, and none of the ordinances will need to be broken." He gave Evansea a nod. "I'll let you alert, who is it now, Carcharodon? He'll need time to make the arrangements. We'll give 'im it."

Raf Ellis gestured for Ellia to take her position at their centre. "According to plan, honoured one?"

A graceful bend of her tail and a rearrangement of her hair from her face. "Whatever could you mean?"

The lot began making their way, the merguard keeping his distance while he sent in an update. Raf swam nearest Ellia.

She asked, "Tell me Raf, what did young Evansea mean about heightened alert?"

He glanced at her with a frown, idly allowing his scooter to pull him along. "Isn't that why you're here? Our young fry over there, he wasn't putting on airs about patrolling. Though I do wonder about that prod. Seems above his age-grade." He dismissed his own speculations with a "Pah!"

A sentry station up ahead indicated the fourth line, and now various buildings of various shapes and sizes began to define the area. Here and there sectioned areas contained curated marine life. There wasn't much merkin activity at this time of night in the working district.

"And the reason for a royal guard to be patrolling?" Ellia prompted.

"Right, right. Well, there have been rumours of attempted break-ins and disappearing merfolk."

Merdragon

Passing a relaxed fish cloud, Ellia swiveled around to swim backwards so she could face Raf. "Burglary in merCity?"

Raf shook his head, "No, no. More heavy stuff. Gene-code access only. That and the people supposedly disappearing are being blamed for it."

"Like old KJB sleeper agents?"

Raf snorted, "You mean KGB."

Off in the gloaming waters, Ellia heard the incoming royal guard squad. Evansea swam closer to the front of their procession in anticipation. His fingers splayed open and closed, open and closed.

Ellia gave Raff a warm smile, "Thank you, Raff Ellis, I think my escort is arriving."

"Look, those aren't the only rumours. Your wings have always been controversial and many of the younger generation haven't seen you in person. Horns have been added to the stories."

"Horns?" she asked, incredulous. "I fought hard, inside and out, to prove I was more a strange beast than a beast minion, despite the dragon descriptor."

"Hey, even down here we're human enough to enjoy conspiracy theories, especially when it comes to the future. Still haven't learned things seldom play out like we think they will. Keep your wits; maybe catch a Cult member while you're at it. Good PR and all."

She gave him a wink and spun herself back around. "PR, hah! I need a halo. Think if I bleached my hair it'd help?"

He snorted and crushed the bubble. "That'd be a shame. Hard to keep up your skulking habits and putting the fear of God into those without it."

"I appreciate the support. Hope I find the source of those rumours, legit and otherwise. You'd think there really was a bevy of seven jealous princesses. We'll see how right you are about the seriousness of my exile." A glint of armour in her peripheral. The squad was coming in fast. "Next stop, merPalace."

The merPalace rose above merCity, a brooding pearlescent mother octopus, an indefinite octahedron with roots that grew down low, then narrowed to a tethering point reaching to the floor of the deep oceanic canyon. Unnatural and older than merkind records, opinions and research results popped up on a regular basis. General consensus did agree that the unnatural effects on the pressure surrounding it were causal. MerCity enjoyed pressures equivalent to 100 metres below sea level to a much deeper level than nature should have allowed. As one approached the floor at the 1000-metre level it did increase to the equivalent of 350 metres. Few merkin could venture so deep without mechanical aide.

Coral grew everywhere due to artificial lighting and genetic modifications. Ellia admired a particularly curly-cued neon shaded variety as they passed. A class project. The city thrived on constant invention. Mersong rippled the waters, lights reflected off a multitude of iridescent scales, and gold flashed almost as often. The coral—she'd missed the incredible variety—the building blocks of nearly every bud-like building, giant shells gleamed, interspersed between. Late in the night as it was, she was eager to see it in its full lit glory. T

hey approached the merPalace at a stately pace, the enneagon of merguards englobed Ellia, replacing Raf Ellis' men. Ahead the merPalace moved like an octopus on relaxants, a living breathing structure. Its gates of entry varied from none to five, depending on time of day and current levels of security. Gate number five, located at the merPalace's peak, stood invitingly open. The single royal merguard waiting, not so inviting.

Ellia randomly threw the question to her new escorts, "Let me guess, Carcharodon?"

As soon as they were within a polite distance, he moved toward them to greet Ellia.

He addressed her sternly, "Honoured one," with a modest genuflection of what the original sentry had involuntarily enacted.

Ellia caught Evansea's hand spasm around the SP.

"Greetings," she replied with respect.

The gateway expanded and he gestured for them to follow him in.

They swam through the filigreed coral reef tunnels, led by the merKing's guide fish, and Ellia grinned despite the grim faces around her—the theory on land currently stated as fact that coral took a long time to form, but down here in the merKing's palace maze, the coral changed daily. But there was a catch. From merQueen to lowliest prisoner, the guide fish, with their sympathetic connection to the coral, were the only creatures, other than the merKing, who could navigate their way in and around the mystery. Many other fish and wildlife swam about, but few ventured all the way in. Those that got lost chose to make a home in their own little stretch of coral.

The guide fish flitted to and fro, their colours brilliant to Ellia's eyes, preening in their responsibility, leading an honoured one through the coral halls. Simple-minded, they couldn't distinguish a disgraced honoured one from a perfectly respectable grace. They swam in changing lead order, circling to the front and

Merdragon

then giving way to flirt with Ellia, shamelessly begging for a touch, conspicuously ignoring the merguards.

One of the smaller guide fish did flit around Evansea for a quick flirt, but an older fish flashed a fin and the small one returned to its duties in a spirt. Ellia assessed Evansea from the corner of her eye. If the small guide fish dared to cozy up to him with the tempting lure of an honoured one in the immediate area, she'd give him a few more moments of consideration.

Consideration she needed to be giving to their current downward direction. She used her lower range, "These guide fish don't typically enjoy going to the dungeons."

Carcharodon turned to face her but didn't slow down. "It is the merKing's directive, honoured one. The merKing retired from Court several hours ago already."

"I wouldn't have minded waiting outside."

One of the guide fish stopped as if to consider her request, but then remember its homework and continue.

"Perhaps you could have, –Evansea, what was the term you said she used?"

"Jack-hammered, sir."

"Mmm, jack-hammered. Yes, jack-hammered the alarms during working hours."

"Fewer people around at this time, less chance of accidents."

A turn down in the tunnels, the descent deceptively aggressive. One of the older merguards grit his teeth. The guide fish swam closer to the ceiling.

"For the same reason, I believe, the merKing gave us this directive."

"Great, first I'm electrocuted and now this."

A brief glance was sent Evansea-ward. "That was an unfortunate misunderstanding. Additional instruction will be given. As for now, Wavestaller," he called to one the guards, "fall back," the oldest one, "this is as deep as you go."

Gratefully he did as ordered. The pressure was increasing.

They continued deeper still, one minute, two, five, another five, the merguards in increasingly varying degrees of stress. Ellia noticed Carcharodon's gill flaps moving less freely. She expanded her own gills, barely noticing the effort. "I'm sure the merKing will understand if you let the guide fish lead me the rest of the way."

Carcharodon raised a hand to slow their forward motion, or was it downward? He assessed his men grimly. "Evansea, merKing is sending the honoured one deeper than expected. You've been undergoing special training; you'll continue the escort."

Ellia snapped a glance at Evansea. "Special training, my assets…"

A different set of guide fish had slowly replaced the original set. These dwelt in the higher-pressure extremities. Of a slightly mellower nature, lonelier in the nether regions, they ignored any possible reproach and blatantly swam into Ellia's cupped hands, under her arms and through her hair.

She trilled, "Charmers and darlings" at them and allowed herself to be led. Evansea trailed beside, not quite as at ease, but not in great distress either. Additional attributes to further consider. "Just how old are you?" she asked.

"Excuse me?"

"Never mind. Young is young." Around another corner and a sudden dip. A large round opening in the floor. The guide fish circled. They'd reached Ellia's destination.

"I see this is where we part, unless you've been instructed to watch me sleep?"

"Uh, no, just to set this," he pulled out a small round disc from one of his vest pockets and set it on the floor between them. "It's a ward to alert security if you choose to cross it."

Ellia tickled one of the guide fish. "I'll be sure to jack-hammer it when I leave."

He hung in the middle of the corridor, hand opening and closing on the prod. Abruptly he imitated the senior guard's genuflection. "My apologies for the earlier misunderstanding."

She curled a tail fin over the lip of the floor opening. "Well now. Apology accepted. Don't worry, I'll be catching a good snooze down here tonight. It's been a long day." One of the more robust fish darted into the hole, and leisurely she followed it down. She popped her head out and sang a "Good-night," with a wave of her hand.

Ellia watched Evansea pause for a moment, turn to go, stop for a thought. This time one of the guide fish tugged on a short strand of his hair. The decision had been made for him. Ellia waited for him to swim out of sight.

"Never met a guide fish friend I didn't like. Now," she drifted down into the cavernous recess she'd been assigned, "to get some sleep in the safest place in the palace."

Night had fallen on the lone warehouse, surrounded by solitude and barrenness. Not a single stream of light escaped to reveal its existence. A brief

Merdragon

crack of the door exposed full power to all lights and systems at play inside. The liveliest system, a living guard, sat on a chair with a tablet in one hand, a rifle on his lap and a water canteen on the foldable table beside him. A soundproof headset covered his ears. A light flashed on the radio-phone device attached to his chest pocket. A tilt of the head gave the impression that the light had included a ping to the headset. He set the tablet down on the table, picked up the canteen, and stood to begin an inspection tour.

A high-pitched scrape came from inside the seacan; the guard gave no reaction. He walked to the far wall and pressed a button. That he followed with a walk to the small, human-sized door. Out he went. Fifteen minutes later the door opened again, and he re-entered the warehouse, breathing now a little heavier, a fine dusty sweat on his face. A rumble from the inside of the seacan raised the hairs on the guard's forearms. He clenched his jaw and swigged a drink of water from his canteen. Grimly he strode back toward the seacan.

Reaching his seat, he didn't sit down immediately, instead he took a big breath, grabbed the tablet and started a walkabout. He took his time, tablet video running. Eyes, bodycam and tablet all in full use as he scanned from top to bottom, top to bottom along the full length of the seacan. There wasn't much to see until he made his way to the other side, opposite the outside door. There, midway along the length of the can, bars crisscrossed over a dark translucent window. He paused spotting it, then began his approach. His footsteps softened.

A metre from the window a voice spoke from within. "Is this the sixth or seventh day you've been pacing around my cage like a mouse?"

The soundproof headset should have deadened the question. He footsteps twitched anyway.

"Or has it been longer?" A rumble vibrated the edge of the seacan. "How long has it been since you last put on your tail?" A dissonance rippled the parched air. "Felt water course through your gills?"

The guard swallowed. Hand shaking, he reached for his canteen and tipped it over his face.

"When was the last time you challenged the currents?" Then as if a thought had suddenly come to mind, "Ah, do I understand correctly? The ocean was too dangerous for you was it, so they sent you to the upside? You carry weapons because your wan strength is perhaps not enough?" The voice huffed in laughter. "Cheer up, boy, there's no water near here is there? Pfft. What do you have to fear, you dried fish?"

It had been nineteen days, five hours, and two minutes to be nearly exact since he'd been relegated to pacing the warehouse and playing guard mutt. The three times he'd been relieved had not been enough.

His weapon snapped into his hand, and before he took a second breath he shot directly at the voice behind the window. The window chipped. Chipped a rough chunk of glass. The voice was hungry. Her voice. And so were her eyes. Ravenous.

The soundproof headset had not been enough. Another voice cursed at the guard through the radio, a waste of breath and electricity.

The air felt bubbly. Ellia pondered that thought with her eyes still closed. Like, really bubbly. Why did that seem wrong? Up her nose, up her gill plates, and all sorts of ticklish places! The giggles burst out in coughs and fits, and her eyes flew open as her body twisted and jerked away from...the air vent. She caught her breath, drift ing in the middle of the room. The bed shell in the corner hadn't held her very well, and she'd seemingly been drawn to the air vent that was now producing a great deal more aeration than it had earlier.

"I wonder who I should be thanking for that?" She glanced quickly at the ceiling. It had closed overnight. "So. On one hand you provide a little reprieve, but on the other hand I should stay here until summoned." The guide fish that had lingered behind with her swam along the floor of her now cell. "Not sure I fully appreciate the message." A light blinked on the console beside the shell bed. "What do you think," she asked the discomfited fish, "should we start singing?"

"Honoured one, I'd be grateful if you restrained yourself." Song was the natural merkind form of conversation, she'd been singing since she'd first spoken to the sentry. The speaker knew Ellia had meant something different.

Ellia tilted her head and said to the fish, "Since when did guide fish start talking?"

"Didn't think you'd lose your manners so thoroughly on that island," the resounding baritone admonished from the intercom. A major transitioned mid-vowel into a minor. There were surface dweller sound techs that would have sacrificed an arm for a chance to study the merPalace speakers.

A graceful swivel and Ellia faced the intercom unit with a touch of chagrin. "Your Majesty, my apologies, perhaps I have indeed forgotten my manners." A touch of seventh.

"Apology accepted. Now, can we switch to visual?" It was not a demand.

Ellia tried to judge the after-effects of the bubble storm on her hair. A quick glance around the room offered little help. Not many guests came this far down.

Merdragon

A sigh came over the speaker. "Vanity." He'd lived with the merQueen for more than the honeymoon phase.

"Manners," was her quip in reply.

"Noted. A steward will be in contact for whatever you need after this conversation. Non-visual is fine."

"When will I get an audience?" she asked, settling in front of the speaker with the guide fish curling up on her tail fin.

"You are still technically in exile. It can't be public."

She reached over to flip on visual, manners be trashed. A gold screen with the royal crest greeted her. "Pardon to Your Majesty, but I disagree. Either I get welcomed back with open arms, or the exile was legit, and I'll just let myself out of here and..."

"Why didn't you respond to my communiques?"

"What are you talking about? When?"

The royal crest glared at her suspiciously. "What were you doing in Iceland?"

"You know what happened?" she asked, a surprised squeak of soprano.

The merKing's words drifted along a mournful minor, "A young one died, for a certainty I know. Cursed genetics keeping our numbers small. What happened there MerEllianna?" The golden tones were plaintive. "This is a step too far even for ex-grace counsellor Danube."

About to respond, the screen went dark. So did all the artificial lighting. And the aerator. The guide fish scurried to hide in her hair. The coral had colour shifted into an unpleasant red glow. A mix of fluorescence and bio-luminescence.

"Alright little one." She glanced up at the ceiling. "Create me an exit, will you?" Time to see how much autonomy the merKing had granted her.

Unexpectedly, instead of the ceiling, the guide fish darted to a spot already opening in the floor. Another guide fish poked its nose up from the underside and beckoned for her to follow.

"Well now, wasn't planning on heading down you guys. Not the type to run from trouble, you know."

The one that had kept her company overnight came to tug on a strand of her hair. Firmly. Ellia put a hand to her scalp and showed a little tooth. The guide fish flipped over and played dead. She couldn't help it, she laughed. "Fine, fine. Lead me down the coral garden path." A wiggle and it darted to the hole to dive down and disappear.

She followed.

On the underside of the hole was an unkept, rarely used tunnel-way. The guide fish darted aside an over-reaching coral branch and Ellia darted after, her much bigger tail sliding against the rough surfaces. A gap in the tunnel wall closed as she passed by, revealing only a glimpse of another tunnel lined with windows. She allowed herself a brief moment of curiosity to wonder why so many rooms and tunnels existed in an area few could easily visit. Down the guide fish led; mid-way along the route, a shift change occurred. She waved a kiss good-bye to her last-night's roommate; it wistfully blew bubbles.

Ellia scraped around a tight corner in the increasingly brambled tunnel. The glow from the coral steadily dimmed and the walls un-defined. She looked closer. No, the walls were, disintegrating? No, she saw, as a branch of coral withdrew into itself and then outgrew into a new position. An "oh" pop! escaped her lips. A time-lapse video in the real. She hadn't seen that before.

"Aren't you a lively bunch." A ripple ran through the coral. Mersong was rare in these deeper sections.

The way cleared a little more for her then. The coral could be accommodating. Neaten themselves up for a polite guest. In thanks, Ellia sang a simple tune between breaths as she continued running—to steal topside vernacular—after her guides to who knew where. It couldn't be the tether, could it? Vulnerable, perhaps, but weak? No.

Up ahead she spotted movement. Her guide fish all disappeared. Ellia slowed. A current swirled around her palm. A current that should not have swirled quite in that way. Her scales tightened. She drifted forward, eyes straining to see in the dimming glow. A section of the impossible red disappeared behind a long, large shape. It grew darker until Ellia realized the regular lighting was actually returning, and it was the contrasting silhouette which stood out sharper against that light.

The shape shifted, and now Ellia could make out a few more details. A light tap of her tail against a sturdy coral moved her closer. She put out a hand to stop herself. It was a six-gill.

"What might you be doing down here?"

A three metre long six-gill shark. One fluorescent eye rolled to look in her direction. Its body shifted, but it couldn't move far in any direction.

"You shouldn't be hunting inside the merPalace. Bad form." A mild scolding. She circled over the beast to see that down the tunnel a large gap had been blasted through the merPalace wall. "Didn't know you guys had learned how to create explosives. I'm impressed."

The six-gill was not. The shark struggled.

Merdragon

"Something particularly intriguing must have lured you inside," Ellia sang, calming the shark. She liked six-gills. Cows with teeth. They visited the valley floor for scraps and vermin, but the lights of the city, and a mild barrier, kept them from being any danger. Not like the ones that had been sicced on Min Soo, bred for viciousness.

"Let's see, shall we." Ellia continued to sing as she analyzed the shark's position. A coral, attempting to seal the breach, had mindlessly blocked off the shark's retreat. Removing the shark entirely would greatly aid in the regeneration process.

A muffled explosion sent a blast wave through the crawl space. Pieces of coral and marine life came flying out of crooks and crannies, the shark banged against a sharp coral edge, and Ellia went tail-over to avoid crashing into shark or coral. The shark thrashed and snapped in pain. A small dead guide fish disappeared into the shark's mouth. The lights flickered back down to half-life.

Ellia's eyes flashed. She had to deal with the shark, now. Leaving it behind would kill it by coral, but the explosion screamed for attention. With a snarl she pulled out the cold dagger from its hiding spot against her chest. Singing a soothing tone at odds with her snarl, she swam to the breach and began to slice at the coral. The dagger accepted no resistance and Ellia grieved. This section would need a transplant. The coral she touched with the cold dagger would not heal itself.

A silent slick and slack, and, in unexpected freedom, the shark gave a grateful snap, rolled its eyes and u-turned itself back outside. Ellia shook her head at the damage she'd done. The gap would remain open until a crew could get down here to fix it. She tucked the cold dagger back into its hiding place. Time to investigate the other blast.

Ellia headed further down the tunnel, glancing back only once to see the coral had cut off her retreat. The breach had been partitioned. It didn't matter. She cared more about the hole blasted deeper into the interior of the merPalace. All around her, little hidey-hole critters scrambled for new places of refuge; she eased past at a fast coast, not wanting to cause more panic.

One more curve to corner, and Ellia reached the carnage. It was dark, and Ellia could taste the blood mixed with the sediment. She snarled in distaste. A dark rough circle lacking any coral glow pointed the way. She dove in slowly, hands outstretched. Echolocation would give her own location away if someone were listening. She tried to imagine the interior terrain based on vague memories and the journey down.

A dimly flashing, tiny light caught her eye. She reached for it and instantly smashed her forehead into an obstacle. A hiss of pain and stars in her eyes. Cautiously she reached up to feel the beam that had nearly ended her. It was attached to other artificial shapes, and she realized the light she'd seen flashing was mostly obscured by the partially collapsed room. Hand over hand she drew herself around and through the damage until she finally saw the whole of the light. A pressure lock warning signal.

If finger snapping were a thing underwater, Ellia would have snapped. She'd heard about pressurized labs in the merPalace. Research and development. The pressure lock had been cracked. A pull on the handle and the door swung open without a hiss. She peered inside and winced at the crack on the inner door too. If anyone had been working in the lab… The bright light streaming from that crack was more ominous than the red of the impossible coral. Eel quick, she slipped to the door and slid into the blindingly lit room. And dodged out of crosshairs just as fast. The crosshairs of the harpoon vibrating in the pressure lock frame.

Blind from the brilliant blue light she sang for a locate. Enemy, solo, at 10, 3, 2, xyz. A flood of chitter, chitter, chitter blurred the locate. She grabbed the harpoon and moved, dodged an immovable piece of equipment, and ducked through another. Her eyes were adapting. The lab was circular. And sizable. Enough to keep the pressure-geared saboteur far enough away to avoid being speared. She was getting closer.

The merkin—the mechanical pressure suit was mer-made, no question—shot another harpoon. Missed by an oarfish length. She smirked, but not when the alarm sounded. She spared a glance at where the harpoon had landed and swallowed her own fire. The emergency pod housed an occupant. A lab tech had been working. And the harpoon had embedded itself into the pod. A panicked face pleaded with her through the glass.

Ellia assessed the pod clamps. The pod should have shot itself up to safer zones as soon as it was occupied, but now she saw one clamp had been damaged. The sound of the pressure lock caught on her ears and she spared a glance to see the harpoon shooter swimming out. A tapping on the emergency pod glass porthole brought her attention back to its tenant. The merwoman grimly pointed after the saboteur, urging Ellia to follow. Ellia turned away, but not to chase. No, to pull out the dagger.

Keeping it out of the merwoman's sightline, she first reduced the harpoon's length to nearly flush against the pod, then sank lower to gingerly cut away at the

Merdragon

damaged clamp. Tougher than the coral, the metal still gave way to the dagger easier than to anything else in the lab.

The merwoman pounded on the glass, increasingly distraught. Ellia ignored her. Focused. The clamp released and instantly the pod shot up as designed.

A sigh of relief. Short-lived. Ellia scratched an itch on her arm. A burning itch. She tasted the water and gagged it out instantly, sealing her intakes. The merslime of a merperson had left her a parting gift. A flash in a gutted corner revealed another one. A flick of her tail and she flew up after the emergency pod, the lab melting below.

Four hours later, Ellia floated outside the merPalace audience room cooling her scales, surrounded by the royal merguards. The coral around her shifted in colour, marking time from nearly obscure turquoise to pinks to gold to black light ultraviolet. The colours were on their third cycle when the guide fish sprang into a flurry of motion, pooled around Ellia and, greatly daring, expressed their fishy affection in an effervescence of fish kisses. Then, with a flurry of bubbles, they schooled away back into the tunnels.

Carcharodon came skidding in at speed and his men shifted around him with questions. Carcharodon raised a hand to forestall the discussing and led four of the merguards through the entry way, and she, momentarily distracted by the fish play, found a smile lilting at the corners of her lips. A hurumph compelled her to follow through the entry, herded in by the remaining merguards, Evansea included.

Expecting it, didn't prepare her for the twenty years of forgetting. The merKing's orb chamber swallowed her and her escort like shrimp swallowed into the maw of the blue whale. A sudden rush of nerves wiped the amusement from her eyes. It had been over twenty years of exile, and well, there was the case of the multiple blasts, a melted laboratory and no suspects in hand. The morning's conversation had ended on suspicion. "Change is a constant," she mouthed to herself.

Floating at the orb chamber's center, the merKing, infamous trident in his hand, observed the world turned inside out. The world spun around the chamber, inverted, each continent, every city, lake and river instantly magnifiable at a gesture from the trident, or input by a technician. Even more impressive—dog-at-dinner drool-level, the envy of every marine geologist, every oceanographer, and every child who ever laid outstretched on a dock staring down, imagining what swam below—the unveiling of every ocean floor around the planet.

The oceans retained their unmistakable water identity, but only in the way of an aquarium. Trenches, peaks, settlements, fault lines, riches and the great desecrations visible at a glance. The great currents, the minors, the maelstroms, the dead zones, and the invaded spaces to be avoided, all laid bare, with merkind titles at odds with surfacers.

The merKing, ensconced in precious metals, the techno exoskeleton of a throne, trim of grey beard and grey hair, muscled like a tank, and wearing a wide band of techno-gold over his forehead, greeted Ellia's arrival with a glower. Merkin sprinted at eye-avoidance speeds around the chamber, actively doing anything to avoid his attention. Carcharodon led his charges nearer.

As they closed the distance, by instinct they allowed the span between each one to widen in anticipation of the merKing's possible wrath. Meanwhile, Ellia slowly and carefully began unfurling her wings, patiently and skillfully avoiding any untoward movement that might be misconstrued by her twitchy merguards. With tail fin countering the motion of her wings, and careful, subtle control of the speed at which her entourage approached, she managed to be at full spread the moment the merKing raised his hand. Ellia placed forearm to parallel forearm against her breastbone in respectful merfashion.

The merKing spoke first, the song sending vibrations to the very outside of the inverted globe, "MerEllianna Nighemere." Her unsung title hung in the air and genetically encoded instincts twitched in everyone within hearing distance. Then the question, bass layered, "Why have you returned?" It could all be show, but she couldn't read him. He had that talent. Uncertainty swam like cold eels in her gut.

The glow of the Earth view reflected off her gossamer wings and the gleaming of her scales made her an alien even here, her home. Void of visible nerves, with careful grace, she curtsied as only a fully winged merdragon could, her entire being engrossed in the task of offering obeisance, every breath held on the balance...and threw the dagger.

It was more of a kindergarten teacher's toss, but instantly the merguards activated their spears in a crackling display, engulfing her in a field of murderous dissonance. The merKing rose with a roar from his throne and a pulse rang from his trident disabling the spears. The dagger landed hilt first in his hand and he growled the command, "Stand down!" Resuming his seat, he snorted, "Fool's theatrics," adding a wave of his trident for good measure.

The merguard had turned off the field, but Ellia remained in her wing cocoon. She hummed to herself inside, "Mother of pearl, that was a near thing. Starting to

Merdragon

wonder if being a lab bat might not be the better choice. I wonder if Min Soo would come see me, preserved in a jar." She giggled at the thought which doused her cold. When had she developed a penchant for hysteria? "Jesus, help me," she prayed.

Wing section by section she emerged from her self-isolation.

The merKing was observing her sternly. "You stopped sending reports five years ago, abruptly show up after a slew of thefts, destroy one of our," he hrumphed and glanced around at his audience, "laboratories and then fling a knife at us. Explain yourself."

Ellia's whole body waved in disbelief, "Your majesty?" He hadn't mentioned Iceland. "Five years ago, I received silent running instructions along with a "watch out for the sharks", who, by the way—those ungrateful beasts— turned on me."

A veritable glower descended over the merKing's brows. "We never sent that message."

"You sure? It's not like it would be impossible, but...I did start working on a get-around for that lock you set. Then someone busted open the island bubble."

A rumble, "A false message..." he tapped instructions into the equipment around him. "The seal, that was necessary. And yes, I can see you were not the one to pop it."

"Still not entirely enthused I didn't have control over it." Her lips were itching into a snarl, but she held them down. "As for the thefts, it'd be pretty dumbfounding of me to drop by after the crime's been committed. Why even suspect me?"

"The same reason you were sent to the island in the first place, your genetic code. You know as well as we do that your living signature was why you were created." He paused for a grumble. "And if you didn't undo the island shield from the inside then Danube's succeeded where he shouldn't have."

A snort escaped her and her wings fluttered. "Sure, an almost master key. Lot of good it does without—"

The trident sparked a minor warning. Ellia's snapped her mouth shut. The merKing spun the dagger in his massive hands. "What about the laboratory? We've heard Sci-Master StarLace's testimony."

"Sure wish the guide fish could at least speak in Morse code. They knew something was up and led me down. Surprised I didn't encounter any emergency crew, now that I think about it."

Carcharodon interjected an explanation, "There was an explosion at the power den simultaneously with the one at the lab. We weren't even aware of the secondary one until the power started coming back up. Then StarLace comes shooting out of an emergency escape tube."

"So, an insider. Reason to suspect me, I guess." Ellia shrugged and leaned back into her curved wings despite the nerves. "Reckless." She let a small bubble slip out the corner of her mouth. The merKing propped his head with the fist holding the dagger. Ellia drew a strand of hair around a talon and the merKing shifted the dagger to a safer position. "Whoever it was came in from the outside, chased in by a curious six-gill." A few intakes around her indicated surprise. "Maybe it was trying to defend the house that feeds it. Got it out, but note to the coral gardeners, the walls will need repairs beyond natural coral skills." A question thrown in Carcharodon's direction, "Has anyone been caught yet?"

He shook his head, "Not yet, hoping you can add to your preliminary report of "There's a guy in a pressure suit who just blew up the lab, but don't go there, go get him, and where's a chemist to get this blasted goopy acid off me.""

"When you've got the scales that I do, anything in the water that itches me should be of major concern to you. And the guy who knows how to make that stuff even more so. Not a great place for pressure suits to have sudden failure."

One of the merguards surreptitiously rubbed a hand against his thigh scales. A few others made similar psychosomatic gestures.

"You look fine now. Anything you can add?"

She crossed her tail fins, "He was a pretty decent shot with the harpoon and knew how to jam the escape pod. Wasn't entirely murderous seeing as how both StarLace and I are alive, especially StarLace. I don't know what he grabbed, but he's certainly not planning on returning to that wrecked lab. There was one spot he made a special effort to turn into irredeemable sludge." Silence and then a light bulb sparked in her eyes, and she snapped her fingers, "The six-gill! Whatever drew him after the thief may lead us to him too."

Carcharodon offered a curt curtesy to the merKing, "Pardon your majesty, this is new information that could prove useful."

"Go, by all means, go," the merKing dismissed him with a wave of the dagger.

Carcharodon pointed at two of the merguards and left the remainder to escort the honoured one.

The merKing balanced the dagger on the tip of his finger, keening its nature with both his natural eye and the in-depth sight of his tech. Realization softened his gaze and he returned his regard toward Ellia in his own turn of disbelief and frank curiosity. "Where did you find this? A rather dangerous little dragon tooth."

Merdragon

"Pfft, a real dragon tooth wouldn't hold long against that." Her eels settled. The merKing had lowered his ruler mask. "I brought it as a peace offering, in case."

"You used this to cut the pod clamp?" She shrugged her wings, "and to free the six-gill, yes."

"The coral gardeners are not going to be happy. We hear it's a rare species down that far."

"They do glow a fierce red."

A section of the orb around them was glowing up, tracking the sun. "Oh? The scientists haven't yet figured them out. Doesn't help them that the coral tend to stay to more standard shades when instruments are out."

Ellia snorted. "They should try singing to them."

"In their suits?"

Chagrined, "I forget too easily sometimes." Other than Ellia, only the merKing could venture so far down unprotected. Sending and receiving while inside mer-sized suits tended to be imperfect. Suit-to-suit worked better than suit-to-surroundings.

"Come," the merKing commanded her, and gestured for the merguards to remain where they rested.

With the grace of a Giant Ray she approached, eyes sharp to immediately arrest her forward motion the moment the merKing required. Closing in, she angled her wings to decelerate, eyes narrowing as the distance between them decreased. There were undercurrents here. Cautious, her momentum approaching zero, she scarcely dared a breath when the merKing raised his hand.

The merKing shrugged himself out of his techno exoskeleton throne, the anchor that kept him at the orb's centre, and gestured for her to remain still. The muscles of his tail rolled beneath silver grey scales as he swam around her, shoulders wide by nearly three of hers. Sure, her wings added width, and her tail added length but so could a kite next to a gorilla. Even though all present could breathe underwater, more than a few held their lungs on the inhale as the merKing released his hold on his trident and reached out with a hand that rebuked Great Whites and rowdy Orcas, and ran that hand over the radius of her left wing. He hooked a finger around the wing claw. Automatic reflex clenched a hold.

The dagger flashed in his hands, once, twice as he pondered. "This dagger has a name." She eyed him calmly.

"The UnMaker."

"The danger is significant." The merKing had it right. The dagger had three purposed targets and she was one of them.

"I didn't earn my title by being a coward," she replied, her position steady against the throne room's currents.

"No, that you did not." He spun the dagger in his hand once more. "We suppose even your naysayers would have difficulty arguing against this. Nice play. We thought it had been lost. You'll have to tell me where you found it." Abruptly making a decision, the merKing released his hold on her wing talon, and with a powerful turn of his tail returned to his throne. Re-ensconced, he instructed her to "Approach the throne." He raised his gaze to direct the merguards, "Withdraw an oarfish length."

The officer in charge did so reluctantly, a grim frown expressing his unhappiness. It wasn't misplaced. The UnMaker was legendary, nearly a myth. It hadn't been used on a titled merkin in hundreds of years, and then only to turn a regular merkin into a surface dweller. Once touched by the UnMaker, all title rights were erased from the genome. The human form became fixed. All merinstallations, above or below, became safe from the formerly title-privileged access. The only consolation for the merguards lay in the merKing's immunity. Once title-maxed and crowned, the merKing became permanently mer. Not that it couldn't cause damage to his flesh or gear.

Noting the reluctance, but satisfied by their obedience, the merKing refocused on Ellia. "We'll ask you to pull in your wings."

Tilting her head at the odd request, she complied anyway. The merKing shook his trident once, and Ellia spun around as a privacy shield of turbulence waked up around them. A blur replaced their view of the chamber and Ellia could only imagine it worked both ways. An active silence muted all outside songs attempting entry. That too worked both ways.

"This is new," Ellia commented.

The merKing leaned smugly in his throne. "It is good to be king." Then he frowned, "Excepting days when I'm presented with the option to execute the daughter of a good friend."

"I was hoping you wouldn't take me up on it. We don't have time to prove my saintliness."

Any bull would have been proud of the merKing's snort. He flicked his tail in annoyance. "We need to speak in private to avoid a panic. Do you know what was in that lab?"

Merdragon

Ellia rested her wing claws on opposite shoulders, and, with delicately clawed hands loosely clasped, she gave the appearance of a genteel lady sitting on a settee waiting for tea to be served. "Not a clue."

"Only a handful of title-heads know. The core node that unlocks the genetic keys for every newly titled or promoted merkin."

Shock. "But that means…"

The merKing tapped his fingers, "Yes, I would be the last merKing."

"Danube, your brother…"

"Most likely his doing, hand in poison-hand with the Cult, yes." He glowered, disharmonics in his voice, "The lab framework has been destroyed, but the original is still intact on the island. Now that he possibly has the core node, all he needs is you or me to get access to the lab inside the island. We can rebuild the frame, but not the node."

"He's been planning this a long time. The Cult maybe longer. While I was tracking my trackers, I overheard Danube spouting about his involvement in my concocting. It confirms father's findings when he tracked the Cult to the island. He always suspected he saw Danube there. Thankfully father managed to get out, plucking me from the lab on his way. Danube's always treated me as an unruly pet that he thought needed a choke-collar."

Her lips curled in distaste. The merKing had sent men to flush out the island, but it had been empty upon their arrival. Sealing it off had been his only option at the time to prevent unauthorized access until it could be properly studied. Later, Ellia had been sealed in under pretense.

"His foster mother should never have pushed him into thinking he had a chance at the throne." A switch by his tail fell victim to on, off, on, off, on, off.

Ellia caught the movement, and for a moment, curiously pondered the switch's purpose.

The merKing continued, "A Cult follower herself with her own dreams of grandeur, most likely. The Cult's been around since merkind first broke away from our slave masters. Danube's no slave-minded fanatic. He's joined their cause to fight for what he sees as a personal injustice. He draws others into the cause by making it their personal injustice." The exoskeleton throne shifted easily as he shifted positions. "Now that you're outside the island's protection—and the island's lost your protection—he can move forward."

The quiet burring of the turbulence shield played background music to their silent concerns.

Ellia's gaze drifted past the merKing in remembrance, "Iceland… What could he have found out there?" She covered her pinched mouth with a clenched fist. "I've seen carcasses. I've seen dead merfolk. We always retrieve our dead." She covered her eyes. "Something extinguished that young mermaid's life-light. She couldn't have been more than sixteen and all that remained was just a small part…" Her hand fell from her face, her eyes wide, puzzled, "There were no signs of a struggle. No resistance, no defense. Just the deathsong." She asked again, "What did he find?"

"Many records were lost in the rebellion. Danube's found something he shouldn't have." The merKing clenched his sledgehammer fists. "Something that may make it possible to bypass both of us."

Her wing claws flexed, "His security's been developing holes, but not when it comes to that secret. I couldn't find where he cached it. Not even the continent."

"Your network's been the source for most of our information, although with your silence I had begun to question it. And to implement steps to fill in the gap, but no one's managed to title-up to your father's rank yet which has stymied our efforts." He keyed in a memo. "I'll instruct the merinstallations to track what they can and to provide you with whatever resources we have."

Nodding acceptance, she asked a divergent question, "Have you found any additional evidence behind the attack on the merQueen? Anything that could convict Danube rather than just send him away?"

A bass grumble stiffened the hairs on the back of her neck. "Other than the necropsy showing that the kraken had been drugged and tortured, no. There is a limited number of people who could have done it, but no irrefutable proof. We'd hoped sealing you out of reach on the island and cutting off Danube's access to the merCity would squelch his ambitions."

"I did appreciate having my title-upgrade released to me before locking me away. Gave me access to all sorts of areas down below. Still didn't magically make me into a mad scientist or genius inventor. If you ever decide to risk opening it up again, I'd suggest an archeologist join the team. I still have one more title-up pending, don't I?"

"I suspect at least one. To be honest, it's probably what triggered Danube's strike, knowing you'd be in reach of an upgrade once you eventually came back. Without the next one, even if I release all my locks on the island, you still won't have full access. At least your current level made your island time less isolated. Despite our recent com-glitch." His grin revealed a grim humour. It disappeared quickly. "I regret I could not release one to your father, he'd already been maxed up."

"How is he? I'd like to see him."

Plaintive minor sevenths burred in the merKing's words, "He's never recovered from the merQueen's song. We're sorry; I'm sorry. He's well cared for in the nursery. The children are gentle around him."

She swayed inside the unspoken, "Thank you."

He waved a never mind at that. "Back to the important issue, the node. Without it no one else is going to have the chance to title-up. Our entire society is built on it. Graduates will no longer gain access to their chosen field's tools or information. Places like the island will be limited to this generation. We will be forced above and those who's genetics can't handle it will die out." The tip of his trident crackled. "The framework can be rebuilt, but the core node cannot."

"If Danube gets access to the island lab, will he be able to title-up to King?"

He sighed, "That's the tragedy. Our sister has the potential, along with a few other relatives, but not Danube. The cursed remnants of the slave masters. We have enough leeway to choose from a pool but not everyone can be anyone."

Uneasily she spun, turning her back on the merKing to look outward. She ran her claws against the turbulent shell. "With Danube at the Cult's helm he's making a mess on land too. He's getting sloppy, interfering with surface dwellers. Even more than past Cult activities." She glanced back at him. "Do you remember your niece, Darya? She may be his reason for Iceland."

Frowning he asked, "You've met her? I did offer Danube the option of having her fostered and raised here. Being raised on land as a merkin is an unhappy upbringing. How is she?"

"She needs artificial stabilizers now, and if she ever has children they won't survive above surface."

A bass rumble disturbed the water. "We'll have to draw him out. You're a known variable versus whatever he unearthed in Iceland. Darya's condition is his hourglass timer."

She returned to the genteel lady's position, running her tongue over her left fang. "Caged dragon into a worm on a hook, fantastic."

"MerEllianna, you may have sparked into existence inside a test tube, but we merkin value you. The Cult, most probably led by Danube even then, had their plans to use you as their master passcard, but they forgot your lineage." His trident crackled and his voice took on an organ's solemnity, "We have not forgotten. You have not once disgraced her legacy. The Honoured One made it possible for us to discover the True Creator and unshackle ourselves from the slave masters. We must remain free. As the Honoured One's partial clone, you honour her memory with your actions."

"Enough, enough, I hope I honour my father's training more than I do the legacy of a person I've never met. The information available on the original Honoured One is patchy and half-mythical." A thoughtful expression crossed her face, "Have you had thoughts of going on the offensive with the Cult?"

A burly eyebrow managed to touch the techno crown, "Are you suggesting it?"

"Father was working on collecting data which I continued collecting while on the island. They're much more involved in surface dweller systems than we've been giving them credit. Political, economic, educational...you name it. They're a major driving force behind the pollution crisis. It may be time to make ourselves known. With the current rate of advancements, the surfacers will find us soon anyway. Best to bring ourselves into the light so we can spot the dark corners."

A few entries into the panels of his throne. "We'll have our ambassadors prepare." He subvocalized to his exoskeleton, setting a few additional commands. A stream of text and images scrolled on one of the panels, set at an angle Ellia had difficulty seeing.

A different wrinkle appeared above the merKing's nose for the first time since their re-meeting. Setting the trident in its port on the throne, he leaned forward and clasped his great hands together. "Tell me, I've learned of something curious. Your departure from the island involved a drylander with whom you have not severed relations." He leaned back to glance at his screens for more details. Both eyebrows rose as he added, "A considerably public drylander. Is that wise? You've made sure he's not a Cult pawn?"

Ellia's tail curled and uncurled at the edges. Her irises sparked around the edges, "Han Min Soo? I am rather attached to him. I did suspect him, but I also did my corroborating due diligence. He's my people now."

"Don't we usually keep our contacts at a distance?" he admonished.

"Can't say I didn't try. Danube jumped on the suspicion train before I even left the island and put his eyes on Min Soo to keep tabs on me. I suspect to use as potential leverage." She watched a stream of bubbles rise to meld into the turbulence. "Minor confession...he is, well, island-spiced."

The merKing stiffened. "Now that. That was unwise."

"It was that or let him die." She kept her cool, but frankly, Min Soo was her territory.

"Death is nothing unusual."

Merdragon

"Twenty years of isolation and another person already dead? I found some unreasonable value in the man." She may or may not have whistled a note of sarcasm.

"The Cult cannot find out."

"Not even Min Soo knows. Depending how things unravel, I may need to unravel even that." Her heart twinged. "Cutting ties." Maybe even pinched a little. "For his sake."

Nodding sympathetically, "You're the one in the field. If you need—." The merKing twitched his ears in annoyance at a sound penetrating through the turbulent shield. His conscious mind caught up with his ears' reaction, and suddenly alert, he looked outward. He grabbed his trident and with a twitch the shield dissolved. At the same moment, an exquisitely sweet sound surrounded them with a hypnotic summoning.

Not wishing to resist the call, despite an additional perk of her title, Ellia languidly turned to see its source.

The merQueen. The voice that had caused the old choir master to retire after she'd married the merKing. The voice that made great white sharks roll over for belly rubs. The voice of the Aurora Borealis. The voice that trembled the merKing's heart.

She floated in front of them, no maid, but a madame, her lavender pink tail scales reflecting any stray ray of light in the room. Her face pale as ice, but her dark blue eyes warm as fresh baked blueberry pie. Her strawberry blond hair glimmered with flashes of pink gold and her techno gold filigree crown held it away from her never-not-beautiful face. Gently she allowed her turbulence piercing melody to fade into silence.

Neither merKing nor Ellia spoke.

"You have a visitor," sang the merQueen.

The sound ran from Ellia's ears down to her tail fin and sent a ripple from top to bottom. She pressed her lips tight together to prevent the happy giggle.

"My Queen," the merKing rumbled and held out his arm. The merQueen reached out for his hand and came alongside her husband. With his trident the merKing carefully gestured toward Ellia, "Our exiled honoured one has returned. We plan battle."

The merQueen stretched her free hand to Ellia and received the merdragon's delicately clawed hand into her own. "MerEllianna Nighemere, you have been gravely missed." She released the merKing's grip and pulled Ellia into a warm motherly embrace. She chuckled low, "Even dear timid Suvi-Makena admits to missing you. Puttering around with her in the sea gardens, she pointed out a few of your souvenirs." The merQueen pulled away to really look at Ellia, eye to eye, "Welcome home, honoured one."

Ellia blinked away her fire tears and carefully hugged the merQueen in return. They drew apart and the merKing reclaimed his Queen's hand.

"How long will we have the pleasure of your presence in merCity?" the merQueen asked, dulcet chords in warm blankets inviting the hearer to stay forever.

It felt like slapping a seal pup to refuse but, "I fear this latest incident indicates the Cult has nearly finished drawing their bow. However, with the thief's catch still in motion it gives me time. I hope Carcharodon apprehends the thief with the item intact." She gestured at the dagger in the merKing's possession. "And with that here, no one will be able to use it against me." She pulled a strand of hair from her face. "The unknown element is what deeply worries me. I have to return to Danube's circles and hope he's become desperate enough to go for the target on my back."

"You have access to our above surface resources, I'm sure the merKing has arranged it. Is there anything we can send with you on your return?"

Ellia's wingtip claws shifted, and her wings re-draped themselves about her. The title was sitting a little bit more comfortably on her shoulders. "I travel light, however there are a few things I would ask of your Majesties."

The merKing chuckled and turned to the merQueen who's eyes had widened slightly. "We have been asked in the plural, no less."

"What is it?" asked the merQueen, curious.

"I would ask the merQueen's boon to borrow her tailor for a very simple, but of necessity, speedily done matter."

"He's yours." She tapped a signal through her own tech to alert him.

"...and?" the merKing prompted.

Loosening a wing, she stretched it out to point out Evansea. "Allow me to borrow that one. I suspect I'll find merguard backup particularly necessary."

A stray shadow flickered across the merQueen's face. The merKing ran his thumb gently over the knuckles of her hand. Silent communication passed between them.

The merKing gestured for Evansea to approach. "Your details."

Pale blue and green streaked hair swirled away from the young merguard's face as he quickly swam near, saluted in the mer way and snapped obediently, "Your majesty, Evansea Krakenkiller, sir. Royal merguard. Specializing in heavy weaponry, equipment-free, high-pressure environments, currently under communications training. A few other areas in which I've only just begun my training, Sire. I have not yet had my first transition."

The merKing inclined his head toward Ellia, "Honoured one, you are aware that not all merkin are capable of handling the serum, or making a clean transition, or even capable of processing the sensation of feet?"

"I'm willing to take the risk if he is. God willing, he handles the transition well and he gets some experience which will prove useful to you, your majesty, in the future. If not, at minimum a resource in the nearby waters would provide me with valuable support."

"MerGuard Krakenkiller," boomed the merKing. Tails straightened within the orb. An official issuance was imminent.

"Your majesty?"

"The honoured one has asked that we send you to aid her in her mission above surface. We will not command it. The serum you will be required to take can be both gift or curse. It is no shame if your body is unable to handle the adaptation. Nor in the potential aftereffects. We do not give your service away, merely lend you for a time. Will you go?" The transition was not mandatory. A rule, a foundational law that bound even the merKing. A free merkin's choice that separated them from their slave past. So many things still bound them that whatever freedoms they could obtain, they held.

"Sire, I will go." His pearlescent blue tail caught the light as he turned to Ellia and offered a voluntary courtesy. "Honoured one, I will be grateful for your instruction."

A smug smile slid into place. "Keep your wits about you. I tell stories."

The merQueen spoke up, "Young Evansea, best go to the Sciences quickly to have done what needs doing. We will know by morning if your body can handle the serum, else all this is moot."

"Your majesties, honoured one," he saluted again and swam past the other merguards who gave their encouraging nods.

Ellia gave her own bow to the royal pair, "If we're all good on the returned exile and no-longer-a-suspect part, I'll take my leave as well, if I may?"

"The guide fish are at your disposal," stated the merKing, "An update will be sent to you if Carcharodon's hunt is successful."

As Ellia headed out, she heard the faint melody of the merQueen, singing to her husband, "A most melancholic reunion." The merQueen had a mother's instincts. She would know a daughter's next stop, now that the merdragon was free to careen about the merPalace at a suitably madcap pace.

A stealthier daughter searched Min Soo's apartment with Danube in her ear.
"You're sure it's not in the apartment?"
Standing in Min Soo's bedroom, Darya ran a hand down the sleeve of a soft as butter suit. "It's not here." She turned to leave, her socked feet padding silently through the door and into the kitchen. She opened the fridge door and scanned the contents. "From the state of the place, the merdragon hasn't been here either for at least a few weeks."
"You're sure?"
"He's only got a single's dishes drying on the rack and the fridge doesn't have the usual super dense cal-loads she's known to keep about."
"So, it is fully possible she's gone running to my brother. You think the boy here is of any use as leverage? Would she have dropped him?"
Darya circled around the living room, examining his award and toy collections. A small five-centimetre sculpture caught her eye. A whimsical wave that practically sang hello.
"Totally worth keeping an eye on," she answered.
"Okay, get out of there for now. Min Soo's driving into the parkade. Maybe he's carrying it on him; maybe she's already got it. I don't want him taken until we know for sure."
Exiting the apartment, she asked, "Do we have confirmation the node is on its way?"
"I'm heading out to collect it now. Then we have to send another supply run to that monster."
The elevator opened, empty. She stepped inside. "You're not leaving anymore guards there, are you?"
"I'm not an idiot. I need every merkin we have. Who knows who has what embedded title-codes. Unfortunately, I can't use surfacers, either. I need that UnMaker back. Riko is an idiot. When I find where he's holed up, I'm going to wring his neck."
Darya didn't respond to the threat. She felt the same urge herself, even if it was conflicted. The merdragon's serum swam in her system. The only reason she could go skulking about.

Merdragon

The elevator dinged open on the main floor and closed behind her as she walked across the lobby. She didn't bother watching the numbers descend to the parking level.

As tailors go, merfolk typically always had unusual requests, but "You want me to make what?"

The doodle Ellia had drawn glared obnoxiously on the tailor's design board.

"Yes, that, in black."

As merkin go, he wasn't much called on either. On the stouter side, with a habit of wiling his days daydreaming in the coral gardens, playing a merkin game of crossword scavenger.

"And you require it by tomorrow?"

"Yes, and you'll notice the concealed pockets. One or two more would be helpful," she added, pointing out a few convenient locations.

He pointed out one section uncertainly, "This, is for use when you are legged?"

She nodded, pressing her lips together to avoid showing her teeth. It wasn't his fault she was twenty years late for a reunion.

"I see…" He inhaled sharply and grabbed a device off the wall. He pointed it in her direction. "Well, quick then, let's get your measurements."

She raised one taloned finger, "Remember, allow for shifting dimensions."

The guide fish groupies had lingered around the tailor's office, and the moment Ellia finished her business they schooled around her. She curved into a ring to corral them in mock netting. Blub-blub-blubbing they spilled out in every direction. The coral around them flickered in a rainbow cycle of pastel colours.

"All right, you miscreants," she sang at them, "this time I need to get to the assisted care nursery."

They circled around her with an air of puzzlement.

"My father, Drayvin merNighe, is he not at the merPalace nursery?"

A senior guide fish took center stage and the others looked to him for direction. He swung his body back and forth a few times and then bobbed up and down with a blub-blub. He swam up beside Ellia's cheek, gave her side-eye, then darted off with the whole school swirling behind him.

Ellia choked up a bubble whistle-laugh and bent nearly double in a hard push to catch up. "You fish are having way too much fun at my expense. Have a little pity, hey?"

Cheerfully they spun ahead of her in a tunnel formation. Merfolk dodged out of their way as they passed. Ellia waved in apology as she chased after the school. Expressions ranged from outrage to sympathetic laughter. A little merbaby boy spun in his mother's arms, and Ellia coo-whistle-sang a greeting/farewell.

They did eventually slow as they approached a quieter toned area. Roomy and consisting of smoother surfaces with increasingly frequent soft sections. The guide fish began to pare down their numbers as they dispersed to other duties. They'd arrived.

A merwoman saw them, and, as she approached, Ellia noted the nurse's markings on her vest. Her name merNataNaeco, old lineage.

"I'm here to see my father." She didn't need to elaborate.

"Of course, come, I'll bring you to him."

The sound of children's laughter slipped out of an area ahead of them. Ellia glanced at the nurse in surprise.

"You didn't expect children to be quiet, did you? It's great therapy for the elderly, and the elderly teach a great deal to the children."

"Yes, I remember. The merKing mentioned it, but I did not expect my father to be allowed quite this expansive privilege."

The nurse guided her around a partition. "In his current state there's little harm he could do and the merQueen specifically allowed for it."

Past another partition and the walls expanded into a comfortably sized, gently lit open area. In one section, two merwomen, hair thin and white, drifted in conversation with an even older merman, thin and frail. A tail's length away five mertots chased each others' tails in a tight game of swim tag. The nurse beside Ellia nudged her to another section. Ellia's breath caught.

Off to the right, and above the entrance, an old merman laughed gently at the antics of the merchildren around him. A wide and thick mechanical ring encircled his waist and held him, as a wheelchair would have on land. A blinking light revealed the monitoring mechanics. Ellia's eyes softened.

Blinking she bit her lip and took in an extra stream of the oxygenated water through her gills. She swam up to his level and greeted him, "Hello, father."

His head jerked toward the sound of her voice. The instant he spotted her he flung out his arms and sang out, "MerEllianna-nana-nana-naa?"

She reached out to hug him. She blinked at the loss of muscle mass. "Yes, father."

Pulling back, she watched as he struggled, frowned and stuttered, "H-how are you child?" Questioning had become an unfamiliar habit.

Merdragon

"I'm well. How are you faring?" She gently took his hand in hers, careful not to prick his thinned skin.

His smile returned. In sing-song fashion he replied, "I'm fin fine, just fine, fin, just fine, just fin fine…"

She interrupted, "What have you been doing?"

"Oh, I, I did something today, I did, I, I… I ate a sea-monster!" he giggled.

"Really?"

In the floating food web attached to his 'wheelchair' Ellia could see the sea-monsters he'd referred to. Food formed in the shape of krakens and volcanos and giant crabs.

A mergirlchild torpedoed into his lap sending them all spinning. Bubbles and giggles filled their section and Ellia laughed, fire tears lost in the melee. Moments later Ellia found herself against the ceiling with the child's face nose to nose with hers. She was being inspected.

"Are you merNighe's friend?" The mergirl asked. Cautiously Ellia answered, "Yes. Are you his friend too?"

The little mertot blinked her brilliant pale pink eyes. "The beautiful lady who sings says she's his friend too, but she doesn't sing for him. Why?"

Ellia's heart broke a little and she tapped the little mergirl on the nose, "Have you ever heard a really loud noise that made your ears hurt?"

The merchild nodded seriously.

"Well, merNighe accidentally heard the beautiful lady singing really loudly and it hurt his ears."

There was no way the merchild would understand that when the merQueen had gone to subdue the kraken that Drayvin merNighe had been one of her escorts and lost his own techno gear during the struggle. Unprotected, her full-strength siren's song had addled his brain into constant, often dozy, placidity.

"Oh. Can *I* sing to him?" she asked.

"Do you like to sing?" Ellia asked.

Opening her mouth into an O-shape, the merchild let rip a quick piercing, leapfrogging run up and down the oceanic scale.

Anxiously Ellia dashed a glance at her father. In relief she saw the arpeggio had had no effect, preoccupied as he was with a trio of mischievous merchildren swimming circles around him.

"Did you ask merNataNaeco if it's okay?" Ellia redirected the question, "You should go and ask her."

"Okay," the merchild said and disengaged from Ellia to swim directly to the nurse.

Ellia watched her go and surreptitiously hid her face while she recaptured her hair into some semblance of behaviour. Once the child had moved on from questioning the nurse, Ellia swam over.

"How is he?" she asked.

The nurse eyed her sympathetically, "Honoured one, I'm sorry, we do what we can, but you've seen for yourself."

"He hasn't seen me in so long. He was happy to see me, but..."

"The merQueen's song burned out key motivation and survival chemicals. We've tried artificial means, but he's losing the ability to even scare himself into taking a breath. We're keeping an eye on him, but I'm glad you had a chance to see him now. We're not sure how long he still has."

Ellia rested a hand on the nurse's shoulder and bowed her head for a moment, "Would it be okay to take him out for a bit?"

"Of course, his ring keeps us notified of any changes to his condition and will provide emergency meds if necessary."

"Thank you, we won't go far." She twisted about and undulated up to her father's circle of entertainment. The little merchild swam just above his head.

"Father? Would you like to go out for a swim-about?"

He tilted his head and then nodded like a bobble-head doll. He stretched out his hand to her and she grasped it tight.

"Can I come?" It was the mergirlchild again.

"What?"

The mergirl sped to the nurse and Ellia heard her ask, "Can I go with merNighe and the scaley lady? Can I, can I?"

The nurse questioned Ellia with a raised eyebrow. Ellia sighed. "I'm taking him to the Sanctuary. She's welcome to join us."

The nurse brought the little merchild to meet her eye to eye, "Racing Flower, remember to stay with the Honoured One." She emphasized the title, triggering gene-obedience. "If you get lost," she tapped the pendant around Racing's neck, "just squeeze this and someone will come and find you, ok?"

The merchild nodded, big eyes intent.

"All right, off with you then. Thank you, honoured one."

"Ellia is fine. Come along—Racing Flower, is it? Let's go visit the Sanctuary."

Merdragon

The Sanctuary stood outside the merPalace, a nearby, simple structure with a simple cross above the entrance, the only indication of its purpose. Racing chattered away beside Ellia while Drayvin swam, or rather allowed himself to be towed, on her other side. Passing through the entrance, Flower lowered her voice with a finger over her mouth.

Ellia imitated the motion with a flash of amused conspiracy in her eyes.

The Sanctuary held many memories and Ellia reminisced with fondness. She could breathe. Finally. She closed her eyes and just was.

Something tickled her ear. She opened one eye. Eat-rinse-repeat, big pale pink eyes stared at her, nose to nose.

"Daddy's here." Ellia drew back, puzzled.

"Do you mean..." The little mergirl pointed, and as Ellia's gaze drifted along the imaginary line, a shadow shifted behind one of the many columns.

Instantly Ellia's wings snapped out into a wall between her charges and 'daddy'.

"Who is it?" she challenged. The light of the Sanctuary didn't allow the shadow to stay a shadow long. A merman of no fearful description emerged from behind the column. Puzzle pieces snapped into place in Ellia's mind.

"Thief."

Two little hands grasped Ellia's wing and, "Daddy!" She flung herself toward the thief. Ellia lunged and captured her inside a wing.

Turning the escapist to face her, Ellia cautioned Racing with a tap on her chin, "Little one, I just need to ask him a few questions, ok?" She turned to the thief, "I won't play it easy this time. Is she really your flesh and blood? Seems convenient for you to be here."

His movements were weak. His head nodded a loose yes, and he tapped the same spot where the pendant lay on Racing's neck. "I didn't expect you, I just wanted to see her before I left, I didn't, didn't expect... This isn't the normal time for either of us to pick her up. I was just resting here, nearby." He avoided Ellia's eyes, "They wouldn't think to look for me so close to the merPalace..."

Racing wiggled inside her confines, but Drayvin's slow lopsided drift upward distracted her.

"Where's the node?" Ellia asked.

He waved in a non-descript direction, "It's long gone. I don't even... I don't know. It's in a homing capsule. Shielded. Small enough to avoid detection."

She tapped her chin with one taloned hand. "Do you know what it was?"

"Do you know how long we'll be safe here?"

The sound of Drayvin trying to sing an old merkin hymn distracted her for a moment. It was one of his favourites.

"What? The Sanctuary?"

He shook his head, drifting closer, his eyes on Racing. "Down here, with the surfacers spoiling everything up top. You know, my grandparents, they travelled freely, but now? What will happen to Racing? Already you can tell the clear difference between merCity and the outside sectors. We have to wear gill filters more and more and we're limited in where we travel, and everything has to be pre-planned, verified and registered."

"That's no excuse to do what you did."

He turned to face away from her, "It's too late to stop it. Maybe now the merKing will be forced to do something." A bitterness crept into his voice, "They said I maxed my title upgrade on the first one. Me, Epifaño, son of two Master levels." He sighed, "It's not so bad," he reached out to play with Racing's hair, "but I don't want it for her. She should be allowed to be whatever she wants. Maybe the node can be modified. Or maybe the surface can provide her with more options."

Ellia allowed the contact. The merguards would arrive soon. She'd activated Racing's beacon before engaging. "It's not wrong to dream, but this wasn't the way. Tell me, you said you were leaving. Where were you going to go?"

"Leaving?" he asked, "Oh, right, leave, well, I don't really…"

"…have a destination?" Ellia guessed. She spotted the ripple of a merguard's approach. "Good. How about you spend some time in the merPalace?"

He looked up startled, "What?"

She nodded toward the entrance, then tilted a glance at Racing, "It's been a lovely visit, but," she tossed a look upward to Drayvin drifting closer and closer to the ceiling perches, "I think it's time I took my father and Racing Flower back to the nursery."

Racing piped up, "Daddy, did you come to take me home early?"

A glance of his own revealed more than one merguard approaching. Epifaño ruffled Racing's hair, "Mommy will pick you up later today. I'm going to be gone for a while but don't worry, daddy will be back with something special."

Before Racing Flower could get suspicious, Ellia flexed her tail and rose to meet up with Drayvin who'd accidentally hooked his arm into a lighting loop. "Racing, sweetie, could you help me out?" Racing bobbed her head in a helpful attitude and swam to Drayvin's other side and pushed his hand so that Ellia could extricate him. Ellia raised a finger to her mouth and whispered, "Do you want me to show you a secret passageway?"

"Really?" Racing's eyes were wider than Ellia had thought possible.

Ellia nodded firmly, "But you can't tell anybody else, except your parents, ok?"

Little fingers wiggled excitedly.

Pulling in her father closer and shepherding Racing ahead, she brought them out through a utility passage that was mostly used for special performances and maintenance. They popped out at the other end of the Sanctuary, well out of sight from the front entrance.

Swimming back to the merPalace, Ellia prompted a stream of stories from Racing. In between her creative buffering, Ellia named the denizens around them with outrageous names to keep the day a happy one.

Back at the nursery, merNataNaeco greeted them and directed nurses to come and collect Drayvin and Racing.

"What happened?" she asked Ellia once the two were out of earshot. "I noticed the signal went off and instantly alerted the merGuards."

"I hoped you might. They're both fine, but we had a bit of an incident. Do you recall when Racing was last at one of her foster parents?"

"If I'm remembering correctly, I'd say about five or six months ago."

"Suggest to her mother that this week might be a good time to send her out again."

"I'll let her know."

"Good. Now I have to go report to the merKing." Ellia rested a hand on the nurse's shoulder and bowed her head for a moment. "Listen, I have a favour to ask."

"Ask."

"I'm going to have to leave tomorrow morning. Will you bring my father to see me off?"

"You're leaving so soon?" merNata asked, startled and concerned.

"My father's ability to comprehend urgency may have disappeared but mine has not. Things are progressing faster than I expected. Will you be there?"

MerNata frowned, but she nodded, "I don't really understand, but I'll do as you ask."

Swimming with the current

The following morning, outside the merPalace, Ellia rolled her shoulders and tried to stretch out her tail without being too obvious. The debriefing and planning from A down into the XYZs had taken a good portion of the night. A few guide fish spilled out of the entrance and dove straight toward her, bopping against her to check on her wellbeing. Ellia nodded to a somber merNata floating behind Drayvin in his swimmer. Drayvin waved and pleasantly greeted each passerby in a happy counter melody. On merNata's other side, slightly above, Evansea's mother—at least Ellia assumed she was—drifted up and down in a pace, poorly containing her anxiety. Grimly proud, she clutched a locket containing Evansea's baby hair.

Ellia heard Evansea reassuring his mother, "Mother, please be at peace. I'll be okay."

His mother patted him on the arm, "I know, dear, I know." She smiled tremulously toward Ellia, inclining her head as they made eye contact, "I'm sure the honoured one will lead you well. Make sure you follow her every instruction."

"Yes, mother, of course."

She tapped him on the chin in admonishment, "Remember to keep your chin down and your head up, your tail straight, but not too rigid, remember to keep it flexible and make sure you eat right, but do avoid that coffee stuff, I hear it tastes dreadful and I'm sure, what is it? Caffeine, yes, I'm sure it won't agree with your system, and watch out for the nuclear test waters, but I'm sure the honoured one won't go there, and," lowering her voice to a whisper so that Ellia barely made out, "your father told me to warn you to watch out for something called a 'zipper'."

"Mother!" Evansea hissed, mortified.

Ellia choked on a suppressed laugh and inadvertently snorted bubbles instead. The guide fish bubbled up in reply and performed impromptu, elaborate choreography that she was sure represented something, but if anyone knew other than the guide fish themselves, she would bet on it being the coral. And the coral wasn't talking.

Drayvin waved both hands in calm delight at the display, and she floated lower so they could be face to face. Self-calming, she smoothed the flat pouch belted to

Merdragon

her waist. The tailor had delivered it just fifteen minutes ago and expressed his desire that she never make public who had designed the worrisomely plain atrocity. Along with that request, he'd advised her of a note that the merQueen had included to be read en route.

Touching her father's arm, she asked, "Father, I have to go now. Will you be okay?"

A faint moue of grey passed across his face, but it disappeared as quickly as it had come.

"I'm fin fine, fin fine, fine, fine MerEllianna-nana-nana-na," he singsong-ed, swaying his head side to side. A glimmer of something urgent passed in his eyes. He gripped her hand for a moment and whispered, "Brave, brave, brave, little Ellianna-nana-na, s-s-s-safe, safe, eh?"

She smiled at his singing of her name and reached out to grip both of his hands in hers. "I will be brave. Make sure you follow merNataNaeco's directions and be good. Watch out for those sea monsters at dinner."

He giggled and pointed at his mouth. With a sad upward curl of her lips, she hugged him as tightly as his state would allow. Her eyes burned at the edges. Carefully she separated and turned toward Evansea.

"Ready to go, merGuard Krakenkiller?"

"Right away, honoured one. Mom, I have to go," he said and pulled himself away.

The coral of the merPalace shone a brilliant golden yellow as more guide fish slipped out and spread into a splendid formation, waving as one giant tail. Less brilliantly extravagant, Ellia's father and Evansea's mother both waved as well, the one calm, the other a little emotional. Ellia knew the merKing and merQueen sat observing the departure from within the orb; Carcharodon had reported an incident connected to a now missing member of the merPalace personnel.

Evansea caught Ellia's incline of her chin and the gesture to leave. He nodded and they set off.

In silence they swam briskly out of the merCity's busy bustle. He'd gone away before, of course, but this felt somewhat different. If he returned, he knew his vision of merCity would have changed.

Waiting for them, in the outlying corrals, a small school of specially bred, domesticated black marlins. These marlins could maintain their 130km/hr speeds for several hours. The source of many a sailor's "true" story when every fact finder knew that marlins "could never." Best in a team, similar to the sledding dogs of the arctic—or going by size, a full-grown racehorse—they lived to run and had a well-trained homing instinct.

Less friendly than the guide fish, only the lead fish in any way acknowledged their arrival. He darted toward them with his sword aimed true, and flashed to the side at the last possible moment. A flick of the tail and he u-turned to flash past them again. He waved his sword to be off and sped to the front of his team. A shiver ran through each set of three in their eagerness to race.

The marlin handler did a quick refresher run-through to ensure that Ellia and Evansea both knew how to manage the marlins. Satisfied with their attention, and answers to his questions, he gave them the go-ahead. In Evansea's eyes Ellia looked confident as she took the reins of the lead team. Evansea got behind the secondary team. Ellia lightly clicked her teeth.

Like a shot the black marlins took off. Evansea's gills gasped and flapped at the sudden acceleration. He'd never been in the position to ride behind the merKing's elite team. It took him a hundred metres or so before he could properly get his gills functioning again. Tail-riding, he couldn't see Ellia's team in front of his and resigned himself to flying blind behind the merKing's rockets.

Glancing once behind, despite the streamline instructions, he saw the merCity had all but disappeared into the gloom of the sea. He refocused on keeping himself in position and never once glanced back again.

Nearing the three-hour mark, the two teams started slowing down and separated from each other. Feeding time. Ellia eased up her control and directed Evansea to do the same. She rose above her team and scanned their surroundings. A school of smaller fish had been reported in the area, according to the sonar songs of the nomadic whales passing through. The black marlins spotted them first and dove for their dinner.

Ellia and Evansea rode above the melee and caught panicked off-shooters.

Evansea snapped the neck of his first and considered it thoughtfully.

Ellia sucked hers down and grinned toothily, "One down the hatch, two down the pipes, three to give you scales." The beginnings of a school-pool challenge game.

He muttered a prayer the fish stayed behind his teeth and swallowed three, one after the other.

A sonar sweep passed over them in the middle of their meal.

"Time to go. You'll take the lead this time."

Merdragon

The black marlins had felt the song too and responded well to Ellia's clicks to leave, despite the still splendid mass of fish swimming around. As instructed, Evansea's team took lead position, leaving Ellia's team to take advantage of the draft created by the leading team. The song sounded again followed by another and another. The nomadic whales had circled and were returning to feast again. Evansea clicked this time, and they were off.

The black marlins swam now at a slightly slower pace. They'd eaten well, and although they would need to rest again, they wouldn't need to stop for another meal until the 'morrow, unless of course, one conveniently passed in front of them. They'd rest only for the chance to switch positions. Evansea and Ellia both caught snatches of shut eye, pulled along by their coursers.

In one stage of being in the second position, Ellia snuck out the message the merQueen had secreted to her. A parasite had been found in the merKing's own throne. Min Soo's safety itched under her skin. If Danube found out, would he nab Min Soo to hedge his bets?

Evansea woke with a start. His ears felt muffled. He broke his streamline and his whole team wobbled. He sank back down, tensed for them to slow, but nothing doing. Somewhat more strategically this time, he rose above the team to see if he could see what had awakened him. Ellia, in lead position, had also risen above her team. She shouted something back to him and that's when he realized his ears were drowning in noise.

She'd warned him earlier, of course; they'd caught the Kuroshio Current. Once they entered there'd be no stopping until they reached the splitting point. The black marlins swam with exuberance, fiercely flickering in and out of formation with a willy-nilly-ness Evansea found startling different from their normal intense drive. He saw Ellia laughing along with them and had to grin. Daring the current himself, he joined in the fun with a few low-key spins and flickers of his own, for training purposes.

He woke next in a tumble of tired black marlins and he flayed about in a confused attempt to straighten them all out. A great rumbling filled the water around them, and Evansea went spinning again as his team dove downward.

A clawed hand suddenly grabbed him by the wrist and hauled him out the panicked melee. A flash of the talons sliced the line connecting him to the marlins. He struggled to regain his orientation. His tail caught on the edge of the current. His shoulder audibly popped as the current tried to wrench him from the honoured one. With merdragon speed, she flung out her wings, beat them down in one muscle tearing pulse, and yanked him into the clear.

She didn't let him go until they were a good twenty metres away. Once she'd released him Evansea rubbed at his wrist and tested his shoulder for functionality. It was still attached but he wasn't sure how much use it was going to be. Ruefully he tried to spot the merKing's black marlins.

"We're on our own now," Ellia spoke up in response to his non-subtle searching.

"It's my fault," Evansea started to apologize.

"No, I set the leader loose as soon as they pulled us out of the Kuroshio. That was my mistake. I didn't realize you were mid-nap." She tail-to-tail tapped him to emphasize the no-harm teasing. "The way home's going to be a slower trip for them, but at least they don't have us hanging on their tails. Your team reacted to that cargo ship," she pointed to a distant hull, "in a willful panic. Any excuse to be off after their school mates."

She nudged his good shoulder with a wing tip, "It's our turn to work off some of that last sardine fest we indulged in."

He groaned and held his stomach, "Don't mention sardines, I may be sick."

"What's your fastest cruising speed?"

"I can maintain eighty for an hour or so," he responded, modestly, proud to be speaking the truth.

"I'm impressed, there aren't many who can. Very well, I'll keep us to that speed, good thing you don't need your arms. Make sure you let me know if you start cramping. The waters here aren't cleansed like they are in home waters."

Evansea stretched out the sleep and the abuse from his spine, ran a muscle warming flicker from tail tip to the back of his neck. "I'm ready."

"Let's go," Ellia replied and led off in the direction of the East China Sea.

It had taken them two days to be kicked out of the Kuroshio and it took them another day to reach their landing destination. Ellia kept them twenty-five klicks off Wido Island until night settled entirely and until even the lesser lights had thinned out. They avoided the beacon lights and swam right up against a convenient pier. Ellia surfaced first and then clicked for him to follow. He breathed out as much water he could from his system and surfaced.

The transition always brought a coughing fit. Worse when you had to keep it quiet. While Ellia kept a lookout, he tried his best, water pouring out from mouth, gills, nose, eyes. A little resentful, he wondered what her secret was. She hadn't coughed once.

Merdragon

Coming up beside him, she rubbed his back and asked, "You good? I think this is the right cove."

He nodded. Time to merguard-up.

Belly and tail brushing against the sand and gravel, Evansea tried to avoid sucking in any waves he'd only cough out again and followed Ellia hand-walking up to the beach. Dragging their tails behind them they left the water, and Evansea groaned silently, mourning the loss of the water's buoyancy. He had a whole new respect for walruses. His shoulder reminded him of injury as he strained to put one hand in front of the other, cursing the dead weight of his too heavy tail, wincing every time a particularly sharp rock caught on his scales.

The waves slapping against the pier distracted him, the sound strange to his ears. Everything sounded strange. Rarely did he ride the surface waves and never had he been so close to an above surface populated area. Even if they watched broadcasts from surface dwellers, the sounds still travelled through water. The sounds he heard now vibrated oddly against his open-to-air eardrums. A cough caught him unawares. His muscles spasmed and he fought to bring his lungs under control.

Ahead of him, Ellia had reached the tree line and pulled herself up into the grass. Evansea, following after, sighed in relief at the smoother surface. His fingers kept waiting for the strands to curl around his fingers like sea kelp. A sigh turned into a spasm.

A few metres farther, a small shack stood, and Ellia headed straight toward it. With familiarity she pulled up a sunken-in rock to reveal a key at its base. The key opened the shack and she dragged herself into the dark of it. What else could he do but follow? He eyed the three steps and apologized to his shoulder.

Inside, Evansea's eyes adjusted, still in mervision, and observed as Ellia pulled herself up on to a padded wooden bench. She shook out the waiting folded blanket and pointed at a similar bench opposite hers. His muscles shook. Up he crawled into a mirror of the honoured one's position. The blanket tumbled out in a mess, and he fumbled to do without the help of a water assist.

Ellia stretched out on the bench like a floppy seal, draped the blanket roughly over herself, and tapped the door closed with the tip of her tail. Darkness. One green flickering eye opened to focus on Evansea. In mersong, oddly vibrating in the above water medium, "We'll transition here. The first time can be…disconcerting. Initiate the change and go to sleep." The eye closed.

The blanket bunched in his fists and his eyes widened when he realized her breath had dropped into dead sleep. His tail flickered uncertainly as he contemplated if he should try and adjust her position or try to imitate it instead.

She stirred from the dead. "Trigger. Sleep. Now."

His spine straightened at the command tone, and he smacked his tail painfully against Ellia's bench. Embarrassed, he scraped his tail as he hastily hauled it back to his side of the shack.

A curved sliver of glimmering green showed for a moment and Evansea heard her growl, "Now."

Without putting if off for one other moment, he twitched the internal muscle that released the implanted serum and closed his eyes. There was no way he'd actually fall asleep, the weight of his body against the bench, the roughness of the blanket and the cold sweat forming from the oncoming transformation. He forgot to account for the days of exhaustive swimming, and frankly, in spite of himself, he sank deep below the waves of wakefulness faster than if it had been more than a metaphor.

The curved sliver of green appeared again, and a slow smile grew below it. The smile stayed long after the green had been occluded.

The next morning, Ellia awoke early to the dawn light creeping its way through the crack under the door and the cracks in the walls. She wiggled her toes and stretched out clawless fingers only to yank them back under the blanket. She shivered. A hardy bird chirped outside, and she heard the comforting crash of the waves against the shore. Remembering Evansea, she glanced over and bolted up.

Dead to the world, he slept with the blanket wrapped around him, feet pulled up on to the bench, oblivious to his transformed self. Some things were predictable, like the pale blue-green hair shifted to blond, and his face shape had remaine, but he'd lost a great deal more mass than she'd anticipated. His limbs, arms and legs, were long. As in looong. He'd top Min Soo by a few fingers. A bare shoulder glowed an inflamed red but couldn't hide the whipcord muscles. She'd have to get some medicine when she went into town.

She tugged the still warm blanket around herself and started searching through the cupboards lining the small storage shed. Out came some simple garments including a pair of shoes and pants, sweater and a coat. Moments later, toes exploring the insides of unfamiliar shoes, she slipped out into the day, closing the door behind her. She tucked her hands into the coat's deep pockets and felt the documents four days had managed to create for Evansea. Legit documents

Merdragon

that didn't claim Korean citizenship but provided the appropriate identifications for traveling within the country. The same delivery method for Evansea's documents had been used to reunited hers with her. If there was one thing she didn't need her own crew to handle, it was this.

It used to be easy to fake a document, if one was even necessary. She remembered her early years when Drayvin had showed her recordings of the discussions from 150 or more years ago, before he had even been born. They'd seen the advances coming. The discussions had been passionate at times, debating whether they should focus on forgeries or infiltration. Infiltration won out by a narrow margin. One of Drayvin's earliest jobs had been to plump up established identities for merkin in various countries.

The documents in her pockets were well worth multiple times their weight in plutonium. A legal place of standing on the surface; an ident as legit as any merkin on the surface was to get until merkind became its own accepted citizenry.

The ocean breeze gave her a stiff clap on the back. Wido Island may have been a tourist destination, ideal for a stranger to stroll through, but she still needed to keep her wits. The sun fought the wind to touch her face and hair, the morning light on autumn colours undiluted by seawater. The clarity of sight and the joy in wind currents... She skipped once, twice, snuck a look around, and threw in a quick pirouette.

They'd come to land near a commercial area, and the smells raised her on her toes, of kitchen stoves, cooked meats and vegetables, secret broths and the ever-present kimchi. Ah, cooked food. Salt defined seafood, but above surface, salt didn't need to be so predominant. Her stomach rumbled in anticipation. With her nose as her compass, she sniffed her way to a place serving early and placed an order for two, paying with the money stashed in one of the coat's many pockets. She kept her Korean language skills to tourist basic.

Breakfast in hand, she returned to the shed by a different route. She plopped herself on the grassy ground and ate, savouring every fleck of flavour. A concerning thought attempted an intrusion, but she waved it off. "He'll be fine. I'm sure Min Soo's fine." Finishing with a final, determined smack of her lips, she dismissed the doom cloud and peeked into see Evansea still sleeping. Second portion in her hand, she wistfully gave it a sniff and reluctantly set it inside the shed next to Evansea. He'd need every bite, and more besides, when he eventually woke up. A bit more sleep would do him good. As would a few additions to the clothing stored in the shed.

She took a second walkabout, this time scouting more of the area before going back to the village. On her second return to the shed, she had more food and had managed to find some ointment she hoped would do some good. A pair of boots, a thick sweater, and long coat to hide some of his length and any walking oddities.

The door hung open. A glance inside. Gone. Breakfast, blanket and Evansea. She set her purchases down inside and began a sweep of the surroundings. The sweep was short. In the bushes, off to the left and slightly behind the shed. A fully grown lost boy, in blanket cape wrapped like a kimbap, crouching with knees folded to his chest and intensely focused on the blood oozing from one of those knees.

She cleared her throat. His head flew up, hair flopping. "Honoured one!" he sang his exclamation, a ridiculously round-toned tenor. He stumbled to his feet and hissed in pain.

Ellia froze.

He wiggled his web free fingers and then pointed down at his feet and bounced, grinning, "I have toes."

"It's strange…"

Worry twisted his pale eyebrows. He glanced down at his feet, touched his neck. "What is it? Do I look weird?" He spun around like a puppy chasing its tail. "Do I have a fin somewhere?" He pointed at his bloody knee, "Is it the blood? It'll heal right? Just like at home?"

Cement lock blocks were ka-thunking into place. "…I've only seen that colour in, oh." An entire chandelier lit up in her mind. "Well then, fry. Yeah, uh huh."

"What's the matter? Colour of what?"

She looked him straight in his blueberry and orange-flecked eyes. "I have been played, well and truly and completely. You, my friend, are going to need to wear sunglasses every living minute, midnight included until we get you some coloured contacts."

He went cross-eyed, trying to attempt a mobius trick. "What's wrong with the colour of my eyes?"

"It didn't shift into a traditional, surfacer's norm. You'll have enough troubles with your looks. Don't need to add that." Without the node, there would be little point in knowing a few home truths. "But now you really need to put on more than that blanket."

He took a step forward. Then another. The dimmer switch for his face spun back up to maximum. "Honoured one, this is sooo cool. I can't wait to try running."

Merdragon

She shook her head in wonder. Evansea was different. Different in more than his physical aspects. She couldn't quite pin it down. Time would tell if it related to his eyes.

"I dropped off some additional surface gear for you in the shed. You've watched the how-to videos, right? As part of your training?"

Still fascinated by his toes and the process of walking, he nodded.

It had been years since she'd consciously thought through the process of walking, one foot falling after the other, after the other, after the other. Now she saw it again in Evansea's gleeful concentrated focus. A strobe light of facial expressions. Focus. Glee. Focus. Glee. Step forward. Step to the side. Step forward. A daring step back. Ellia quick jumped to prevent the fall, a hand between his shoulder blades. It took more than the regular amount of muscle to give him support. She guided him to the shed, pointed to the pile and the medicine. Outside she waited on standby in case he needed instructions not covered by the lab vids.

The door opened, and his first words in something close to relief were, "No zippers."

A smirk crossed her face, "One danger at a time. Speaking of which, did you," she sniffed, "yup, you did. Any problems with the ointment or bandaging? Can't have you walking around in public with a bloody knee. Your looks and teetering are going to be eye catchy enough."

Necessities taken care of, they set out slowly to get Evansea fully adjusted to his legs. Walking along beside him, Ellia kept careful watch, but after the third hurried whisper from a passing couple she took another head-to-toe overview of his appearance.

"Evansea?"

"Yes, honoured one?" he replied, coming to a swaying stop so he could turn to look down at her.

She pointed over to a tree with a bench beside it. "Go, sit over there and avoid making eye contact with anyone."

"Certainly, honoured one," he replied.

Twenty some years of not having that title spoken at her every day and now Evansea seemed fixated. She waited until he reached the bench then entered a nearby shop. An eclectic shop, perfect for visitors. She picked out a ballcap from one end, chose a pair of sunglasses from a rack near the register, and just as the junk food section caught her eye, she heard a middling commotion coming from outside. Quickly she paid, cut off a couple about to exit with an apology, and stepped out to see a group of people blocking her view of where Evansea had been situated.

The sound of camera shutters snagged on her ears. Smartphones were up, accompanied by whispers of "so cute" and "handsome". Not the horror she'd imagined but not fantastic. High school students on a trip together had gathered, and, sneaking a peek between them, she had to blink at the toothache inducing sweetness. Evansea, kneeling on the ground, petting and making faces, cooing nonsense and generally emitting photoshoot adorable, at his first meeting of a dog. She shook her head. After the guide fish gushing, she should have expected it. Maybe she should have asked if seals tended to trail after him too. Raising herself up on her toes she estimated the crowd quantity and the likelihood of its mass increasing. A higher percentage than preferred.

Casually she stepped toward the college grad female owner of the dog and greeted her with a pleasant nod. Intentionally in English, "Nice dog."

The girl gave her the classic inspection of who is this person, and do they have relationship rights that I don't know about with this target I am attempting to flirt with? Do I have the assets to defeat this potential rival? "Thank you," about covered the entire silent conversation.

The dog's cold nose bumped against Ellia's knee and she reached down to pet its head, brushing against Evansea's fingers in the process. Ignoring her "Keep your eyes down" instructions, he looked up, wide-eyed with wonder, "Honoured one, it's a dog..." Ellia gave him a quick shake of her head; he'd sung it. Lips pressed shut, he slowly rose to his feet giving the dog a final pat as he did so. Ellia nodded her farewell to the twenty-something-ish and led the way out of the semi-circle. A breeze of sighs ruffled Ellia's irritation.

Not saying a word, she walked a ways before handing Evansea the hat and glasses. A few left, right, left, right angled turns later she could only hope they'd lost any aegyo-seekers.

In English, "Keep those glued to you from now on." She refused to crane her neck to see his reaction. "Seriously hoping I don't regret making you my choice. Should have chosen Raf Ellis. Do remember to speak either Korean or English. Do you have French in your pocket? According to your passport you're Canadian. You did get the sleep-teach before we left?"

"Didn't need to on the languages, I've got aptitude, so they've been loading me up, I think I'm on my twelfth one now, but" he hung his head, "I forgot, just now."

"Understandable..."

Merdragon

"What's that?" Something had distracted him. A shiny, new, something.
They dodged from one shiny thing to another and Ellia let him. By day's end he'd mastered the walk and developed his own signature style. He'd even managed to try out "the run".

That evening, lights out, she brought him back to the beach. He was a merguard, trained fighter for the merKing. On the shore Ellia retrained him to use his legs rather than his tail; retrained him to fight using different elevations rather than the varying dimensions and orientations allowed by water; retrained him to apply his advanced skills on land. She had her skills, he had his; might as well use them, no shame in admitting his top game was different than hers.

Slumping down in the rocky sand after hours of practice, Ellia slipped off her shoes and dabbled her toes in the cold waves. She cautioned Evansea, "Remember, if it rains or someone splashes you, the water isn't going to magically transform you back into mer-form. You control the change. However, and I know they told you this, but I can't emphasize it enough, if you land in water deeper than you can stand, your instinct will be to swim or breathe. Don't. You act on that instinct and you will change."

"Yes, honoured one," he replied carefully in Korean, matching her choice. She'd been throwing him language curveballs, too. He pointed out at the seaweed line left by the tide, "Because of tides?"

"The ocean has a different face when viewed up top. And that's another thing, keep the respectful speech, but drop the "honoured one". In Korean you'll have to come up with a different honourific."

"Sir! The team's been highjacked."
"Highjacked?!" Danube Sr. slapped his hand on the technician's chair and leaned over to see the screen.

The technician pointed at a night-vision view of the desert warehouse and a cargo helicopter. "There. See that?" Three people in utilities, armed and—most telling—not pointing their weapons at the four-legged being walking in their midst.

The chair's stuffing grumbled under Danube's grip. "Where's the pilot?"
No words, just a zoom-in on the cockpit. The pilot was fine. Finely prepping for flight and under total compulsion. No maydays, no attempts at starting an ammo exchange, nothing.

A long stream of words spat from Danube's mouth in shades of sewage and whistle shards that made the technician cringe in actual physical pain. Danube straightened, still spitting out an occasional pitch of ice-picks, and began pacing. On each about-turn he glared at the table holding the stolen node. A message symbol appeared on the lower corner of the technician's screen.

"A message, sir."

"Play it."

"Read only, sir."

Danube stopped his pacing and glared at the technician. "Read it then."

The technician opened the message and did. "HO - mK MSH il inj".

With a trembling hand Danube rubbed his eyes, his complexion deepening in colour. "Again."

Voice shaking, the technician repeated the nonsense. Danube slowed to a full stop. His face lost all expression and his colouring downgraded to neutral. "What was the name of that fool who took Joon Ho's place?"

The technician pulled up a file on his screen. "Han Min Soo, sir."

"No, switch that around to merkin standard." *Danube picked up the node and began rolling it between his hands like a basketball.* "This confirms where the winged spawn's been. I refuse to use her title," *he spat.* "She's met the merKing and that idiot was part of the conversation. MSH. Min Soo Han." *He spat again.* "'il' has to mean the island and the only reason our spy would risk revealing his position is if "inj" means what I think it does. Injected."

"Sir?"

"I'm not going to lose anyone else to that thing we dredged out of Iceland. Track it for now and we'll address this," *he tossed the node up a few centimetres into the air,* "with Mr. Han's assistance. The cat's not going to follow instructions without the UnMaker. Mr. Han will be more manageable. The merdragon has the UnMaker. If we get this Min Soo, we'll have both a spare key and a remote control for the test tube brat. Once I get what I want, I'll send her out to clean up that nuisance piece of toxic garbage." *Danube pulled out his phone to place a call.* "Darya? Get a team to collect Min Soo Han."

A few questions, updates and instructions bounced back and forth until Danube finished with, "The merdragon can blame herself for injecting her newest pet with the island's current access keys. Getting past that ridiculous door won't be a problem, and with the node, we won't need the Master key inside."

Merdragon

On Evansea's second leg day, Ellia took it easy. His groans and winces did little to keep his grins down to manageable, and despite the uncoordinated gear, or perhaps because of it, he was not blending into the background. They stood with other early morning travelers, waiting for the ferry ride back to the mainland. Upon its arrival, boarding, Evansea maneuvered to shield Ellia from the natural jostling. She frowned to herself when one particular jostle touched on his wrenched shoulder.

Under the noise of the ferry, she made a note to herself, "Bodyguard behaviour needs a little redirection and rebranching."

Arriving on the mainland, they caught a bus heading toward Seoul. It creaked when they stepped on. Evansea gleefully took in the sights, engaged with shopkeepers and smacked his lips in satisfaction every time he tasted a new dish. He'd developed from the reserved merguard who'd first electrocuted her. Ellia clicked her nails in concern at his transformation. He did manage to mellow a degree or so by the time they reached Seoul. The training she'd run through with him had shown he hadn't lost his merguard abilities, but she wondered if Evansea had reacted in a mild, unanticipated way to the serum.

Observing from the store where she'd purchased a tourist's temp phone, and seeing as how his glee had settled a little, Ellia decided to overlook the oddity for now. She placed a call to Riko.

He answered, "Who is this?"

"Riko-ssi, you have got to work on the phone mannerism," Ellia chided.

"Honoured one? You're back?" He sounded almost happy.

"Update me."

He swore, "I know nothing 'cept your plaything's about to get torn right out of that nest you two got and I ain't contemplating what they plan on doing once they get 'im."

The phone casing cracked in the palm of her hand. "Elaborate, fast."

Rapid-fire he told her the plan in progress. Riko would've had to be texting to not hear the growl growing in Ellia's throat.

"Listen carefully, you're going to drive down to my present location and pick up a parcel, then—"she laid out her instructions finishing with, "Fail to deliver and you'll never get rid of the burn marks." With the subtly of radioactivity she added, "A reminder that without the UnMaker, Darya's chances have decreased to me."

"Yes, honoured one."

Click.

She double-timed it to Evansea, short-hand briefed him, then grabbed a waiting taxi. Driving off, the phone screen lit her face in the steadily decreasing daylight, thumbs in full war-mode as messages sent her mini-fleet into action. An hour's drive and she took scope of her surroundings. As good a place as any. She tapped on the driver's shoulder, and, paying him, she stepped out onto the street.

The streetlamp earned a rolled eye. "Your cons are outweighing the pros right now, you understand?"

Closing her eyes, she visualized the maps she'd been memorizing. "Good place to jump should be," she opened her eyes to turn, "in that direction."

By the time she'd reached her launch pad, night had properly fallen. She dialed the phone and started running.

Gravity?

Two and a half months after finding the good-bye note, Min Soo received a call on his phone from an unknown number. Six months ago, as a celebrity with a recognizable voice, he would have ignored the call and let it go to voicemail. An hour ago, he'd been in the middle of prepping for an event when Artist Gabriel had sent him to the roof with his gliding gear. He answered the phone, "Hello?"

"Min Soo! It's me, Ellia."

His eyes rounded in shock, "Ellia? You, you're..."

She interrupted, "No time for that, there's some serious unpleasantness heading your way. Interference is in place, but they're also trying to minimize attention. You've got the gliding gear?"

The sound of wind blew harsh against his ears from her end. "Yeah, I have it, and getting a little chilled here on the roof."

"Hold off until they start taking down the door before you take the leap."

"I'm doing this in the city?" Flustered, "Are you sure? I suspect that's illegal. And dangerous."

The sound of a wind gust distorted her words. "... shish kebab. I'm already on my way, Min Soo." He heard a flap of her wings and a breathy, "Head southeast and do try to avoid helicopters and floodlights."

"Did Artist Gabriel tell you about the event I'm supposed to be at tonight. Do Hyun's on standby."

He heard a mild shriek, a sudden steady blowing and a few fading squawks. He thought he heard a faint, "Silly thing, get out of my hair." A sudden snap and Ellia's voice came back at regular volume, "Min Soo? We still connected?"

"Yeah, you okay?"

"Stupid birds. Distracted flying, I don't recommend it. See you soon."

The call ended and he eyed the phone and then the roof door suspiciously. "So, was that a yes or a no?" An inhale and a sigh that came from the deeps. "The glider was your idea, Min Soo, transformer time."

The glider in question had gone through some improvements since he'd first flown it. He tugged on the straps to make sure they were snug, and snapped out each spring-loaded wing before pulling them back in. Ready, he attached an earpiece to his ear and secured his phone. He walked out to the parapet and crouched down to wait.

And waited. And shifted his weight to the other leg. Decided to put on the goggles and gloves.

The training sessions he'd received kept him from jumping at every sound, but the tension rose with every passing minute. He shifted again. Adjusted his goggles. One minute or one hour, he was starting to wonder if the whole thing was a waking, perverse, wish fulfillment dream. Anything to see Ellia again, to know he—he shifted again—that she—he stood up.

The doorknob rattled.

He didn't wait. He leapt up onto the parapet and kicked off into the dark, out of sight before the door-rattler got past the barricades. The glider wings snapped out on a prayer and on cue. He hooked his loose foot into the horizontal support. A relieved smirk touched his lips, and with renewed confidence, he brought to mind every bit of Ellia's instructions. A vagrant current found a wing tip. He nodded at his reflection in a window and caught an updraft to keep himself aloft and flying east.

The conversation was one-sided.
"Mr. Han's gone, sir."
"Nope, nothing on the pavement."
"We've got Eric in the news 'copter?"
"Understood. We'll follow the drones."

A stray floodlight kissed the edge of a wing; Min Soo slipped quickly sideways and hoped no one had been paying attention. Riding an up-current alongside another glass encased building, he came around the corner. Suddenly the odd heartbeat thump sound he'd been wondering at came into full force. A helicopter.

He nearly stalled in his effort to pull back, floundering, falling. Cold spikes drove up his spine as he shut down the panic and focused on straightening out his form. Regaining some control many metres lower, he took an angled look at the helicopter and realized it was heading away from him going south. It had just passed in front of him, hidden by buildings. Now he had a bigger problem. Altitude. He'd lost a bad amount of it. Soon any random glance upward would catch sight of him, coming down without a landing plan or permit.

"I'm sure I saw him. Turn around."

Merdragon

"Get the drones up."

"Where is that flying fox?" He grit his teeth trying to think of an alternate emergency plan. Something better than landing on a rooftop dinner party.

Then he heard the distant thump, thump sound of the helicopter again. Behind him.

"Ellia, where, oh where are you?" He craned his neck to catch a glance between his feet, over his shoulder—nothing. The glider didn't give him a lot of freedom to just turn and look around like Ellia could. He swallowed convulsively, his hands getting damp inside his gloves. The gloves kept his hands warm and tight on the handling grips, but he really wanted to wipe them off along with the cold sweat developing on his forehead, despite the November temperatures.

The hissed "Ready!" was his only warning. Diving sideways under him, Ellia snatched the tow rope and pulled. Hard. If his harness had been even a little loose, he was sure he'd be out of it. His eyes teared up behind his goggles as the wind whipped against every bare spot of flesh. Around the next building she flew like a bat on nitro, and Min Soo held on for dear life, barely managing to keep from spilling air.

"He was absolutely right there. I swear I saw green scales."
"Sir! It's her. There's not a chance we're going to catch him now."
"Drones almost have him? Yes, sir."

Around another building, face to face with a drone. She dove for a dark space like she knew its name. The wind howled after them, clawing to keep up. She dropped the rope, climbed ahead of him, doubled back. Blind to his rear, he heard the sound of a mechanical whine and metallic crunch.

In front of him, a drone dropped into view. He couldn't stop. Coming up over him, Ellia spun and baseball thwacked the drone with her tail. Another crunch as it cracked against a concrete wall. He kept going and pretended the red dot had been his imagination. His stomach clenched as she slid beneath him to grab the rope, twisted once to give him a fiery grin, and up she pulsed her wings, climbing, climbing. She dropped the rope again and he lost sight of her.

"Fall back?"
"Changing tactics. Leave off."
"Darya?"

Min Soo's phone rang in his ear. Automatically he answered it, "Hello?"

"Hi, stranger," Ellia's voice melted in his ear. The sound of her wingbeat came down from over his right wing. "You doing okay?"

His hands squeezed hard on his handling grips. "It's good to see you."

Ahead of him her tail abruptly dipped, and one wing jerked. She'd tripped midair. A silent response.

"Ellia?"

He saw her crush the phone with her clawed hand and open it again to let the crumbs fall away. She glanced over her shoulder, and he saw her eyes burning with their signature green fire. He felt an old familiar paralysis kick in at that moment, but then she twisted, and by some quick mean feat she suddenly faced him, snaked her hands up behind him, pulled herself up until they were a mere breath apart. Then tucked in her wings. The glider creaked at the sudden additional weight.

Min Soo swallowed hard, paralysis tingling along his extremities. "Ellia, what are you doing?"

"Hiding," she answered unexpectedly.

"Hiding?" he blurted out.

He felt her tail fin curl itself around his feet. The glider wobbled, and Ellia slid against him making some adjustments to their joint balance.

Heart pounding, Min Soo took a gulping breath and tried to stay calm. "Hiding. Explain. Please."

Mercifully Ellia closed her eyes, but then she snuggled up to him to speak directly in his ear, "One is better than two; reflective, pearlescent wings are more conspicuous than black fabric; I'm exhausted from pretending to be an aerobatic fighter jet. Good to see you too."

He closed his eyes and muttered something unintelligible. The smell of seawater filled his senses. Which reminded him of landing. "Where, um, are we going to land?"

With innocent surprise she asked, "Haven't you been paying attention?"

He frowned and opened his eyes to try mentally GPS-ing the streets and buildings below. Her face kept getting in the way. "I'm not sure. To be honest, I'm a little disoriented."

She leaned her head back rather alarmingly in Min Soo's opinion and scanned the cityscape. Her arms tensed against him.

That's when he noticed. "What are you wearing?"

Merdragon

She raised her head and gave him a wink, "It's my LBD."

Years of international modeling experience came to the rescue. "Little black dress?"

"Yes. Bank a little to the right, would you?"

He complied automatically, still not sure where they were. Then he noticed something else, skin where there should have been scales. A narrow-eyed inspection revealed her rather pinched face. In disbelief,

"Are you crazy? What are you doing?!"

"We don't have time, my ~whistle-click~. The glider's good for it and I need to be able to walk once we land. Gotta get the prince to the ball on time."

"Are we even...?"

"Your manager's probably met Artist Gabriel or Ampara by now." She bit her lip, and he felt her grip tighten around him. "Have to focus now, 'kay? Just keep flying straight."

Refusing to shut his eyes, he witnessed the fine dust falling away from her into the wind, dust that glimmered as briefly as ember flying from a campfire. He clenched his jaw shut. Questions would wait. Including a translation of whatever she'd called him. And why he'd suddenly become a target.

Stolidly he flew as Ellia transformed against him. No leisurely change, she was shredding herself hard. His chest grew hot, and he heard her start keening in that unbelievable voice. It hurt to listen; he couldn't imagine how it hurt to endure. The sound began to fade, but he couldn't be sure if it had simply gone beyond his hearing range. With relief he realized that it coincided with the sensation of feet curled around his legs and the complete dissolution of her wings. Her face made him less happy.

"Ellia? I think I recognize this area. If I'm right, that over there, with all the lights and cars, is the place I'm supposed to be."

The hands that were clasped around him felt blunter, no talons to rip him open. It terrified him to think of how weak those hands might be. Her feet too, instead of her tail fins, were wrapped around his and felt fragile in comparison to her fierce tail.

Tiredly she spoke with a rasp, "I need to turn around." The flames in her eyes hadn't dimmed. "This is what we'll do..."

Flying high, wireless, she pretzel-ed herself, first twisting her lower half and then her top half. Min Soo stayed as solid as possible, counter-balancing the air-slips she repeatedly caused. Finally, it was his turn. He took a reassuring breath, calmly released the handling grips and wrapped his arms around her as snuggly as his long arms could manage. He felt her weight the instant she released her grip on the glider struts to grab the handles. The glider shuddered as control transferred from one master to another.

As soon as her hands were firmly in place, she aimed them down toward a dark copse of a mini park. Across the street, Min Soo spotted a dark van that strongly resembled his, just as Ellia tilted them and began a downward spiral. Min Soo shut his eyes and focused on holding Ellia tight, fighting the dizzying effects of circle after circle. Lower and lower until the muscles in her back clenched in an aggressive straighten and stall. He opened his eyes and shook his feet free with a quick snap, hit the ground with a skip, hop, and Ellia braced them against a tree to end their momentum.

Arms locked around her, surrounded by a tiny pocket of privacy, they breathed together, recovering.

He spoke first, "Let's not do that again."

She tapped his arms, and he slowly unclenched his death grip. "I agree. Not for another week at least." Turning around she reached for a strap, "Let me help you get that glider off and folded up."

Clicks and clacks, unsnaps and a groan as Ellia lifted the glider off his shoulder. He stretched his neck and cautiously rolled his shoulder.

"Nice landing." Min Soo snapped around and winced as he felt his shirt graze the raw skin beneath.

Artist Gabriel in full black, nondescript and grinning. Strolling up behind him, Ampara in a full length dark grey coat loaded with pockets.

"Anyone have a spare coat and shoes for me?" Ellia asked.

Dismay replaced the grin. "Señorita Ellia, I regret, the necessity did not cross my mind." He gestured toward the second van now visible behind Min Soo's manager's.

Ampara sniffed, "Pfft, it is but a few steps away."

"So much love. Thanks, Hugh."

Min Soo glanced down at Ellia's bare feet then knelt down on one knee. He gave her a sardonic half-smile. "It's the infamous piggy-back again. I thought I was safe." Mockingly he added, "and you're not even Korean."

"If I was still in, you know, my other, uh, gear, you'd be princess-hauling me, so don't complain."

"The conversations I have with you are never going to be normal, are they?" he asked as she draped herself over his shoulders.

Ampara snorted and picked up the collapsed glider.

Merdragon

"Probably not," she agreed, and oofed as Min Soo stood up.

He started walking, frowning at the lighter-than-normal-for-her weight of her frame. She'd seemed a good deal heftier when she'd come careening toward him like a heat-seeking missile. Experimentally, not thinking, he squeezed her legs to confirm his concern.

Draped over his back she breathed into his ear, "~whistle-click~ you may be, but I'm no market chicken to be tested for tenderness."

He nearly dropped her; the whistle-click held a suggestive note. The gurgle from her stomach gave an entirely different suggestion.

Artist Gabriel checked the road for traffic and waved at them to cross. "Come. While you get attired, we will make sure to provide our Ellia with sustenance. Come, come."

"What about whoever was chasing me?" Min Soo asked and set Ellia down beside the rearmost van.

Ellia balanced on the balls of her feet, a hand on the door handle, and gave him a sideways look. Suspiciously apologetic. "You like dolphins, right?"

"Sure, who doesn't?"

"Keep that in mind." She nudged him toward his van. "Go. It'll be hard enough getting yourself gussied up in there without wasting more time. You're going to be exceedingly fashionably late. The hunters will have to wait if they haven't already jumped ahead."

Almost, almost he refused, but then the shifting of her bare feet on cold pavement and the goosebumps developing on her arms convinced him. "Fine, fine, I'll go, but I want to see you before I head in there," he said with gesture toward the other rear entrance of the event.

"I'm not taking off, don't worry. Go."

He swiveled on his heel and went.

Ampara opened the van door for Ellia before Min Soo had even taken two steps. "Time's short. Riko says Darya and Danube are here. Claims he knows nothing about the node. Jun Sung and I are going to try tracking it down while they're aiming for you and Min Soo."

It didn't need a reply. She jumped into the van's stripped down, warm interior. Ampara closed the door behind her. Her eyes beelined on the mini buffet.

"Ellia-nim! You're here."

She snatched the densest, calorie and nutrient rich thing she could find before turning toward the greeting. Evansea.

"Wow."

He spun in the chair, dressed—she thought about it for a moment—yes, expensively.

"Is it good?" He frowned and shook his very recently trimmed and styled hair. "Honoured one, that Riko is not to be trusted." A napkin lay crumpled in a trashcan nearby. He'd been at the mini buffet while waiting for her.

She chewed fast and reached out to pat him on the arm. "Mmhmm, good, and stop calling me that. Did he give you any trouble?"

He tugged on the lapels of his designer suit jacket, "I believe his tongue may recover." The wristwatch he wore sent a shard of light in Ellia's eye, blinding her with a wink. He shook it clear of his cuffs. "Señor Seung and Monsieur Ampara seem nice. Smart too. Riko dropped me off with them at what I think was a men's clothing store, and," his voice hushed down, "they gave me the passcode phrases, but they're not like us."

A glass of something sweet and sticky washed down the last of Ellia's first dish. "They know not to ask questions. Do avoid volunteering any answers. I give them enough goodies to make it all worthwhile and friendly for all of us." She narrowed in on another delightful stomach-full and started fast snacking. Her eyes roamed over the van's accoutrements and gear. "I like them." A napkin served its purpose, and she stood to a slight stoop to walk the couple steps required to reach the clothing rack. Shoe rack included.

Behind her Evansea asked, "What's the operation? These clothes seem like they'd stand out more than blend in."

As she prepped, she told him why and what for. It took as long as she needed to turn into a celebrity's minion.

The driver door opened. Ampara peered in around the edge of the seat, "Getting chilly out here and Monsieur Han's stepping out of his van."

"Intro music," Ellia said and whistled final instructions. The side door slid open and Ellia stepped out. Evansea followed and the van springs sighed in relief.

They'd entered by the rear door and found their way to the silk and glitter. Ellia and Do Hyun stayed along the walls while Min Soo, dressed in multi-textured black, and a glinting green diamond necktie pin, met with those reporters officially attending. Cameras flashed—and flashed twice as often after spotting

Merdragon

Evansea. In shades of tropical ocean, he lingered with energy near Min Soo's side, a mystery steadily attracting attention.

Standing along the wall with Min Soo's manager, Ellia commented, "Do you ever feel like a hobbit in the elf kingdom?"

"Until they burp or fart," he replied.

Ellia burst out laughing. A few glanced in her direction and she cut the laugh short.

Wiping a tear from the corner of her eye, "Especially when they've been indulging in some good old home cooking, oh man."

"Shh!" he warned as Min Soo approached with an unhappy expression.

To his manager, "I forgot my cellphone at home. Do me a favour and get it for me, would you?"

Torn between his duties at the event and his personal duties toward Min Soo, he hesitated. Ellia patted him on the shoulder, "Don't worry, I'll watch he doesn't let anything loose."

He snorted. Furtively he checked if Min Soo had caught on but only impatience marred the professional perfection. He nodded and hurriedly left.

Min Soo watched him go, "He's a good guy. Have to make sure he doesn't get in trouble for this."

"He's not going to be happy when he finds you've got the phone stashed in your inside pocket. Did you spot our target?"

"No, Evansea did. After this I'm expecting a full introduction. He's got some skills."

"Where?"

"Next floor up. Who is he? Evansea says he has an entourage."

"Well-muscled, I bet. It's Riko's father, Danube Sr. I'll meet you up there."

Min Soo stood still as a photograph, pale white skin, black eyes following as Ellia invisibly passed through the moneyed gowns, domestic and foreign alike. "I happen to come with muscles too, you know." He mused on her invisibility; it served a purpose, but he did not like it. Evansea's exclamation of amazement carried over the general hum of the room, and Min Soo raised a corner of his lip in sarcastic amusement. The plan progressed.

Spinning on his heels, he returned to Evansea's general vicinity, brushing past a slight grip on his sleeve. Evansea, who'd gathered a circle, flashed him a smile while shamelessly attracting attention. Min Soo allowed the unrelated anger that had been slowly building leak onto his face as he strode up to Evansea and briefly grasped his elbow. He leaned over with a carefully constructed sotto voice intended to carry, "Cool it."

With an equally constructed face of injured innocence, Evansea jerked his elbow out of Min Soo's grasp. "What the matter with you?"

Ears perked up, eye corners were in full use, the infamous façade of Han Min Soo could possibly be about to express a genuine emotion.

Min Soo's lips quivered into the hint of a snarl, "We need to head to the roof."

"Hey, yah, great idea. I heard someone say there's some really cool water fountain up there, let's go." He bowed, or rather bobbed in his energy to the circle, obstructing an outstretched hand, pale blond hair flopping over his eyes. "I'll be leaving first, thank you."

Speculative eyes followed the pair. Nearly twins in presence and build, one dark and ramrod straight, an obsidian pillar, expressionless, the other as flighty as concert laser lights, changing shape and darting from one topic of interest to another. Evansea jostled against his black pillar companion and pointed out another muscle standing near an exit.

Min Soo gave Evansea a distasteful frown with a hair of a nod. A clap on the back directed him away from a camera man. A clumsy elbow marked a woman whose face Min Soo tried to attach to a memory. The memory slipped, distracted. Who was Evansea? Min Soo gave him a raised eyebrow but quickly followed it with a mirror trained ugh.

Trusting Evansea would follow, Min Soo made his way to the glass elevator. He stepped inside with two other passengers. Evansea slid in just before the doors closed shut. Min Soo let the tension suffocate the lift as it struggled to rise.

The doors opened and Evansea jumped out. He threw out his arms, and Min Soo dodged with a "Yaa!"

Heads turned and neighbours signaled to each other. A repetitive night of posing for cameras and schmoozing to get ahead had a chance of being upgraded with a new boss-fight sequence.

"Rockin' amazing!" Evansea grabbed Min Soo's shoulder and surreptitiously pointed out an older man, whispered, "That's Danube," and his men. Louder, "It's a pool with a fountain!"

A fountain and pool, in November. Ice themed with music and lights. Nobody was swimming. Evansea didn't need to point out Ellia.

A server passed by and Min Soo grabbed a drink to occupy his hands. Evansea jostled against him and Min Soo grit his teeth. "Watch it!" he spit out the corner of his mouth, playing the game with his eyes focused on the other side of the pool. He didn't much like the aggressive lean in Danube's stance. Nor the fact that he'd seen him before.

Guilelessly Evansea bounced in front of him and started walking backwards. "What's your problem bro, loosen up." He jumped back beside Min Soo and shouldered him into a stagger. A titter and a few tut-tuts added to the rising ambiance. Talk hadn't stopped. Min Soo heard his name, saw a camera flash.

He grabbed Evansea's arm, "If that's Danube Sr., I've seen him before. He said he knows my family." The words didn't travel far.

The message did. Evansea draped an arm over Min Soo's shoulder, then danced back as he was shrugged off. "I'm just playing bro, come on." He spun and started charming his way in Ellia's direction. A black hole and an orbiting blue diamond comet, their deadly gravity drew more and more attention to an oncoming collision. Event security was being drawn in with every inevitable stride Min Soo took.

"Give back what you stole." That was Ellia's voice pleading.

"Meet me during regular hours at the office and we'll discuss it." Too many cameras. Danube wanted Min Soo, not attention. He inclined to add, "I'm not the only thief. If I can't have my dagger, I'll take yours."

"You're a busy man, you're never available," Ellia protested volubly, innocence frustrated beyond endurance.

Danube's phone buzzed in his pocket and he stepped back to answer it. Ellia signaled Evansea.

He leapt forward and clapped Danube on the shoulder, knocking the phone from his hand. A guard went for it. Min Soo raised a hand to his head in feigned horror and helpfully went for it too. A well-placed toe-kick sent it under Ellia's accidental heel.

A crunch and a collective gasp.

Apologies all around, Evansea, Min Soo, Ellia circling, moving. A hand grabbed Min Soo by the elbow, and he looked down. He frowned; a cannon ball blew through a memory door. The girl from the advertising shoot, from months ago. What was she trying to do?

"Come on, security's here, let me get you outta here." Her eyes pled with him; he took a step.

A guard flew between them, breaking her hold. Min Soo retraced the trajectory—Ellia. She gave him a bizarre swish of her hips before turning back to Danube. A touch on his arm and suddenly Ellia's movement made sense. He stumbled back into a low table, conveniently taking out the knees of one of

Evansea's opponents; he flashed a grin of thanks. Min Soo stumbled over the table toward Ellia. A splash caught his ear, Evansea must have scored.

Only, Ellia's expression said not.

He spun around.

Waves sloshed against the side of the pool, and people had pulled away but were now drawing back to see the damage.

Ellia was beside him, tugging on his sleeve. "He can't swim."

Startled, "You mean he's not a...?" He shrugged out of the jacket and kicked off his shoes.

"I'll explain later. He needs help now."

With a last glance at her, he tossed her his watch and dove into the pool.

Deep, but not Olympic pool deep, Evansea waited, serene as an esoteric emperor with a hand raised for rescue. Min Soo took the offered hand and put in the extra effort required to return them both to the surface, up to the edge of the pool. Helpful hands reached in to pull them out and Min Soo pointedly refused to look at Evansea. A senior server had towels at the ready and all three of them were escorted to the side as police officers finally arrived to sort out the scene.

Climbing down the service stairs, Ellia asked, "Did we keep them occupied long enough with our performance?"

"All we needed was a director to yell cut," Min Soo quipped to Evansea.

The senior server, or rather Artist Gabriel, replied as he opened the door on the third level down from the top, "Last message I received, Riko got them past the initial security, but then I disconnected to come assist you. A marvelous brawl."

In the darkened halls, Gabriel handed Min Soo and Evansea a pair of bathrobes.

Evansea took his and clapped Min Soo on the back. Min Soo visibly winced. "You know, once I heard that the hon-," Ellia hissed at him, "I mean, uh, noona? Yeah, noona and you were, well, that. I looked you up before we came back," hiss, "and the... For a bit there I thought you were really mad for real."

Min Soo gave an almost laugh, a slightly explosive huh, "It was easy playing off your idiot act."

Ellia took the bathrobe from Min Soo and opened it up for him. "We'll take another service exit this time. Gabriel, I'll get them home. You go check on Ampara and Jung."

Merdragon

Min Soo interrupted, "Ellia, I've met Danube—that's his name, right?—before, at the gallery, months ago. He said he knew my family."

Everybody paused.

Ellia spoke into it. "Okay, I'll look into it. I've mentioned before that holding surfacers hostage isn't really our modus operandi, but there's always a first time."

They started hurrying down the hall again when Ellia asked, "Wait, we have wheels, right?"

Later, courtesy of a mildly miffed manager, back at the parking garage beneath Min Soo's apartment, Ellia scouted ahead for other tenants before signaling the all-clear for the two bathrobed men. The three of them got into the elevator and she stood, fancifully she thought, as a wildflower bookmarked between mystery and mischief. She was certain the security guard on CCTV duty choked on his night duty lunch. He couldn't see Min Soo had already started to shiver.

They arrived at the apartment door, and Ellia put out a hand to stop Min Soo from keying in the entry passcode. She gestured to Evansea, "I realize you've made each other's acquaintance, but allow me to be a bit more formal. Evansea, I'd like you to meet our host, Han Min Soo-ssi."

Taking his cue from Ellia's manner, Evansea bowed courteously, "Pleased to meet you, I am in your care."

Ellia turned to Min Soo, "Min Soo-ssi, allow me to introduce you to ~whistle~mersong~, merGuard to the merKing."

In introducing Evansea Krakenkiller, she did so properly. Quietly, but with full respect to his name. The sound echoed of a sunset sky over calm bloody ocean water. A sound that sent proper shivers through sound insulated floors and walls.

She translated it into sounds Min Soo could reproduce.

"Evansea Krakenkiller," Min Soo repeated, sounding out the unusual name. In a slight daze, he opened the door and they filed in. The door shut with a click. Then his eyes widened, "Mer what? To what mer what?"

Shaking himself out of his own gobsmacked state, Evansea bounced on his toes then circled Ellia to put his chin on her shoulder, "I'm hungry."

Ellia side-stepped to lose him, slipped on her slippers and tsked him. To Min Soo's raised eyebrow, she reminded him, "Remember my dolphin question?" She crossed her arms and toed a spare set of slippers to Evansea. "He's reacting unexpectedly to the transformation serum. There are various reactions, but I haven't heard of it affecting personality. Down under he's a rather earnest, straightlaced type, but since he gained legs, he's become a playful, but still deadly, puppy. Heart's still good, and he did particularly well at the event tonight, so I'm keeping him. It would be terribly shameful at this point for him to be sent home. Not sure if his earnestness would tolerate it."

"Transformation serum? Is that what you use? Is he like you?" She could see the questions rising as the whole day began unwinding in his head. "He's staying with us." That last wasn't really a question.

She gave him a pat on the shoulder. "Time to get out of these wet clothes and take a hot shower. Evansea'll last."

As necessities were dealt with, Ellia stepped aside and placed a phone call. "Artist Gabriel?"

"Señorita Ellia?" he sounded tired. "No luck. Jung and Ampara are safe, but Riko bailed midway."

She closed her eyes and breathed through her nose. "Did they find anything?"

"They were keeping something in Mexico, but they've lost it now."

"Mexico? Do you think it was the node?"

"Is the node sentient and capable of moving on its own?" "Don't be ridiculous. It's basically a juiced up hard drive, not a replicator."

"I don't know what it is then. Honestly, I don't think things are going well in Danube's camp. There's another player, and I think it scared the bravery right out of Riko when he found out his father no longer had control over it."

Ellia paced. The door to the bathroom opened. Min Soo and Evansea traded spaces.

"Did they find out anything else?"

"They heard chatter about getting Min Soo because he had some keys. It wasn't clear. The alarms were going off at the time."

She rubbed her forehead, "This is giving me a headache. Listen Gabriel, find a safe place and hole up for a while."

"I'll send up a prayer and see what other info I can find. Be safe." And that was that.

She tossed the phone on the coffee table as Min Soo came out of his bedroom. "Updates?" he asked.

"I need some sleep. I can't think anymore. Juggling too many fish in the air."

Min Soo shook his head, "With metaphors like that, you do need sleep." He eyed Evansea happily crunching on an apple. "What about him?"

"He's a merguard. He'll find his own spot." She said it loudly enough for Evansea to hear and nod.

Merdragon

Tiredly she added, "If anyone needs me, I'll be dead, sleeping." For the first time she headed toward the bedroom made for her, entered and shut the door behind her.

Two sets of eyes followed her and clearly heard the sound of a well-placed heel on a mechanical bug, crunch.
Min Soo tilted his head for a water drop second of thought. A step came unconsciously. Suddenly Evansea stood in his way.
"Where are you going?" Evansea asked.
Min Soo noticed Evansea's oddly coloured eyes for the first time. "To make sure she's alright."
"But that's noonim's sleeping chamber," Evansea replied. His form of address had changed again.
It had been an excessively long day after months of regularity. "Yes, and?" Min Soo replied obtusely. He took a step to the right, then to the left, and finally stood back at centre, frowning at the blocking Evansea.
"And she's honoured one." Evansea said, as if that explained everything to the foolish top-sider. His arms akimbo, firmly braced on his hips, he stood resisting Min Soo's model dignified attempts to pass.
The statement twigged a topic of curiosity Min Soo had been chewing on ever since he'd heard the phrase from Riko, and now from Evansea. "I've been wondering about that. What is, and why is she, addressed as honoured one?" Merkind whatsis might come out in the story.
Evansea's face clearly showed Ellia had warned him about oversharing. "What did she tell you?" A game of mum's the word at work.
"The first time? A mythical story about a lonely merman and a solitary lady dragon." Min Soo replied and turned toward the kitchen to get himself a glass of water. He followed it by leaning against counter.
A little dumbstruck at first, then Evansea started snickering. "What, you don't believe her?" "
Since that's just the first of a wide span of well camouflaged truths and half-truths, frankly I don't know what to believe." He hid the wince from the almost forgotten night-flight's after-effects.
Evansea hopped up to sit on the counter and rubbed his hands together with glee, "Allow me to illuminate your mind, but first," he leaned closer to Min Soo and peered down at the cup, "could I get one of those?"
Min Soo shrugged, winced, filled another glass and handed it over.

Evansea tasted it, smacked his lips. "Could I get some salt?"

"Haven't seen Ellia do that, at least not since the once," Min Soo commented, sliding the saltshaker Evansea's way, who promptly dumped a proper tablespoon's worth into the glass. Considerably more than Ellia's delicate shake.

"She doesn't need to, just like she doesn't need any artificial serum." He shifted on the counter and swung his legs in a way that reminded Min Soo of Ellia. "Bro, these leg ends are so small an' bulky at the same time, not like my tail." He wiggled his feet and curved them toward each other.

"You know, she sang my full name to introduce me, I rarely hear that, maybe less than my title, we all get them, titles I mean, as soon as we pass our first graduation. I don't even think about it most days, but it's there and it's like your ID passes, license to drive, ID to drink, to work, blub, blub, blub. There are tests you have to a pass to get to the next upgrade, maybe like a promotion? Did you know that Danube's got Gracious? They had to put all sorts of safeguards against him getting access when they exiled him." He made an odd motion with his mouth and neck, like crunching on a shrimp and spitting out bubbles from gills. It caused a coughing gag reaction.

Min Soo reached out to pound him on the back. "You okay?"

"Gah, yeah," he returned the back-pound and Min Soo stumbled forward to one knee with a hiss.

Evansea jumped off the counter with a good thump, apologetic, "Man, sorry, bro, still getting used to all this. Did I really hit that hard?"

Min Soo waved him off, "Nah, just starting to feel the effects of being swung around the skies of Seoul." He grabbed the back of the couch and pulled himself up to lean against it.

"Hah, I've never actually seen her fly," Evansea said wistfully.

"Really? How's that possible?"

Evansea glanced toward Ellia's door and lowered his voice. "We live underwater, remember? She's the embodiment of an old legend, not someone we go on daytrips with; she's part of the history lessons we study growing up. I was still in nursery when she was around." He lowered his voice even more, "Not everybody knows this, but being a merguard...her adopted father...his title is Current Director."

The term didn't translate well, Min Soo shook his head puzzled.

Evansea tried to explain, "You know, like water currents..." He tried to swish a non-existent tail, "What's a good reference? Spy master? Only, instead of only observing the water currents, he manipulates them. He was her teacher and she only ever got fostered out to other top-level max-titleds."

"That's enough," Ellia's voice was firm.

Evansea jumped and Min Soo's back spasmed. "Aw, noonim..." Evansea protested, inadvertently using the form he'd used talking about her to Min Soo.

In the dim light her eyes glittered warning.

"Yes, honoured one," he corrected himself, repeating the odd genuflection Min Soo had first witnessed from Riko.

Ellia waved her hand in forgiveness, "Noonim is fine. Go to sleep and let Min Soo alone."

"But he said he wanted to enter your sleeping chamber!" Evansea couldn't help protesting again.

Min Soo looked at him startled. Were half-truth tall tales a merkind way of life? The longer the tail, the taller the fable?

"I doubt he said it in quite that manner," Ellia chided. In the brief moment Evansea turned his head, Ellia shot a wink in Min Soo's direction. It was his only warning. "Min Soo, you coming?"

Mannequin-faced, he straightened up and sauntered after her as she turned back toward her room.

They left Evansea bewildered on the other side of the door. Min Soo could say he was equally bewildered. He was 99.5% sure Ellia's actions were not the suggested ones.

"Remove your shirt and sit," she said, crouching down next to the bed.

"Excuse me?" He did neither.

She turned back around and lifted out a medical kit. A raised eyebrow and unbridled mischief danced in her eyes like New Year's fireworks. His lip twitched. He pressed them together in a total failure of an attempt to suppress the smile coming up in. Three. Two. One.

A flutter of her hand beside her neck evoked what he could only imagine would have been a flurry of bubbled laughter. She put a finger to her lips and pointed at the chair. "Seriously, though, I almost forgot about the battering you took tonight. I've got some salve and stinky patches for you to sleep in tonight. It'll mitigate the damage."

He sat with a sigh at the vanity-desk and delicately pulled off the button-up nightshirt he'd put on after his shower. A habit he'd only taken to with company. He watched her as she went about the nursing business.

"What's really the deal with Evansea Krakenkiller?" The salve she was slathering over his shoulder cooled the burns he hadn't even noticed.

He hadn't had a chance to see the damage to his back. If Ellia's grimaces were an accurate indication, he wouldn't be doing any shirtless modeling for a bit.

"You noticed, didn't you? Chitter, chitter, chitter, stealth circle, circle, circle, attack and chitter, chitter, chatter. A dolphin." Her hair swung and a strand stuck in the salve. "Sorry, ugh. Not the conditioner I need." She handed him the container of salve. "Here, put this on your chest while I slap on these patches. You're going to need a few." The surface of the round, squat vial had been marked by a simple line-design, flowing in irregular patterns all the way around. He sniffed it. Almost odorless. "A thin layer is all you'll need wherever the skin is raw or broken," Ellia advised. He nodded and began applying.

He heard the sound of a package being ripped open, and instantly a smell struck his nose. The chair creaked with his swift turn to defend himself against whatever horror Ellia had unleashed. "What. Is. That. Smell?"

"About-turn, it's for your own good."

"Did I do something wrong? Have I angered you in some unforgiveable manner?" he asked, leaning away, trying to distance himself from the square patch he could see her dangling in the mirror.

"The smell dissipates fast, but I have to get it on you before it does. The stuff has to penetrate down to your muscles." Without mercy she slapped the first one on, and then more than he cared to count. He had to close his eyes, pinch his nose, and persevere until the all-clear.

A knock came on the door. Ellia went to open it.

"Honoured one?" pause "Ohh…" Min Soo heard the bounce return to Evansea's footsteps as he sang out, "Good-night!" The sound of the balcony door followed shortly after.

"Hmmm," Min Soo replied with a particular nasal quality. He opened his eyes and released the death grip on his nose.

Ellia stood by the open door. The message was clear. The time for his goodnight had arrived. He stood to his feet with a last glance at his graffiti-stickered torso. A careful sniff revealed his nose had either adapted or Ellia had been telling the truth. "Thank you."

"Best thing now is sleep. Good-night, Min Soo, and sorry about all of this."

He did not like that tone. "No, I won't accept an apology, and you are not allowed to disappear." He paused in the doorway and crossed his arms without

Merdragon

letting them rest against his chest. "I never get the full story from you. If you disappear permanently, I might die from curiosity."

The sound of a whale song interrupted any reply Ellia may or may not have made. She snorted instead as Min Soo face-palmed with the ointment-free hand. "Ignore him. It's just a lullaby. Go to sleep and I promise I won't disappear. At least not until tomorrow morning."

"Good-night," he replied, giving up with a sigh, and left with his arms held awkwardly away from the rest of his body.

The first thing Min Soo heard the next morning was the text message beep from his phone.

"You're trending. Paparazzi are camped outside your apartment. Don't do anything stupid." It was from the agency.

He rolled out of bed and stopped. A roll of the shoulders and a back check in the mirror testified to an injury free yesterday. The bed was empty of patches, and he verified that none had migrated to other body parts. With a frown he checked the date on the phone. It matched his memories.

"Ellia?" he called out. He opened his door to see a blanket wrapped Evansea perched on the back of the couch. "Hey, you jumped into a pool last night, right?"

Evansea nodded at him with eyes that said, "Of course, or is this a surfacer memory thing I don't know about."

Min Soo turned around and pointed at his back, "I can't find the stickers Ellia glued on me anywhere. Is that normal?"

"Total absorption. We don't do garbage like you guys do."

"Right. Okay, a mer thing. Any, uh, idea about the compatibility?"

Ellia's voice came around the corner, "Relax, Min Soo, it's no different from giving meds to someone with the blackest, black skin who's on the string-bean spectrum versus someone who'd easily be confused with a giant snowball. If you're human, you're human." She came into view with a towel on her head and continued, "Yes, our DNA, etcetera is a little more programmed, but if you prick us, do we not bleed?"

He twisted in his skin. "That actually feels really good. Why don't you sell it up top through a cover company? You'd make a fortune."

"We do send up stuff all the time, but in idea format. Problem is the Cult keeps running interference. I advised the merKing on this last trip that it's time he sent ambassadors out and about. Have you heard any news yet this morning?"

"Company warned me I'm trending and on the paparazzi radar."

"Good. Contrary to the merKing's new plan, Danube does not want to make merkind presence known. His plans work better in the dark. That's why last night's little ruckus included Evansea."

Min Soo crossed his arms and legs to lean against the kitchen counter. "Mind explaining?"

"They can't kidnap you if there are cameras tracking your every move. I don't have that kind of manpower, especially with the other things I'm trying to track down." She gestured at Evansea, "With him hanging around you, Danube daren't do anything too outrageous because he suspects, rightly, that Evansea is inexperienced up top and might give everything away. He might risk it if nobody was watching," she smiled, and Min Soo finished the sentence, "but cameras."

She nodded and that was how it went. Min Soo attended all his obligations and Evansea bounced around like a demolition-grade maypole ball.

"You sure we can't get to him?" Danube Sr. asked, his face sour.

"Only one way to get the cameras off him and that flamboyant barnacle. The merdragon won't be able to interfere." Darya handed him a tablet with her suggestion.

Danube skimmed the data. A finger tapped at a particular point. "Are you sure we can swing the assignment paperwork? It will expose some of our contacts."

"As sure as anything can be."

"Do it."

Three days later of feeding the piranhas, Ellia sat drinking her mid-morning coffee in the apartment while eyeing Min Soo fidgeting in the apartment. A sedate form of fidgeting. Casual, cool, dignified. He had a question he needed to ask.

Her phone notified her of a message.

A glance and she sat up. Riko'd sent it. "Military service, now." A picture followed. She zoomed in and almost broke the phone.

"Min Soo, call your agent."

He frowned, but dialed asking, "What am I calling about?"

"The military hounds are on their way to collect you for boot camp."

"But I'm not due until next August." "

We can use it, but your PR has to get on it." His agent answered and he quickly gave him the heads up. He didn't stay connected long.

Merdragon

While he was on the phone Ellia dashed to her room and pulled out the LBD that had held more than the merQueen's note. She unsealed one of the many pockets and pulled out a perfume sample sized vial. Two exquisitely small devices floated inside.

Returning, "We have two choices. I can break your arm and defer your enlistment." She shook the vial pinched between her fingers. "Or you just go with it." Shrug. "A fracture would probably have you brought in anyway, and maybe get a contempt ruling thrown at you."

Evansea popped up out of nowhere, as usual, and raised Min Soo's arm, analyzing. "I could do it quick and clean."

Min Soo yanked his arm back, "I'd rather enlist." He crossed his arms, and asked, "Why aren't we fighting this, Ellia, legally?"

She pulled up the photo and showed it to him. His face went white. He swallowed hard as his face flushed back past warm.

"Yeah, I thought I was so smart putting that tracker on Darya's car. Silly me, she'd already placed a night camera in a tree while we went for our joy-flight. So, either you go or your career as you know it is over."

"Why are they doing this? Why are they after me?"

"Evansea?"

"Yes, honoured one?"

"Go watch on the balcony for their arrival."

She shifted impatiently until the balcony door closed. A long thin whistle escaped through her teeth. "The basic, incomplete explanation is that the stuff I gave you that prevented you from dying and then drowning, left a substance in you that Danube needs so he can get access to areas he's been blocked from on the island." She raised a hand to prevent him from interrupting. "Danube, on the other hand, has something crucial to the continued existence of merkind." A hiss escaped her lips. "Imperfectly, I'd say you're bait."

"Bait?!"

"You weren't supposed to be. No one else should have known what I did, but the info proved juicy enough for the worm that planted the parasite in the merKing's system to risk exposure." She took a breath and put a hand on his arm, "I planned to have it flushed, but we're in this boat now. You willing to walk into the waterfall?"

His face had gone marble, the black moons of his eyes divining her soul for the truth. The fridge gurgled in the background. A crack of white broke the marble façade—his lop-sided grin. "Does this mean I'm getting promoted?"

She slapped his arm, "Fine, yes." Shaking her head, she opened her closed hand to reveal the vial she'd been holding. Carefully she unscrewed the top and allowed the viscous liquid to carry one of the tiny devices into her hand. "Anything external will be easily discovered. This is a little gift from the merKing." Pulling the hair away from one ear, she pressed the thing hard against the bone behind her ear. She pulled her hand away, bloodied.

Min Soo handed her a napkin. "Is the other one for me?"

A nod. "It works as a tracker and communicator. It's supposed to be undetectable to a standard exam, as long as they don't get overly suspicious. Still good? It hurts, but it's fast, like a bullet."

He pulled over a chair, sat down and exposed his neck. "Hurry up or I might embarrass my vampire history."

"Tsk, tsk." She shook her head and tilted the vial to shake out the twin device. "Fine. Funny guys like you deserve everything they get." Her eyes narrowed, and with a touch of sympathy she put one hand on his shoulder as she jammed the device into place.

To give him credit, he didn't slug her. "Bullet?! Bullet??!!" His hand was a vice grip on her arm. "That. That. That was. Blessedly short."

She tapped his vice hand. "Time to go deal with open-ended business and gather the minor bits you need before they come."

An hour or so later, Evansea stepped in from keeping his watch. "Hey, they're here."

Min Soo strode out of his bedroom with a small bag. "Ready."

"Last chance to change your mind," Ellia warned.

"No, that was before you shot me."

"Haha, let me see..." he turned to show her his profile and her smile faded with a sharp hiss. "Ah, this is not brilliant." A bruise had developed.

"What is it?" he hurried to one of his convenient mirrors. "Well, that's going to be difficult to explain. Can't hide it with makeup either."

Ellia covered her eyes to give herself a chance to think. "If they see that they're going to worry about a head injury." She started pacing.

"You didn't get one?" Min Soo asked, disturbing her pacing.

She shook her head and pulled aside her hair to prove it. "Nothing."

He took another look in the mirror, cleared his throat and ran a finely shaky hand through his hair. "There is a potential solution..."

"Well, spit it out."

Merdragon

"It, uh, requires lipstick," he said with a squint in her direction.

"Lipstick?" She frowned and thought it through.

"Evansea? Go stall the elevators."

He shook his head confused but went.

Ellia eyed Min Soo, and making a quick decision, she ran to her room, grabbed the first stick to hand and ran back. A fast glide. Min Soo hadn't moved.

She eyed him cautiously, "You sure about this?"

"I don't have any other ideas, and it's a pretty stereotypical thing, to be honest." He shrugged as if it was par for the course, but a little red was colouring his ears. He pointed at the bruise, "Might as well do the worst one first."

She leaned back, "Excuse me, what? First one?"

He swallowed visibly and shifted his gaze to a spot on the wall.

"Just do it already."

She tilted her head and stared at the bruise slightly behind his ear. She'd have words for whoever had designed that little device. She leaned. He held his breath. She pulled back. "I can't do it. This is a ludicrous solution."

"You're kidding me, right?" His eyes drifted down to meet hers. "It's the best one we have on short notice. Your personal fan is not going to be able to hold off the elevators for long."

Her mouth twisted. A whistle out. A whistle in. "Guess these teeth are better for it than in my other form, here goes."

A few silent moments later she pulled back and inspected her work. At least she tried to with her heart thumping away at a less than healthy pace. Min Soo's pulse had increased as well, based on the tempo-keeping blood vessel near the scene of the crime. She turned to face the other direction to recatch her breath, and emotional solid ground.

Min Soo coughed, tried to clear his throat, tried again, and stirred behind her. She took a breath and turned back to face him. He cleared his throat again and pointed at the target, "How, how'd it turn out?" His face flushed red.

Drawing on her liar skills, she nonchalantly covered her mouth with a tight fist. If nods made sounds, hers would have sounded like a short-burst machine gun. "Looks good. Yup." The liar skills were for her face, not the words.

He ran a hand through his hair, mussing it up even further. He eyed her with thoughts building up inside twin black holes and took one step closer. The distant sound of the elevator door pinged in the taut silence. "Objective number two," he muttered, "make it believable." He lowered his head and went straight for her lips.

The doorbell interrupted next.

They pulled apart and Ellia gave him a quick scan. And a pat on the shoulder. A nod.

A knock on the door followed the bell.

She watched Min Soo take another step back, shake his head and clear his throat. He gave her his own nod then turned to answer the door.

Enlist in more

Seven weeks later, Min Soo's feet were back on the sands of a beach he never thought to trod again. He stood with his squad, their commanding NCO giving orders. He hadn't known until this morning he'd be here now. He hadn't told Ellia directly—he'd already been caught talking to himself once or twice—but he trusted she already knew.

"Alright men, Han Min Soo and Guk Joon Ho, you check out the cave, Ho Jung Hoon and Sung Min Ho, find the crash site," he pointed out the other two pairs and commanded, "you two go scout the perimeter and you two come with me."

They split up as instructed. Shuffling through the sand, Joon Ho asked, "So what's in the cave?"

Min Soo told the truth, "It's got some rough furniture in the front, but there's a tunnel that leads further in that I didn't get to explore when I was here last."

Joon Ho surged ahead, "Last one in gets latrine duty!"

Shuffling behind him, Min Soo uttered a token protest but made no effort to catch up.

As he'd threatened, Joon Ho reached the entrance first and boldly stepped inside. Min Soo brushed the empty door hinges and wordlessly wondered who'd removed the door. Had Ellia been back? Why had she removed it? If not her, who? He followed Joon Ho inside. Other than the wind's attempts to make itself at home and an animal or two's attempt to do the same, the place had remained unchanged.

Joon Ho spun around in the centre and clapped Min Soo on the shoulder, "Man, you have all the luck. Crashing on an island with a place like this waiting?"

Pulling their packs off they knelt on the dirt floor, pulled out headlamps from their gear and attached them to their helmets. Min Soo stood up first and jerked his chin toward the tunnel entrance, "Ready?"

Joon Ho held up the glowsticks he'd pulled from his pack, "Breadcrumbs."

Min Soo gave his usual huff laugh and let his partner take the lead, again.

The same exact seven weeks later that Min Soo had reached the island, Ellia was actively not thinking about things she shouldn't be thinking about while stowed away inside a place with edges that were not playing nice with her ribs, spine and especially her toes. She hadn't spoken to Min Soo in several days, since their communications connection had broken when she'd gone out of range. A spasm threatened her big toe. She sent relaxing thoughts in its direction while distracting herself with a mental layout of Danube's yacht.

"The scans are still coming back empty?" Danube's voice.

"Sir, the scans are set on extreme sensitivity. There's nothing within ten kilometres that we haven't identified. The live net is being recycled through at irregular intervals. A few barbequed fish, but nothing large scale."

"Father,"—Ellia lip curved down. Of course Darya had chosen to disregard the merdragon's peace offering— "we still haven't managed to track Riko, but our other—can we still call it an asset?—may have arrived on the island on its own."

He swore hard enough to rattle Ellia's hidey hole. "Our key's scheduled to land on the island today! Get a message out. Nobody lands." The sound of a hatch closing ended the walking update.

Ellia wiggled her toe. Now with everyone distracted by "the asset" she could swipe the node. She un-contortioned herself out of her hiding place and crept through the halls, front-brain working on avoiding the guards on ship while her back-brain kneaded on Danube's words.

A surge of yacht speed interrupted her skulking. She grabbed hold of a hatch frame to brace against barging into a crew twosome. Listening in, she waited for a distracted moment in the early courtship conversation and slipped past, low. A light buzz burred behind her ear. Her back-brain transferred the kneading responsibility to the mid-brain. Padding barefoot, she felt the vibrations of engines pushing their max limits. She reached a decision fork and chose the engine room path.

Three levels down, she spotted two crewmen standing in front of a door clearly defined as her destination. Mid-brain was knocking on her front-brain's door. The men were armed. She hadn't had a proper meal in two days.

In the island tunnel, Joon Ho's light bobbed from one side to another as he scanned for anything of interest. Unlike the tunnel Min Soo had squeezed through before escaping the island, this tunnel opened up quickly until their lights became as effective as two stars in the dead of night, in the Redwood forests. The pathway however was not so wide. It meandered without railings, only occasionally returning to kiss a wall. Thankfully, it widened in other stretches to create comfortable landings.

Merdragon

At one landing they came to a multiple split. Joon Ho gestured to the one on the far left, "Let's try that one first."

The odd deadness of Joon Ho's voice made Min Soo grimace. It should have drifted or echoed. Joon Ho glanced around nervously and reached into his pack to pull out a glowstick. "Breadcrumbs." He turned to face Min Soo. Blinded, Min Soo threw up his arm to shield his eyes from the headlamp and his partner quickly corrected his mistake.

Joon Ho spoke behind the blinding negative spots, "Is it me or does my voice sound weird down here?"

Min Soo blinked repeatedly, trying to adjust his vision. A faint vibration behind his ear gave him some reassurance. "Probably some porous rock down here or something. Don't tell me you're getting cold feet?"

"Nah, I'm plenty hot, thanks. Must be that porous rock or whatever. Sorry about the light. Your vision back to normal yet, good enough to continue?"

"I'm good." He dropped a glowstick. "So we know which path to return to."

Glowstick settled they took the left tunnel, Joon Ho first as usual, Min Soo taking the rear. Behind them the glowstick continued to shine in its solitude. Abruptly the dark swallowed it.

"You're here."

The moment Ellia opened the hatch her mid-brain passed forward the dough. Danube hadn't gone to the control room. He'd circled around without worrying about skulking. To wait in the engine room. He stood in front of her now, hands empty.

"Beginning to think you missed the tide."

"Where's the node?" She locked the hatch behind her. One surprise at a time.

He dismissed the question with a wave of his hand. "Unimportant. We have a mutual dilemma."

The engine room vibrated with power, but the dough had formed into bread. The burring behind her ear told her Min Soo was not where she'd left him.

Deeper into the maze, Joon Ho and Min Soo discovered another landing and left another glowstick. Once out of sight, darkness swallowed that one too.

Up and around the two wandered, both unwilling to admit their fears. The radio crackled and they both jumped. Joon Ho grabbed his, and Min Soo froze in place beside him, waiting incoming orders. The radio crackled with static, and the commander's voice came through, garbled and undecipherable.

Joon Ho responded, "Sir, there's interference. If you can hear me, we haven't found anything. I think we need a lot more light and some surveying. It's a freaking maze. We'll head back out now. Joon Ho out."

Min Soo nodded his head in agreement, his light flashing up and down against the cavern walls. If either had been paying just the least bit more attention, they might have caught sight of the darkness, but like horses smelling home feed, they paid less than ideal attention to anything other than the path back. Min Soo kept his goosebumps under wraps, but even knowing this was Ellia's stomping ground, the creep factor was rising by the footstep.

They retraced their steps back to the last landing. Joon Ho made it a couple steps head start out of the tunnel before Min Soo's headlamp caught up. Their lamps played around the landing, searching. For the glowstick.

Joon Ho's flat voice trembled oddly, "I remember this landing, we came from over there," he said, pointing to the correct path.

Min Soo noticed a rock outcropping he'd mentally marked earlier. His voice wasn't much better than Joon Ho's, "I agree."

"Probably some rat found it," Joon Ho commented without prompting.

Min Soo's headlamp bobbed.

With the courage of those who face their fears, they both went down the path, not voicing their hope that the next landing would still have its glowing direction giver.

Unfortunately, that hope arrived as dead as their voices. The next landing's glowstick was gone too.

"You don't suppose the other guys are down here playing with us, do you?" Joon Ho voiced hopefully.

"If they are, that's a sick joke to play, and they are so eating rat," Min Soo retorted.

"Yeah...raw..." Joon Ho's voice trailed off a sound cliff.

A new sound caught Min Soo's ear, "Did you notice the sound of water flowing around here before?"

"No, whyyyy..." Joon Ho voice died as the ground gave way.

"No!" Ellia cried out.

"What's wrong?" Danube stepped closer. In concern?

"You sent Min Soo to the island, didn't you?"

His brows flared up, "You're only finding that out now?"

Merdragon

"I've been holed up inside your yacht for the last three days. I'm getting off now. Disengage the security." She embodied hunger.

Danube stepped back, arms akimbo, and sneered, "That won't work on me. I fed you with a syringe, don't you remember?" He laughed cruelly. "I developed an immunity to that hunter's stare years and years ago."

"I will change right here and now and breathe this boat into a fire ball."

"Didn't Drayvin ever teach you to negotiate?" He scolded. "You don't want to destroy the node."

"Danube…"

"Settle down for two seconds. I don't like you, but right now our goals are momentarily the same. I admit, Iceland was a miscalculation. Our broken history books failed to tell the full story."

"That's what you meant by asset. What is it?" Ellia whistled out.

"I'm keeping the node here as collateral." He flipped a switch. "I'll rely on you to deal with history. Shame you don't have the UnMaker."

Min Soo lunged to grab Joon Ho's hand, pack, anything, but a thick cable suddenly snapped around his waist and yanked him back, hard. Frantically he tried to pull away, grasping at the cable, but his fingers slowed as it moved around his ribs like a thing alive. His attention snapped back to his own survival as he moved his hand to the warmth behind him. His fingers brushed against fur. A chuffing chuckle blew hot air against his neck. He stilled.

The chuckle came again and sent chills so severe through his spine Min Soo thought it might break. Then he realized it wasn't him shaking, but the thing behind him.

The warm air, hot enough it should have calmed his chills, carried the smell of brine and rancid meat. "My, my, my," murmured the darkness in a woman's contralto voice, smug and nasty, "who is this handsome toy come to pay me a visit?"

"What did you do with Joon Ho?" Min Soo demanded, knees shaking behind his bravado.

"Was that your useless companion?" the voice asked, amused.

"Yes, the man who a second ago got sucked down into that hole."

"Are you worried, little man? Why shouldn't I flush useless trash into the ocean?"

"What?" Min Soo exclaimed and strained to pull away.

The cord tightened. Hot breath chilled his ear, "You, however, I wonder how useful you will be?" Min Soo's back vibrated with the rumble of the voice's purring.

"Who are you?" he asked.

"Shall we play with a riddle or two?" she asked with another chuckle.

"Why don't you simply tell me?" he asked reasonably.

"One of three, made to be,
ask, seek, and knock;
Broken now, remind me,
Which was locked in rock?"

The riddle explained nothing. His brain reached for anything. Could Ellia hear him? Ask, seek, knock? The door? Its image came to mind, the door that had disappeared from the entrance, the magnificent door covered in indistinguishable designs glowing in the dark, designs that burned their images into the subconscious until the day that a monster stirred at his back.

"You're the sphynx," Min Soo blurted. Internally he wondered, sphynx?

"Aren't you the smart little man?" She replied, voice flat. "Should I let you go?" Dust flew against his face as she shook herself like a lion might. A whirring noise whined in his ear as she groaned out a stretch in the darkness. The cord around his waist loosened and she strode around into the light of his headlamp.

She had been magnificent, once. The whirring and whining he'd heard came from a metallic exoskeleton that caressed her skull at the eye socket and rode down her neck along her spine and spidered down each leg. One foreleg was entirely mechanical, gleaming and worn. He shuddered as he spotted the cord that had seconds ago been wrapped around him. It flexed and hissed, flicking back and forth, back and forth, anchored in the place of a natural tail.

The scars on her human face stood out in hideous relief, stitched together by the metal of the dark exoskeleton. What little of her fur existed, bristled between her roadmap of battles. The lion's tooth on the upper left gleamed black against the light of his headlamp, silver etchings glinting faintly within it.

He shifted his gaze, the lamp's light following, to avoid angering her, and fell on the one thing that would, her wings. At least that's what he thought they'd been. Now they were stumps that rose on occasion in a forgotten attempt to beat the air and wind. Her mechanical claws scraped against the cave's stone floor, and he quickly refocused on the space between her two front paws.

Merdragon

She snarled, mocking him, "Pretty, handsome boy, afraid of a little ugly?" Her tail snapped at air in her annoyance. "Didn't they warn you about me? Didn't they?!"

"No one knows you're here; they don't even know you exist," he replied, intent on what those claws could do.

Her throaty laughter purred through the cavern, and he wondered how her voice sounded so alive when his still sounded so dead.

"Don't you now? What did that traitorous tramp accomplish? Burn and bury me for millennia, will she? Dead now, isn't she? Tell me," she asked, crouching low to face him eye to eye, "I've tasted merfolk; how do you unmodified humans taste?"

"Less salty," he quipped.

"Ah," she sighed out the syllable, stretching her neck.

He went for his knife. Too late. One swipe of her natural lion's paw, Min Soo flew into the wall. He scrambled, winded, along the wall as she stalked forward.

The spot behind his ear burred. "Min Soo! Stall for time, I'm coming." Ellia had heard him.

The sphynx froze and perked up an ear as if she'd heard something too. Min Soo struggled to think as his lungs fought to recover from the knockout. He held back a reply to Ellia's message as the sphynx lowered her head with a sideways sway and leaned into snuffle at his ear. A blood-flecked golden eye swiveled in its socket and snared his gaze.

"Don't do that again, either of you, hmm?" she growled, the closest thing to a non-question he'd heard so far.

He nodded cautiously, not entirely sure what Ellia intended he do. How did one stall a sphynx?

"Shall we presume your partner survived?" she continued, withdrawing a step, misunderstanding what she'd detected. "How long do you suppose it will take for him to have these caves crawling with ants?" The snake tail swung around and snapped at him like a herder. "Shall we go?" A venomous coo.

Breath back to as normal as he could manage, Min Soo used the wall to haul himself back up to vertical. Air screamed past his face and his helmet flew off his head. The headlamp went dark.

"If you can't see, neither can they, am I right?" Heat leaked from her organic parts. Her cold tail curled around his throat. "Have you ever wondered how well snakes see in the dark? You won't go hying off, will you?" The tail's metallic scales slid against his skin possessively. And read his pulse.

"Nervous, are we?" Her mechanical paw fell on his shoulder and the tail slinked away. "You think those spindly things you call legs would be capable of walking, or should I just remove them and bring you along as dead weight?" She laughed, chuffing behind him in the dark.

He started walking, hands braced in front. The sound of metal against metal spiked the hair on his nape. Any minute he expected to feel his fingers smack into a wall, or her teeth, but seemingly wanting to keep him moving, a nudge here or a click of her tongue warned him of obstacles...most of the time. She didn't much seem to care about his toes or his shoulders. Biting his lips, he kept back the yelps of surprise. He could practically hear her grin and the curling of her lips with each new scrape or bruise.

In the dark they walked, his hesitant wide steps and her odd gait of three organic legs and the one mechanical. It threw his own steps out of sync, not to mention his spatial orientation. The walk in the dark reminded him of the much tighter, but more companionable path he'd taken with Ellia under the cauldron. It reminded him to blink.

How long a distance they travelled, in the dark he couldn't tell, but on one blink he managed to dodge a low hanging stalactite without the sphynx's warning. Noting his increase in vision acuity, the sphynx urged him to walk faster, nudging him with her mechanical paw. More of a shove, he stumbled but managed to stay upright, blinking repeatedly, trying to interpret the contrast between the black and grey shades.

They turned a corner and Min Soo raised his hand to shield his eyes from the light. His eyes adjusted and the light became considerably less bright than he'd first assumed. He realized something else. The source of light came from the door. The magnificent, hardy door that had kept the typhoon at bay those many months ago. The door that had shown him, in his memories, the sphynx. The image had changed.

The sphynx shoved him forward and spat, "Why don't you open it?"

Dirt smeared into the cuts in his hands, and he stared at her from his knees as she padded to one side of the phosphorescence. Like a cat she ran her long tongue over her one black fang, impatient. His eyes flitted over the door and frame, searching for some hint of danger. Why didn't she open it herself? Not seeing any, he placed a hand opposite the hinges and pushed. Nothing. Eyes glazed he looked questioningly at the sphynx.

She scraped her metal claws alongside the frame of the door, and he flinched as a chunk of broken rock hit his face. "Well?"

Merdragon

A spot of blood dropped over one eye, and he winced as he wiped it away to examine the door again. Still as magnificent as ever, the new patterns shone brightly in the dark. The only source of light. He traced them with his eyes, searching for an open says-me. He swallowed the dry dust of nerves and fished for a clue from the sphynx. "I'm not merkin. I can't open this door." Ellia hadn't told him how to be a key.

The mechanical paw stopped its sharpening against the rock wall, and Min Soo tucked his chin down as the sphynx rested her claws, pinpricking on his scalp.

"Dare treat me like a fool? Do you think because I am damaged that I can't smell the blood-contained keys?" The pressure increased until he was sure she'd broken skin.

Releasing him, she snaped her tail at the door and sent dust flying. The dust settled and with a voice of deceptive gentleness she began her question quietly, "Once more only do I ask, will you" —her volume increased— "willingly open. The. Blighted. DOOR?!" The last word a roar. Min Soo clamped his hands over his ears and cowered, her words reverberating against the sound suctioning tunnels.

Blood or sweat dripped down his face, he couldn't tell which, and he couldn't stall anymore. Gingerly he began running his hands over the patterns of the door. She'd insulted its magnificence. He closed his eyes in silent apology, feeling the embedded patterns, following each one to its end. If only he could open it, but he couldn't even find a keyhole to pick, if that was even an option. Gritting his mind, he focused all his thoughts on opening the door. And then he felt it. A buzz where he imagined the bone implant to be. So faint, he prayed the sphynx hadn't sensed it. It cleared his thoughts, and he realized the sphynx had completely psyched him out. He should have been asking why she wanted in, not how he should open the door. As soon as he thought the question, he fell forward, losing his balance. The door had released its stubbornness.

Fingers scrambling, he grabbed for a handhold, but like a sledgehammer, the sphynx slammed full-bodied against the door, crashing it inward and knocking him through to the other side. He rolled like a tumbleweed with a thought—why had he apologized to the door? His nose brushed up against more phosphorescence embedded in etched walls. The sphynx left nothing but a gust of wind as she brushed her hind feet at him and scampered past into wherever the door had led them. He pulled back from the wall, biting back a groan. His eyes stung from the dirt she'd flung behind. That and the feedback cackle.

Min Soo groaned, head reeling, and raised a scraped hand to his face. In the phosphorous light the blood shone black against his pale skin. He shook his head and groaned again. The last minutes or day, he couldn't be sure, replayed in his mind and his brows furrowed. He sat up and rubbed the back of his hand over his eyes. He stopped, "Wait...blasted snake eyes! She just pulled the same trick Ellia warned me about." He shook his head again and ran both hands through his military cut hair.

Proverbial granite reformatted his jaw line. He glanced back toward the dark tunnels and then back the way the sphynx had disappeared. Bracing against the glowing walls, he stood himself up and shook out his stiffening bruised muscles. One eyebrow rose, and the granite chiseled itself into a sardonic smile. "So, try to find my way back in that deadening darkness and maybe meet Joon Ho down inside a rabbit hole, or...?" He rubbed the back of his neck, "... or play secret agent and figure out what that, that, thing is trying to do down here."

Sifting through his gear, he dug around for anything useful, but nothing. The sphynx and her tail had been thorough. He brushed off the dust he'd gathered on the floor, crossed his arms and squared his shoulders. "Ellia, if you can hear me, I'm going to follow that sphynx beast thing and find out what she's up to." His lips curled, lopsided, "Come find me, you fire breathing merdragon. I'll keep her distracted until you get here." He tilted his head and waited for a response. Nothing. He'd been spouting bravado into thin air. Uncrossing his arms, he clapped his hands together once, took a big breath and set off on the exhale.

Ellia tore through the water, driven by the one word Min Soo had managed to slip out, "Sphynx." She'd flown until the potential to be spotted by the military and any civilian became too great. Now, the roar of water replaced the whistling wind. The roar decreased as she finally began to slow, approaching the back side of the island. Another type of whistling caught her attention. A scarred scouting dolphin searching for a human.

She whistled inquiry. To make sure it wasn't Min Soo.

He responded with a wave of his body and a fast chitter. Happy to know he'd nabbed her interest, he spun back in the direction he'd come and indicated she follow. A few spins made sure she actually did before he put on his speed.

She heard the pod before she saw them. Heard the standard rescue codes. Her escort dove into the festivities, broadcasting notes of success. With much nose prodding, chittering and rollovers, the pod invited her inside to the core. The dolphin on carry duty gave her a resigned eye roll. They'd found a man, and if she guessed right, they thought he was alive enough to try and rescue. Internally her clock screamed.

Merdragon

First, she sent one of the dolphins back the way she'd come and hoped he or she stayed on task. It was like sending a mischievous toddler on a mission to grandma's house. Simple commands, simple instructions, lots of motivation and hoping for a dearth of ice cream trucks. She hoped Evansea had managed to finish the yacht take-over.

Next, she checked his vitals. The dolphins hadn't misdiagnosed their patient; he did still have a pulse. His breath, however, was iffy, and swallowing water with every other wave wasn't helping matters. A green flag popped up in her mental topography of the island. A powerful pulse of her tail and she rose to hip height. There, an upcropping, an orphaned part of the island. Wrangling the dolphins into rough order, she beelined it, and deposited the patient on the rocks. She made sure he would live for at least the next hour and coaxed a portion of the pod to remain while a few more were sent out to hunt for additional rescuers. She could only pray for the best. A brief song of good-bye to man and pod, and she dove down under to swim away from the island.

Not too far away, just to the edge of the larger subsurface footprint of the island. The true edge of the island, dropping off into a subjectively narrow crevice. Ellia dove deeper, singing to map out the dark. The song etched the multiple openings onto her mental map. Tunnels from which streams of solidified magma fell like frozen waterfalls.

Ellia approached one of the openings and allowed the temperature of the water to give a report while also allowing her own heartbeat to settle inside of a whale's heartbeat. Hypothesis reached, she bared her teeth unhappily and darted in.

Ten steps or so down the glowing tunnels, Min Soo glanced down at his boots. Sound had returned to normal, and the fine sand shushed loudly between his soles and the hard floor. He kept going but tried hard to listen for the sphynx. Instead, between the shushing footsteps, he heard the murmurings of water and mechanical goings on. A faint paw print urged him forward.

The further he ventured, the more the glowing walls changed. Doors appeared at intermittent intervals and the phosphorescent growth petered out to be replaced by light from the walls themselves. As he turned a corner, Min Soo touched the smooth surface of the wall. Whether from his touch or simply a place of transition, the light in the walls began to shift and move in blotches. The change tripped him up for a second. He took an experimental breath, reached up to the ceiling and a strand of projected seaweed curled around his fingers. His breath sighed out.

A muted bang distracted him and, eyes narrowing, he set off again. Seconds later the bang was followed by a short mechanical wrrr. He slowed his steps and frowned down at the shushing of his footsteps. An idea traipsed in, and with a quick glance around, he removed his boots. The socks came off too. A grim smile touched the granite. No more shushing.

Boots in hand, he cautiously continued. Around the next corner, a door offered itself up as a possible route for the sphynx. Min Soo considered it for a moment, but it didn't match the distance of the bang he'd heard earlier. Uneasily he glanced back the way he'd come. The tunnel was as manmade as any regular hallway but given to irregular patterns of curves and turns. Curves equaled short sightlines which translated to vulnerable sightlines. Sweat dripped from the edge of his hairline down into his collar and a shiver quickly followed. He dismissed the door and tracked onward.

He approached the next bend, bare feet leaving silent footprints in the sand. Ears intent on any sound, he reached the curve, paused with a breath, then peered around the corner. Nothing. He sighed and stepped around only to see the next curve's secret come partially into view. A heavy-duty doorframe. He snapped back out of sight. If wishful thinking worked, his ears would have grown at least a few centimeters. The frame promised a door.

Artist Gabriel's training regimen tapped at his psyche. The sphynx's tail worked on his spine. He slumped back against the wall, clasped his hands together and raised them to his forehead mouthing a silent prayer. He hadn't heard whistle or growl from Ellia since her last message. He had to trust she'd arrive before the sphynx tranced him into submission and served him up for her supper. Lowering his hands, he glanced around the corner, set his boots down and, staying low, he began sidling to the next curve.

The door came into full view. "An airlock?" he mouthed. With a violently damaged keypad.

Ice shards sent a shiver up his spine. Shoulder check. False alarm, the hall was clear.

Farther down the hall he could now see, windows. Fatalistic courage in each bare-footed step, Min Soo crept past the airlock and sidled up to the first window. A look. The room was clear. No sphynx. He sighed audibly. Another, more thorough scan of the room confirmed his first assessment. He tilted his head, raised an eyebrow and slowly rose to his full height. One long silent step took him

Merdragon

back to the airlock's defunct keypad. Another whiplash inducing glance to ensure the sphynx's continued absence. He put his hand on the door. "I hope that thing you stuck behind my ear works on this door too."

Eyes wide open this time, he internalized one word, "Open."

A silent clock ticked in a timeless vacuum.

Time resumed with a click behind Min Soo's ear. The airlock swished open. He breathed a thank you and hurried inside. The hatch closed behind him before he could issue the instruction. His toes curled on the hard floor and he brushed his feet against his pants to wipe off the sand. The spot behind his ear was buzzing. Buzzing in sync with the control boards in the room. Was this where Ellia had been the day he'd crashed on the island? She'd mentioned something similar.

Absent-mindedly Min Soo rubbed a hand against the buzzing spot. A light blipped red on one board, then another. On the far side of the room two boards sounded additional blips. A video display turned itself on and Min Soo drew closer. The display showed a camera view of the subterranean halls, rooms with machinery Min Soo couldn't interpret, and notably, satellite views of the island. The satellite view caught his attention. "Is this live? It's still daylight. 1700 or so?" Lettering appeared on the screen but not in a language he could recognize.

Hot breath hit the back of his neck. "How is it that a fool like you holds a master key?"

Ice shards paralyzed him.

A thump and the sound of steal claws scraped the floor. Dust drifted down from the ceiling. He groaned.

The sphynx chuckled, "Forgot to look up, didn't you?" Her tail snaked over his shoulder and forced him to turn. She wasn't looking at him. Instead, she'd already redirected her attention to one of the many control boards. The dead serpent of a tail clamped him to her side. He shuddered as his bare hands brushed against her coarse and patchy fur.

She hissed in amusement, one eye refocusing on him as she ran a tongue over her unmodified canine. "Was it not fortunate I was feeling rather satiated when last we parted? What's a master key without it's designated living host?"

Min Soo couldn't move his mouth to ask what sort of master key she thought he had. Her eye filled his vision. The rumble of her malevolent purring sent the ice shards flowing through his veins. "Tell me, what is one plus one?"

His mouth answered, "Two." He couldn't tell if her purring vibrated the floor or him.

"What is your mother's name?"

He cringed, his jaw muscles tensed, but he heard his own voice give into the command. "

What is the colour of the sky?"

"Blue," he answered, mystified.

"What is your lover's name?" His breath hitched before answering, honestly, "I don't have one."

"Hmmm…" the hesitation visibly disturbed the sphynx.

Min Soo could smell fish and death on her breath as she leaned in closer. The tawny furnace of her eyes bled into his vision. Her purr was devolving into a growl. "And what is the opposite of open?"

His mouth opened, but his vocal cords froze on the answer. A spark lit in the mental space filled with cannon balls and closets. He could fight this!

An inexplicable expression ran across her face. The growling stopped. She blinked one eye, then the other. Min Soo started to breathe again. She asked, "Off?"

Primed, he answered, "On." The room clicked.

The chuckle started low in the sphynx's chest and rose as the paralysis dissolved from Min Soo's body. He spun around to see all the control boards doing exactly as instructed. They'd been on backup before. The master key had just unlocked the entire room. What exactly had Ellia given him? Did she even know how much access he seemed to have?

The sphynx tsk'd with a sneer, released him and began scanning each board. At the third one she rose on her hind legs and began making entries with her claws, adept as any human fingers. Min Soo slumped against a board and rubbed worriedly at the spot behind his ear. He eyed the controls around him, but the displays might as well have been Mayan.

"W-wha," his voice stuttered. He stopped, covered his face with one hand, cleared his throat then started over, vocal cords in control. "What are you doing?"

"Now my dinner's asking questions?" she scoffed.

A glance dismissed him. Her tail, on the other hand, whipped over to flip a switch on an adjacent board. Instantly a holographic globe appeared spinning leisurely over a mostly bare consol. As Min Soo watched, the few red lights scattered around the globe began to multiply. Frowning, he reached out to touch one located near the Hawaiian Islands. The globe stopped and responded with a secondary layer that gave a zoomed-in window of the red spot. Along with a text and graphs he couldn't read.

Merdragon

"I don't understand." His ear buzzed. The text transmuted into Korean. "대박, wow." A light went on in his mind and he opened his mouth to turn off the consoles. Another mental lightbulb stopped him. Turning off the consoles would only last until the sphynx made him turn them on again. It wouldn't help her temper either. He'd be early dinner instead of a stalling obstacle. Reading subvocally could prove more valuable, Ellia might hear him.

The text was not an easy read. Geological terms made note of global thermal routes and energy transfers, oceanic pressures and currents. At least that's what he thought the words meant. "Hope this means something to you," he added to his litany.

He pulled back and the globe resumed spinning. Red dots had continued to bloom across its surface. A flashing alert above the globe which read "Fail-safes disengaging." Min Soo repeated the words out loud as a question. The sphynx didn't respond. The frown on his forehead was growing permanent.

"What are you up to? Who are you working for? The Cult?" He'd overheard Ellia use the term with Evansea.

That elicited a response. Of laughter. Uproarious laughter. And her attention. She straightened from her hunch over her present console. Straightened up vertically on her hind legs to stretch toward the sky above the subterranean. He caught a glimpse of the grandeur the Egyptians had tried to emulate in their monument. Her ruin returned upon her fall back to all fours.

She leapt over the console that separated them and swaggered up to him. "Do you think your whispers reach beyond the silence of this base?" A hiss of laughter. "Work for the Cult?" She chuckled. "Work for the Cult?!" Spit flew. "Does the tiger work for the rat? The cockroach? Do you know what they wanted?"

He shook his head, no.

"Tell me what all men desire, despite the lies they tell themselves getting it?"

It only took a few seconds to connect the dots. "Power."

She purred, "Hmmm, what else is a fool but the one who seeks power above all else for his own high ideals or base desires?"

Min Soo turned the question back, "What do you want?"

The laughter faded entirely from her face. "Can I not choose death?" "
You want to die?" Min Soo asked.

She stretched her neck before replying. Her lips curled into a sneer. "Do you think I will die alone?"

His toes curled against the warm floor. The red dots blinked on the globe like flaming death skulls. "You can't want to destroy the planet?"

Huffing laughter, bitter as strychnine, "Can't I?"

A warble from a console on the opposite side of the room interrupted her. The dead tail snapped around him like an iron noose.

"What did you do, you wretched worm!?"

Clutching at the vise around his neck, Min Soo didn't have an answer. Water had begun to rise on the other side of the room, partitioned off by a force field. He wished he'd had something to do with it. He hoped the large circular frame flashing on the drowning side did.

About the time Min Soo had encountered the magnificent door, Ellia had been baring her teeth at a mental flip of a coin. There was no predicting the frequent release of the magma; once the pressure gauges hit critical, the vents would open. The ancient engineering process both powered and preserved the island.

Through the artificial, almost frictionless tubes she swam. Years and years ago Ellia had been in these same tubes, but that had been out, not in. In the pitch-black darkness, she sang the lullaby tune Evansea had sung on Min Soo's balcony. Drayvin claimed he's sung it on their way out and had used it whenever she got fussy. It rang in the tube, painting the darkness with directions. A darkness that was beginning to give her the warm, not-fuzzies. In the pitch black she sped up, risking a few bruises against the risk of cooking.

The water began heating up her scales, and her gills flared in displeasure. A deep glow highlighted the perfection of the tube's curvature and Ellia tightened every scale. She plastered her wings against her body and explosively exhaled out her gills.

Not the most efficient form of propulsion, but it boosted her into the central chamber as the vents began to open. Up she dove, eyes arrowed-in on the flashing eel escape path. The hole zagged, then zigged, leading to an irising hatch. Seal-friendly, easy to open, she popped through and let it shut behind her.

Cooler water here, she flopped down on the floor, setting off a puff of sediment to reveal the gleaming obsidian beneath. The insulated floor reassured her as she caught her breath, her tail floating up to wave on its own. Equipment filled the room from floor to ceiling. Mostly somnolent equipment. One solid unit beeped and blooped, lights flickering and needles fluctuating. Ellia pushed off the floor to examine it closer. In the twenty years she'd been on the island, she'd only heard of this place, never entered. She picked up a small clip and shoved it in her hair. The coolness of the water eased the pain of her gills while her brain clocked up.

Merdragon

The timer in her head ticked and toked with the silence of a grandfather clock at two in the morning. A few roosters were adding to the ruckus. She stuffed them all into a mental closet so she could make some scientific observations and educated-guess adjustments to the equipment. At one station she pulled out a cable and considered it with narrow eyes before she held it against the spot just behind her ear. Her tail curled stiffly, and sparks flickered in her eyes. A few additional lights switched on; a curly cue pattern of phosphorescence began to liven up the blasé walls. Ellia ignored the inherent hopefulness, disconnected and swam upward again to a slightly more intricate hatch. An iris of pearlescent metal with hazard lights flashing.

What's going on?

Ellia extended her hand, claw-tips extended, and tapped the centre of the doorway's iris. Instantly it cycled open. She rode the flooding rush and took in the scene at fast forward speeds. The smugness of being "authorized personnel" disappeared before she could enjoy it. The field had formed as she'd intended.

On the other side, the sphynx glared at the unexpected arrival. Her tail twitched. The tail she'd wrapped around Min Soo's neck.

The sphynx's hackles had risen to meet Ellia's threat. Her lips curled up into a surprised snarl. "You?" It crescendo-ed into a roar, "Murderous traitor?!" The field rippled between them.

Ellia held back a response to the challenge and sidled closer to a nearby set of controls. She had to find the right one.

The sphynx leapt over a control board, swinging Min Soo carelessly against it. Ellia winced in sympathy with each impact.

Up against the field, the sphynx hissed and spat, "Who's a bottom feeding, scum spewing, patricidal viperfish? You? Who murdered the simple-minded krakenman with a twist of deception and then came for me?" She scraped her metal paw along the barrier sending sparks and rivulets along its water running surface. It wasn't intended to hold back a worker. "Who tried to take me apart?" Her face changed, became sorrowful, "Weren't we sisters...?" It changed again, she snickered, "Who was such a sucker...?" It changed again, earnest, "How was I to know it was your favourite merchild? Should I have given it a swifter death?"

Hiding her reactions behind a face of stone, Ellia held herself from correcting the sphynx's misconstruction of Ellia's existence. Mistaking Ellia for the original merdragon could be a good thing. If she could use it to her advantage. She had no interest in re-educating the sphynx, not with her tail around Min Soo's neck. This time-frozen anarchistic psychopath might give her a useful history lesson instead.

Face shifting to pure rage, the sphynx rose on her hind legs until her head nearly met the ceiling, towering over Ellia, then landed back on all fours with her full weight, dust billowing. She whipped Min Soo forward and grabbed his shoulder with her metallic claws, piercing skin. With a wicked smile she nuzzled his neck, one eye on Ellia's face as she gave him a taste test with her long black tongue. Min Soo craned away in disgust as she smacked her lips.

Merdragon

"How tasty will this one be? Not merkin, is he?"

Leaning against a set of controls, Ellia's claws dug deep, leaving permanent graves, and a growl thrummed at the base of her throat. If she could just get a few programs going.

"What do you want?" Ellia demanded, fire wrapping around each word.

"Want?" Sphynx replied, lowering herself to the floor, Min Soo firmly under her forearm, playing—a cat with a mouse. "I have a fully bodied meal right here, whatever more could I want?"

Ellia eyed a control surreptitiously, but the sphynx caught it, "Do you not think, my traitorous sister, that the minute you do, that this one will not gush organs from his neck to his groin? Think you not that I will delight to dine on his living flesh?"

Min Soo's reaction buried an arrow in Ellia's chest. Working so hard to avoid distracting her. She slapped a temporary staple on the psychic wound. "He'll last you a few days at best, probably spoil from lack of salt before you're done. What do you really want?" One set of talons busily buried themselves in the controls behind her as her tail swung back and forth.

The sphynx constricted her tail until Ellia worried Min Soo would pass out.

Ellia baited, "Come on, sister, scared of a little tag on this side of the field? Your score's with me." Danube hadn't been kidding about the regret she have over the missing UnMaker. The lack of wings had to be due to UnMaker work; she could have used it to finish the work already begun.

Breathing in tiny gasps, Min Soo opened his eyes to arrow in on Ellia to shape the word, "No."

The sphynx snorted and she loosened her grip enough for Min Soo to grab a breath. "Your worthless carbon life?" Her chest heaved with deepening laughter. Spit flew as her brays devolved into jagged hissing. "Betrayed by my makers? Betrayed by my slaves? Buried alive to dream of death by my sister?" Her eyes twisted, a piece of hardware sparked, and something snapped in the cybernetics buried along her spine. Hatred glitched out like pixelated sewage, "I-I-ah! B-br-b-broke program-am-am-ing. Now. Now. Now. I put. To fire. The programerssss. And. Their. Spawn."

"You can't," slipped out Ellia's mouth.

The sphynx leapt to all fours with a roar. "I can!"

Ellia dug down hard with a claw tip. All the controls on the air side went dark.

With lightning speed, the sphynx narrowed in on Ellia's hands. "You will pay for that," and she buried a single mechanical scimitar of a claw clear through Min Soo's abdomen.

Min Soo's whole body spasmed in pain, his gasp the loudest scream Ellia could imagine. Her eyes burned with fire-tears and only her claw tips kept her from leaping through the barrier.

The sphynx held him up in front of Ellia. "Do I not know your weaknesses, little sister?" Her tail retracted from Min Soo's neck and leisurely ticked time, back and forth. Back and forth. "I did not anticipate your living, breathing self, but I have not forgotten you in the millennia I suffocated in that miserable excuse of a volcano." She spat to the side. "What? You couldn't make sure it was hot enough to deep roast me?" She sat back on her haunches as Min Soo's bloodstain grew. "Will you not breach the barrier, dear sister, and give up that side of the room?" She chuffed, "Once you're on the ground like a helpless fish I will release what's left of him." She shook him like a dead eel.

"Alright," Ellia cried, with more of a whimper than she'd intended, "I yield." She had to get to Min Soo before he bled out or the sphynx chose to do more damage.

Wing stubs flexed as the sphynx huffed backwards. Ellia drew closer to the barrier and sank down to the floor. First one arm came through, then her head and shoulders. She hand-walked from the support of the water into the dry, enemy side. The moment the tip of her tail came through, the sphynx threw Min Soo to the opposite end of the room and stalked toward Ellia. Her whole body slinking with murderous intent, and Ellia scrambled, flopping and slipping backwards until she hit a wall.

There was no space to fly so she coughed. A minor spit-fire to warm things up. She cleared her throat, thought of the little challenges good old dad had issued, coughed again, and this time she caught the decent sized fireball with the tips of her talons. It gave the sphynx reason to pause. Ellia guessed she could dodge it, but was she willing to allow for the collateral damage?

"In here I may not be able to fly or swim, but I can still cough up a good-sized defense, sister," Ellia warned.

The dead tail swayed in a contemplative breeze. The sphynx looked over her shoulder at the bleeding Min Soo, then twisted her neck back to consider Ellia's handicapped, but still formidable state. She stretched out her neck to work out a crick, then raised the claw she'd used to skewer Min Soo. With a dainty lick she sampled his blood from the retracted weapon. Abruptly she turned and leapt through the barrier, abandoning the stalemate.

Powerful strokes drew the sphynx to the first panel. With a few judicious key stabs the barrier between the two sides solidified into a clear glass slate.

Ellia diffused the fire ball. Her full attention zeroed in on Min Soo. She triggered the change.

She started to slither toward Min Soo, and blackened flesh smeared the floor behind her like a poisonous snail's trail. Intentionally she juiced her internal system, pushing it beyond anything she'd ever attempted before. Min Soo was bleeding out. Blood surrounded him on the floor, growing at a pace barely restrained by his clutched hands. Ellia pressed her lips together to keep from keening in her haste to change as her tail audibly tore in two. Crawling, claws digging into the floor, hauling herself toward Min Soo, her left wing caught on a console and snapped clear of her shoulders. Black ash smeared with sweat on her face as her scales died. The right wing followed the left.

Incapacitated, Min Soo wept like the dead. Eyes wide but drifting. His face, her target. She ignored her claws as they broke off, betraying her as she tried to get to her knees, slipping in her blood, smashing an elbow on the blood slick floor, tasting iron in her mouth. She'd recover, Min Soo might not.

Again she brought her knee forward, this time careful in planting her raw skinned foot squarely on the floor. Freshly re-shifted muscles twinged as she rose into a crouch, and gritting her teeth against the pain, she stumbled the last couple of meters to Min Soo's side.

She placed a hand over the hand Min Soo was using to staunch what he could. Carefully she felt along his back for the entry wound. Wet and slick, the blood oozed without restraint. His blood pressure had to be nose-diving. She dreaded to think about his organs.

A few options tabbed up in her mental PC. His eyelids eclipsed dual black holes. "~whistle~, hey Model-nim, I'm about to get a little fresh with you. Hold still, won't you?"

"Sea wench," slid out the corner of a wan grin. A clammy sheen had crept over his tan.

Hands shaking, first she removed his tattered overshirt, folded it lengthwise several times then wrapped it around his waist. She undid his belt with another quip, used it to tighten the makeshift bandage and keep it in place. His hand clenched and slackened of and on throughout the procedure, but the gravity of his eyes stayed constant on her face, like the Earth holds onto the moon, like a drowning man insists on the approach of drifting flotsam.

Satisfied as she could be with her rough fix, she spared a glance to see how the sphynx was faring. Out of her element, but breathing with an air mask, an extension of her exoskeleton, Ellia could see her bringing controls and sections of the island long dead to life. What mattered to Ellia was the sphynx's lack of attention in their direction.

"Min Soo?" she sotto voiced, redirecting her own attention back to him.

"Hmm?" he replied, eyes glazed over, his breath shaky.

"We have to get out of here now," she said, bending down to slip her arm under his shoulders to haul him up.

His other hand gripped her arm feebly. "Don't you have to stop her first?" he asked. "Volcanos."

Hauling him up as gently as she could, her own muscles still uncertain, she answered, "No, first we have to get you out of here."

Stubbornly he resisted, draped over her blood smeared shoulders and wobbling on his feet, refusing to take another step.

"Min Soo-ya, ~whistle~, trust me, okay?" she pleaded, craning her neck to meet his eyes, "Trust me."

His head gave an infinitesimally small bob and reluctantly he took a step. A heavy step. Ellia took most of his weight on her shoulders and half dragged him to the door. As the door opened, the sphynx cackled after them, "Enjoy your last moments, dear sister!"

The sound echoed in their ears even after the door closed behind them, the laughter of a millennia gone mad, psychopathic sphynx.

In the tunnels made for feet, Ellia and Min Soo hobbled forward together, Ellia confident in her direction, Min Soo dragged along. He stumbled against her when she stopped at a door with a symbol clear to anyone—a red drop of blood. The door opened and Ellia dragged him inside. She lugged him onto an amped up armchair and hurriedly began rummaging through drawers, sparsely supplied. In one drawer she found what she'd been hunting for, a container with three ping-pong-sized balls.

She hustled back to him, and without his yay or nay she popped a ball into his mouth. His jaw moved to swallow, naïvely, when his eyes flew wide in survival terror.

Merdragon

Ellia clamped a hand over his mouth, "It's a healer. I know, I know it feels like you've got a baby octopus crawling inside your mouth and down your throat, but give it a moment, the numbing should be kicking in now..."

A tear crept from the corner of his eye as he fought the violent urge to gag the whole thing out. His muscles spasmed from loss of blood and instinct. Ellia felt his face slacken. He slumped against her hand.

"Thank You, God," she whispered as she gently rested him back in the chair and hooked him up to an IV-line of blood substitute.

Satisfied, she returned to her surveying of the infirmary. Short work later, amongst other things, she found a lab coat and pulled it over her still raw shoulder. The blood had already turned to black dust and fallen away, but her skin shone the unpleasant red of a fully realized sunburn. Another shirt and a box of cleansing towelettes in hand, she returned to Min Soo's side. Setting the items on a counter nearby, first she removed the belt that had held Min Soo together, then removed the blood-soaked shirt to reveal the mess the sphynx had made. "I'm sorry, Min Soo, I'll make this up to you. Never would I have given you that communicator if I'd known it'd interact with the other stuff I slipped in your broth."

With the towelettes she cleansed the area around the wound to reveal the oozing puncture being stitched together from the inside, greatly decreasing the outflow of his precious bodily fluids. Without the island seasoning she'd given him months ago... She snipped it from her thoughts. Ellia pulled him forward to rest on her left shoulder as she examined and cleansed the entry would on his back. His skin cold against hers, she removed his bloody undershirt, his dog tags clicking together. "You're not cut out for this. It was unfair of me to drag you into it. Why the controls gave you my authorization..."

Like a mother dresses a sick and sleepy child, she nudged one arm and then the other into the clean tunic she'd found, popped his head through the wide neck opening and gently rested him back down. "I have to get you out of here so I can deal with Ms. Nasty Kitty."

She stood back up and her face shifted away from the guilt and gentleness. From somewhere in her rat's nest of a hair-don't, she pulled out the hair clip. Pressing the sides, the not-a-clip lit up with five green lights in a row. She pressed the first light, and the rest began to pulse, each to its own tempo.

Her patient stirred in the chair, and she tucked the clip, for lack of a better word, into her lab coat pocket.

"Min Soo? You awake?" she asked, patting him on the shoulder.

"Hmmm! I'm alive? What happened?" he asked, still fuzzy.

She placed a metallic bowl in front of his face, "Get ready to heave, darling."

He opened his mouth to say something, but suddenly convulsed instead and out flew the ball, red, black and spent. Hesitantly he went to touch it but drew his hand back before making contact.

Ellia shook her head at his look of intrigue, "I'll debrief you later. Now we have to make an exit."

As steady as a newborn foal, he stumbled his lanky self out of the chair to his feet. Instinctively he clutched at his gut, then pulled up his shirt to see the unbandaged, and decidedly less deathly looking wound.

Holding the door, Ellia called, "Come on."

He followed, grimacing, but capable of moving on his own. "You're not just going to leave that thing here, are you?" he asked as they hurried through the tunnels at sub-optimal speeds.

Out came the not-clip. "She can flip as many controls as she wants, this remote is the self-destruct. See these blinkers? The reason I didn't extend your spa session."

"The whole island?"

"Don't worry, your friend got washed out to sea into the loving fins of a pod of dolphins. And your comrades have been recalled."

They'd reached the land-side entry. The one with the magnificent door. Min Soo brushed his fingers against it, "I think I'll miss this door."

"As will I," Ellia replied and opened it.

Hand raised, about to knock, Evansea stood on the other side. Bulkier.

"What are you doing here?" Min Soo asked.

"Uh, I came to help. Carcharodon's got Danube and his crew under wraps. Am I too late?"

Min Soo chuckled quietly and rested straight-armed against a dusty wall. "Man, not sure what pills you popped to get all jacked up, but you still wouldn't be able to handle that beast in there."

Ellia came up beside him and laid a warm hand on his neck. A feverishly warm hand. Her words passed him on their way to Evansea like honey dripping down glass, "If you have to knock him out, get him off this island. You know the shortcut." And she slammed the door shut.

Merdragon

Evansea and Min Soo both lunged for the door, but the phosphorescence had shifted to a sickly orange. When Min Soo tried to access the door, the connection snapped like a whip inside his head.

"Ouch!" he yelped, hand over the spot behind his ear. It smarted like an elastic band against his fingers.

"What happened?"

Min Soo banged a fist against the door. "That sea wench locked me out! Ellia! Unlock this door now!"

Faintly, he felt the buzz, and with a sudden surge of hope he tried the door, but instead he quite literally felt her voice say, "Vertical emergency exit for me, Mr. Handsome. You're not going to make me carry you again, are you?"

He pulled back from the door, face reflecting the sickly orange and slumped to the ground with a dejected shake of his head.

Evansea asked, "What's going on, bro?"

Min Soo punched at the ground, weakly, methodically. "She said something about a vertical exit."

"That's good, isn't it?"

"She can't do it. She can't change. You didn't see her shred herself last time she transformed. She doesn't have the mass."

Evansea pulled Min Soo up to his feet. "Look, I have to get you out of here. She's an honoured one, legendary merdragon and all, she can handle herself."

Grabbing Evansea's forearm with a vice grip of desperation,

Min Soo vehemently disagreed, "No, she can't. You didn't see that malicious thing."

"See what?"

"The sphynx."

Evansea's eyes widened to saucer proportions. "What? No tsunami way. Ellia didn't say anything about that. The sphynx died, old history ago."

Min Soo shook his head, "No, she's the one Ellia just locked herself inside with. We can't leave her."

Evansea snapped a capsule under Min Soo's nose and scooped him up over his bulked-up shoulder. Setting off at a fast jog he muttered to nobody in particular, "Argument's over. If the sphynx is here, only the merdragon can stop her. Even if only half the stories are true. We are not getting in the way."

Singing in the dark

Ellia hurried back the way she and Min Soo had come. He'd gained an instinct for her lies. Her bones felt light, and gravity a little gentler. Her mass was severely depleted. She pulled out the not-clip. The one light had turned red. She'd managed to slip that lie right past him with a partly, mostly true fib of hope.

"I'm sorry, Min Soo, the self-destruct is more of the Earth-sized variety and I'm not its current handler. This flashy thing is my inside scoop on the sphynx's countdown."

Around the next corner the infirmary came back into view. Inside she pulled out drawer after drawer. "Come, come my souped-up vial of calories and chemicals." A metal dish clattered to the floor. "Wait, expiry dates." She spun around, "Let me see…" The not-clip double beeped. "Kraken spit. Okay, counting down from ten, if I can't find the juice, that's it, I'll do without."

At two and a half, "There you are." Concoctions like the one she needed were made to order. A couple presses of a button and a vile coloured, tar thick fluid dripped into a beaker. She sniffed it. Appetite and disgust collided like a steakhouse and a dump truck. Her feet already moving, she glugged the stuff with moans of serious conflict. "Maybe this won't be suicide."

Outside the control room she shrugged off the coat and pulled out the timer, the third light had just turned red. One light left. "Way to go, leaving it to the last minute, hey? Your future so important you had to stop for a snack? Pfft." She wiped her mouth, smearing blackness across her face. The stuff felt like a lead balloon in her gut. A glance inside the control room. "Did you think your subconscious would figure out how to break that barrier all on its own?" She cracked open the door and hummed a little tune to herself. "You wouldn't have given up the control room for Min Soo's life if you didn't have a plan." The whale lullaby lilted out of her with a little siren-ic melody to counteract the leaking growl.

The sphynx barely deigned to acknowledge Ellia's lowball entry.

Ellia settled herself on the floor against a console and closed her eyes. The melody mutated. Mutated into the song sung by the loneliest whale. And mutated again. Grew louder. It flowed in duplicitous subversion. Polyphonic and choir-master despised. An external buzz joined into the merdragon's duet.

Merdragon

She opened her eyes. The barrier shivered. It attempted a third harmonic. And broke.

The instinct to change tore at her like a riptide. Impossible to resist, she drifted in it with the flow of the flood. Distracting herself with sideways thoughts, Min Soo's elusive smile, his long lean form safe on Danube's yacht, his warm cello voice in her ear telling her to, "Smarten up and get out of there!" Her eyes flew open, and she shook herself out of the mesmer moment. The place was primarily made for merkind. When the barrier crashed, water, not air had filled the room. The last of her air supply had ended.

Like a dream where two plus two doesn't equal four, Ellia struggled to reach the far wall without breathing, without swimming. Eyes darted from the oncoming sphynx to her goal, the second part to her program. She frantically grabbed hold of the nearest console and pulled herself forward, but not fast enough.

The sphynx snagged Ellia with her mechanical paw and blood danced in the water. Ellia's shoulder audibly popped. Air burst from her lungs. She clamped down on her lips and tumbled wild, crashing hard into a wall console. The sphynx pushed off with her hind legs, and Ellia scrambled to get away, push-pulling one-handed.

From the corner of her eye, she spotted the sphynx aiming for her with a kill strike and Ellia rolled desperately away. A miss. A tail strike followed. Hard against Ellia's back with the force of a homerun batter's win. The impact knocked the wind out of Ellia, and her peripheral vision started to darken. That's when her tunnel sight spotted the control bar she'd been aiming for, two metres away.

Fighting core survival, the DNA dry-triggering of the change, she pushed off against the floor and stretched. Her scalp screamed. The sphynx snarled her claws into Ellia's hair and ripped upward. Against the ceiling. Into an air gap.

Ellia heaved in air; vision returned. A jackhammer kick against the ceiling. It drove her past the swinging sphynx. She spotted the control bar again and slammed into it with all her strength and crushed it. Control had been returned to the island. Control returned to Ellia's pre-programming. A much more limited self-destruct. Limited to the island.

Lights began flashing red and yellow. The sphynx screamed behind her mask and dove toward Ellia with eyes gone beyond mad. Ellia dodged away between the legs of the console and scrambled toward the iris she'd originally entered. The sphynx got there first.

A stand-off. High noon at the OK Corral, and the sphynx didn't need to move a muscle. Oxygen deprivation would shoot Ellia in the heart. Better than melting into lava.

If a person could sweat under water, Ellia would have been dripping. She hung in the water, blood providing the dripping and an arm that had no drawing power. The sphynx wasn't smiling. It seemed Ellia had already pulled enough fast ones to make laughter a bad option. Her eyes spoke curses.

In her head Ellia heard Min Soo's voice, "You crazy sea wench, hurry!"

She couldn't be sure of the reality, but she replied anyway, "It's my last prayer."

"Ellia, fight!" His bellow rang in her head. A secondary buzz, and she heard, "Stupid island, don't you have an emergency procedure, or what? There's a person drowning in your control room. Initiate rescue!" Why hadn't she thought of that?

Ellia's eyes closed, her muscles went slack, and air bubbles rushed out her mouth like escape pods. The sphynx stirred uneasily. A round metallic ball, oddly buoyant, began to spin in a far corner. The sphynx drifted toward Ellia's limp form with a cautious stroke. The ball spun faster. Tail twitching, the sphynx kicked herself forward.

Like a lightning strike, the ball knifed toward Ellia and cycloned around her. The sphynx snarled and gouged the floor in her haste to reach Ellia. Too late, the cyclone spun straight up like a bullet, and a medical emergency iris opened above them to suction Ellia up inside it.

The sphynx tore at the iris edges, but she was too big to follow. Power strokes churning water, she charged toward the airlock. The water pressure was too strong. She couldn't get it open. The opening mechanism crumpled under her hammering. Psychotic, but clever, the sphynx jumped from one console to another, reading, reading, interpreting the warnings flashing at each console. Her tail snapped and twitched. Sparks snapped in the water and her snarls came unsteady and unhinged.

The little metallic ball, cousin to the baby octopus Min Soo had swallowed, deposited Ellia in the infirmary. Duty complete, the little ball sped back to the control room to return to its medical emergency standby position.

Fortunately, the stretcher on which the little ball thought it had deposited Ellia wasn't there. It had been moved away from the little ball's programmed expectations. Ellia hit the floor with a thud. A CPR level thud that knocked the water out of her lungs. She inhaled air like a blacksmith's bellows. Pain arched up her arm as she turned the wrong way, and slipped as the dislocated arm refused to support her. The stars she saw were not the types to admire on a long summer night.

"Come on, come on, hurry." Min Soo's non-stop litany brought her to her feet.

Still a little gaspy going out into the tunnels, she patted her stomach, "Please absorb faster, I have a deadline."

Running toward an emergency exit her memory swore existed, she felt the floor beneath her tremble. An enraged roar followed. It spurred her on faster, skidding around a corner, through a door and up actual stairs. Two flights up she found the e-pod. The door slammed open below her with an enraged scream. Claws shredded stone. Green eyes met tawny. Ellia slammed a fist against the giant red button.

The barebones e-pod shot up the vertical shaft and burst onto the surface, high up on the cliffs. She stumbled out and the earth rolled like a wave beneath her feet. The smell of sulfur and volcanic gases filled the air, and she took off running. Desperation drove her toward the cliff edge, rocks slashed her bare feet, and the half-digested lead balloon stitched pain in her side. With a last sprint she leapt off the cliff.

Well offshore, seven kilometres away, and steadily moving farther, the yacht coasted between the island and the military vessel. Min Soo paced the deck. Evansea stood by, sat down, stood up again, walked to the railing, slumped to the deck and jumped up again. Movement caught Min Soo's attention and he dashed to the telescope at the railing edge.

Bent over the scope, he scanned the island cliffs.

"She's out!"

Evansea sagged with relief. He didn't want to be known as the merkin who abandoned the honoured one. He raised up the binoculars he had hung around his neck. He swore and grabbed the ship's phone.

"Carcharodon, brace for impact. The island's going to blow and it's going to go hard."

He pulled a yellow, fist-sized capsule from the bag over his shoulder, muttered a word at it and threw it over the side. The instant it hit the water, an underworldly warning shrieked.

Oblivious, Min Soo's entire being focused on Ellia. "Come on, come on." He didn't even notice the words out of his own mouth. He watched as she leapt, and held his breath, muscles taut, willing her to change. A wave unbalanced him, and he lost her for a moment then caught her back in focus. He sucked air, hard. Framed by the lens of the telescope, her wings sprung out to catch the wind.

But it cost her. Nearly skeletal, scales dull and patchy, the tail a strand of itself, and one arm dangling useless. Her wings beat with determined desperation.

The blow hit her before he heard it, and Evansea slammed him down to the deck as the pyroclastic blast decimated the island. Smothered beneath Evansea, he felt the giant hand smash against the yacht, propelling it forward, damaging vessel and human skin and bones. He held his breath for the outcome.

Sudden silence.

He pushed against Evansea. Debris fell around them as he scrambled clumsily, slipping to where the telescope had flown off its stand and lay against the bulkhead. It rattled in his hand, useless.

He looked toward the island and yelled, "Ellia!" or thought he did. The volcano had become a dome of glowing rock steadily being crushed into itself by a barely visible field.

Evansea rolled up from the deck and grabbed Min Soo's arm. Min Soo saw his mouth move, but nothing. He tapped his ears and shook his head. Evansea nodded with a grimace of frustration.

Min Soo pointed toward the island and mimed Ellia. Mimed going out to get her.

He got a stern frown back from Evansea along with a shake of his head.

Frustrated, Min Soo mimed gills on himself and then covered the imaginary gills with his hand. He sucked his cheeks in and pointed out to Ellia's last location. He clasped his hands together, begging.

"You sure?" Evansea mouthed.

Min Soo's fervent nods convinced him. He stepped onto the edge of the railing and dove down into the ocean. Min Soo slumped to the deck, head in his hands and prayed.

Epilogue

The island that exploded outward, then abruptly imploded back down into a solid lump of rock, gained a large amount of attention. When it happened simultaneously with aborted volcanic murmurings worldwide, top-level scientists took serious note. When unknown individuals popped up claiming to be ambassadors of a previously unknown nation, with substantiating evidence, scientists connected dots and governments scrambled.

Min Soo sat in a room with an empty table for his only company. He'd been escorted to the room three days in a row. It had been eight days since he'd last seen Ellia.

The door opened.

A senior officer walked in. A senior officer radiating lethal authority. "Private Han Min Soo?"

He snapped up into a salute. "Sir, yes, sir."

"You know Ms. MerEllianna Nighemere?"

"Yes, sir." Not knew, but know. That had to mean she was still alive, right?

A folder landed on the desk. "Sign that and you'll be sent back to your unit."

Min Soo opened the folder and read the single page. The whole of his experience was now classified. He hadn't planned on an exposé. He signed and handed back the folder.

The senior officer barely glanced at it. "A piece of advice. You've got friends in high places. Keep them. Any questions?"

"No, sir."

And that was that. Min Soo's lips were locked with a signature.

He was quietly returned to his unit, a restructured unit. News bites filtered into every conversation; he tried to ignore them. Rumours of military personnel vanishing; shipping lanes randomly closed; government and corporation purges. He didn't care.

His commanding officers kept him busy. Sent him for extra training. Sent him to get medically examined, often. Sent him to for regular psych-checks. Didn't ask him any questions. Min Soo only had one.

Acknowledgement

I have to thank my father for refusing to read this book until I had finished the first draft. Having read too many partial manuscripts, he finally had enough of that angst and put his foot down. Thanks, dad.

As well, I thank my brother and my dear friends for being my beta readers. You stepped out of the ordinary, into my imagination, and responded with respect and kindness.

Finally, I thank my mother for waiting, and always encouraging me to keep putting one foot in front of the other, no matter the circumstance.

About the Author

Laura Lahtinen is a Finnish-Canadian who currently lives in Canada's Fraser Valley, BC. She loves tea, her dog, and sings to herself when riding down the highway on her motorcycle. If she could convince her dog to join her for the ride, she'd finally have a singing companion. From go-kart tracks to dusty archives, fabric stores and newspapers, and learning more than she ever could have wanted about wildlife scare tactics, land surveying, and spreadsheets, she finally decided to write down all the totally unrelated stories piling up inside her head.

This is her debut novel with many more brewing… just like the tea most certainly forgotten, again, on the kitchen counter.

Manufactured by Amazon.ca
Bolton, ON